WHEN THE
FLOOD
FALLS

WHEN THE FLOOD FALLS

THE FALLS MYSTERIES

J.E. BARNARD

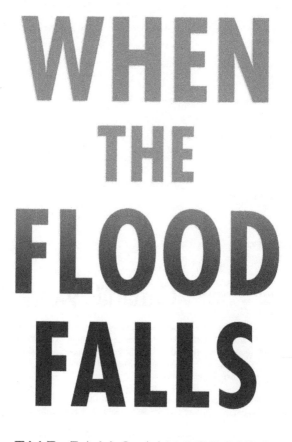

DUNDURN
TORONTO

Cover image: ©istock.com/Oleh_Slobodeniuk
Printer: Webcom

Library and Archives Canada Cataloguing in Publication

Barnard, J. E., author
      When the flood falls / J.E. Barnard.
(The falls mysteries)

Issued in print and electronic formats.
ISBN 978-1-4597-4121-8 (softcover).--ISBN 978-1-4597-4122-5 (PDF).--
ISBN 978-1-4597-4123-2 (EPUB)

      I. Title.

PS8603.A754W54 2018   C813'.6   C2017-907240-4
                                                  C2017-907241-2

1   2   3   4   5   22   21   20   19   18

We acknowledge the support of the **Canada Council for the Arts**, which last year invested $153 million to bring the arts to Canadians throughout the country, and the **Ontario Arts Council** for our publishing program. We also acknowledge the financial support of the **Government of Ontario**, through the **Ontario Book Publishing Tax Credit** and the **Ontario Media Development Corporation**, and the **Government of Canada**.

Nous remercions le **Conseil des arts du Canada** de son soutien. L'an dernier, le Conseil a investi 153 millions de dollars pour mettre de l'art dans la vie des Canadiennes et des Canadiens de tout le pays.

Care has been taken to trace the ownership of copyright material used in this book. The author and the publisher welcome any information enabling them to rectify any references or credits in subsequent editions.

— *J. Kirk Howard, President*

The publisher is not responsible for websites or their content unless they are owned by the publisher.

Printed and bound in Canada.

VISIT US AT

 dundurn.com | 🐦 @dundurnpress | 📘 dundurnpress | 📷 dundurnpress

Dundurn
3 Church Street, Suite 500
Toronto, Ontario, Canada
M5E 1M2

For Ruth

CHAPTER ONE

The glass wall gazed blank-eyed over the clearing, each of its nine panes backed by thick, pale drapes. No woodcutter's shack here, but a huge, glossy house built of stripped and varnished logs, each as wide as Lacey's waist. The porch pillars were sanded tree trunks and in the arched front door was carved a relief of saplings. More show home than family home, more Neil's flavour than Dee's. Why had Dee kept it in the divorce?

Spruces ringed the glade, their roots lost in tangled undergrowth, while before the house, all was austere. Red rock shards filled zigzag beds punctuated by spiky shrubs, their jagged edges scraping on Lacey as she gave the doorbell a final push. Dee had coaxed her for weeks, leaning on the good old university days and shared misadventures in her daily texts and voice mails, to set up this reunion supper, and now she, not Lacey, was late. Six years of separation due to careers and spouses was supposed to finally end, but Dee wasn't home.

As the last echo of the last chime died, Lacey retreated from the stone-paved patio to her shabby Civic to lean on the fender and contemplate her options. They amounted to two: leave now, or wait until Dee either showed up or replied to her messages.

Five minutes. She would give Dee that much. She glanced at her watch to mark the time, crossed her arms, and settled into the alert idleness learned through years of conducting stakeouts on the Force. Catalogue every detail. That was how you knew when something had changed. The flutter of a drape might indicate someone hiding inside, or that a rear window had been opened for a stealthy escape, sending a draft through the rooms. A barely registered movement beyond a hedge could signify someone sneaking out, or in. A man in a mail uniform wasn't always delivering letters and flyers. Not that these scattered acreages along the hillside would have home delivery. On the edge of wilderness, an hour from Calgary, at the feet of the Rocky Mountains, a mailman would stick out like a neon Popsicle on an igloo.

As she leaned there in the still glade, the forest rustled toward her from all sides. Tiny sounds — leaves or birds or little rodent feet going their secret ways through last year's leaves — whispered isolation. She might be alone on the hillside, save for the sharp corner of a roofline higher up. She should be on her way back to Calgary and supper, although it would mean crossing that lone bridge over the rushing brown river again.

Locals expected the last of the snowpack to surge through sometime next week. Until then the river would keep rising, bringing down whole trees and threatening the bridge. Blinding, turbulent water, Lacey's worst nightmare, and right under the windows of her new jobsite, the not-quite-finished Bragg Creek Arts Centre and Foothills History Museum. Lacey knew even less about art and history than she did about security-camera wiring, but being Wayne's gopher brought in some pay and kept her most desperate worries at bay, at least during working hours. She couldn't ask more than that of her new life. Not yet. Was that shushing sound the river tumbling over its banks, or just the breeze through the spruce tops? Where was Dee?

Only three minutes had passed. The emptiness was getting to her. Too much open space after a decade in the overpopulated Lower Mainland, where even the wilderness trails were rarely empty. It was a two-minute drive down the hill into Bragg Creek. She could grab a burger at the bar, the only eatery that wouldn't look askance at her dusty jeans, workboots, and faded T-shirt. Okay, two more minutes and then she was going. She scanned the front of the house again.

Still, no drapes fluttered, but this time she recognized something odd she'd overlooked in her annoyance. Dee loved the sun and the wide-open sky, fir trees piercing the blue, birds fluttering past her windows. Loved to watch deer wander through the yard to nibble on anything she planted. She had gushed about all that to Lacey when she'd first moved out here, six, maybe seven years ago. That explained the spiky shrubs, anyway. Not deer food. Why, now, were all the windows shrouded in heavy drapes on a celestially sunny day, when small birds were squabbling around a seed tray suspended from the porch overhang? All these Dee loved, and yet she had blocked them out.

Lacey straightened up, surveying the house with the keen ex-cop's eyes she hadn't fully brought to bear earlier. No visible windows were open, but that could mean air conditioning. No drapes had been disturbed since her last scan. If the back of the house wasn't as closed in, maybe Dee was merely protecting expensive upholstery from sun damage. Circling the house would fill in the two minutes nicely. A single glance inside could ease the half-formed worry that her old friend might be lying injured inside, victim of an accident or worse. Times beyond count as a constable, she had undertaken welfare checks on strangers, saved a few, and found some past saving. She could not let this one pass her by.

Returning to the carved front door, she turned left past the vast windows and around a massive fieldstone chimney stack. Each window she saw was securely locked and swathed. French doors on the rear terrace had their blinds turned down too tight to see anything at all between the slats. Impossible to guess which rooms lay beyond which windows. She'd seen grow ops less carefully cloistered.

A plank deck connected the terrace and the front patio to a triple-car garage. A high post-and-beam pergola supported a riot of blossoms in hanging baskets well above the reach of a deer's teeth. Garage doors: all locked. No sign of forced entry anywhere, no signals of distress. Just an unfriendly house devoid of its current resident.

She skirted the sage-green deck furniture and looked again over the rear yard. The spruce circle was wider here, leaving space for a tended lawn and opening a gap where a woodland path ran up to a wider trail. A wire-fenced dog run attached to the garage was deserted, but the stainless steel water bowl was half full. Maybe Dee had simply taken a dog for a walk. She'd always had a dog. Young Duke, a honey-haired Labrador, had hiked the Algonquin Trail with them when he was a gambolling pup, barely knee high. He'd be old now, and slow. Maybe it was a slow walk, and this search and speculation were only the old habits of a cop's brain that had not quite retired six weeks ago, when Lacey's resignation letter landed on her staff sergeant's desk. The RCMP had been her life for most of a decade, and now it wasn't. Her head needed time to adjust to civilian life, to stop seeing criminals behind every closed curtain. Dee had simply gone for a walk and lost track of time.

Blue sky reflected on glass in the garage's rear wall: a window inside the dog run, above Lacey's head. Impossible to tell from here whether it was covered or not, but she bet not. Dee's vehicle was probably parked in there right now, supporting the walk theory. Finding out would fill in another minute or two. She jiggered an oblong patio table, one end at a time, down the wide plank steps and into the dog run. When it was firmly in position against the garage wall, she scrambled up and peered in. What would Dee think if she came home to find her old friend perched on a patio table, peeking into her garage?

Whatever Lacey had subconsciously hoped or feared, the garage held no answers. A second small window high up in the end wall cast enough light to show her a gold Lexus SUV and a rack holding two bright plastic kayaks. The third space was empty now of whatever Dee's recently divorced skunk had driven. Did that SUV mean she had gone for a walk, or did she have a second vehicle that she now parked in Neil's spot? Had she gone away with someone else? Why wasn't she calling back or replying to texts?

As Lacey turned back to the house, to the deep shade of the front patio, she blinked. Just for a second, she had flashed back to coming home to her old house in Langley, checking that all the drapes were shut tight the way she had left them, and scanning the street for Dan's car before she risked opening the door. She knew all too well what she'd been afraid of then. Was Dee afraid of her ex-husband, too? In the warm afternoon sunshine, Lacey shivered.

Half a mile away, in a wide vale, Dee Phillips crouched on the trail beside a gravel road, balancing with the help of a gnarled walking stick. Her ankle stung with the strain, an inescapable reminder she had pushed herself too far, too hard, too soon. But this was her first time here on foot since the accident. Her first time sitting alone with the memory of Duke. Six months ago today, almost to the hour. "I'm so sorry, old friend," she murmured to the wind-tossed grasses. "I should have left you home that night. You couldn't keep up." There was no answering whimper, no sense of that whitened muzzle pushing into her hand. No presence here at all. Here, if anywhere, his spirit should have lingered, waiting for her to come back. He was gone, truly and completely.

She was groping in her jeans pockets for a tissue when the rumble of a truck engine approached. Scrambling to her feet, she whistled. The auburn plumes of two setter's tails bobbed up among the Saskatoon berry bushes at the edge of the trees. Bright muzzles turned toward her. "Beau, stand," she yelled, panic lending her voice power. "Boney, stand."

The truck rumbled closer. The dogs stood, poised and graceful, waiting for the next order. She kept her hand up to reinforce this one. *Please don't let them break now. Not here.* She risked taking her eyes off them and looked over her shoulder for the vehicle. It came in a dust cloud, an old red Ford more rust than paint, and slowed to a crawl as it neared the trail crossing. Just Eddie Beal on his way home from picketing the museum. He leaned out the open window.

"All right there?"

"Yes, thanks."

"You mind them young dogs, now. Hockey jocks are back at the Wyman place."

Was that thrice-accursed Jarrad among them? There was no point asking Eddie. He could name every dog for miles around, but his egg customers were the only humans whose names he cared to remember. Well, and hers, though only since the museum had begun construction. If she let him get one more sentence out, he'd be on her about that again. She backed up a step, stifling a grimace as the weight on her ankle shifted. "I'd better get them home," she said. "No sense taking chances."

He waved and drove on, with no sign he'd noticed her tear-streaked cheeks. Although with Eddie, you could never tell. He was an odd man any way you sliced him. She called Boney and Beau, lavished praise when they came bounding up, and was groping in her pocket for treats when her cellphone dinged. Clutching the walking stick in the crook of her elbow, she swiped the screen. *Supper Lacey*, read the reminder. Along with three missed calls, one voice mail, two texts. It couldn't be coming up to five thirty already.

Apparently it was. She had ignored the first reminder half an hour ago, sure she would get back to the house in time to tidy herself before Lacey arrived. She'd used to run the whole hillside trail in less time. Today, too strung up to remember her ankle brace, she had been hobbling by the halfway mark. A stubborn commitment to this pilgrimage had forced her onward. She looked up at the hill path and groaned. The longer, gentler way would take her the full half hour back, every step more agonizing than the last. The short way ended right across from her backyard, but the first bit was a steep uphill and needed two good hands and two strong, flexible feet. Why hadn't she asked Eddie for a lift? If Lacey knew she was on her way, she'd surely wait. Maybe. Lacey hadn't been eager to meet up at all. It had taken weeks of loosely disguised begging to get her here, and she might not wait for the reason behind it if she thought Dee had simply overlooked their supper date.

If she wouldn't help …

Dee pushed that thought aside. Lacey would help. It was in her bones. But explaining these months of terror over the phone, especially when it might not be real, might be a by-product of the pain pills and nightmares ... that was something Dee couldn't face. Lacey just had to stay around long enough to listen. Hitting redial on the last call from *McCrae, L.*, Dee held her breath.

The phone's vibration caught Lacey with the patio table halfway up the steps. She braced it against her legs to answer. Dee's number. At last. Relief gave way to a swell of anger and a sharper voice than she intended. "So, you remembered."

"I'm so sorry. I did remember. I even have pineapple chicken in the oven. Are you still near my house? The thing is, well, I can't get back."

"You're blowing me off even though you already started supper?"

"No! I mean, I really can't get back. I took the dogs for a walk, and I guess I never told you I broke my ankle. It's not fully healed and I walked too far, and now I just can't make it home on foot. I'm less than a kilometre away by the trail, but almost five by the road. I hate to beg a favour if you've hung around waiting already, but can you please come and get me?"

Ten minutes later, Lacey was creeping along a back road that, according to Dee's directions, would take her around the hill. She'd have to let the dogs into the back seat. Drool and paw prints and that smell that would cling to the cheap upholstery for weeks, almost as bad as cigarette smoke. But this was what you did for old friends. The Civic bobbled over washboard gravel and once shivered as its undercarriage grazed a high spot. Didn't Alberta believe in paving its roads? Or at least grading them. No wonder people out here drove pickups and SUVs.

Finally, here was the white-painted rail fence Dee had mentioned. Lacey signalled and turned. This bit of gravel was marginally smoother, running parallel to the hill's steep, treed backside. In the other direction, up a gentle rise, half a dozen opulent log homes sprawled in their own clearings, the westerly sun slanting off their many windows.

So the land wasn't quite as deserted as it had seemed. Good to know. Or bad, she supposed, if you were an environmentalist concerned with protecting wilderness from development. Dee would be two kilometres along, at the crossing of a marked trail. WATCH FOR HORSE-BACK RIDERS, the sign would say.

She spotted the sign, but couldn't see Dee. A slash of red proved to be an Irish setter poised motionless at the road's edge. Behind him, another sat by a dusty stump that struggled to its feet and became Dee, leaning hard on what looked like a tree branch. As Lacey stopped the car, the closest dog lifted its lip in warning. The other moved in front of Dee. No RCMP canine-handling course was needed to read their protective instinct. Rather than trigger further aggression by approaching on foot, Lacey waited in the car while her old friend hobbled forward.

"So what happened?" Lacey asked, once the dogs were stowed in the back — so close she could feel their hot breath on her neck — and Dee had eased herself into the passenger seat.

"I was stupid," said Dee, fumbling with her seatbelt. "I wanted to come be with Duke where he was hit by a car last winter. Physio's been going well so I thought I could walk this far. Didn't think about the rough ground or the slopes. My ankle's the size of a grapefruit already."

"Put it up on the dash to ease the swelling." Lacey took her foot from the brake and set off slowly to avoid jolting Dee's foot. Duke was dead, then. Getting hit by a car was often a faster, kinder death than many old dogs could expect, but hard on their owners. "How'd you break your ankle?"

"Jumping into the ditch with these two lads. Duke wasn't fast enough. This road's usually deserted after the last commuters get home from Calgary, but that night a car blasted out of a side road, fishtailed on the gravel, and would have creamed us all if we hadn't dived over the snowbank. And there went my ankle. Bone, tendons, and all. I yelled at the stupid car but it was long gone. Didn't stop or even look back. When I crawled up to the road, Duke was lying there with a shattered hip."

"Did they catch the driver?"

"Eventually." Dee closed her eyes. "I couldn't help much. Too stunned to even notice the colour or make. I was more worried about freezing to death. I'd fallen on my phone and it was toast. I couldn't stand up, couldn't do anything except cover Duke with my jacket and hope someone would come along soon." She sniffed. "Soon is relative in those conditions."

"But somebody eventually came?" Lacey turned onto the washboard road and slowed to make the Civic jiggle as gently as possible over the corrugations. She'd had enough injuries herself to remember the pain of jiggling.

Dee winced. "Yeah, somebody came, and just in time. In normal January temperatures, wearing jogging gear, I'd have been hypothermic in minutes. But a chinook blew through the night before, brought the temperature up thirty degrees by morning, and it was still near zero at dusk. Boney and Beau huddled up with me and that helped. Ironic, though: I'd been on top of the world four hours earlier, shaken hands on a huge East Village development deal after lunch, and was freezing to death by suppertime, with a useless phone and my dog dying at my feet." She let out a sour laugh. "From development tycoon to Darwin Award candidate in half a day. I was damned close to falling into a frozen sleep when rescue finally arrived. The devil on horseback, as they say."

"The devil being your ex-husband?"

"Neil? No chance. He never comes out here anymore. At least ..." Dee hesitated. "I don't think he does. He slimes around my office occasionally, trying to winkle deal tips out of my staff, but not when I'm there. This was one of my uphill neighbours, Jake Wyman. He was literally on horseback, out riding, and on the road only because he thought the hill trail would be too slippery for the horse in the dark. I'd hardly seen him since I handled some property for his ex-wife, and he might have been holding a grudge. Although I'm sure he would have helped, anyway. You don't pass by on the other side out here, especially in winter. People would die." She sighed, with gratitude or maybe resignation.

"I owe him a lot. He wrapped me in his heavy jacket and then called his groom to get the horse, a blanket and transport for me, and a mug of hot tea, plus a vehicle to take Duke to the emergency animal hospital. While our other neighbour drove me to Calgary to get my foot X-rayed, Jake took Boney and Beau home for me. He didn't mention his ex during all that, although when he came to get me from the hospital the next day he asked if I'd give him her current address. He's not one to miss a chance."

A wife who didn't want to be found by her ex-husband was a smart wife, in Lacey's book. A woman was at highest risk of being killed by an ex-partner in the year immediately following separation. One reason she was a province away from Dan. Not that she thought he would come after her, but then she'd have said he would never raise his voice, much less his fist. After that first time, who knew what he was capable of? She swung the car onto the paved road, ignoring a back-seat growl and the prospect of herding these hostile setters into their pen for the night. "Did you give this Jake the information he wanted — out of gratitude, maybe?"

"Of course not. Any lawyer would know better. I suggested he write to her in care of me and he said he would think about it. He never brought it up again. His chef brought me meals every day for the whole next week, which was a godsend because I was woozy with pain pills and grief, barely able to stand. Jake came every day, too, checked if I needed anything, and took Boney and Beau out running with his horse. He still does. They love it, and I sure can't take them running right now."

"And the reckless driver?" As she signalled for the turn up to Dee's road, Lacey realized she'd been driving beside the churning river and had not let it get to her. So that part of her cop's focus hadn't deserted her. Information gathering ahead of emotion. Always. "How did the police get him?"

"Tip from a neighbour, and he surrendered himself a couple of weeks later. Too late to tell if he'd been drinking, but the hockey players around here party hard during the midseason break. They're mostly rising NHL stars with too much money and fame and not much responsibility, except to their team. Anyway, he's going to court next month."

"On what charges?"

"A bunch," said Dee. "Reckless endangerment, I think, and something like careless use of a vehicle. I'm a real estate lawyer; driving offences aren't my strong suit. Nothing for killing my dog, though. He didn't hit me, and a dog's life doesn't count in the police's eyes. But I'll get to make a statement, and I won't hold back on what his actions did to my life. That's my driveway coming up."

The dogs, to Lacey's relief, went directly to their pen and took turns gulping the water left for them. She closed their gate, helped Dee up to the deck and around to a side door, then finally got her first look inside the vast varnished house. Mudroom first, cluttered like all of them with boots, coats, shelves stacked with miscellany. The kitchen beyond it was all varnished wood, black granite countertops, black appliances. That was her first impression, quickly displaced by the enticing aroma of baking pineapple. "Mmm."

Dee hobbled to a stool. "Should be almost ready. I didn't mean for you to make supper, but if I just sit here and give orders, can you finish the meal prep?"

"Sure. You do remember I can't really cook, right?"

Dee laughed, just a small one, and some of the tension left Lacey's chest. With Neil out of the picture, the Dee she knew might yet emerge from the shell of perfection that had seemed impenetrable on their last visit. Her earlier reluctance to see Dee seemed silly now. She'd expected to come here, hat metaphorically in hand, with her police career and her marriage in tatters behind her, grovelling for house-hunting contacts from a woman notorious for having her own life together. Not that she was revelling in Dee's misfortunes, but they were a timely reminder that rain fell onto even the most organized lives. Friends got out the umbrella for each other. Today she was holding the umbrella, even though it meant dog drool in her car and exercising her culinary cluelessness. "What do I do first?"

Half an hour later, the pasta was drained and Dee was tossing the salad. She was still propped up on her stool and alternating between ice wraps and warmth for her ankle.

The dogs barked steadily at Lacey from the moment she stepped outside, growled while she poured their kibble over the fence into their bowls, and only stopped barking at her back once she was inside the house with the door shut. No welcome there. "I gave you a ride home, you ungrateful mutts," she muttered, but not loud enough for Dee to hear.

After that, she descended into the basement to bring up bottles of wine that would go well with the pineapple chicken. "Not that I can tell one vintage from another, anyway," Dee confided. "The one we're having tonight has fruity elements that I figure won't be horrible with chicken or pineapple, and that's the extent of my wine lore."

The basement and as much of the main floor as Lacey glimpsed through archways off the kitchen were more homey than the house's facade. The furniture was comfortable, if expensive, its neutral hues livened up with textured throw pillows and blankets. The rooms were dim, though sunlight haloed every curtained window.

"Do you mind if I open some drapes?" she asked after setting down three bottles of white. "It's a lovely evening and I don't get to be outside much, between work and the commute from Calgary."

Dee flipped over a few bits of leafy greens before answering. "Uh, sure. Just remember to close them tight before you go. I can't be hobbling after you."

"Seems like you wouldn't need drapes much out here." Lacey slid back the kitchen curtains. "No neighbours close enough to peer in." After a moment with no reply from Dee, she went on. "I was careful about my window coverings in Langley, never more so than when Dan first moved out. He wasn't handling things well, and I was always conscious that he might be outside somewhere, watching my movements." She let her voice betray some of the fear that lingered from those dark winter weeks. Let Dee know that it was okay to be afraid of her ex, if that's what she was afraid of, and that the fear was nothing to be ashamed of.

But Dee didn't rise to that bait. "I always said he wasn't good enough for you. Are you pouring that wine or not?"

The pouring went on well after the meal had ended. In the vast living room, before they settled onto soft couches amid the colourful cushions and throws, Lacey again opened the drapes, partly to watch the spectacular view of distant mountains and partly to see how Dee would cope. She resolutely ignored the ribbon of turbulent brown water winding through the valley and thought that as long as she couldn't see the bridge from here, she might be able to ignore the risk that it would be closed by morning. She sank into softness as Dee brought out a photo album of their hike through the Algonquin Trail with puppy Duke. They toasted him and reminisced until the second bottle was done and spruce shadows came creeping across the terrace. The sun was going down, the forest closing in.

Dee limped over and closed the nine sets of drapes with their power cords, then stood fussing with all the edges she could reach to make sure nobody could peer in through a gap. She said, half into the curtains, "You're likely not in a shape to drive, even if you are an RCMP-trained expert with thousands of patrol kilometres a year. Stay here tonight. I've got extra toothbrushes and stuff upstairs, and your choice of spare bedrooms. And your commute to work will be really short in the morning. Hell, stay all week and be my legs. I might need a lot more wine brought up to get me through this last crush before the museum officially opens. If I'd known how stressful being the president of the museum's building committee was going to turn out,

I'd have evaded the honour. Will it all be ready before the gala on Friday, do you think?"

"The security stuff will be," said Lacey, setting aside for the moment her leap of joy at being offered any bed that wasn't her old patrol buddy Tom's much older rec-room couch. Between three weeks of crash space and him lining her up with AWL Security Services for the museum job, the favours were adding up fast. "Wayne is driving himself and me hard to get every metre of cabling in and every uplink tested, inside and out. I can't speak for anyone else's job." Dee, she noted, was still standing, her hand clutching the edge of the last curtain. She didn't want to be here alone tonight. Would she say why if asked outright? "I shouldn't drive tonight, you're right. Can I take you up on the bed and the toothbrush? If you make the offer of a longer stay tomorrow, when we're both stone sober and wide awake, I promise to give it due consideration."

"Spoken like the cautious old McCrae of our university days," said Dee, taking her hand down from the drapery. "How could you have faced that dangerous job year after year when your personal life is more carefully calculated than an insurance actuary's?"

Soon Lacey was settling into a luxurious upstairs bedroom with magazine-quality décor. Dee's master suite, from which she had retrieved pajamas and other sleepover necessities, was twice the size and even more lavishly appointed. Its occupant, though, was not much different from the old Dee, who still walked her dogs with messy hair and no makeup, who teased and laughed and reminisced. She would not care if her old friend didn't arrange the matching throw pillows quite as artfully on the bed in the morning.

Despite the relaxation brought on by the wine and the soft cuddling of the pillow-top mattress, Lacey had a hard time dozing off. The stresses she'd held at bay all evening were niggling again: her lack of a home, her uncertain post-RCMP job and future, Dan dragging his feet on both the divorce and selling their house in Langley, and yes, whatever had Dee so frightened she wouldn't leave a drape open day or night. The nighttime sounds of the surrounding forest, so soothing by day, whispered ominously by night of beasts on the prowl and hinted at the wildness in the hearts of the trees. Trees like in the fairy tales, whispering, surrounding human habitations, cutting them off with impenetrable hedges and …

At some point along the restless path to full sleep, when the trees were stooping over her bed, clutching at her shoulders, she roused to find Dee bending over the bed, shaking her shoulder and whispering urgently. "Lacey, wake up, please. Please wake up. There's someone on the deck and the dogs aren't barking. Please!"

CHAPTER TWO

For a long, frantic minute Dee shook and whispered at Lacey, but her friend didn't stir. She had to wake up, to listen and look and scare away the footsteps on the deck. Unless it was all another horrible trick of Dee's over-worked imagination, a side effect of the pain meds and the stress, and there was nobody out there at all. Dee crept to the nearest window and slid the handle over slowly, slowly, willing the wood not to stick or squeak. As soon as the frame opened enough to admit a thin line of nighttime air, she stopped. Bending down, she edged her ear to the crack, pulling back her hair to hear better. Anything? Anyone?

There! Another footstep. A man's boot heel, surely. She sagged against the windowsill, torn between relief that she hadn't imagined this and terror at the confirmation that the prowler was real and outside right now, maybe trying to get in. After a slow, deep breath, she slid the handle back over to block out the night and shuffled the two paces back to the bedside.

"Lacey! There's someone on the deck. Please wake up!"

"What? I'm awake."

Dee repeated herself. This time Lacey seemed to take it in. She swung her legs out of bed and reached for the lamp. Before flipping the switch, though, she stopped. "This has happened before, hasn't it? Is this why you really wanted me out here tonight?"

"Not the only reason, but yes, I've heard someone other nights. Never seen anybody." *Please believe me, please believe, please go look and make them stop.*

"Okay." Lacey's face was a white blur in the dark room. "Here's what we do. Don't turn on the lights just yet. You got your cellphone up here? Take it and lock yourself in your bathroom. If I'm not back in five minutes, or you don't hear me calling out to you and you think somebody has entered the house, call the police. You have 911 out here?"

"Of course." Dee wanted to explain that it would take ages for them to get here, but Lacey was already halfway to the stairs, her borrowed pajama pants flapping against her legs. She swung around the newel post and paused, one hand on the banister.

"Any weapons in the house?"

Dee shook her head, then realized she'd only be another shadow in the deep dark of the guestroom and said softly, "No."

"Lock yourself in," Lacey repeated and sank away, her footfalls mere whispers on each carpeted stair.

Left alone in the blacked-out upper hall, Dee lowered the hand that she had stretched out after her friend without realizing it. The night crowded her, squeezing the breath from her throat and swallowing the last shreds of comfort left by Lacey's presence. She crept to the top of the stairs and crouched, listening with all her might to the faint sounds of movement through the house. Lacey must be peering out the doors and windows before she stepped outside. With a thrill of horror, Dee realized she had not told Lacey where to find a key. Would her friend open a door, walk outside, and risk being locked out, at the mercy of whoever was out there? Or risk leaving a way in for a prowler intent on reaching Dee?

She couldn't just lock herself in the bathroom, leaving herself no escape route. She could go down, give Lacey the keys, then hide on the main floor, where there were at least three ways out if she needed them. More if she counted windows.

"Lacey?" she whispered down the stairs, as loud as she dared. But of course there was no response. She crept three steps down, peering into the gloom below. No hint of starlight filtered through her drapes, which were drawn shut obsessively well. No way to know if someone was outside any particular window or door except by moving aside the drape. How many nights had she done just that — crept downstairs to peer out while trying not to move the cloth noticeably, always dreading being confronted by a face peering in?

Her ankle twinged, a reminder to keep moving or sit down. Which would it be: go downstairs and stand ready to help Lacey, or go hide and let someone else face the terror she was shirking?

Dee Phillips, she told herself fiercely, crouched in darkness on the third stair, *You have survived broken bones, a broken marriage, law school, and the most cut-throat profession in the so-called civilized world. You will not hide while someone else defends your turf for you.* She stood up straight, clutched her cellphone tight and the railing tighter, and descended, step by cautious step, into the abyss.

Lacey peered out past the curtains on the kitchen window, the last one on her circuit. Nothing moved that she could see. And surprisingly, she could see plenty. The circling spruces made a dark palisade, but the open spaces gathered what light sprinkled down from the stars and the sliver of moon. Her night vision was operating at full strength after her long grope through the blacked-out rooms. Three stubbed toes, a smacked and stinging elbow, and one fast grab at a lamp that had teetered as she reached past it. That was all she'd gained so far. Was it time to turn on the outside lights, assuming she could find the right switches? She moved toward the mudroom, bumping her hip bone on the black granite countertop, and let her fingers drift along the wall. Switches — which ones did what? She didn't press any to find out.

She slid aside the blinds on the mudroom's exterior door. Still nobody. Just the furniture on the deck and the hanging baskets above. A few shadows large enough to hide a man, or a deer, if it stood quite still. She could walk outside and yell for whoever it was to show themselves. Say the cops were on their way. They probably should have called the police right away, but if it was only a deer going after the flowers, she'd feel like a fool. And an even bigger failure. Only a few weeks off the Force and she couldn't handle walking around a house at night? She'd have been laughed off the job, if she were still on it. But there was a difference, a confidence, to walking a perimeter with a heavy flashlight, heavy boots, a heavy vest, and a dispatcher on the other end of your radio. Here, she'd be walking out in Tweety Bird pants and T-shirt and bare feet, if she couldn't find her workboots in the dark, strange house. The dogs still hadn't made a sound. She couldn't tell from this angle if they were asleep in their shelter or lying drugged — or worse — by the gate. Going out there was the next logical step. Or rather, putting on her workboots was. She tied the laces in the dark, tucking in the trailing ends in case she had to chase down a prowler.

Hoping Dee was doing as she was told, Lacey opened the door. The river's roar ran like ice water down her spine. A scant second later, the dogs' howls split the silence, letting her know just what they thought of an interloper daring to open a door of their mistress's house. Which made it an even bigger mystery: if someone really had been prowling in the yard, why had the dogs remained silent?

Behind her, Dee's voice calmed the dogs.

Lacey spun. "What are you doing down here? I told you to wait upstairs."

"I decided I couldn't hide out and let you defend my turf for me." Dee sounded half defiant and half scared out of her mind. "Did you see who it was?"

"I didn't see anybody. Or any movement at all until I opened the door and the dogs freaked out." Lacey peered hard at Dee, but the dark within the room hid her friend's expression. "Are you 100 percent sure you heard somebody on the deck? Because the dogs are obviously fine, and they're very much defending the place right now."

"Oh god," said Dee. "Not again. Please, Lacey, can you just walk around the house? Make sure nobody's tampered with the windows or anything? I'll tell you everything when you come back in."

"All right, but I want the outside lights on. I've tripped over enough stuff already."

Lacey stood silent on the deck, eying the ring of ominous darkness beyond the terrace lights. The dogs, vigilant in their pen, watched not the dark treeline, but the interloper on their deck. Likely they sensed her tension but, obedient to Dee's shout, they didn't make a sound. She was thankful for that much. Five minutes outside, examining each door handle and window latch by the strong beam of a flashlight, showed that nothing had changed since her afternoon's perimeter check. No scrapes or scratches, no smudges save those she had left herself when trying to peer in earlier. She made a thorough job of it again, circling the garage and the dog pen, conscious with every step of the dogs pacing her inside their wire fence. The river's menace washed louder over her nerves. She shivered and didn't try to tell herself it was just the midnight chill on her bare arms.

As she came in the mudroom door, she called out, "Just me."

Dee was making tea, her silhouette edged by the light

from the stove hood. She poured the boiling water with intense concentration. "You didn't see anyone."

"No sign of anybody." Lacey locked the door and drew the blind, but left the outside lights on. "You ever think of getting motion-sensor lights? They'd be a deterrent."

"They're on the garage, pointing down the drive."

Impossible to read her emotions from that clipped sentence. Lacey prodded for another response. "More of them would be good. On the deck or over the backyard?"

"Animals would set them off all night. And I can't afford them, anyway." Dee's voice was strung tighter than an off-key violin. Her hand shook as she pulled mugs from the cupboard. "You want canned milk with your tea? I bought some special, just like the old days. It's in the fridge."

"Heavenly," said Lacey, as she reached for the glossy black refrigerator handle. She kept her eye on Dee, though, and saw well enough when her friend blotted her eyes on a cloth napkin. Dee, crying? It was almost unthinkable, like the Hoover Dam springing a leak. "Hey, now, take it easy. We'll figure this out. Sit down, get your foot up, and tell the big mean ex-cop all your troubles. For real this time."

It took a good few minutes before Dee looked up from crumpling the napkin between her fingers. "It might all be my imagination, although heaven knows I listen hard enough. And tonight I was sure I heard boot heels on the deck. Not just once, but from my room and again from yours. Maybe I've been staying awake too much, stressing, and my mind is playing tricks on me. God knows I need a decent night's sleep. I don't think I've had one in months."

"What is it that keeps you awake? Pain in your ankle, job stuff, fear of a prowler?"

"It's not just a fear," Dee snapped. "Somebody *is* prowling around my house at night. Somebody the dogs don't bark at."

Lacey's domestic violence meter clicked up another notch. The blinds had indeed been an early clue. "Neil? The dogs wouldn't bark at him, would they? Did he ever hit you, Dee? Or threaten you?"

"Never. He might have thought about it a few times, but he'd have worried about breaking a nail." Dee pressed the napkin to her eyes again. Her voice came out muffled under the drooping cloth. "He left me in the most humiliating way possible, and he has nothing to gain by sneaking back here at night. In fact, since I pay him spousal support, he might even lose by being so stupid."

Potential gain wasn't the reason most men stalked their exes. It was blind, irrational rage that motivated such behaviour. Lacey had seen that all too often on the job. Women who were stalked, terrified, beaten. Killed for the crime of leaving. For an instant Dan's face flashed up, those nights when she'd shoved a dresser across her bedroom door in case he tried to get into the house while she was asleep, before she had the locks changed. Why did Dee blithely assume Neil was any safer? Lacey took a breath and a sip of milky tea, refocusing. Go back to the evidence. See what was there.

"Okay, you're sure someone has been here some nights. You've heard footsteps when there shouldn't be any. Has there been any concrete evidence afterward?"

"The first time I heard them, a few months ago, there were boot prints in the snow the next morning. Down from the path in back, past the dog run to the porch, and out the same way. I hadn't looked the day before, so I don't know if it was a neighbour walking by that way to see if I was home, or if it happened that night." Dee lowered the napkin. "But I heard someone."

"I'll accept your word on that. And the next time?"

"Another time there was dried mud on the deck when I woke up one morning. I hadn't come in that way, so it might have been done the day before." Dee's eyes, red-rimmed and etched around with fine lines, flickered over each of the tightly curtained windows. "Not conclusive, I know. But another time I very distinctly heard footsteps right on the porch. I wasn't even asleep yet, just lying in bed in the dark, watching the moon over the snowcaps down south. I lay there wondering if I'd heard what I thought I heard. Then they started up again. I ran to the window first, didn't see anyone, so I ran downstairs. Whoever it was had gone by the time I got the lights on. Or they were hiding in the trees, watching me." Dee shuddered. "I went out for a good look around at first light, but I couldn't see anything unusual. No mud, no snow to leave footprints in.

"Now I stay awake night after night listening for them to come back. I can't tell you how many times I've gone from window to window, like you did tonight, looking out, always afraid I'd see someone looking back. I tele-commute as much as possible rather than come home to an empty house. Especially after dark." Her voice rose. "I've been getting away with it because the museum open-ing is so close, and it's my job to make sure our corporate sponsorship is well managed. But that excuse is going to run out in another week, and then my real job will be on the line. If I lose my salary over this, I'll lose the house, too. Everything." She clutched Lacey's hand. "I need to know, 100 percent, if it's in my mind or if there really is, or has been, a prowler. Please say you'll stay with me. At least until the Centre's big opening gala."

"I'll stay," said Lacey without hesitation, "until we've sorted this out one way or another. Now, drink your tea. If there was someone out there tonight, they will have realized that you're not alone, and they won't come back. In the morning I'll have a good look around, and we'll talk over everything, identify anybody who might think they have a reason to creep around here at night. The lights can stay on for tonight, and tomorrow I'll see if Wayne has any spare motion sensors he can loan me."

"You won't tell him why? I can't have people at the museum site talking about me. I can't look weak right before the opening."

"I'll tell him there's a bear or something bugging the dogs at night. Okay?" Lacey lifted her mug and paused. "You do have bears out here, right?"

"Bears, cougars, other predators."

Including humans, Lacey thought, but she didn't say that. Neither did she say just how disturbed she was by Dee's near-hysterical fear of a possible prowler. Either Neil had left her more afraid of him than she was willing to admit, or she was utterly overwhelmed by her job, her divorce, her injury, and now the crush of the museum's grand opening. The stress of any two of those might bring on some paranoid imaginings to a woman living alone in the forest. Dee was never one to be crushed that easily, but she'd carried this terror alone since there was snow on the ground. If she cracked now, it wouldn't be surprising at all. That wouldn't happen, though. Lacey would be here to keep her fear at bay until the museum was successfully opened for tourists.

As she followed Dee up the stairs a few minutes later, having very visibly rechecked every door and window, she thought that Dee might never sleep again if she ever shared the third possibility that sprang to mind: that someone might be prowling out there, careful not to leave evidence, not trying to enter or to do obvious harm, but deliberately playing on the frayed nerves of an isolated woman recovering from an injury. But gaslighting some-one needed a motive. Who stood to gain if Dee fled back to the city and sold her log McMansion at a loss?

The following morning, Dee surprised her again, this time by saying, as Lacey followed the smell of coffee to the kitchen, "You know, I never realized how crazy I would sound until I heard myself trying to explain it to you. I've been alone with this for so long I've lost all per-spective. Thanks for not telling me I was nuts last night, but I kind of am. So I've got an action plan."

That was more like the old Dee: action plans at an hour when other people were barely able to open both eyes at the same time. Lacey accepted the offered mug. "And your plan is?"

"First, I'm going to refill my prescription for anti-anxiety meds. I was taking them for a bit after the accident but they ran out months ago. Second, you're going to — if you will, that is — help me get my bike down from the garage rafters. I always used to go running or biking to burn off the stress, but I've gotten away from the habit. My physiotherapist even suggested I try biking again, but I was busy and just put it off. Now I know I need that stress busting, and after yesterday I realize running is still a long way off. So biking it is."

"Those ideas both sound sensible. Er, do you still want me to stay for a few days?"

"God yes! You're the first breath of sane air in this house for months. Do you have a mountain bike? If not, I can borrow one for you."

"Mine's at Tom's. I can bring it out tonight when I fetch more clothes."

"Great." Dee slapped the top on a travel mug. "I'm off to the office. But I'll be back by eleven for a press conference at the museum. See you then." She headed for the back door, then paused to un-clip a secondary ring from her car keys. "You'd better have a door key. I'll get my spare back from the neighbour if I get home before you. House is the maple leaf one and the square, plain one is for the garage. *Mi casa, su casa.* Just like old times." She flashed a smile so confident, so at odds with last night's fright, that Lacey couldn't quite stifle the idea that Dee had been a bit too deep into the prescription pills already.

CHAPTER THREE

They were working inside the loading bay, stringing camera cable up above the ceiling tiles, when Lacey got around to asking her boss about loaner lights.

"And who is your roommate that I'd trust them with my equipment?" Wayne's voice was dry in the way that every sergeant's voice Lacey had ever heard was dry, like he couldn't quite believe a rookie was asking such a stupid question, but then, what better could be expected of a rookie? She flushed without meaning to and found she was standing at parade rest without having consciously shifted position. Working for another ex-RCMP officer was supposed to ease her transition back to civilian life, but it reminded her every day that she hadn't been strong enough, in the end, to cope with the strains of a cop's life. Quitting on Wayne wasn't an option; she needed something besides *RCMP* on her resume. And now she needed to stay near Dee, too.

"Dee Phillips," she said.

His flat stare assessed her. "Well, aren't you the savvy operator? Moved in with the boss of the whole job, just like that."

"We were university roommates. She heard I was out here and offered me a bed until the Centre's wired. Saves me the commute from Calgary." She eased out of the formal stance and repeated the request. "May I borrow two motion-sensor lights to monitor her yard for a few nights, please?"

"No."

So much for that option. Maybe there were cheap versions at Canadian Tire. She could rush in right after work to buy some and whatever tools she would need to install them. Getting back to do it before dark would be tricky, especially if she went to Tom's to pick up her stuff.

"No," said Wayne again. "Since she's the president of this whole job, we should do better by her. Get me photos of the area you want covered and I'll draw you up a plan. There are five or so spare lights in the van you can take. Is her house close enough that you can get there on your lunch break?"

"Yes, sir."

He nodded, his mind already moving to the next task. "Get me the small crimpers from the van, and a half-dozen AV ends."

Lacey headed up the stairs to the staff exit and pushed open the flat steel door. A camera flashed in her face. She froze for a nanosecond, but the photographer was merely testing his equipment. Of course — the press conference Dee had mentioned. Out on the freshly laid lawn, a half-dozen microphones and cameras ignored the usual nutty protester by the road and focused on a grizzled cowboy in a battered beige hat and boots. He looked a hundred years old. The slender blonde leaning on his shoulder was barely a third his age. Her perfect teeth were aimed at the cameras while the fitful breeze flung strands of her glossy hair across the cowboy's weathered face. His hand rested on a sturdy wooden sign that gave, in authentically rustic burnt lettering, the facility's twin titles of Arts Centre and History Museum.

The woman looked faintly familiar and the cowboy not at all, but then Lacey had been on this job for barely a week. The only person she could name in the throng was Rob, the curator/manager of the new facility. With his pleated khakis and frosted dark hair, he stood out among the worn jeans and hard hats that infested the building. She veered behind a log pillar to avoid the media and came face-to-heels with a pair of scuffed workboots on a ladder. A workman on a ladder and a second up another ladder were stretched to full height, hooking a rolled-up banner between two of the fat logs that made up the building's colonnade. Similar banners hung between other sets of pillars, with a pull rope strung between them all.

A videographer with a shoulder camera was the only person paying any attention to the workers, panning up their ladders, gathering background footage. Lacey edged past him, glad to be incognito in grubby civvies. No reporters today would demand comments on the Capilano River bridge incident or ask if she was part of the class action lawsuit against the RCMP. That life was behind her.

She followed the colonnade toward the parking lot. As she stepped clear of the building, the river assaulted her ears with its menacing rumble. Surely that brown, churning mass of water was a foot higher than yesterday? It was nothing like the happy, shallow blue stream she had seen last week. She turned her back on the swollen river with a shudder and breathed deep of the fresh mountain air. It smelt faintly of fir trees and strongly of good, clean mud, much better than the usual building-site odours of varnish and diesel. She unlocked the van, leaned into the rear door, and was groping for the right crimpers when a convertible shot into the parking lot with a squeal of tires. On instinct she noted the particulars: late-model BMW M6, bright orange, Alberta vanity plate Y-MAN4.

The Bimmer skidded to a stop in a swirl of dust. Three buff young men leaped out, hurdled over the row of newly planted shrubs, and stampeded over the sod toward the entrance. Beefcakes on the hoof. The media pack swung around to meet them. By the time the next camera flashed, the blonde was in their midst, draping her hands decoratively over a muscular forearm and leaning back to let her blond locks flutter over another man's brawny shoulders. The old cowboy, abandoned, wandered toward a nearby bench. A shabby woman there shuffled sideways, making room for him while she fumbled a cellphone toward her shaggy brown curls. Lacey's eyes slid back to the photo op, where Blondie was basking in the camera-flashes like a starlet on a red carpet. How was this promoting the new facility?

A shriek shredded the quiet morning, so loud it echoed from the hill across the road. As Lacey spun to find its source, the shaggy woman lurched to her feet and stumbled toward the press, screeching. The cowboy jumped up, one hand reaching fruitlessly as Shaggy hurled her phone over the heads of the reporters. It bounced off an athlete's shoulder. Media heads and camera lenses whipped toward the disturbance. Lacey's feet were already moving, impelled by the old cop habit of running toward trouble, but Shaggy reached the scrum first. She batted a microphone away and was shoving a reporter aside when Rob leapt into her path. She staggered to a halt and slumped, weeping, onto his shoulder.

The media pack surged forward, blocking Lacey's path, giving her the pause she needed to recall she was a mere civilian now, with no official standing to intervene. In any event, the threat seemed to be over. She retreated.

The cowboy came up behind Shaggy and waved his hand at the crowding reporters. They shuffled backward, but not far. Peering between the shoulder-cameras and microphones, Lacey watched the unlikely trio of shaggy woman, grizzled old man, and dapper Rob put their heads together. After a very short conference, Rob led Shaggy back to the bench. The old cowboy strode toward the reporters. Lacey expected a plea for mercy on the distraught woman but he said nothing. His hand flicked again.

The sound of thunder was probably her imagination, but the scrum felt it, too. They parted ahead of the old man like the Red Sea before Moses, leaving the athletic youngsters stranded on the grass. Even Blondie scuttled sideways, leaving the old man and the young ones in a circle of empty lawn. Whatever he said was too low for

Lacey to catch, but the Bimmer's driver took a sudden step backward. His tanned face paled. Scenting blood, the media stepped forward the instant the old man turned away. Rob left Shaggy's side and drew them off.

"Ladies and gentlemen," he called over the murmur of the breeze, "the banner reveal is delayed a few minutes. I'd be happy to take questions now on the development of this wonderful new facility and the opening gala for our first-ever exhibition: A Century of Western Canadian Hockey."

The reporters, with some backward glances, shuffled toward him, leaving the old cowboy once more seated on the bench with the shaggy woman. He no longer looked like a thrower of thunderbolts, but as perplexed as any man stuck with a crying woman. Lacey dodged around the re-forming scrum to crouch beside Shaggy. If there was any more trouble from this disturbed woman, she might help keep it off camera.

"Can I help you?" she asked Shaggy, who was still sobbing, although into a large white hankie that was probably the cowboy's. "Are you hurt?"

The woman sniffed, dark curls tumbling over her shoulders. "Sorry. Got out of hand. I'll be fine."

"Are you sure?" The woman nodded, lowering her head until her droopy hat brim hid her tear-streaked face. Okay then. Since she showed no signs of leaping up or screaming, Lacey scanned the scene for other sources of trouble. There were none. The protester, his sign still held high, was staring from the roadside, just off the property. The media pack had followed Rob to the front entrance, where he was gesturing at the rolled banners high overhead. Nothing to see here, folks. Nothing for Lacey to do with her old, hard-wired police reactions. She went back for the crimpers, counted out the cable connectors, and headed for the staff door.

Fifteen minutes to fetch tools from the van. Not a good way to impress Wayne. He might think she was out here kissing up to the old cowboy, whoever he was — clearly someone the reporters respected and, since he was front and centre at the press conference, a power at the new museum.

Near lunchtime, she left the building by the front entrance. The media and the ladders were gone. The unrolled banners of outsize hockey players fluttered between the log pillars. She turned to view them from across the lawn, recognizing the ubiquitous Calgary Flames jersey on one as well as the Vancouver Canucks jersey she had been only too familiar with in the Lower Mainland. The opening exhibit upstairs in the east-wing gallery held more kinds of hockey memorabilia than she had ever suspected were made: sculptures, posters, comics, bronzed skates, and old uniforms. The walls were mostly bare, awaiting paintings and photographs on the same theme. Why a hockey exhibit in a cowboy-themed tourist village like Bragg Creek? She knew too little about art galleries or hockey — or cowboys — to hazard a guess. She left the Civic in the lot and set off on foot, staying on the side of the road farthest from the river.

Away from the building, the noise was louder. At the corner where the bridge came across, where she usually turned to head back to Calgary, she couldn't avoid the sight of the water any longer. Big branches and other debris churned up against the bridge abutments. The largest pieces hit with a crack before swirling away, barely a foot below the bridge's underbelly. She watched in sickened fascination until a car came along. The driver honked at her and she jumped, stepping hastily off the pavement beside the uphill turn to Dee's house. After two minutes of steady walking, she was turning up Dee's long driveway through the spruce trees. She let herself in by the mudroom door, noticing gratefully that the dogs were not in their pen to make a fuss. As she stepped into the house, though, a setter loped over from the living room, planted its feet, and growled at her.

Dee's voice came behind it, sharp with fear. "Who's there?"

"Me," Lacey called back. "Sorry, I didn't mean to scare you. I walked up." When the dog turned away in answer to Dee's call, she followed him into the living room. "You missed the excitement at the press conference." She stopped. Dee was huddled on the couch, her faced blotched and her nose red. "What happened? Are you hurt?"

"Not hurt bad, but I wrenched my ankle a bit. Again."

Lacey scanned the room at light speed, but nothing seemed disturbed. Not an intruder, then. She breathed. "If it hurts enough to make you cry, maybe we should get it checked. Where's the nearest medical place?"

Dee blew her nose on a soggy tissue. "Nothing closer than Calgary. And anyway, that's not why I'm crying. Can't a girl shed a few tears after she's nearly been run over for the second time?"

Lacey perched on the corner of the massive coffee table and leaned toward her friend. "This happened today?"

"Yeah. I was walking with the dogs down toward the Centre when some assholes came speeding down the hill. I grabbed Boney and Beau and jumped into the ditch. When the dust settled I couldn't get up right away. I just sat there, shaking."

"Tell me you called the police."

Dee lifted her chin. "No need. It was Jake Wyman's car."

"The kindly millionaire? He tried to run you over?"

"No. He lets guests drive his cars. It was another stupid bloody hockey player behind the wheel, I'm sure. They think they own the world."

"Three jocks in an orange BMW, by chance?" Lacey wasn't surprised by Dee's nod. The timing fit. "They burned into the Centre's parking lot while I was out there. Probably right after they passed you. If I'd known, I'd have nailed them."

"I'm sure Jake has thumped them down by now." Dee eased her shoulders from her blanket. "I called Rob's phone right away to tell them not to hold the press conference. Jan answered. She'd have told Jake first thing."

"Who's Jan? That shaggy-haired woman with the piercing shriek?"

"My uphill neighbour. Old friend of Rob's, and she's known Jake forever, too. I heard her yell his name and then she was cut off." So Jake Wyman was the old cowboy. He didn't dress like Lacey's West Coast idea of a multi-millionaire, but that explained the reporters' deferential distance while he told off the punk driver.

"Your neighbour was cut off," she told Dee, "because she threw the phone at the jocks and then tried to beat them up. She had to be restrained."

Dee sat up. "Seriously? I hope she's all right."

"She said she was. She looked a wreck to me."

"I'm sorry I told her. It just poured out of me when I heard a friendly voice. Like when you walked in. What else are friends for?" Dee grabbed a fresh tissue and mopped her face. "Why are you here? Need lunch? Leftover chicken and salad in the fridge. One of us will have to get groceries soon."

Lacey explained about Wayne's offer. "You'll feel safer tonight if I can get those lights installed in the right places after work. And I'll get your bike down, too."

"No rush on the bike." Dee unwrapped her legs from the blankets. "I'm too shaky to try riding today. But I'm so glad you came home. I feel saner already. I'll do food while you do photos, okay?"

As Lacey moved around the outside of the house, trying to balance the need for prowler protection with the story she'd told Wayne about the dogs, she wondered at Dee's sudden mood shifts. Was it just the stress, or had she become a bit, well, unstable? Was there any prowler, or had she imagined the whole thing? She'd said she had suspected that of herself; now Lacey suspected her, too. But they had to proceed as if there was evidence to be gathered. If nothing triggered the extra lights by Friday, the day of the museum gala, they could discuss that again. And she'd have three more days to evaluate Dee's mood swings. Wouldn't that be a touchy conversation — suggesting that Dee needed to see a therapist.

CHAPTER FOUR

Back at the Centre after lunch, Lacey copied her photos to Wayne's laptop. He skimmed through them and, using his finger on the touchpad, drew arrows and circles on the relevant images to show where she needed to install the lights. "You'll have to use extension cords for now, and I can't spare any. We'll wire them in properly if she wants to keep them. Go load them in your car before you forget. And bring this list of stuff from the van. We'll do the art vault this afternoon."

Extension cords weren't exactly high security; they could be unplugged if someone managed to sneak under the motion-sensor panels the first time. Lacey made a mental note to make sure the sensors covered wherever the cords came from. If the lights went on just once, they'd prove Dee hadn't imagined the whole thing and demonstrate the need for greater security. She'd convince Dee to spend the money, or Wayne to delay billing for the work, or something. She went out into the brilliant afternoon, shuffled around the equipment per her instructions, and headed back inside to meet Wayne at the elevator that would take them into that holiest of holies in the art world: the vault.

Located deep in the sub-basement, poking its rear end out under the parking lot, the steel-encased, climate-controlled room was reachable by only one elevator, and only if the right key card was used. It was also at least ten degrees colder than the atrium. Standing in the small elevator lobby across from the shining steel vault door brought goosebumps up in waves on Lacey's bare arms. She tried not to rub them while Wayne briefed her on the security. Only those key cards held by Wayne, Rob, and the board's president and vice-president would allow access down here. The elevator would not leave if the vault door was unlocked, something staff members would know, but illicit entrants would not. Those top four high-security cards could override that rule and call up the elevator to some other level, trapping intruders until police arrived.

"It's almost more anti-vandal defence than antiburglary," Wayne said, handing up a screwdriver as she balanced on a small plastic stepstool to adjust the angle on the camera above the elevator door. "That protester outside could be the visible tip of a lot of local resentment. Who knows what some shine-swilling bush hermit might try for his fifteen minutes? Since Mayerthorpe, nobody takes chances with disgruntled farmers."

Lacey nodded, although she thought Wayne was overstating his case. Mayerthorpe, Alberta, was where four RCMP officers had been picked off by a mean man with a grudge. The bright, touristy environs of Bragg Creek seemed a different universe from that of such men. In reality, the two small towns were hardly a half day's drive apart, and there was plenty of bush around here to harbour angry nutters. The lone protester didn't look angry enough to worry about, but then, some of the worst mass murderers in history had seemed nice enough to their neighbours.

When the two lobby cameras were cable connected and their angles adjusted to his satisfaction, Wayne unlocked the vault with his key card and a numerical code and pulled the shining door open. A wave of deeper chill flowed out, reminding Lacey of a morgue fridge. Peering past Wayne, she caught her first glimpse of the inner sanctum: ten metres by fifteen of white walls and floors under a six-metre-high ceiling, with lighting so intense it bleached out every shadow. One side of the room held bare, open shelving of varying depths and widths, the other a long frontage of vertical panels, each half as wide as a standard door, with a drawer pull in the middle and three slots for labels above that.

Lacey gestured. "What's behind those?"

"You, in a minute." Wayne lifted a remote control from a wall mounting and pushed a button. With a hiss of hidden hydraulics, one panel moved smoothly out into the room. Behind the polished metal front was attached a rigid-mesh construction half as long as the room and almost as high, with a handful of movable hooks hanging randomly from its expanse. "They'll hang pictures on these for storage," he added. "All computer hydraulics, and the software programmer is the biggest pain in the ass I've met in five years." It was the most personal commentary he had let slip so far. He pushed another button to send the massive rack back to its resting place.

"Where do we start?" Lacey set down the plastic stepstool and tugged her tool belt into position. They tested and focused the motion-sensor camera over the door, a second camera facing along the shelving, and a third aimed along the front of the hydraulic racks.

"One more," said Wayne. "Take everything and go tight up against the end wall."

When she was in position, he pointed the remote. The rack closest to the wall rolled out with a whisper of steel wheels and a hiss of overhead cables, cutting off Lacey from the rest of the vault and giving her a long moment to either panic or admire the posters taped up on the mesh, presumably by the construction crew. Jayne Mansfield's cleavage made a change from the hockey players on either side, but none of it distracted Lacey from the claustrophobia that was never far below the surface ever since the underwater incident all those years ago. She concentrated on breathing steadily. There would be no panic, no sign of weakness, not when Wayne was finally showing signs of accepting her. At least she could see through the mesh. A solid wall would have sent her through the roof.

When the motion stopped, she sidled along the rack to its back end. The plastic stepstool's feet bumped along the mesh behind her, bouncing away only to rebound off the cement wall and back again. She wiggled past the rack's cold steel end plate, reached back for the stepstool, and angled its leading legs into the gap. It stuck. Ignoring with difficulty the visual weight of all those other mesh monsters pressing in on her, she yanked. The stool moved a bit. The rack moved too. It rolled in toward Lacey, dragging her plastic stepstool sideways, pinned between the end plate and the wall. She shoved hard against the end-plate but the rack kept coming, cutting off her only exit. She backed away, yelling for Wayne.

If he answered, his voice was lost between the overhead hiss of hydraulic cables and the underfoot whisper of the rack's wheels. The stepstool collapsed with a whine of tortured plastic.

Her butt bumped the rear wall and still the rack came. She squeezed sideways, trying to fit between the end wall and the next rack. There wasn't enough room. Nowhere to go.

"Wayne!"

The rack reached her hands, flat out at arms' length. She leaned on it with all her might, but still it came.

Her elbows bent. Her wrists were bending …

The hiss stopped.

The steel behemoth stopped, too, so close that she went cross-eyed at the blur that was her reflected nose. Her hands pulled back from the panel as if it were electrified. She closed her eyes and clenched her teeth, each quiet breath a victory against screaming.

Wayne's voice came from a long way off. "McCrae? Are you okay?"

Deeper breath. And another. She tested her voice and heard it say calmly, "Yes." Just a bit stressed by nearly being crushed to death in an enclosed space, but she couldn't say that out loud. In Wayne's book that would be whining. Ex-RCMP officers did not whine.

"I won't risk turning the power back on," he called. "Can you push?"

"It weighs a ton."

"It's balanced like a dream. Once started, it will roll like a baby stroller. Now push."

He was right, sort of. It took a lot of will for Lacey to put her hands against the rack again. But with him pulling from the front end and Lacey's feet braced on the wall behind her as she pushed, the monster began to move. She kept pushing as it rolled smooth and slow, unwilling to wait even a step behind the first chance of freedom. When it cleared the opening, she slipped out of the gap and past the pin-up posters to the widest spot in the vault's corner. If she'd had Jayne Mansfield's cantaloupes on her chest instead of these fried eggs, she wouldn't have fit back there in the first place. She swallowed a hysterical giggle.

"I'm clear," she said. "Next time, you take the back, okay?"

"Nobody's going in there again until the installer adjusts the auto-close. It should take a good shove to get this to move. Not like a CD player."

"CD players only pinch your finger." She might have been crushed, and even if she'd survived, she'd have been out of work for ages. Was she eligible for workers' comp in Alberta? She wasn't an official resident yet, just a temporary migrant from B.C. without a Calgary address or an Alberta health card. And here she'd thought the threats to life and limb had been left behind with her

RCMP uniform. Deep breath. And another. She wasn't crushed. No whining. "Do we put it back by hand, too?"

"Nope. Go turn the power back on. We need to know if it's one rack or all of them." He pushed buttons and watched the immense racks slide out into the room.

Lacey took her turn tapping the racks to start the auto-close sequence, pushing her fingers past the fear of touching those polished plates. The merest tap was all it took to start the racks. Nothing stopped them once they started except cutting the power at the switch box in the elevator lobby. Anyone hanging up a painting could get dragged sideways and mangled, like the stepstool.

Wayne wore his old impassive ex-cop's expression, but the flint in his eyes matched the steel vault door. "We're done in here until that's fixed. Go download the elevator log so I'll know who to yell at. Then you can take a break."

Glad to escape the cellar that could have been her tomb, Lacey grabbed the log-reader gizmo and went, hoping she would remember where to shove the reader's little flat plug. Wayne had shown her yesterday, but her hands had developed quite a tremor since then, and her mind wasn't much better.

Fortunately the elevator gizmo co-operated, scrolling up a neat list of card numbers on its little screen. Wayne's key card number, the only one she recognized besides her own, was last, as it should be. The elevator hadn't moved because the vault door was open.

Wayne came out and closed the vault. She handed him the card reader and suppressed a shiver as the elevator doors closed her in. She hadn't so much as remembered her old claustrophobia at lunchtime, but that was then. Deep breaths. At least it wasn't underwater. Being trapped underwater in an enclosed space would have been her most terrifying RCMP shift come back to life.

As Lacey stepped out onto the flagstone floor of the atrium, her goosebumps receded before the balm of sunlight pouring through the south-facing wall of windows. The rattle and clunk of distant power tools displaced the vault's preternatural silence. Voices murmured from the Langdon Theatre overhead and the Natural History Gallery across the way. Paint fumes rose from the classroom level beneath the theatre, heading for the varnished log-roof beams three storeys up. No way to feel enclosed here, overlooking the sun-kissed Elbow River with its churning, brown current that set up an echo in her stomach. She pulled her eyes from the water, willed herself to stare at the landlocked front entrance instead, and reminded herself that she had not died. If nearly a decade in the RCMP had not cracked her, she would not cave on her first civilian job because of a near miss. She was fine. She would be fine when she had to go back into that gap later today. Or tomorrow. She would be fine. Deep breaths.

Something bounced off her head and pinged against the elevator. More construction crew humour? She stepped aside.

"Hey, up there! Whatever you're dropping, quit it."

A baggie fluttered down, spilling triangular orange pills. From the landing half a flight up, a woman reached through the railing after it. Shaggy brown hair blurred her face. A baggy shirt and a loose skirt disguised her body. Add a droopy hat and here was the mess that had interrupted yesterday's media event. Dee's neighbour. What was her name?

"My pills," Shaggy whispered. "Please."

"You won't want the ones that fell on the floor." Lacey scooped up the baggie with its lone remaining pill and went up. She knew prescription speed when she saw it, and who but an addict carried Adderall in a baggie like it was trail mix?

Shaggy's hand shook as she fumbled the little orange pill to her mouth. "Please," she whispered again. "Call Rob."

Gladly. Drug addicts were no longer part of Lacey's job description. She pulled her phone and, lacking Rob's direct number, called Wayne instead.

"There's a woman on the west stairs above the atrium, asking for Rob. Can you let him know?"

"Will do," he said. "Tell her to wait there."

Lacey turned her head away. "Tell him to hurry. She's popping ADD pills from a baggie. Long-time abuser by her shakes." If the woman flipped out, she would have to be restrained. What legal cover did a mere security installer have if she took down an out-of-control addict? She turned, saw the woman glaring at her, and hoped her words would be forgotten as soon as the little orange upper kicked in.

Fast footsteps thumped on the glossy log stairs above them. The curator swooped down to sit beside the druggie. "Honey, you were supposed to stay off the stairs. You promised!"

Stay off the stairs? Stay off the Adderall, more like.

Shaggy leaned her head on Rob's shoulder. "The paint fumes were killing me. The elevator didn't come. I thought I could do it. I'm always better in summer."

"Yes, you are," said Rob, patting her hand. "But it's not really summer yet, and you promised you'd be careful if I let you come around today. What's Terry going to say to us?"

"My fault," the woman whispered. "Take me home."

Rob's patting stopped. "Oh, dear. I can't, honey. Not right away. I've got to head off that shipment of paintings from the Petro-Canada collection. The vault's not going to be ready this afternoon. But maybe Ms. McCrae wouldn't mind." He looked up at Lacey with a pleading smile. "Jan lives just up the hill. It would be a five-minute round trip. Nice afternoon. Lovely scenery. I'll take her van up after work."

Jan — that was the neighbour's name. "I'm on the clock."

Wayne's voice came from the foot of the stairs. "You can take her."

Lacey swallowed her impulsive protest. Hiring her was ex-sergeant Wayne's favour to his ex-constable, Tom, to whom she owed three weeks' lodging, the job, and — more than once over their shared years on the Force — her life. Tom's reputation was, in part, riding on her shoulders here. If Wayne wanted her to haul this addict home instead of doing any of the rush jobs that had to be finished by Friday, she would do it.

Rob helped Shaggy to her feet. "Jan, just tell Lacey where to go once you get into the car. Okay?" He passed her arm over Lacey's rigid shoulders. "Hang on to the railing, honey."

Lacey turned under the limp arm and supported Jan around the waist. Wayne came up a few steps and took the other arm. Nobody mentioned the little orange pills on the carpet, but Lacey made a mental note to go back later and make sure they were safely disposed of. Prescription speed in candy colours — just what you didn't want scattered around a building that would soon be open to school tours.

Wayne steered them all outside and deposited Jan on a bench in the shade. "Get your car, McCrae. I'll stay here."

When Lacey returned, Jan was sitting up more or less straight, her back to the varnished log wall. Drugs must be kicking in. She could probably drive herself home in another five minutes, except that two former Mounties couldn't let an obviously impaired woman operate a vehicle. Lacey got her buckled in and steered the Civic to the road, savouring the early summer scents of clean mountain air, newly leafed trees, and the glacier-fed river. After those terrifying moments in the vault, being outside was a balm, even if the task at hand was one she should have left behind with her badge.

"Where to?"

"Turn right onto the road, then left at the bridge." Other than that, Jan kept her mouth shut and stared straight ahead. Occasionally she trembled. Lacey turned uphill past the first log-and-glass mansion. It was not flying the flaming C of the Calgary Flames hockey franchise, but the next two houses were. She hadn't noticed them on her way downhill to work this morning. This high-end rural route was clearly a hockey neighbourhood. Did local support explain the museum's hockey exhibit?

At a hand gesture from her passenger, she turned off the road a bit uphill from Dee's drive, following paving stones around a modernist house that was all glass and angles. It, too, had a Flames flag hanging from a sunroom cantilevered out over the steep hillside. She stopped on an oblong of paving, as close as possible to the only visible doorway.

"I can manage now." Jan groped for her seat belt, fumbled it open, then struggled with the door handle. Getting her feet outside took a lot of concentration, and once they were on the ground, she sat there breathing heavily.

"I'll see you to the house." Lacey unbuckled and went around the car. Jan stood up, swayed, and clutched Lacey's arm.

"Just to the porch." Jan hobbled over the paving stones and eased herself onto a chair.

Lacey's phone rang. "McCrae."

Wayne was terse. "Vault guy's unavailable. Take off early. See you in the morning."

Crap. Two hours' pay down the tubes. He'd have found something else for her to do if she hadn't left the building. Or did he know she was too shaky to work, anyway? Did he despise such weakness in an ex-cop? Would the next message be telling her not to bother coming back? She could end up working mall security by the weekend.

At least malls tended to be large, open spaces, almost like here. She looked out over the valley. The museum, with its nearly fatal vault, was a toy building down below, but behind it the river churned. Was it eating at the riverbank beyond the museum's terrace? Was that the next fear she would face — being trapped down in the classroom level while murky water beat against the windows? She shuddered and turned away. Never again.

Jan was squinting in the sun, enough Adderall behind her eyes now to lift the sag out of her face. Lacey revised her age estimate down to the midthirties. Almost a contemporary.

"Thanks for the ride." Jan walked almost steadily to the door. She didn't fumble her key in the lock at all, just strode on through as if her previous shakes had never happened. The door shut behind her, leaving Lacey alone on the paving stones with the sweet June breeze whispering through the treetops and the museum far below, tiny and too postcard-like to have caused such mayhem in her life by three o'clock in the afternoon.

Even though her body was crying out for a nap after the disturbed night, she hated the thought of going back to Dee's, to the barking dogs and the omnipresent rumble of the swelling river, not to mention whatever mood Dee had swung into by this time. A long, winding drive out over the open plain would feel great right about now, but driving would not get the motion-sensor lights installed. If she did those first, she could run into Calgary for extension cords and pick up more clothes from Tom's at the same time. With luck, she'd even miss rush hour traffic.

Except, she realized, as she backed up the car to leave the sharp-edged glass house behind, she had yet to inquire closely into which individuals really might be out to get Dee, in case she hadn't imagined the whole thing. The suspect list might start with Dee's ex, Neil, but it had to include that protester outside the museum and the rich man up the hill. Just because he was helpful with the dogs didn't mean he was truly a friend or ally. And the man who'd killed her dog last winter — she was set to testify against him. That was motive enough for some people.

All this was in Lacey's mind as she sat across the black granite breakfast bar from Dee two hours later, eating some divine pasta Dee had imported from one of the trendy restaurants down in the hamlet. There was a glass of wine to go with it, of course, a crisp California chardonnay. But, mindful of the impending drive into Calgary, she wasn't having any beyond a sip of Dee's to see what she was missing. Someday, she might lose her overzealous adherence to alcohol limits, but not while her life remained in this highly unstable state. Getting busted for .08 would be a serious handicap to finding a proper job, not to mention house hunting and eventually moving.

"We have to take this seriously," she said past a mouthful of succulent seafood and sauce. "Start with the protester. What does he hope to gain, with the Centre nearly finished? What did he lose because of this project your company helped finance?"

"The rural municipality approved the museum's development. According to his handouts, he thinks the arts are a waste of time and money. It's not an uncommon attitude in Alberta. I heard a rumour, too, that he'd had his own plans for the land, but his proposal was outvoted. It was before my time on the board, though, and I don't think he blames me for it. He's careful to stay off the edge of the property, so he's doing nothing illegal. Just a nuisance." Dee paused for a sip of her wine. "I hope he gives up when we open. It won't do the tourist traffic any good." She clearly thought the protester harmless; Wayne thought him a potential mass murderer. Lacey thought she'd better investigate a bit further, as soon as time permitted.

"What about Jake Wyman? You said he had a grudge."

"I said he might have been holding a grudge. He hasn't acted like it, though. And he's never asked for his ex's address again. Maybe she got in touch with him and he just hasn't mentioned it to me. Not my business. I wasn't involved with her divorce; I wasn't her friend. I just manage her property while she's out of the country."

"Any other legal matters that might have led to a grudge? Someone you outmanoeuvred in a development deal, or whatever you real estate lawyers do?"

"I don't see how. My listed address is a postal box, not my house. And anyway, lawyers don't stalk each other. We sue."

"Is there any possible way Neil could benefit by driving you to sell this place?"

Dee groaned. "Again with Neil. I know you didn't like him, and yeah, you were right. He's shallow and vain and manipulative, with an ego bigger than Castle Mountain. But to come after me? It would take too much of his valuable time to drive all the way out here. He might miss out on some breaking deal or glam social event."

"You were right about Dan, too," Lacey said, surprised it was so easy to admit. "He's a rule follower to the core, and that core is a true-blue chauvinist. He couldn't stand me outranking him at work, and he took it out on me at home." She wasn't ready to go into details about his methods, and hurried on. "Neil's in real estate, too. Could he get the house back if you felt you had to move? Maybe to sell for a profit?"

"In this market? He wouldn't touch it. I had to take a second mortgage to pay out his share, and now the market is slumping, so I'm stuck with it. Besides, his girlfriend's house is bigger." Dee shook her head. "If it's him, I'm counting on you to catch him at it and make him explain. Beat it out of him if you have to. Not that you'll have to. He's a coward at heart. When he sees your car in the drive, he'll know I'm not alone and he'll call off whatever little plan he has. If it's him."

"Unless he's driven by jealousy and thinks you have another man in here. Who knows what he'd do then?"

"He wouldn't care. He doesn't love me. Sometimes I wonder if he ever did."

There was nothing to say to that, so Lacey said nothing. She spooned up the last of her seafood sauce, moved her plate to the dishwasher, and said, "I'd better get on the road if I'm going to be back to plug in those lights before the mosquito hour. Will you be all right on your own for a bit?"

"I've got lots of paperwork to keep me entertained. And I'm sure there will be another half-dozen crises at the Centre that'll have to be dealt with tonight." Dee's voice was light, but the lines were back around her eyes, and she couldn't stop herself glancing at the open window. Would Lacey return to find the house buttoned up tighter than a meth lab again?

CHAPTER FIVE

Jan clattered pots into the kitchen sink, squinting a bit in the light from the west-facing window. The evening sky glowed, brilliant as midday this close to the summer solstice. The mountain shadows would take hours to creep as far as her house. It felt like the day could last forever. "I can't believe how crystal clear everything is," she said over her shoulder. "Every sound, every sight is crisp and clean. As if time has slowed down, giving my brain as long as it needs to process every signal. Those pills are killer."

"You said you weren't going to take any today because they made you shake so bad." Her husband brought the plates from the table, his strong, stubby fingers shoving them into the dishwasher with ominous vigour.

"I know, Terry. I know. I just … forgot, okay?" Sunlight kissed the suds in the sink, bright and glistening as seafoam, seducing her eyes, wafting her thoughts onto distant voyages.

"You forgot? Why am I not surprised?"

Pulling her gaze from the bubbles, Jan stared at him instead. Tanned face, brown curls, strong neck, sturdy torso in a *Search and Rescue* T-shirt. He looked like Terry, but his expression was hard. Why was he objecting to this prescription? He had supported her through dozens of other treatment trials over the years, in full knowledge that there were no guarantees. This was the only one that cleared up her mental fogs. Maybe he just didn't understand that.

"When I was crashing down there alone on the stairs, it seemed like the only way to get enough energy to keep going. And they really feel wonderful. They give me back my old self for a few hours. My old brain."

"You've said that about other treatments. So much for your old brain." Terry flung cutlery into the dishwasher. A fork missed the basket and bounced through the racks to rest by the heater element. He bent to retrieve it, his shoulders as wide as the countertop. His muscled arms easily reached the dishwasher's back corner. "You could have phoned Rob for help. He was right there in the building. He'd have come for you."

"I forgot my cellphone in the van." Jan swiped suds over a lid, holding on to her temper as tightly as she gripped the wet dishrag. If Terry realized she'd been too messed up to remember that her phone was in her pocket the whole time, he'd never let her go down to the museum again. "And yeah, before you say it, I know I should have had it with me. It was just a bad day, okay? They happen. And one of the workers phoned him for me. No harm done."

No need to mention that the worker had called her a drug addict. Terry was already against the pills. She was sure he had come right out and said that at some point, even if she couldn't remember exactly when. If it was important her super brain would fling it up to visible altitude any moment now. What was altitude in brain terms? What artists painted the inner workings of the brain? Likely Picasso onward. Nobody before that had believed much in an inner consciousness. Except maybe Hieronymus Bosch? Her mind clicked through its mental catalogue of art images until something else crashed into the dishwasher, sending her heart racing.

Terry was halfway across the room before her head turned. "I've got to get ready. Have you seen my hiking boots?"

Jan's head reeled from the sudden shift back to snarky reality. "In the garage, right where you left them last week."

Terry padded sock-footed toward the mudroom. "Where's Rob with that van? He said he'd be right up twenty minutes ago."

"Probably some last-minute emergency at the museum. He was uncrating exhibits when I left this afternoon. Maybe one of them was damaged, and he's got to mess around filing insurance claims and getting photographers out there and stuff. Fine art insurance is killer."

He turned at the door. "I know you're really wired when you talk about art as if you still had a job."

"You shit!" Jan slammed the last pot into the sudsy water.

After a pause he said, "Sorry. That was insensitive."

While he was in the garage getting his boots, she forced herself to breathe in deeply and then breathe out slowly to a four count to temporarily calm her raging brain and ragged nerves. Why was he hating these pills? Or maybe it wasn't the pills, just the situation. Terry's SAR gear was in the van, which she had abandoned because she hadn't managed her energy or medication properly this afternoon. He already ran his life around her needs, and this one night a week he liked to go out and test his fitness, away from her endless small requests for help. No wonder he was irked about not having his gear. Not about the pills at all, but about maybe missing his one night out. And he thought her brain wasn't working. Hah.

When he came back she said, "You're right, Rob's late. And I'm sorry I left the van this afternoon. Will you miss anything important if you don't get there right at seven?"

He looked at her warily for a moment, then accepted her peace offering. "Just the rope-and-harness review, and I'm not leading it tonight, thank god. Some of those bozos couldn't tie a knot to hang themselves with. Heaven protect any lost climber who depends on them for rescue."

She squinted once more out the window. "I see the van now."

Soon Rob came scrambling in the patio doors, his artful dark hair still frosted with construction dust. "Sorry I'm late. Absolutely fatal day at the museum. Jan, honey, how are you doing? I expected to find you comatose on the sofa."

"She took a magic pill," said Terry, yanking his second bootlace tight. "You coming, or will you walk down to your car later?"

"Almost there, dear boy. Honey, we have a crisis. Since you're wide awake and thinking straight, can you please bend your mind to how we can hang the opening show when our insurer won't sign off until the vault is ready? I can't bring paintings in without insurance, and you know it's disastrous if the donors and loaners don't see their darlings on the walls on Friday."

"The vault's not done? I thought it was finished today."

"You were crashed when the bad news hit. Not only is the temperature control still not working, but the racks are hypersensitive. Wayne put the bottom floor on lockdown for safety reasons."

At the door, Terry cleared his throat.

"Oh, coming," said Rob. "Anyway, call Dee if you have a light-bulb moment. I gave her the inside scoop this afternoon, although Camille got to her, too."

"That woman is a menace."

"That she is. I'm utterly thrilled you're standing tall, hon. Dare I hope you'll come finish your tour tomorrow?"

"Not tomorrow," said Terry. "She'll be sleeping off the magic pill. And you'll be the test subject in a noose demonstration if you don't get your ass back in the van." He walked out. Rob gave Jan a bemused quirk of his eyebrow.

She shrugged. "He's on a hair-trigger today. At first I thought it was the pills, but now?"

"Could be he's just tired of getting his hopes up, honey. You've been around this treadmill so often since you got sick." Rob darted across the room and kissed her temple. "Cheer up. If it works, it works. Even if it works part of the time, it's better than before. Right?" The van's horn tooted and he hurried out.

Quiet descended. Jan sloshed at the last few dishes, but could not get drawn in again by the play of light on bubbles. No matter how wired her brain was, her body was using up energy her cells couldn't replace quickly enough. She dragged her afghan out to the deck and nestled down on a lounger to watch the sunset. Bird calls trickled up from Dee's treetops below. The fragrance of roses drifted down from Jake Wyman's gardens up the hill. The evening ahead seemed alternately a beautiful dream and unbearably slow. Every time she thought she was comfortable, some muscle somewhere would twitch or tense up and she'd have to shift position. Her mind ran over and over the same old things. Could she have handled Terry better? Why was it on her to handle him, anyway? But could she have said something nicer? He was clearly at the end of his rope over her illness. Like she wasn't? It was her life and career in the crapper. Round and round and round until she was ready to scream, "Change the playlist, damn it!"

She needed, craved, a mental challenge to distract her. Maybe she could come up with a solution for Rob. She knew almost as much as he did about the selections he'd made for the opening show, and she had five years' more experience dealing with fine art insurers back when she still had a job. That thought triggered a rerun of Terry's snarky comment and she briefly lost track of her new goal. She forced herself off the lounger and leaned over the railing to see if Dee's SUV was still in her drive. If the dogs and the vehicle were home, so was Dee.

Soon she was huffing a bit on the gentle uphill slope of Dee's driveway. The dogs heard her coming and waited patiently, quietly, as usual sensing her need for a less boisterous welcome. After a short rest on the steps, she made her way around to their pen. They covered her hands in sloppy kisses and shoved their heads over the fence for ear scratches, whuffing in their chests as her fingers found the sweet spots. Doggy breath mingled with the scent of sun-warmed spruce. Behind her, a door opened.

"I thought I heard someone," said Dee. "You didn't walk down, did you? It's been ages since you could do that."

"I did walk." Jan came up on the terrace. "I'm all buzzed from those stimulants the doctor wanted me to try. Seeing how far I can push myself."

"You're walking farther? You want me and the dogs to come along, help you get home again?"

"Nope. I'm here to rescue your opening-night show, find a way to finesse the insurance."

"You pull that off and I'll give you a luxury weekend in an all-natural health spa." Dee led the way indoors and plugged in the kettle. "Too bad Lacey isn't back. She'll know what's up with the vault."

"That woman who works for the security installer? She's coming here?" Just great. On top of the pills and the near fight with Terry, now a woman who thought Jan was a drug addict. If only the walk down had not left her legs quivering like manic jellyfish, she could have headed home right this minute. Maybe after a rest.

"Yeah. I invited her to stay a while. We were roommates in university."

"How soon will she be here?"

"Not sure. She's picking up her stuff in Calgary. She said she'd met you?"

"Yes." *The nasty cow called me a drug addict, practically to my face. I can only imagine what she said about me.* "She seems a bit … brusque."

"She didn't used to be that way," said Dee. "But she just left the RCMP, and I think being a cop really hardened her — the outer shell, at least. That's partly why I invited her to stay for a few weeks. The old Lacey is still in there, but she'll need some space to sort of depressurize. To stop thinking like a cop first and a person second." She waved Jan into the vast living room. "Sit here. You may be feeling great, but my aching bones need my comfy chair."

"It all depends on these two gallery entrances," said Jan a few minutes later, pointing to the curling corner of a blueprint. "If they're fully covered, the insurance requirement is satisfied for anything in there. If Rob only brings in the exact paintings he's chosen for the opening show, they can all go straight into the gallery. The rest can stay in Calgary until the vault's fixed. You'll pay for the extra week's storage, but that won't be as bad in the long run as pissing off Jake and all his oil baron buddies on Friday night."

"That's almost too easy," said Dee. "I see Lacey's car coming up. She can tell us pretty quick if the gallery can be ready."

Jan glared out the window. Her legs were rested, hopefully enough to get her home. She could cut out now, avoid the McCrae woman's judgments and silent sneers. But before she could make an excuse, the dogs went ballistic in their pen. Dee hurried out, calling over her shoulder, "I've got to shut them down before Camille phones to bitch again. Do the tea, will you?"

Too late for an unobtrusive exit. In the kitchen Jan pulled mugs from the cupboard and the tea box from its shelf, wondering how often she would visit this familiar room after tonight. She and Dee had only gotten to know each other properly after Dee's accident. Apart from Camille Hardy, whose notion of friendship did not include any women with interests beyond hair, nails, and clothing, they were the only women on this road. They'd kept each other company during some short, cold days and many long, dark evenings of the winter. Would their friendship survive the arrival of Dee's old friend? She brought the mugs to the living room as Dee and Lacey came in the front door, and smiled politely while Dee made the re-introductions. "I hear you'll be staying for a while," she said, trying to keep the anxiety and anger out of her voice.

"Yes, a while," said Lacey, with an odd glance at Dee. "Dee says you have an idea to save the opening show. I'll be glad to pass it on to Wayne if it's at all feasible."

"Hopefully you can tell us that," said Dee. "Show her, Jan, while I get the teapot."

Jan nodded. "You'll have gathered by now that the insurance runs on kind of a points system. All we have to do is up the points on the main gallery and keep the pictures in there."

"Okay …"

"Wayne didn't explain any of this?"

Lacey shook her head. Jan paced while she tossed out the basic information about fine art security that anyone working in the field ought to have known. To be fair, the woman was new at her job, but it was hard to cut her any slack. She hadn't cut Jan any, just made a snap judgment about the pills and reported it to her boss as fact.

Dee came back with the teapot. "Do you have a plan to fix the gallery?"

"We got a little sidetracked," said Jan, pushing aside the plans to make room on the coffee table. "Anyway, Lacey, the main gallery upstairs doesn't have enough layers of security as it is now. Just the locked main door, right? A glass one, so it could be broken through."

"Yes, and the cameras. But it's good enough for those pottery and glass things in the next gallery. They've been up there for a week."

"Those are new ones, by local artists." If this woman couldn't tell the difference between a pot fired yesterday and a hundred-year-old painting by a Canadian master, she had no business working in an art museum.

Dee frowned at the plans. "Round-the-clock security will run into big bucks."

"Rent-a-cops make that much?" Lacey leaned forward. "Maybe I should try that after all."

"The companies that rent them out make a bundle," Dee corrected. "The guards don't. We'd need two shifts per night, two guards per shift, say ten thousand for a week. Hell on the budget. And someone has to set up their routines and check up on them and so on, costing more valuable time. Three days to the opening gala and now this."

Jan abandoned the struggle to sit still. She paced to the fireplace and around the sofas over there, shaking her fingers, her words coming almost faster than her brain could keep up with.

"If we can harden the gallery sufficiently, Rob will need half a day at the storage vault to personally verify each painting's accession number and make sure it gets onto the truck. Leaving it up to the storage folks risks getting a wrong picture, one that won't fit in the wall layout or whatever. We can do it. I can help him."

Dee looked at her funny but only said, "So what can we do to the gallery? Cameras inside as well as on the doors?"

"Not enough." Jan made a second, faster lap of the living room.

"Cameras *and* motion sensors?"

"Nope. Those are the same thing, they record what's going on but don't do anything to stop it. There's gotta be a way. Gotta be a way."

"Jan! Sit down. You're making me dizzy."

"Oh, sorry. Wired." Jan's voice came out too high, too fast, and she wound it down with an effort. The security woman had that bad-smell look again. "Better call Terry. Get him to take me home."

"But we don't have a gallery plan yet," Dee pointed out. "Look, sit down and drink your tea. That will calm you."

"Calm me. Yes." Jan sat and sipped her tea, but her brain was still zooming around. Around and around and around. Too bad it couldn't fly to the top of the hill and back. Maybe a quick pass over the Wyman estate would tire it out. Wyman. Jerking forward, she slopped her tea. "Jake Wyman! He has live wireless monitoring

24-7. How hard would it be to tie in the gallery cameras to his monitoring system for a week?"

Dee wiped up the spilled tea with a napkin before it reached the building plans. "Lacey?"

"I don't know." Lacey put down her teacup. "I'm too new to this work. But if it could be done, why would he let the museum piggyback on his security system?"

Jan giggled. "He would do more than that if Dee asked him."

Dee gave her a look. "He's only being friendly. It's because we're both newly divorced in this community of couples."

"Whatever." Jan found herself looking right at Lacey for pretty much the first time all night. "Anyway, he will because he has a lot invested in seeing the museum succeed. It's got two million dollars of his money in it already. Plus he convinced some of his oil buddies to cough up artworks out of their personal collections. Modern hockey art mostly, but there's a huge Joe Cadot canvas to anchor the north wall, that's being brought over from some horsey place near Spruce Meadows." She was talking too fast again. She took another big swallow of tea, wondering if Lacey had ever heard of the self-taught Métis painter who some critics called the prairies' answer to the whole Group of Seven. Her mind skittered off on a tangent, totting up other prairie painters she'd include in a mythical group. William Kurelek? The Regina Five? But they were abstract artists, not landscape. W.L. Stevenson from Calgary. Who was that other Métis painter? The other Joe … Her mind had stopped answering. She looked up to find that the conversation had moved on without her.

"Jake is a retired oilman," Dee was telling Lacey, "and a major hockey fan."

"With poor taste in wives." Jan giggled. "At least the last one. She was board president before Dee, and she got him to donate to the museum to get it started. Then she ran off with a pro hockey player. From a team Jake owned, too, just to rub it in. She and Camille Hardy were best pals, pease in porridge." There was something wrong with that comparison, but she couldn't figure it out. "That log monstrosity on the corner down there? That's Camille's." She gave an exaggerated shudder, grinning at Dee. "Dee just *loves* being on the board with Camille."

Dee made a face. "Camille thinks her ideas ought to carry as much weight with me as they did with our esteemed ex-president. I pity her husband. He and Jake both got played by hot, young blondes. But this gossip isn't getting the gallery sorted."

Lacey topped up her teacup. "What will the overnight security be after the museum is operational? They won't move all the paintings back to the vault every night, will they?"

Dee groaned. "My god, you're right. The overnight electronic monitoring of the galleries is scheduled to start Thursday. We can just add a few nights to that contract instead. Why didn't I think of that?"

Because I came down here in a tizzy, Jan thought, feeling suddenly deflated. Rob had not intended her to get all fired up. She should have stayed home and rested, so she could help him out by going to Calgary to make sure the storage place packed up the right artworks. That would have been much better for all concerned. She stood up slowly, feeling the familiar tremors creeping down her thighs. The pill's illusion of strength was wearing off.

Dee drove her the two hundred feet up the road that she had walked down with relative vigour only an hour before. The sunset was more beautiful, the bird calls softer, the evening breeze sweeter still, and she was falling fast back into the abyss from which the magic pill had yanked her this afternoon. Jan tried to apologize for getting wound up, to explain how the pill and the desire to feel competent again had pushed her. But the old disconnect was back between her brain and her mouth, and the sentence she planned vanished in the middle of a word. Dee knew this kind of thing happened, had accepted it as part of Jan. But now she had a choice of friends. Why would she choose to hang around with someone who couldn't even finish a sentence without being jacked up on Adderall?

Jan said goodnight and crept into her house feeling even more stupid, more a waste of space than she had this afternoon. There was nothing left to do but retreat to the sunroom, cuddle into her afghan, and try to rest until Terry came home. He'd be eager to tell her about his evening. At least she could act like a good wife for a few minutes, if she could stay alert that long. From peak performance to a dead crawl in the last twenty minutes. The pill gave a spiteful twitch to her spine, and she sat up with a gasp.

"Take only *half* the pill next time," she said out loud, and leaned back down with a faint smile.

CHAPTER SIX

Later that evening, squinting against the sunlight from her bedroom window, Lacey tossed her second knapsack's worth of work clothes into drawers. After stashing her small toiletry kit in the nearest bathroom, she checked the other rooms on the top floor more thoroughly than she had the night before. Two more bedrooms, a lounge area overlooking the vast living room, and the huge master suite at the other end, overlooking the garage. The best view down onto the deck was from Dee's ensuite, a room larger than Lacey's kitchen in B.C. It wasn't ideal, but if the lights came on, they could see anyone escaping up to the trail. Lacey's room looked down the driveway. She was pretty sure the tangled underbrush around the spruce trees would keep anyone from running off that way, although they might dive into it to avoid the lights and creep away later.

With the sightlines established, she went downstairs to find tea waiting and Dee on her phone, sitting through a long rant from that Camille woman they'd mentioned earlier. Shameless eavesdropping revealed that Camille wanted an annotated list of all the loaner paintings in the opening show, with full biographical details on the artists and the current owners. She clearly expected Dee to order Rob to drop his thousand-and-three other jobs to compile her list. After repeated suggestions that Camille consult the printed catalogue for the opening show, which was readily available down at the museum, Dee finally disconnected.

"Damned grand-standing tramp," she said.

"You really don't like her."

"Usually I can take or leave her, preferably the latter, except that she's on the museum board, too, and therefore impossible to completely avoid. Today she's really pissed that Jan interrupted her moment of glory at the press conference." Dee guzzled her cooling tea. "Also, she really is a tramp, not that it's a crime, but it's really low class of her. She drapes herself all over her husband's protege in public. Mick's a nice old guy, mentored this kid practically since his first pair of skates, and now that the little jerk is a hotshot NHL player, he's got Mick's wife nibbling his ear in front of Mick's friends and neighbours. It's impossible to avoid knowing she's got her teeth into more than that. Mick deserves better. Sorry, another call about the gala."

So Blondie this morning was the woman everyone loved to hate around here. Hot gossip. Lacey shuddered. She'd heard plenty of cop-shop gossip in her time, but really tried to avoid the junior high kind of nastiness. She tuned out the next phone call and watched the last vestiges of sunset trail away from the sky. Three days ahead of the event, the museum's opening gala schedule was already too familiar. Friday daytime was for media tours and interviews. The evening portion would involve select local dignitaries, donors, and celebrity guests swilling pricey booze and watching some kind of upscale variety show. Lacey might not be employed for long after Friday if Wayne didn't thaw toward her. He could easily replace her with someone more electronically apt, who didn't need to be coached through the use of a power screwdriver.

Ten minutes later, Dee popped out her earpiece and yawned hugely. "That's enough for tonight. Anyone else can talk to my voice mail. I'm so glad you're here, Lacey. I'll sleep like a log now that you've got my back. But we've been talking about me and my troubles ever since you got here. What on earth is going on with you? Leaving Dan and the RCMP both in the last six months? This is not the old cautious McCrae."

Lacey drained her mug, buying time. How could she summarize all the events of the winter? One too many puke-inducing sexual abuses of children. Disgusting domestic violence calls. Her growing disillusionment with the Force and the eternal argument with Dan over starting a family she didn't want. The whole mess with young Dominic and old Gracie that finally smashed her commitment to the job. And then the final fight with Dan, and the terrifying week that followed. It was too much to condense, but she had to say something.

"The Twitter version: I'm halfway divorced, halfway between homes, and in a temporary job. Also broke while

I wait for Dan to sell our house and for my RCMP pension payout to arrive. Is that one hundred and forty characters?"

"Hell if I know," said Dee. "I've never picked up a Twitter habit. Ninety-nine percent of my day is confidential, anyway. Nothing to tweet about. But you're living at Tom's? And he got you the job with Wayne? Is he still married or are you two …?"

"We are not. I like his wife. And his kids. I've been sleeping on their rec room couch for the past few weeks, working for his friend just over one. When the museum security is finished, I might be reduced to mall security guard. Who knows what I'll be able to afford for a home on those wages. Calgary is almost as expensive as Vancouver."

Dee squeezed her hand across the coffee table. "Aren't we a pair? All that golden promise from our university grad party and poof! Where are we now?"

"We," said Lacey, "are in one hell of a nice house, thanks to your rising real estate stardom."

"Stay with me as long as you like. It's bound to be safer than staying at Tom's. Sooner or later, you know …"

Lacey did indeed know. Once you've had a man's body and found it good, he never seems quite as out of bounds as before, even if he is married now. Between shift work and the fights with Dan, she'd gone months without sex. It didn't need saying out loud, but one extra beer when she and Tom were both tired to death, and they could skid right off that narrow rail again, rationalizing it as they had before: just stress relief.

"Just as well you're here now," Dee went on. "You can come to the gala as my date." Her phone buzzed, then, and after a glance at the number, she added, "Aw, shit, I have to take this one last call. Back in a sec." She left the room.

Lacey took her mug back to the kitchen and stared out into the late twilight at the dog pen. Were the dogs staring back at her, waiting for her to come within biting range? She stepped into the dining room, where the French doors framed the rear terrace and the wooded hill. Yup, all these open drapes — Dee was much calmer tonight. Either the pills were kicking in, or she'd been able to get a grip simply by knowing she wasn't alone. In the living room, the vast windows displayed the Rocky Mountains, coldly blue against the amber streaks of sunset, their jagged tops still partly shrouded in snow. She stood there admiring the million-dollar view, wondering whether going outside would set off the dogs, until Dee came in from her office beyond the wide log staircase. She looked even more exhausted than before.

"Poor Rob. One of these days Camille Hardy will get taken down to size." She dropped into an oversized armchair. "And I hope I'm there to see it."

"You used to be the one doing the sizing. Getting mellow in your old age?"

"Not at all. But steering this museum through the construction phase requires a certain amount of diplomatic tongue biting, more so since Camille is tight with Jake, who's the single biggest donor. She was tighter still with his ex-wife, the ex-president. Even so, I can't let her drive Rob insane. His competence is the only thing standing between the museum and utter disaster. Look, I've got to get to bed. You have everything you need?

Watch TV if you want; it won't bother me. But please close all the curtains before you come up."

Dee may have slept well, but Lacey did not. She checked all the door and window locks, leaned out of windows to make sure the motion-sensor lights were still plugged in, drew all the drapes, and at last went upstairs to bed. Her bedroom curtains she left open, and the window, too, so she'd hear anyone on the porch. Then she lay staring at the glossy log ceiling, as much as it could be seen in the absence of streetlights. She hadn't counted on every outside noise being quite so loud. Creepy rustlings and other unfamiliar wilderness sounds mocked her through the half-open window. Would footfalls stand out above all that background noise? No comforting hum of traffic here, no sirens or horns blaring, none of the nighttime concerto of Surrey or Calgary. No gunshots, either, which was nice. Peaceful country living.

She was drifting off at last when something thumped against the porch beneath her window. She leaped out of bed and leaned out, but all was dark. What had happened to the motion lights? She ran downstairs in the dark, silently to avoid waking Dee. She switched on the porch lights at the front door and dashed outside … in time to see the rump ends of two small deer disappearing into the underbrush.

In the morning she met Dee by the coffee pot. *Power Women Weekly* would surely approve of Dee's intimidating perfection, from the spotless shapely pinstripe skirt and jacket to the sleek chignon. If that Camille woman had ever met this Dee in a boardroom, she would think twice about making demands. Dee was filling a steel travel mug and clearly ready to click out the door on her business-class heels.

"You're up early," she said. "How'd you sleep?" Lacey confessed to rousting the two small deer. Dee grinned. "Hazard of the neighbourhood."

"You're in the city all day today?"

"In and out. I'll be back to the museum, but first there's a vital meeting for my big East Village development. I'll likely be home for supper, but if you're hungry first, help yourself to anything in the fridge or freezer. Or there are a couple of decent restaurants down the hill." Dee waved her mug in the general direction of the hamlet. "Not as many as before the last flood. Quite a few businesses never re-opened."

"That bad?" Lacey tried to imagine flood water spreading over the peaceful valley. Down beside the churning river, she could envision it all too clearly, but the water didn't look that high from here, staying inside its banks as far as the eye could follow them. That would be reassuring if she hadn't seen a lot more gravel and boulders and trees down those banks just a few days ago. All below the water now.

"Oh, yeah, definitely bad. The Elbow River took out a swath of riverbank just upstream from here and detoured straight along Whyte Avenue into the business district. A once-in-five-hundred-years flood, except now they're saying it'll be more frequent than that. It made a major mess and everyone's paranoid it'll happen again despite the expensive flood mitigation the province is doing."

Lacey shared the villagers' paranoia of flooding waters. She shivered.

"Cold?" Dee glanced at the clock and gathered up her stuff. "Coffee's ready, espresso machine's there if you'd rather. You know where the tea stuff is. You have plenty of time before work. No commute."

"I think I'll go for a run," said Lacey. "Where's good?"

"My old route is out the back, on the trail behind the dog pen. Go uphill past the next houses and follow the wall around Jake Wyman's place. Watch out for horse droppings up there. The trail eventually drops behind the hill and reaches a back road." She took a deep breath. "You'll recognize it. That's where I … where Duke … the accident happened. Then the same way we came back the other day. About six kilometres total. Stay on the pavement, though, not on the river path. The riverbank could be undermined in places."

No fear of Lacey not staying as far from the water as possible! "Sounds great."

"Oh, and watch out for thundering herds of hockey players."

"Huh?"

"Running, riding, biking, anything to keep in shape. There are half a dozen staying at Jake's place for the Stanley Cup Finals, including whichever nitwit was driving yesterday. You'll meet them at the gala. Hot today and gone tomorrow if you're looking for some no-complications sex. Every girl's answer for the post-divorce blues."

This morning's Dee was so chipper it was surreal. "Including yours?"

Dee smirked. "Maybe. But let us not be distracted from more important matters. I bet you don't have an evening gown to wear on Friday night."

"I'm not going to the gala."

"Of course you are. We need a security presence in case something goes wrong with the door locks or whatever. Or if Eddie sneaks in with his protest signs. I already talked to Wayne. You're his rep for the night, and my date. I'm not coming home alone at two o'clock in the morning when I could have my own personal bodyguard."

"I suppose you also fixed it so I'm getting paid to attend?"

Dee grinned. "Natch. Don't worry, I'll find you something not disgraceful to wear. Go run. And watch out for deer."

"Hockey players and deer. Check. If I meet a deer on the trail, what do I do?"

"Make some noise. They'll get out of your way. Bears are unlikely this late in the spring, and you're too big for a cougar's lunch. I'd say you should take the dogs, but they know you don't like them."

"It's mutual. Between the bears and the dogs and who knows what else, I was safer on the mean streets of Surrey."

Five minutes later, Lacey stood on the red-gravelled path beyond the dog run, conscious of two sets of hostile canine eyes on her back. The trail ran downhill from here as well as up, its contours quickly lost amid the aspen and spruce. She would investigate that direction after work. Any prowler had to be leaving his vehicle within walking distance, in the yard of some empty house or on a road where the trail crossed it.

For the moment she turned uphill, walking and then jogging, her legs and lungs settling into their familiar rhythms. Lush spring undergrowth sprawled onto the path, the low bushes bursting with small wild blossoms. Instead of the familiar Surrey fug of traffic fumes, car horns, and emergency sirens, all around her were pine-scented breezes and birdsong. It should have been soothing, but her brain could not let go of Dee's problem. Was there danger? From where, or from whom? Could she stop it before Dee got hurt or went completely around the bend?

Jake Wyman's estate wall crept alongside, its brown bricks deliberately blotched with grey to play optical tricks with the surrounding woods, like those paintings of tree trunks that suddenly became spotted horses. An open stretch revealed the imposing reality: interlocked brick twice Lacey's height, interrupted only by wrought-iron gates that were secured with motion-tracking cameras and a keypad lock. Nothing visible through the gates except more trees. Multi-millionaire privacy. Up here, there was not a single other access point from which Dee's prowler might come. On one side, the wall, on the other a thickly treed slope with snarled, spiky underbrush as far down as the eye could penetrate.

Soon the trail turned downward, and she left the civilizing presence of the wall behind. This side of the hill felt more isolated, even lonely. When had she been so alone before? Her previous wilderness experiences were hiking the Algonquin Trail, continually meeting other hikers, and skiing the busy trails at Whistler with other locals and tourists. For most of her adult life, the RCMP was at her back, in spirit if not in fact. There was a void behind her now, almost tangible in its emptiness. No spouse, no partner, no fellow officers to cover her moves at a moment's notice. Just Dee. And when Dee no longer needed her? She shut her mind to the questions and simply ran, red gravel crunching beneath her feet, her eyes alert for branches, bears, deer, horse shit, or other hazards of life on the eastern fringe of the Rockies.

The burn-off effect worked, as it always had. By the time she passed the spot where she'd picked up Dee and the setters, her head was clearer, her body calmer. The gravel road stretched peacefully ahead in the sunshine, devoid of vehicles and yet comforting in its tidy signage, trimmed-back shoulders, and other signs of human encroachment on the wilderness. She was alone, isolated for the moment by choice, but human habitations were close enough for comfort. Then she turned the corner, and there was the river.

She found she was jogging on the spot, watching the distant line of brown through the intervening trees. This far up the long slope of the road, she could tell herself it was not rushing water she heard but the wind among the spruces, and yet her heart thudded as if she teetered on the edge of the torrent. She could not force her feet forward. Crouching on the gravel shoulder, resting her elbows on her knees, she struggled to get her breathing and heart rate down. The breeze rolled over her and birdsong filtered through the nearest trees, and her whole body shuddered with completely irrational panic.

The sound of her own voice jolted her. "McCrae, you cannot be this much of a wimp." It was the voice in her head that had gotten her through the gruelling training at Depot. The voice pushing her to run just one more circuit, swim one more lap, haul one more classmate up from the bottom in the dive-training course. This time she'd had to say it out loud, just to get her own attention.

Her head came up. "Okay, McCrae. Enough with huddling on the dirt like a scared rabbit. You are genuinely afraid of ever being trapped in a sunken boat in murky water again. But this is not that situation. This is a peaceful morning run in beautiful country. Why are you terrified of that water way down there?"

The answer rang through her head as loud as if she'd screamed it. *Dan.*

And just like that, she remembered. They were walking through the river park on a grey spring day in the Lower Mainland. The drizzle had lifted while they were staring into their cups at Tim Hortons, not talking about the unthinkable, the literally unspeakable half hour two weeks earlier. The day she'd told him at knifepoint to leave the house before the neighbours called the cops on them and destroyed both their careers. He'd left, then, but she'd ended up handing in her resignation the next week, anyway, fed up to her scalp with the barely veiled hostility her male subordinates offered their first female shift boss and the lack of official or unofficial support against any of it. This was her first face-to-face meeting with Dan since, and they weren't talking about that devistating half hour. Domestic calls made up half their workload, too many to pretend there wouldn't be a next time.

It was his idea to walk instead of sit. Fresh air, a fresh angle on their problems. Counselling would be a fresh angle, she'd said. I'll think about it, he'd responded.

They walked shoulder to shoulder into the park, away from the few damp dog-walkers, stepping around puddles on the paved trail, while the leaves dripped and the river rushed past, swollen by spring rains farther up the Fraser Valley. He wanted to move home while they worked out a friendly separation. Give his shift buddies time to get used to the idea or they'd ask too many questions. She wondered out loud why it was more important to avoid questions than to face the fact that he'd attacked her in their own kitchen. He'd said, so calmly she didn't believe she was hearing right until it was almost too late to react, "They'd ask fewer if I was a grieving widower." And he'd shoulder-checked her sideways, off the path and onto the slippery riverbank.

Sitting on that sunny gravel road under summery blue sky, two months and four mountain ranges away from Dan, and at least a kilometre from the nearest river, Lacey held out her hands, checking for scrapes across her palms from that desperate grab at the sodden bushes to keep herself out of the murky, swirling Fraser River. He'd helped her to her feet, swearing it was just a bit of horseplay, something to break the icy distance between them. There'd been no further mention of his moving home, or of counselling. A sleepless week later she'd called Tom and arranged to be in Calgary immediately following her exit interview from the RCMP.

After a bit, obedient to the commanding voice in her head, she got to her feet and headed back up the road at a slow trot. There was, she remembered, a short path up from where she'd picked up Dee. It ran steeply up the hill and crossed the main trail near Dee's backyard. She'd barely have time to shower and get down to the museum on time.

The busy morning that followed kept her from thinking too hard about anything. Well, except about pushy Camille from the press conference. The woman poked her shapely nose into every area of the building. A handful of similarly streaked blondes followed her around, their high voices echoing acros the vast atrium like the yapping of a dozen purse puppies. Later they clustered in the outer office, watching through the glass wall as their leader flipped her hair and waved her arms at Rob, no doubt to punctuate some impossible new demand. Camille, the perennial headache.

Lacey focused on adjusting the camera over the elevator door, which, she noted, was the same brand that covered Jake Wyman's back gates. Nothing but the best around here. She went from that task to the next, working around the swirl of activity in and out of the theatre. Rehearsals were nothing to do with her. She would see the show on Friday with Dee.

Dee was at the museum by late morning, calm and focused in the midst of a storm of queries from volunteers and workers alike. Yesterday's despair might never have happened, save that the tension in her thin shoulders relaxed fractionally when she waved to Lacey. The mere presence of a police officer often had the same effect at an accident scene. People trusted you to handle it. You got good at projecting an air of calm competence even before you knew what you were up against. Fake it till you make it — just like Lacey was doing with this job for Wayne. Except that any of these workers or volunteers, or the nasty Camille, might have it in for Dee over some museum-related issue, and how could a stranger like Lacey hope to sort out the merely irked from the dangerously angry? Her phone went off; Wayne sent her down to the studio area to code keypads.

Whatever else might be said about this job, it was giving her insight into how artists worked. This corridor beneath the theatre seats held small studios for rental by the hour, as well as a large room that could be divided for holding art classes. The inevitable messes could be cleaned up in a sloping stainless steel sink that was longer and a bit wider than a coffin. Two middle-aged women stood over the sink, sorting sculpting tools into bins. Occasionally a piece would roll down toward the drain with a pattering of plastic on metal.

Beyond them, a short hallway connected the clay room to the theatre's working underbelly, where scenery and props could be stored and artworks crated up for shipment. This hallway was lined with personal lockers, each with a keypad that needed coding according to Wayne's list. Here artists could store their tools and masterworks between sessions. These were not ordinary bus station or even high school lockers, but cubbies ranging in size from breadboxes to deep, skinny spaces for stretched canvases. Across the aisle were walk-in closets tall enough to hold life-sized sculptures. Some of them contained rolling carts up to waist high, with a tool shelf at the bottom and a square flat top where the sculpting was done. One of the sorting women stepped on a cart's bottom shelf and pushed off with her other foot, rolling across the floor, clinging to the flat top and laughing as she banged against the big window that opened onto the elevator lobby. No one else came into the area except a few lost rehearsal attendees. The women redirected them to the backstage stairs, pointing the way around by the corridors instead of letting them crowd past Lacey and her toolbox in the short, more direct hallway.

Lacey smiled her thanks. Signage wasn't her department, but if it wasn't installed by Friday, she might spend all night retrieving disoriented guests and actors from the bowels of the building. Good thing she knew it so well by now: two asymmetrical wings connected by the third-floor skywalk and the main floor of the atrium. One wing held the galleries, with art at the top and history at the bottom. The other wing was two floors — a theatre with classrooms and other utilitarian rooms beneath. Theoretically only the actors would be down there. The offices and kitchen under the atrium would be swarming with caterers and staff, but that left a lot of odd corners and back halls where partygoers could get themselves lost. Accidentally or on purpose.

By noon, she was inside the atrium's information/security kiosk, kneeling on the floor with her head under the counter, twisting camera cables into a switching box. The midsummer sun beat through the immense window wall onto her back. Sweat glued her waistband to her skin and curls of hair stuck to her forehead. In the confined space, fresh glue and paint fumes assaulted her nose and throat. Beyond the windows, the river's rumble echoed down her spine. When businesslike heels clicked across the paving-stone floor and stopped behind her, she backed out of her confinement with great relief. Even the dire Camille would be a welcome interruption at this point.

"Security?" Dee tapped her ubiquitous travel mug on the varnished log countertop. "Can I have a safe-walk escort, please?" Lacey breathed deep and looked up at the sweat-free, wrinkle-free perfection that was Dee after a turbocharged morning.

"You need an escort? Has something happened?"

"It's the protester out front. Rob and I have an appointment, and last time, he stood in front of Rob's car for ten minutes. We're taking mine, but he knows it and may stop us again."

"I can't move him out of the way. We can't touch him as long as he stays on public property."

"Just distract him. If he's busy explaining his cause to a possible convert, he might let us sneak by without a hassle. You don't have to identify yourself as anything but a curious construction worker."

"I look the part." Lacey stood up and stretched out her back. "You want me to walk you to your vehicle first?"

"Rob and I will sneak out a side door." Dee waved at Rob and picked up her travel mug. "Give us three minutes to get into position, then go out and distract." She and the curator disappeared down the stairs to the studio level.

Lacey hung around inside the front entrance, watching Mr. Protest march up and down the shoulder by the parking lot exit, waving his sign at passing cars as they slowed for the turn onto the bridge. With his muddy rubber boots, greasy ball cap, and an equally filthy green plaid work shirt half-covered by a straggling grey-brown beard, he could play a hillbilly in any moonshiner movie. He might be a nuisance, but was he dangerous?

After the three minutes were up, she strolled along the wide sidewalk of blue Rundle-stone slabs, wishing she were a smoker. Smokers could ask anyone for a light and then strike up a conversation. As a law enforcement officer, she had never needed an excuse. People were either flustered or flattered, depending on their conscience. Now she had no uniform, no authority, and no cigarette. She was going in undercover, an irony considering that one among her barrel of motives for leaving the RCMP was being rejected for undercover work. She kept her hands loose at her sides, fighting her instinct to be visibly ready for action.

"Much traffic today?" she called as she approached.

He shook his shaggy head, eying her up. After a bit he slurped his tongue over his teeth and said, "Nope. Midweek's not the busiest. Couple of guys honked, though."

"Shows they're paying attention, huh?"

"Yup. Darn waste of taxpayer money, this place. Here, have a pamphlet." He tugged a trifolded yellow sheet from his shirt pocket. "Explains all about it."

"Thanks." On the cover, in bold font, were the words, *Make Jobs Not Pots.* Lacey opened the sheet and scanned enough of the crowded paragraphs within to grasp the gist of his argument. Art didn't bring jobs or economic benefits to the community. "You wrote this yourself?"

"My brother did it. He's good with words." He reiterated the main point a couple of different ways before asking, "You gonna be working here long?"

"Another few days, I expect. Only started last week." That was true, and it should reassure him that she had no vested interest in defending the museum. "You gonna wrap up when the place opens, or keep picketing it all summer?"

"Gotta talk it over with my brother. We take turns."

Two nutters. That was news to her. Did Dee or anyone else here know which was which? Lacey leaned her butt against the guardrail, settling in for a chat and, not incidentally, turning Nutter #1 away from the parking lot.

"I'm Lacey. Which brother are you?"

"Eddie. Eddie Beal. My brother's Eben."

"How'd you get started, anyway? I never heard."

"We been protesting this since it was before the regional municipality two years ago. Big waste of money and ties up land that could be used for industry. Something to bring jobs to the locals." Beyond him, Dee's SUV was backing out of its parking space. Did she count as a local? Not likely.

"This place won't hire locally?"

Eddie snorted. "We got a few of those artsy types living out here, might teach the odd class. Only other workers are the secretary — she's from up Springbank way — and the boss guy from who knows where. Plus whoever he hires to shovel sidewalks next winter."

The SUV rolled up behind him. Lacey said, before he could turn, "What kind of jobs would you rather see?"

"Me and Eben wanted a chicken processing plant. Lots of small farmers hereabouts raise their own birds. Need someplace to get them plucked, gutted, and frozen. Right now they're hauling halfway to Rocky Mountain House."

"That's quite a ways," said Lacey, without a clue

where Rocky Mountain House was. The SUV, not quite pausing at the stop sign, rolled onto the blacktop and turned to cross the bridge. Dee was off. The threat assessment was not finished, though. Eddie or his brother, or both, lived nearby, and their grudge against the museum made them prime prowler candidates. "Must have made you and Eben mad when the RM backed this place instead of your idea."

Eddie slurped his teeth again. "You bet. Bunch of us went up there arguing at the council meetings but they paid us no mind. We tried to take them to court, block the transfer of the land, but they got the case thrown out. Too many lawyers on their side. Too much money against us." He waved his *No Pots* sign at a passing truck. "Our kind scraped by out here eighty years before the tourists found us. We just want to live on our own land, raise our kids in the outdoors, grow our own food, and cut our own wood where we still can. This art building brings more tourists to buy fancy coffee and pots. If we grew our own coffee or used our own clay, we might get something out of it. But we get nothing. All it does is makes Bragg Creek look better to outsiders, so more rich folks want to buy up old family acreages and split them up for big, power-sucking houses."

That pretty much described Dee's house, and those of her neighbours. Whether Dee had been involved with the court battle or not, she would be considered one of the enemy. Did Eddie know who she was, where she lived? Or just that she was around the museum enough for her car to be recognizable? While Lacey groped for a way to ask outright, her phone rang. Wayne, wanting to know why she hadn't finished in the kiosk. She rolled her eyes for Eddie's benefit and waved as she walked back to the elitist log-colonnaded building.

Gazing at its picturesque backdrop of lush young trees and rolling hills, with the southern Rocky Mountains snow-tipped in the distance, she wondered in what universe people would build noisy, smelly chicken-processing plants on land that was not only prime for tourism, but mostly upwind of the shopping district.

Indoors, Wayne gave her the cold eye for dawdling outside, so she didn't ask if he knew the protester had a brother picketer. Thanks to the pamphlet, she had Eddie's full name and home phone number. She scribbled his truck's licence plate number beneath them and shoved the paper into her back pocket. Later she would find out what Dee, Rob, or anyone else around here knew about Eddie and Eben. As a last resort, she would pull a favour with Tom and get him to check the brothers' records. If either was likely to be a danger to Dee, there would be a clue somewhere.

CHAPTER SEVEN

No alarm, false or otherwise, disturbed Lacey's third night at Dee's. After breakfast, she walked down the hill road to the museum, stoking up her supply of fresh mountain air and wide-open views before she had to face that vault again.

Her precaution was not needed. The vault's master programmer had not yet returned Wayne's call. His office said he was out of the country and blamed an unspecified time zone difference for the delay. Wayne fumed, but the vault lockdown was maintained. Instead, he sent Lacey hopping through a string of small finishing jobs that likely wouldn't have been done for a couple of days yet. It was well past lunchtime before he called a halt.

"We'll go late tonight, McCrae, so get out for some fresh air. Meet me in the loading bay at," he consulted his watch, "three o'clock. If I'm not there within five minutes, come tap on my van window."

Lacey was not going to make any comments about ex-sergeants who needed afternoon naps. A nap sounded good to her, too, but Eddie Beal had been picketing out front earlier and she had more questions for him. Five minutes later, with no sign of Eddie or his rust-bucket truck, she perched on a guardrail with her back to the river and her phone to her ear, talking to Tom. She'd already given him the gist of Dee's prowler situation when she picked up her knapsack, so she cut straight to business.

"Hi, Tom," she said. "Do you know anyone at Cochrane detachment? Dee can't remember the name of the constable who took her prowler report back in April. They may not have opened a file."

"I'm heading out on a call, McCrae. I'll check the staffing list back at the office."

"Also have a person of interest. Ask what they know about Eddie Beal. Unofficially." She gave him Eddie's home address and licence plate, promised unspecified future favours that they both knew he had little chance of collecting, and hung up. She jogged awkwardly, still in her workboots, over the bridge and through the townsite to the gas station. After dawdling at the chocolate bar display while waiting for a customer to leave, she dropped a bar and a toonie on the counter and asked the scrawny young clerk if he was a local.

"Yeah. Need directions?"

"No. I was just wondering about that guy picketing the new museum."

He looked at her blankly.

"The big building over the bridge?" She pointed out the window behind his counter.

He looked over his shoulder. "Somebody's picketing that place? Cool. What for?"

"He thinks it's a waste of money." And this was a waste of her time. She gave it one more try. "Do you know a guy named Eddie Beal?"

"Any relation to Jasmine Beal? She's in my little sister's class."

"No idea." Lacey took her receipt and went around the corner to the mall boardwalk. Where would Eddie Beal shop if not the gas station? A grocery store and liquor store anchored the far end of the horseshoe, while this side was for tourists: candles, ice cream, souvenirs. The connecting strip included a bistro, an art store, a western decor place, the post office, and a bar.

Thirty minutes of dawdling from store to store, pretending to look at stuff she had no interest in buying, brought no useful information. A man in the art store, who had sized her up as a non-buyer the instant her workboots hit his varnished plank floor, knew about Eddie's protest but dismissed him as a harmless crank. He turned away from her the instant a real customer walked in. The liquor store clerk tried to interest her in coming to a Scotch tasting. The bar waitress brought her a burger and salad, but no information about Eddie.

"He don't come in here daytimes," she said past the stud in her lip. "Maybe try the night shift if you're interested." Which she clearly was not. Women didn't tip women well, and she was saving her smiles for the men at the next table in their shiny, expensive mountain-biking gear.

That left the grocery store and barely half an hour before Lacey had to get back to work. She scarfed down the food, left the money on the table, and hurried down the boardwalk. Inside, she buzzed the aisles looking for bottled water and prepackaged sandwiches to sustain her through the long night's work. There were two tills open and she picked the one with the older cashier rather than the sulky teenager. As the woman ran her few purchases over the scanner, Lacey started the routine again, more comfortable by now with non-official snooping. She smiled at the cashier.

"Do you live around here?"

"Sure do. Need directions?" That question was a standard one in this tourist area. For the seventh time, Lacey said no.

"I was wondering about that guy picketing outside the new museum. He a local, too?"

"Who, Eddie? Sure is. Lived here all his life. Why?"

"Just curious. I saw him with his sign, wondered if a lot of people here share his feelings about the artsy place."

The cashier shook her head. "You want a bag for these? Well, to answer your wondering, nobody cares. More jobs would be good, but they could always build their chicken plant on another piece of land, couldn't they?"

"That's what I thought." Lacey glanced over her shoulder, but there was nobody waiting behind her. "Someone said Eddie was a bit of a loose cannon, maybe even dangerous?"

The woman laughed. "Eddie Beal? Somebody's pulling your leg, lady. Unless they confused him with his brother. Eben gets hot under the collar, all right, been known to take a poke at some who got in his way. He's the idea man, though. If anyone finds a way to get new industry in this part of the RM, it'll be Eben."

Taking a poke at people who got in his way. Lacey had met more than a few of those on patrol. They started off yelling, did some shoving, and finally a punch was thrown. Misdemeanours brought about by temper. Such a man wouldn't bother with prowling around at night. He'd march right up to the front door and pound on it.

"A live wire, is he? And Eddie's not?"

"You got that right. Eddie's the slow and steady sort. Takes a lot to get an idea into his head, but once it's there he just keeps on truckin' until the job is done."

"Thanks." What if the job this time was stalking Dee for his brother? Lacey took her bag and turned away, then turned back. "Do they look much alike, Eddie and Eben?"

"Identical twins. Have a nice day now."

CHAPTER EIGHT

After a shaky morning and a late lunch, Jan made her way down the hill to the museum. She parked, locked up, and made a firm promise to the van that it would get home before Terry got back from his office in Calgary. Up the shady north face of the building she walked, over the deep-blue paving stones to the log colonnade and under the giant hockey banners. She paused inside the huge atrium for a deep breath and got a lungful of construction dust and paint fumes instead. Oops. Better to have done that outside.

Reflected sunlight from the river wavered over the varnished log walls and the deep-blue Rundle-stone floor. Only one thing marred her pleasure in the soaring space: Lacey over by the west stairs, glaring at her like she was a blob of pond scum. Lovely. Couldn't the woman let go of a bad first impression? She turned away without waving and took the elevator up to the top floor, relieved that the half pill this morning had behaved as she had hoped. She could stand upright without holding on to walls and her hands were not shaking. Neither was her mind. Half was the magic number.

Rob awaited her on the atrium skywalk with a clipboard, a digital camera, and a pair of wiry workmen. He led them all into the bare gallery.

"You're to stay right up on this floor, Jan," he said, looking her firmly in the eye. "No running around. These guys will do the heavy work. The hooks are already up. Camille will have to sign for the shipments, being the only director in the building this afternoon. She says she'll be in the theatre straight through. Just go to the top entrance and wave, and she'll come right up. The Cadot and two others are coming direct from the owner's place. They could be here any minute. Any questions, you call me, even if I'm still driving."

Jan flipped through the clipboard's paperwork. Hanging layout all correct — a page of neat, numbered squares and rectangles for each wall — and the last page was an index matching those numbers to paintings.

"How'd you get Camille to agree to take my orders?"

"She thinks signing makes her important, that an oil baron will believe she personally has charge of his precious paintings. As if he'll ever see the form unless there's a need to assign blame. But what that woman doesn't know about galleries! Anyway, if you need a rest, use the lounge past the potters' gallery. I opened the fire door there so the air is fresh for you. Got everything you need to hang around up here for a couple of hours?"

"Cellphone, fully charged. Water bottle. Snack. Sweater. Extra pen. Even a paperback in case I have a long wait for the truck." She waved the clipboard. "And your layout looks fine."

"On paper. If you really hate it once you see the living colours side by side, you'll tell me? It's not too late to shift some smaller pieces around. I can't afford to have anything not exactly right."

"It'll be okay. You're that nervous about this opening, huh?"

Rob clutched his frosted hair in both fists and shook his head dramatically. "Babe, I'm dying. Haven't eaten in a week. All the fat cats will be here, and if one damned finicky thing goes wrong, I can kiss my permanent contract goodbye. I'm tired of being an itinerant art historian. I want stability." He waved toward the gallery's glass doors and the river view beyond. "I love this place. This building. This village. The small minds that fear we'll kill their old community centre but are too polite to tell me so. The lady at the coffee shop who feeds me leftover strudel from her brother the Bavarian chef. Even the oil boom cowboys don't get on my nerves. I look out my office window, listen to the water burble by, wonder which mountain trail I can bike up next weekend. It's my spiritual home."

"Not to mention the steady job keeps the student loans people off your back."

"That, too." Rob's phone beeped. "Gotta go. You are a lifesaver, hon. I couldn't be in two places at once, and the only way to get the correct paintings from Calgary is to go myself. Did you have to take another pill to be here?"

"Half," Jan admitted. "The other half is in my pocket in case I start to crash. If I have to be dragged home in a state of collapse for the second day in a row, Terry is apt to divorce me. He won't be happy that I chose to spend another afternoon here. Being out today pretty much guarantees I won't attend the gala."

"Do you want to?"

"You know the perfumes and stuff will make me sick. So does Terry. He's just tired of going stag when most people will have someone on their arm."

"I'd offer to be his date, but I'll be working. See you later, babe. Phone me if there's any snags."

She watched him hurry away. Dear Rob. Best of her friends from UBC, working at the museum partly on her recommendation to Jake's ex-wife. He was one of the only people here who had known her before she got sick. He never made her feel like a burden, only like an old friend with new limitations. Speaking of limitations, she had to respect them, too. Even though the magic Adderall was keeping her pumped, the ideal position for oxygenated blood to reach all her major organs was lying down with feet raised. She moved slowly to the wide-open lounge past the pots gallery and stretched out on a varnished log bench. Nobody was in the theatre lobby across the atrium, so she had no compunction about putting her feet up on the bench's arm. It wasn't the most comfortable resting place, but it gave her a unique view of the small carvings that decorated the beams and railings: here a pair of bear cubs peeped out, there a sleepy owl. The elevator across the way dinged, disgorging workmen, along with a new guy and a trolley carrying an immense Styrofoam-and-slat crate. The Joe Cadot, centrepiece of the opening show, had arrived.

Camille appeared in the theatre entrance and followed the trolley across the atrium skyway. She hovered as the huge painting was carefully uncrated and, when the new guy handed an electronic clipboard to Jan, she snatched it. "I'm the signatory," she said. "Jan, I assume this *is* the correct painting?"

Jan nodded, keeping her thoughts to herself about people who signed for things they had no clue about. "There should be two smaller paintings with this batch," she said to the new guy. "An Allen Sapp and a Vaughan Grayson."

"In the truck," he said, and, to Camille, "You want to come down and sign for those, lady, so I can get back on the road?"

Camille pouted. "If I must. Jan, can't you …?"

"No," said Jan. "I stay with the Cadot until it's hung." She didn't need to consult Rob's chart, but she made a show of it anyway before pointing the workmen to the back wall. Then she said to the new guy, "Sorry, but I have to see each painting before anyone can sign off on their delivery. A Vaughan Grayson may not be worth as much as a Joe Cadot, but it's still a unique item with an important place in our show." The guy shrugged as if he had expected that, and off he went with the trolley.

Camille glared at Jan. "Now I suppose I have to hang around until that Neanderthal shambles back up here. I'm in the middle of rehearsals over there."

Jan swallowed her first snarky reply, surprised how fast it popped up from brain to tongue tip. Magic pill. "What's hung here will showcase the facility's high standards, not only at the gala, but for the whole summer. Surely you can spare two more minutes."

Camille stalked away.

Jan turned back to see Rob's efficient workmen already in position. The immense frame, bigger than a billiards table, was gently connected to its hooks and hoisted into position. Joe Cadot was the best of the Western Métis painters, as well as one of the bestselling. His photorealist landscapes each contained evocative human touches that caused many an argument over whether he was a true photorealist or merely a neo-Victorian romantic. They were eternally popular with the rugged oilmen and ranchers of Alberta and hung in many Calgary boardrooms. This one featured a wintry glade where men and horses huddled at a campfire beside a frozen pond. Weathered hockey sticks leaned by a tree and skates dangled from a low branch. A good choice to anchor the hockey show. What luck Jake had convinced his buddy to lend it.

While waiting for the next two paintings, Jan looked around the gallery. When she'd been up here the other day, the borrowed hockey memorabilia had still been in crates. Now it was placed in display cases, hung in clusters in the corners, and even standing front and centre, in the form of a life-sized mannequin wearing a vintage blue-woollen jersey and stripped leggings. She was about to risk bending down to read its label when a familiar face on the portable screen behind it caught her eye. It was Mick Hardy, or, to be more specific, Mick's rookie card from many years earlier. Beside it, in the same frame, was another rookie card. The hockey player was wearing a helmet and visor so that only his chin was visible, but the label informed her that the player was Jarrad Fitch, Mick's protege. He was also the hockey player who'd caused Dee's broken ankle last winter. She gave him a slit-eyed glare on principle. Below the cards was a reproduction newspaper clipping, topped by a photo of Mick with one arm around his wife and the other hand on a much younger Jarrad's shoulder. Jarrad had grown to manhood since then, his whole face and body so matured that his younger self was only recognizable in the bone structure around his eyes. Camille looked pretty much the same as now, while Mick appeared old enough to be, if you didn't know better, a proud father standing between his children.

The story below was loosely familiar: a summary of Mick's twenty years in the NHL and his retirement to focus on bringing hockey to kids, applying his years of experience by leading skills camps for teenage hockey players. Based in Ontario then, he'd seen the potential in Jarrad while watching a regional midget tournament and taken the boy under his wing. The article quoted him on the occasion of Jarrad's World Junior Hockey win; how did it feel to see his protege wearing the same medal he'd won himself three decades earlier?

There was no mention of Mick having married, and Camille's name wasn't in the photo credits, just the words *his wife*. Jan thought about that while she circled the gallery, casting her old professional eye over Rob's floor layout. What was it like to be valued only as an arm decoration for an older man? Camille and Mick had bought the corner house below Jan and Terry's maybe six years ago, not long before Jan's first big relapse and the life-shattering diagnosis. Their settling into the neighbourhood was a blur while Jan was fighting to save her barely begun career and marriage, but she thought Camille had been a lot nicer then. Quieter, as befit the small-town librarian she had been before Mick rolled into that small Ontario town and swept her into a speedy marriage. That made up the total of Jan's early memories.

Camille had always been in Mick's shadow then. Maybe the nice Camille was still in there somewhere, but from what little Jan had seen of her in the past few years, now she was all about the luxury lifestyle Mick's fame had wrought and clutched at every iota of privilege that being his wife might confer. Witness her snit-fit over waiting five minutes to sign off on the next paintings. Which should have been up here by now. Jan headed for the atrium and saw the elevator light go on. Finally. Time to call Camille back from whatever she was up to in the theatre.

The officious blonde stood at centre stage, half-draped over her pet hockey player, Jarrad. The kid — a man now, surely twenty-three or more — had his hand on Camille's thigh. Not groping, just resting it there like her thigh was a piece of furniture, another gilded support for his golden life. Another man yelled at them in the melodious monologue of a professional actor. The gist was quickly clear: Camille's star turn at the gala was as an adulterous wife caught with her lover. How crushingly blatant. Poor Mick. Even if he didn't attend the show — and gossip said he was not coping well with his new pacemaker — all his friends and neighbours would have the affair thrust before their eyes. Grinding her teeth for Mick's pending public humiliation, she stepped into the sound-and-lights booth and flipped the clearly labelled in-house mike switch.

"Camille, the next paintings are here."

An hour later, after the first full truckload of Rob's selections from the secure storage warehouse had been checked in and hung, Jan at last remembered who else would be upset by Jarrad's presence in the building. She went back to her bench in the lounge and called Dee. The call went to voice mail. She left a message, but under the circumstances, that didn't seem sufficient. When she turned back to the gallery and saw Lacey hurrying away from it, her first impulse was to flee in the other direction. She reminded herself that Dee must be warned, and yelled instead.

"Lacey! Wait." Ignoring the pinched nostrils, she paced a few steps closer, slowly, conserving energy. "I just left a message for Dee, but if you spot her coming in here this afternoon, get to her right away and tell her Jarrad is here. It really won't do for her to run into him without warning. Thank you."

She walked away, head high, proud of herself for her control of voice and face. No trembling, no tears, just the professional woman she used to be. But when she got into the gallery, the old bone-deep tremor was starting. The afternoon's running around had cost her, and approaching that distasteful friend of Dee's had eaten the last of her energy. She would have to take the second half of the pill after all.

She reached home just before Terry, whipped pasta onto the table, and then was too jittery to eat. She poked the food around on her plate while she glossed over her day and asked about his. He wasn't fooled.

"You took another pill, didn't you?"

"I split it in half. And I lay down with my feet up partway through the afternoon. You'd have been proud of me."

"That's what half a pill six hours ago does to you? Don't make me laugh."

She jumped up, grabbing her plate. "So I had to take the second half later on. Big bloody deal. I was down there longer than I expected."

"You're turning into a drug addict before my very eyes and I'm not supposed to say anything?"

Jan screamed, "I am not an addict!" and flung her plate into the sink. Mushrooms and sauce splattered up onto the window in a hideous melange. She stared at the mess, hands to her mouth to stifle more screaming. What was happening to her?

Behind her, Terry said, quietly, "That's the pills talking right there. Mood swings are a known side effect."

She turned, tears pouring down her face. "I can't give them up. I can't. I have to walk, to talk, to *work*. I'm nobody without a job, Terry."

He put his arms around her. "You are not nobody. You're just running on a permanent energy shortage. These pills are fake energy. They're using up what little power you can generate much faster than you can replace it. Surely you can see that. Smashing things is not you, honey. There's got to be a better way."

"There is no other way," she sobbed into his shirt. "I've tried them all. You know I have."

"You haven't tried a wheelchair," he said, holding on to her shoulders as she pulled away. "Hear me out, now. Just standing up and balancing uses almost every muscle in your body. It's energy wasted. We could get you a sleek, office-style chair and you could cruise around the house and down to the museum as much as you wanted. I can rent one tomorrow and you can ride it to the gala. A queen on her rolling throne. You can save all those nice folks from Jake pumping them for his ex's location. You know he's gonna do it, and he'll think he's being sneaky about it." He paused, waiting for her to smile at the picture of the rough-cut tycoon trying to tiptoe around a subject.

If he hadn't mentioned the gala, she might have been distracted. She might even have been persuaded to try one out. But to appear in front of all those elegant trophy women and hard-driving oilmen in a wheelchair? There wasn't one sleek enough in the world for that. She pulled away.

"I am not a cripple. No wheelchair. No gala. Now leave me alone."

"But no more pills, either?"

She threw his plate into the sink on top of hers and didn't flinch when both of them broke.

CHAPTER NINE

It was after six when Dee returned with a massive stack of pizzas for the overtime workers and volunteers swarming the building. Hurrying to help carry the food, Lacey quietly passed on Jan's warning. For a microsecond, Dee froze. Then she looked hard around the parking lot, closed the car door with her hip, and headed back indoors, where the aroma of hot cheese drew everyone in the building down to the kitchen in record time. Nobody gave her a second glance, and she seemed to have recovered completely from the fractional pause outside. Whoever Jarrad was, he was not going to have an impact here and now. Lacey put him out of her mind, inhaled three slices of chicken taco pizza, and got back to work.

It was eleven o'clock and daylight hadn't yet left the western sky when Lacey finally left the building, slumped in the passenger seat of Dee's Lexus. One more chore awaited before bed: choosing a suitable evening gown. She dumped her filthy work clothes on the floor in the mudroom, scooted up to the shower in her skivvies, and stepped into the massive master bedroom ten minutes later. Dee was in the walk-in closet, a room with more floor space than Lacey's old bedroom. Surrounded by racks of clothes and shoes, she was flipping through hangers holding a rainbow array of dresses, some of whose skirts trailed on the floor.

"No trains," Lacey said immediately. "Do we really have to do this?"

"Yes, we do. You're representing the museum and Wayne's company at the gala, and you'll need to blend into the crowd. Plus you want to look tasty in case opportunity presents for your post-divorce fling. Where Jake goes, hockey players follow like lambs."

"Jocks aren't my style," said Lacey. "But maybe they're yours. This Jarrad that Jan warned me about, was he your post-divorce fling?"

"I wouldn't touch that jackass with a tire iron. Anyway, he's Camille Hardy's boy toy. I told you about her fooling around with her husband's protege, didn't I?"

"Yes, but …"

Dee shook something blue and frilly off its hanger. "Try this one. It's probably not your style, but the neckline ruffles will disguise your lack of boobs." As Lacey's head was enveloped by the fabric, she added, "My post-divorce fling was a nice enough guy up visiting Jake during the All-Star break last January. We had a great sexy weekend, then he went back to his team and I broke my ankle. End of story. Although, if he shows up at the Stanley Cup party on Saturday, I might treat myself to a second helping as a reward for surviving the grand opening."

"There's a party on Saturday, too? Don't you people ever stop?"

"Last fall, when we picked the gala date, we didn't know the Finals would start so late. Or that the Flames would be in them. What were the odds? And that dress is definitely not you. Too cowgirl." Dee flung something bronze and rustling at her. "Try this. More a winter style than high summer, but we can skip the jacket. Anyway, you should come to Jake's party with me. Lashings of food and drink, and plenty of single men."

"I'm not invited. Also, I have to be up early Sunday for a picnic with Tom's shift and their families. The more people I meet in Calgary, the better chance of finding another job when this one finishes." *And a place to live when I'm not needed here*, she didn't add. "Those folks live in my wage bracket, and they're police families. They kind of get me, which pro hockey players and oil barons don't."

"And it's a bit too soon for Cautious McCrae to start flinging with wild abandon. Fine." Dee looked her over with a critical eye. "Bronze is a good colour on you, but the cut is completely wrong for those hips."

"And these boobs. You have some, while I make Kate Moss look overendowed. Face it, there's nothing here that will fit me. But while you're on this fruitless quest, you might as well tell me more about Jarrad. Would he have any reason to hold a grudge, to wish you ill?"

Dee's hand crushed the shoulder of a crimson-silk sheath. "He's the one who killed Duke last winter. I lost my temper with him once already over that." She shoved the sheath aside just a little more roughly than it deserved. "Now I avoid him. His trial is next month and I won't give his defence team a second chance to discredit me as a witness."

"You don't think being a witness against him makes him your enemy and a potential prowler-slash-stalker?"

"I didn't know it was him. Someone else identified his car. He can't make it all go away by frightening me into silence any more than Mick could fix it by hiding the car in his townhouse garage in Calgary while the little brat flew straight back to the States. Jarrad might not like me, but he has nothing to gain by stalking me. Plus he's been away ever since January. He plays for the St. Louis Blues."

Maybe that was the accepted story, but if that team had played the Calgary Flames, he'd have come with them. Or to Edmonton — that was only a few hours' drive from here. There would be a record of when and where the teams met. Without dates for the prowling incidents, though, Lacey couldn't line them up against the game schedule. She could only arm herself with as much information as possible against future threats.

"Will he be at the gala tomorrow night?"

"He's on the program, in a skit with Camille. I can only imagine how horrendous it will be." Dee turned with something greenish in her arms. "Try this silk. Shimmery olive will be great against the theatre walls."

"Point him out to me right away," said Lacey as she stripped off the bronze dress. "I want to keep a close eye on him as long as you're in the same building."

"Please do. If you see him anywhere near me, come right over. I want a credible witness to any words we exchange."

The green silk was the one. Its draped neckline disguised the absence of cleavage. The matching handbag was big enough for her key card, cellphone, and other paraphernalia she would carry in her dual role as elegant guest and security presence. She was more ready for the gala now than the actual building was. Tomorrow would be another hurried day of finishing up small jobs and troubleshooting glitches in all the high-tech security programs. She hung the green silk on her closet door and went to bed.

The first glitch appeared by nine in the morning. The elevator security program, which was only supposed to lock down the elevator if the vault door was open, had fixated on a different door once the vault level was locked off. It kept defaulting to locking down the elevator whenever the caterers propped open the loading bay doors. Tonight, not only catering staff, but actors and musicians, too, would use those doors throughout the evening while the building was full of high-wattage guests who didn't like to be kept waiting. Eventually Wayne gave up trying to debug the program and simply unlocked the vault level, with strict instructions to Lacey to turn it back the instant the caterers left the building that night.

Lacey nodded. If nobody knew the bottom floor was accessible, nobody would bother to go down there. Camille was the likeliest candidate to try to show it off to an art donor, but hopefully she would be too busy once the party got rolling.

All day the bitchy blonde and her shrieking friends got in people's way, interfering with the children's choir's dress rehearsal, harassing the caterers, and criticizing the placement of pictures in the main gallery.

En route to the kitchen for a coffee refill, Lacey narrowly dodged a trampling by five sets of spiky heels in a cloud of expensive perfume. She found Rob gently beating his head on a cupboard door.

"Bad time?"

"That woman." Rob fluffed the front of his frosted hair. "And her blasted posse. I keep reminding myself they'll be off on some fabulous holiday by this time next week. May Ms. Hardy forget to return. What can I do for you, Lacey? More bad news from Wayne?"

"Not that I know of." She pointed to a line in the gala program lying nearby. "Do you know what this Jarrad Fiske looks like? I want to recognize the performers so I don't try to run anyone out of the backstage area who belongs there."

"All I know is hearsay: he's the guy our esteemed vice-president was groping in the theatre. Nobody has introduced us. I'm only the hired help in their eyes. Especially that Hardy woman."

"She hasn't deigned to notice my existence at all," said Lacey. "Considering how she runs Dee up the walls, I'm getting off lucky."

"You are indeed." Rob held out the coffee pot. "Dregs?"

"They'll do me," said Lacey. She went off to the theatre to identify the man Camille was groping. The only man present was one of the teachers from the elementary school, trying to corral a handful of rowdy boys into the back row of the choir risers. She didn't have the heart to interrupt his Herculean efforts, especially since he might not know Jarrad by sight, either.

Around three o'clock the interchangeable blond board members dispersed. Wayne, with a few last-minute instructions, let Lacey go, too. She found Dee home ahead of her, sleek and gleaming from her up-swept hair to her tawny silver pedicure. In a short silk dressing gown over a body stocking, she looked like a flawless apparition, bearing little resemblance to the red-eyed mess of three days before. She hustled Lacey through a light meal, into the shower, and then into a chair before her well-equipped dressing table.

"Updo," she said firmly. "You can paint your nails while I pin. Cocktails at six thirty. We need to be early."

"My hair will take an hour?" Lacey was joking, but Dee didn't laugh. She brushed a bit more furiously, spread some goop on her palms, rubbed that through the hair, and brushed some more. Whatever the goop was, the result was rather nice. Lacey's unruly front curls lay smooth against her forehead, with the wayward strands at the back neatly tucked and pinned. After layers of ex-pensive, nearly invisible makeup were added and dust-ed and the pale-olive dress was drifted into place, Lacey stood staring at her mirror image. "I'm undercover as a trophy wife," she said, looking over her shoulder to check the drape of the gown. "Or a two-grand hooker."

Dee lifted one arm to be zipped into a silvery-bronze sheath. "Ready? I want to go approve the arrangements before Camille gets down there to demand changes. We should have offered danger pay to the whole staff, or in-sured against rage-induced aneurysms."

CHAPTER TEN

Friday's secret half pill got Jan through part of the day. To disguise that small dose, she cut up a whole bunch of pills and dumped them back into the bottle. If Terry didn't take her word, if he was counting the pills, he would find it harder to be sure. At least for today. Tomorrow she would not take any. Or maybe just a quarter, if she really needed it to get on her feet for Jake's Stanley Cup party. She'd been on the lounger in the cantilevered sunroom all afternoon, soaking up the warmth while hiding her eyes from the bright day, swapping between dark glasses and an eye mask. Rolling over amid the pillows and afghans was an effort. She did it anyway for the sake of changing the view from uphill, into the setting sun, to downhill, so she could look toward shadows. Shadows suited her today, with everyone she knew heading for the museum when she would be staying home alone, again. The gala guests were friends, neighbours, Terry's co-workers. They shared more of his life than his own wife did. What if the contrast between cranky, frumpy Jan and some sleek, tennis-playing harpy got to be too much for him? Would he walk out? Would he force her out of the house into a tiny apartment in Calgary, where she'd eke out a miserable existence on her ever-ebbing divorce settlement? Would he stay with her out of guilt and have a long affair, or a bunch of them? Would she end up like that cellist in that movie who had ALS or something and was left to wither alone while her husband started a family with another woman?

She pushed the thoughts away. Emotion was energy and she had none to spare. Terry was a decent guy and he loved her. She had freely chosen to help Rob yesterday, chosen to overclock her mitochondria with the stimulant pills, and now she was paying for it. Tonight's dress would do for some future party. Although it was hard, today, to think of any occasion that would be worth three days' rest beforehand, plus a whole day's effort to pace the getting ready, followed by however many days it took to recuperate.

Today, with the nausea and the muscle aches and the brain fog that smothered any train of thought and made television a too-bright, too-loud horror, all she could do was gaze out the windows on the shady side of the house, watching the neighbours depart in their gala finery. She had her bird binoculars to hand, but birds moved too fast for her exhausted and uncoordinated brain to follow them. People she could keep in focus for a bit longer.

First Dee and her guest came out, lifting long, shimmering dresses above the gravel driveway, tucking their glamorous skirts into the Lexus. Their golden chariot drove slowly down the hill, vanished behind the trees at the curve, and reappeared when it turned into the museum parking lot. Dee had barely stepped out of her vehicle when Jake Wyman's beloved old Mercedes rolled smoothly into Dee's driveway. If he was hoping to casually offer his escort to the museum, he had missed his chance by scant minutes.

Terry came in from his post-work run, glowing with health and sweat. "Get you anything before I shower?"

"Could you warm up my rice bags?"

"Still having chills? This must be your worst crash all year." To his credit, he didn't mention the pills. He took the flannel-covered lumps to the kitchen. The microwave hummed. Although Jan listened hard, she couldn't make out any sound of him pouring out pills for counting. When he brought the heated rice bags back, he looked past her and asked, "Is that Jake's car at Dee's place? Did he convince her to be his date?"

Jan tucked the bags back under the afghan, shaping one around her feet and laying the other across her aching thighs.

"She didn't wait for him. You think he's after her to be Wife Number Four?"

Terry shrugged. "Or just being a good neighbour. He's been great with the dogs. Those mutts like him as much as they like you." He left for his shower. Jan closed her eyes, giving them a rest from the glare outside. If he went to the gala without asking about the pills, she would not have to decide whether to lie to him or not.

How much time passed she wasn't sure, but Dee's setters started barking. At first it was just one yap from

Boney, but Beau quickly joined in. So many days, she had lain right here listening to them — this was their intruder alert. A bear? She reached for the binoculars again and scanned as much of Dee's yard as she could from this angle. Nothing. It must be in the trees, or on the trail. Jake had just missed it; he was turning out of Dee's drive. He hadn't gone far when Camille backed her butter-yellow Bimmer onto the road with utter disregard for anyone coming down it. Jake hit his brakes at the last second, and then his horn. Camille waved a hand in a way that might have meant anything and sped off down the hill. Going to give Dee a hard time because her dogs were barking? Jan swung the binoculars back to Dee's yard.

Terry came back, showered and dressed in his lightweight summer suit. "What's up down there?"

"Bear, I think. I can't see it, though. Can you go look from the bedroom? If it goes after the dogs' supper you'll have to shoot off a banger at it." Terry loved his pen-sized bear-banger launcher. With the extra elevation on his side, he could lob it over the intervening trees and pop it off right behind Dee's house. Hopefully the bear would run, and the dogs would not be too upset by the explosion. It wasn't the first time they'd been close to one, but their sensitive ears would hurt. Terry had barely gone when Mick and Jarrad the boy toy appeared on Dee's deck. Jarrad was supporting Mick. What on earth were they doing down there? And dressed for the gala, by the looks of it. They must have walked up the trail, an insane feat considering Mick's weak heart. "It's not a bear," she called after Terry. "It's people. I think Mick's in trouble."

She sat up for a better look and trained her lenses on the pair, watching as Jarrad helped Mick into a deck chair. He dragged the chair out to the terrace, into the sun, and dropped to a crouch beside it. Terry came back.

"I think it's his heart," she said. "Should we call 911?"

"If it's an emergency, Jarrad will be dialing already. Is he?"

"Nope. They're just sitting there, maybe talking. Mick's not grabbing his chest or anything."

"Probably just taking a rest, then. I can stop on my way down, offer them a ride. You need anything before I go?"

"I'll be okay." Jan's wrists ached from holding up the binoculars, but she kept watching. If Mick got suddenly worse, she could call for help faster. "He should be home, in bed or in front of the TV. Not dragging himself out to watch Camille humiliate him on stage."

"Perils of marrying someone half his age. Not showing up would enrage her." Terry kissed the top of her head. "You know where I'll be if you need me." A couple of minutes later, his van rolled up Dee's driveway. Jarrad hurried to meet it. Terry didn't even get out, just talked from his seat and then drove away again. Jan fumbled for her phone and hit his number as he pulled into the museum lot below.

"You were supposed to help them."

"Didn't want help. Jarrad said he'd walk down for his car in a minute. They're adults. They can manage." Jan swung the glasses back. Sure enough, there went Jarrad now, jogging easily down the drive, leaving Mick slumped in the chair with his head in his hands.

"Okay, I guess you're right. Have a good time. Say hi to Dee for me, if she stands still long enough."

Jarrad came back at the wheel of his vintage red Corvette. He helped the older man into the car. Mick was far too frail to be out of the house. He'd have to face the humiliation of Camille's "acting" with Jarrad, too. Poor Mick. That was one part of the show Jan was only too happy to be missing. And that was the last of the neighbours, the final distraction. It had helped her, though: Terry had left without mentioning the pills. She wanted to feel victorious, but shame crawled like ants across her oversensitized skin. Was she really an addict, even though she had hardly been on the Adderall a week? Would her marriage be destroyed by this latest failed treatment attempt? She busied herself rearranging her blankets and rice bags. Then she distracted herself by trying to think of a famous painting whose sky matched the translucent turquoise glow off to the east. Today the fixed world of long-dead artists was easier to face than the ever-threatening present.

CHAPTER ELEVEN

As they locked the SUV in the museum parking lot, Lacey said, "Now remember, point out Jarrad to me, so I'll know when to run over to you and be a witness. Couldn't I just bounce him early?"

"I wish, but he's on at the end of the program." Dee looked around. "His car's not here. He won't come before Camille does, anyway. Unless she saw us passing and chases us down, she won't have much time to alienate the waiters before some celebrity arrives to absorb her attention."

Indoors, Lacey introduced herself to the evening's uniformed security personnel. The two men already had their assignments and patrol routes from Wayne, more proof, if it were needed, that Lacey was surplus to requirements. She was only here because Dee had asked for her, only responsible for locking up at the end of the night. Quite a comedown for a woman who, a month ago, was supervising a full shift of constables in one of

Canada's largest, busiest urban-rural detachments. Dee was a lot calmer for her presence, though. She'd had three full nights' sleep and that had to count for something. The motion lights hadn't tripped once. No prowler. Was it just that Lacey had scared them off, or had there ever been one? The matter must be thrashed out soon.

Camille Hardy arrived like royalty, flouncing over to the kiosk to demand the vault be opened so she could show the state-of-the-art security to potential art donors. Lacey refused. Camille ordered, citing her status as board vice-president. Lacey was about to call Dee over when she appeared and stymied Camille instantly by pointing out it would not do the museum any favours to demonstrate a malfunctioning vault. That the vault was technically accessible because of the software glitch somehow never got mentioned. Then an early guest arrived and the vault was forgotten.

Camille was soon surrounded by her posse, at which point Lacey realized no borrowed evening gown could disguise this ex-cop as a trophy wife. These women reeked of money. It was a toss-up what cost more, the ten shades of streaks in their hair or the designer gowns on their sleek bodies. Every dress, every head, was in a hue to complement the decor, making the posse *en masse* a shimmering blur. Even their lipsticks blended. Their names, when Dee introduced them, were a similar blur: Tiffany and Tami (spelled out lest Lacey mistake it for a common "Tammy"), Twyla and Chareen. Women of a kind virtually unseen in the male-dominated world of the Mounties. Was it too late to return to the Force, retreat back to that orderly life where her street-earned skills had been respected and her hairstyle unimportant as long as it had no trailing ends for a suspect to grab?

Jake Wyman, his leathery face grinning above his western-cut tuxedo, stepped around the posse and charged toward Dee. If ever there was a bull in a china shop, he was it, from his string tie down to his gleaming black cowboy boots. Dee greeted him with both hands held out.

"The museum's patron saint. Jake, this is my friend Lacey McCrae from Vancouver."

"Nice to meet you, young lady," he said, and shook her hand. "You gonna bring her to my party tomorrow, Dee-Dee? Nothing fancy like this shindig, Miss McCrae. Just a buncha folks watching the hockey game. Beer and pretzels kinda thing." Imported beer, no doubt, with a German pretzel-twister flown in for the occasion. He turned away without waiting for an answer. "Camille, honey. How's that old man of yours doing with his new pacemaker? Getting back on his game?"

"Hardly," said Camille, with a slight curl to her perfectly painted lip. "He's so sure he'll have a heart attack that he'll barely leave his recliner. I had to push him out the door for a little walk with Jarrad."

"Time for photos, ladies," said Dee. The expensive women flowed upstairs with Lacey trailing them. They clustered by the theatre so the photographer and videographers could capture the opening moments for posterity. Caterers lit fires under chafing dishes and whipped covers off trays of chilled canapés. Wine corks popped. The string quartet stationed in the upper-east lounge lifted their bows. The grand opening gala was finally under way.

As the theatre lobby filled up with guests, Dee found a moment to introduce Lacey to another neighbour. "Terry Brenner, Jan's husband," she said. "Terry, please make sure she knows what Jarrad looks like, okay?" Then off she spun into the throng.

"You're Dee's date?" Terry offered his hand.

Lacey shook it. "Don't let the dress fool you. I'm the bouncer."

"It would be a thrill to be rousted by someone so elegant." He steered her toward the bar. "Let me introduce you to the people most likely to cause trouble: the hockey contingent. Not that they'll set out to create havoc, but they're all big and physical and think they're invincible. So they break things, including themselves, through simple hijinks."

"What are they doing in an art gallery, then?"

"Catering to the whim of Jake Wyman. Every year he rewards top-scoring youngsters with a week by his pool. Golf and horseback riding by day, parties and loose women by night. Except around here, all the loosest women are married."

"Ouch."

He shrugged. "Bored young wives of rich old oilmen, it's bound to happen."

"That what happened with the first patroness of the museum? I heard she ran off with a hockey player."

"Pretty much. Jake's my boss, though, so let's change the subject before I say something I shouldn't." Terry wedged them into a cluster of muscular young men. "Guys, meet one of the only single women in the room. Lacey McCrae, meet ..." He rattled off a list of names.

The young hockey players shook hands politely. No posturing for reporters here. They were barely into their twenties, brawny, well fed, and her height or better. Definitely eye candy, highly suitable for some women's post-divorce fling. But, as Dee had often pointed out, Lacey was constitutionally incapable of flinging. Nor had she ever gone for younger men. This lot looked so young, in fact, that she couldn't help thinking sex with any of them would feel like child abuse, regardless of the legal definition. If one of them was Jarrad, she hadn't caught the name, and it was impossible to discreetly ask Terry to repeat it.

"Which teams do you guys play for?" she asked instead. After that, smiling and nodding seemed all the response necessary.

Before anyone thought to ask her a question in return, another athlete joined them. "Jarrad!" said someone. "Mick with you?"

Lacey glanced over to the bar, where Dee stood between a pair of distinguished older men in suits. No risk of a confrontation at the moment. She turned her attention back to Jarrad. Camille Hardy's boy toy was slim, dark, wiry, and barely her height. He couldn't be mistaken for any of the taller, brawnier young men around her. She couldn't see any particular attractiveness in him, either. Why would a rich, gorgeous woman like Camille bother with a sulky boy ten years younger? Was it just to spite her husband?

"Barely. No thanks to the bitch queen." He flicked a hand toward the bar, where Camille had joined Dee for yet another photo op.

Bitch queen. Did he mean Dee or his lover? Either way, he had all the class Lacey had expected from a pro sports type. She slipped out of that group and wound her way through others to the theatre doors. A glance inside told her nobody was in their seats yet, so she set off across the atrium bridge on a self-appointed patrol. The main gallery held a smattering of well-dressed drinkers ogling the artworks. In the pottery gallery, some young people were taking selfies beside the NO FLASH PHOTOGRAPHY sign. A handful of guests watched the musicians in the lounge, or stared out across the atrium. She went down the east stairs, disturbed an absorbed couple in the Natural History Gallery, and chased a handful of choirboys out of the settler's cabin. Crossing the atrium's stone floor, conscious of the river beyond the great glass wall, she descended to the classroom and studios corridor. Now designated temporary dressing rooms, this area seethed with performers in varied states of preparation and pre-show jitters. Dodging musicians and a double line of fidgeting child choristers, including, she noted, the bunch from the cabin, she took the backstage stairs up. Sidling past the stage manager and his crew, she climbed up the auditorium's side stairs, past row on row of seats, then checked the private boxes with their grey curtains. All in order, and nothing for her to do but return to the theatre lobby to scan for potential trouble.

Not much had noticeably changed. Dee flitted from group to group, waving a wine flute whose level never dropped. Jake Wyman had Jarrad cornered by the bar and was prodding his shoulder with a stubby finger. The other hockey players remained a group unto themselves, bantering and occasionally shoving each other. At least they weren't swinging from the exposed log rafters. Everything seemed peaceful, and the elevator hadn't glitched up once. No need for keys or codes so far. The music stopped, a bell chimed over the sound system, and people began moving toward the theatre. The last smokers trailed in from the terrace. Performance time.

Dee came over to Lacey. "We're in a box on this side," she said, leading the way. "Any trouble so far?"

"Nada. Were you expecting some?"

"With this crowd, a delayed elevator is a crisis. An exaggerated sense of entitlement is in their genes. Plus, you never know with the hockey jocks. Some of the younger ones you'd swear have never gone out in public before." Dee took one of the box's armchairs and waved Lacey to another before whipping out her phone for a last-minute check of messages. Terry Brenner came and collared the third chair.

"Bounced anybody so far, Lacey? Here's hoping the hockey players will behave with Jake in the same box. Although he'll be grilling them again."

"What does he want from them?"

"His ex-wife's address, I bet," said Dee, her thumbs busy on her phone.

Lacey blinked. "Does everyone know he wants it?"

Terry nodded. "The players were discussing it earlier. Everybody's afraid to tell him in case he sends muscle, but nobody wants to refuse outright, either."

"Why not?" It was hard to imagine the old ranch-hand fellow had the vindictive streak necessary to send thugs after the man who stole his wife. But maybe there was some cowboy code of conduct involved.

"He's a part owner of a team," Terry said, "and knows owners and management everywhere. He could cast a chill on a fellow's career."

"But would he send a goon squad?"

"I don't see it myself, but these guys are young and impulsive and judge others by their own reactions. Some player a few years ago went so far as to hire a hit man to go after his agent. Didn't succeed, and later said it was all a misunderstanding, but still. And that's far from the only scandal that's still raw. All that money they get so young makes them targets for scammers and wild-living hangers-on. And the sex abuse scandals — those are hard for the whole sport to rise above."

"Sex scandals? With the groupies?"

"You mean like the rape accusations that make the news in the States, against basketball and football players? Not so much in hockey, whether it's not there or just not public. But young players being abused by coaches and others around the arenas. That has happened far too often. One guy was a serial predator and went through half a dozen junior teams before anyone reported him. There were also rumours about the guy whose player hired a hit man, but nothing proven there." He scanned the audience below them. "Sheldon Kennedy — one of the most respected player whistle-blowers — was reported to be coming tonight, but I don't see him."

Dee tucked away her phone. "He's got a kids' camp this week or something. I don't think art galleries are high on his priority list, anyway. Lacey, in the next box up from Jake is Mick Hardy, our local hockey legend. Camille should be with him, but she's backstage making the actors and MC crazy. Mick didn't do the cocktail hour. Having heart trouble, so he went straight to his chair."

"Poor guy," said Terry. "It's a real comedown for a lifelong athlete. I should probably go sit with him, but frankly he depresses me, trying so hard to pretend he's doing okay."

Lacey looked over her shoulder. On the landing behind them, a videographer was alternately zooming in on famous faces and panning over the audience. Another video camera on the opposite landing half-blocked the stairs down that wall. Dee pointed out a provincial Cabinet minister and a media personality in the box below theirs. The house lights darkened. Rob stepped up to the microphone to express gratitude for all the hard work put in by the board and volunteers to bring them to this auspicious moment, then introduced the prominent radio personality who would be the master of ceremonies. The MC told the usual kind of jokes before introducing the first act, the children's choir.

"The 'we did it all for the children' element," Terry said.

The choir managed to keep their lines and their voices together, and the kids received enthusiastic applause as they filed off. They were followed by a mix of professional and amateur acts, including Camille's posse posing as giggly, wiggly statuary in a mock artist's studio. If there was a point to their performance, Lacey didn't catch it. She was trying to spot Jarrad in Jake's or Mick's box. He was in neither, and she was wondering if she should go downstairs to see what he was up to when the curtain came up on him, wearing a bright-green doublet and lip-locked with Camille, who had draped a scarlet tunic over her golden gown. As a stab at Mick, it could hardly be more obvious. All that was missing was a giant letter *A* on her front.

Dee leaned over to Lacey. "I've got to go down for the finale."

"I'll come, too."

"No need. Jarrad's on stage and there are plenty of witnesses down there if we cross paths afterward." Dee edged behind the box curtain.

"Lucky her," Terry muttered, and Lacey had to agree. Camille's star turn was worth skipping. She was shrill, Jarrad was wooden, and only the pro actor was believable, investing his role as the cuckolded king with rage and grief at the betrayal. Lacey looked over at the box where the ailing Mick Hardy sat, but he had retreated behind the curtain. No doubt hiding his face in anticipation of just such curious looks from his so-called friends. Poor man.

CHAPTER TWELVE

As Dee hurried down the west stairs, a lone security guard at the kiosk looked up, nodding to her as she passed. The classroom level, in contrast to its earlier chaos, was now deserted. Most performers had already done their turns, changed their clothes, and gone up to the bar, or in the case of the children, gone home to bed. Her heels clacked on the easy-clean beige floor tiles. In the theatre above, two hundred people rustled, coughed, and whispered, yet down here all she heard were her own footsteps. Unease prickled up her spine. Her prowler could be someone connected to the museum. Maybe she should have brought Lacey down with her after all.

She shook off the shiver. Her immediate problem was how many minutes she had to repair her face and gather her thoughts for the presentation. Cutting through the clay room, she slipped through the short corridor to the packing room, presently the adult performers' deserted green room. From here, the carpeted stairs led her silently up to the backstage area. Camille's shrill voice assaulted her ears, followed by the smooth bass modulation of the professional actor. From what little she could see of Jarrad out on the stage, he was in his usual sulky pose. His voice was equally uninspired. He'd have no post-hockey acting career. Rob was in the wings on the far side, wincing and looking at his watch. The stage manager stood near the stairs, one eye on his clipboard and the other on a digital readout.

Dee whispered to him, "How long until the presentation starts?"

"Twelve minutes. Be back in nine."

"Thanks." She retreated down to the classroom designated as the women's dressing room. The hush enveloped her once more and she sank into a chair before the rented makeup mirror, grateful for these few minutes of peace. The culmination of two years of work was being celebrated overhead, and all she could think of was that she would soon get her life back. There would be other duties yet, cheques to countersign for the last tradesmen and tonight's event expenses, but her main workload was over. Three nights of decent sleep had restored much of her inner calm. She could look forward to more of that, as it seemed Lacey had scared off the prowler with her mere presence. A low-stress weekend stretched out ahead of her for the first time since that horrible day last fall when Neil had made his affair blatant. Suddenly, this weekend could not start soon enough. She sat up straight, lightly dusted her face with powder, laid fresh gloss over her long-wear lip colour, and made for the door, ready to get that presentation over with so all those people would go away and let her get home to bed. Striding into the hallway, she ran into a man's broad chest. He grabbed her arm. She shrieked.

"Dee-Dee. Did I hurt you?"

"Jake." She sagged on his strong hand. "You scared the life out of me."

"I saw that youngster leave the stage and didn't want you to run into him alone down here."

"That was kind of you." Dee looked around but there was no sign of Jarrad. A small mercy for her pounding heart. "Do you mind escorting me to the backstage stairs?"

"Pleased to, ma'am." Jake placed her hand on his arm and let her set the pace. "I'll stay behind the stage and take you upstairs when you're done. Can't have you getting lost while all those nice folk will be waiting at the bar to toast you."

"You mustn't wait." She was almost sure he didn't know about the presentation, but it would look contrived if he appeared from the wings when his name was called. "There's a great finale planned and I want you to tell me how it looks from the audience. Will you promise me to hurry straight back to your seat?"

"Yes'm." If he'd been wearing his usual cowboy hat, he'd have tipped it.

Five minutes later she stood in the glare of the spotlight, backed by the full board of directors, while Camille escorted the museum's most generous patron down the auditorium stairs to read the plaque that would soon adorn the main gallery upstairs. The Wyman Gallery of Western Canadian Art received its formal name to thunderous applause. The show was over, the celebration in its final phase.

Afterward, Dee circulated through the sunset-streaked theatre lobby with a glass of champagne she couldn't make herself drink, deflecting congratulations onto Rob, the workmen, the other board members. Her face ached from smiling and her feet longed for their fuzzy slippers, but at least her ankle wasn't throbbing. Thank heavens for comfortable evening flats and the long rest during the show. At last the crowd thinned. Jake came to offer her a ride to the private supper planned for board members and VIPs.

"Thank you, but no," she said on a stifled sigh. "I need to stay here and see the caterers out. I'll catch up." He protested, but eventually she was able to cross the fast-emptying room to trade her warm champagne for a double of single malt. She sank into a chair by the river-side windows, too tired to care that she was almost alone. The rushing water outside reverberated in her limbs as her muscles unwound. Like getting a massage from nature. Lacey was around somewhere and Jarrad was not. The little monster had vanished right after his performance, and not a moment too soon for her frayed nerves.

Terry Brennan's reflection walked toward her in the vast window. "Any more of that Scotch?"

"Tell the bartender to give us the rest of the bottle and a few more glasses. Anyone left now deserves a drink."

Lacey arrived, the green silk rustling as she strode across the space. "You're almost the last people here. I thought Camille Hardy would be playing the diva post-show, but I haven't seen her."

Terry looked around. "Now you mention it, I haven't seen her or Mick. Maybe they're having a flaming row backstage."

"No Jarrad, either," said Dee. "If anyone's having anything down there, it won't involve Mick. Have you seen how bad he looks tonight? He could never get down those stairs."

Just then Rob waved at them from the theatre entrance. "I think this guy is having a heart attack."

They arrived at the farthest row of private boxes to find Mick lying back in his armchair, his face as grey as the curtains. Dee picked up his wrist. His skin was slippery with sweat but his pulse seemed steady. But then, he had a pacemaker, didn't he? She had no clue what kind of pulse would signal an attack in a mechanized heart. She looked up helplessly and Lacey took over, her face a professional, neutral mask. She must have looked like that on the job every day, but it wasn't a face Dee was used to.

"Mr. Hardy?" Lacey spoke calmly. "Let's get your feet up. That will help. And we'd better call you an ambulance."

He nodded weakly and whispered, "My wife?"

"I'll find her," said Rob. Terry was already connected to an emergency dispatcher on his cellphone. He relayed questions about Mick's condition. Dee stayed at Mick's side, holding his hand and murmuring soothing words in the intervals between repeating his whispered answers for Terry. Mick should have been at home resting. Instead he'd been dragged here to be publicly humiliated by his wife and her lover, neither of whom had bothered to check on him afterward. How long had he been sitting here, unable to rise, unwilling to call for help? Even in the final throes of her own marriage, she would never have abandoned Neil if he'd been ill. Camille Hardy deserved to be slapped senseless.

Camille arrived as Terry brought the paramedics from the elevator. She stayed back until they had her husband on a stretcher, ready to move. Then she said, "You would go and spoil my evening, Mick. If anyone sees Jarrad, tell him we'll see him at home." She stalked out, her golden skirt swinging.

"Bitch," Dee muttered, as the elevator door closed. She led the way back to the theatre lobby. The last bartender was rolling trays of used glasses toward the elevator. She snatched back the half bottle of Laphroaig and grabbed clean glasses from behind the bar. Settled by the windows, the hush of an empty building enfolding her, she raised her glass. "To Mick. I hope he makes it."

"Mick."

After a swallow, Terry said, "Rob, come up to the house tonight. That way neither of us has to drive, and we can drink to this evening being bloody well over."

After the caterers left, Dee sat with Terry on the river terrace while Lacey set the alarm system and Rob walked the outside perimeter to test all the doors. Thunder rolled through distant mountain passes, but down here the air was so still she could hear mosquitoes whining in the trees. The river had risen since this afternoon, deceptively smooth over its wide, rocky bed. Would they close the bridge by morning? If so, she'd be down here sandbagging, because another foot of water would threaten the offices and the whole lower level, including the vault. The architects had designed against a once-in-two-hundred-years flood, and here they were, on the brink of another once-in-a-thousand one while the 2013 flood's destruction was still raw. Would any of the locals show up to help sandbag here when established homes and businesses were at risk? She made a mental note to investigate renting some of the new water-filled tube dams. It would hit the budget hard, but not as hard as being flooded before they'd even opened the doors.

Overhead a few high clouds blotted the stars, but enough moonlight came through to shimmer on the water, mesmerizing her tired eyes. Terry hadn't said a word, just sat there thinking his own thoughts, a bulwark against the chill sliding down the valley from the snowy peaks. She hadn't felt so safe outside at night in months. The gala was done, the museum formally converted from a work-in-progress to a working cultural building. The water would soon stop rising. She could wind down and start to enjoy her summer.

When Lacey and Rob reappeared, she wasn't ready to leave. Driving up the hill would end this peace, this freedom snatched from the cage of cars and buildings. The unknown prowler had trapped her indoors as surely as if he'd locked her up. She tested her ankle. No grinding, no pinching. The flats had really helped. She could walk up to the house. A fence of friends was better than getting back into her car right this minute.

"Anybody up for a moonlit stroll?" she asked. Not waiting for an answer, she hoisted her gown up past her calves and led the way across the parking lot, past scattered cars and SUVs that waited for owners unlikely to return until morning. "I don't care how ungraceful this looks," she said, twitching her skirt. "So nobody tell me, okay?"

"Good thing the river didn't get any higher," said Rob, "or the ambulance might not have made it."

Terry, falling in beside Dee, said, "It's not supposed to crest until sometime Monday, but there's rain in that breeze. Could bring the whole snowpack down at once, like last time. Got your emergency supplies laid in, in case the bridge closes?"

Behind them Lacey gasped. "Oh god, the bridge might actually be closed? For how long?"

"Not to worry." Dee turned to see that her friend's face had gone even whiter than the moonlight. "They'll give us notice if it looks like it'll rise that high. Anyone who's got concerns will have time to leave."

"But is there another way across? Will we be trapped?"

Terry looked back, too. "If it comes to that, Jake will have his company's chopper parked on his lawn for the duration, and you can hitch a ride out on the daily grocery run. No mere flood can interfere with his feeding of the hockey squad."

They crossed the main road and started up the hill, the men exchanging idle comments about people and moments from that evening. Lacey was silent. Dee ignored them all, wandering along, letting the night air flow over her skin. So many months since she had walked outside at night. How she'd missed this. At her own driveway, she turned. "Goodnight, lads. Thanks for the company."

Lacey followed her. As the trees closed in around them, thunder rumbled in the west. When the dark house loomed into view, Dee's steps slowed.

"You okay?" Lacey asked.

"Real life is rushing over my grave. I can't believe I forgot to leave some lights on. If you weren't here I wouldn't have the guts to walk up to my house alone. I'd have gotten Terry and Rob to come up for a drink, just so I wouldn't have to turn that knob without back-up." She took a few more slow steps up the drive, willing the gatepost sensor to pick up her movements and illuminate the long, dark lane through the trees.

"The new lights will come up when we reach the steps," Lacey said. "You should get Wayne to give you a quote on a permanent installation."

"Sure." *And have him think I expect a steep discount in return for expediting his museum invoice.* "As soon as I pay down the second mortgage I had to take to buy out Neil, and clear off the legal bill for my divorce. Even at insider rates, it wasn't cheap." The garage light came on then, and the LED posts along one side of the drive. She moved a bit faster and reached the house — her cage — with only a slight racing of her heart.

The first of the new lights didn't come on until her foot came down on the step. She paused.

"It's just because you're shorter than me," said Lacey from behind. "Go on. The next one should come up any second now." Then she grabbed the back of Dee's dress. "Stop."

"Why? What's —" Then Dee saw it too: a chair from the deck, blocking their path around to the mudroom door. The wind could not have shifted that chair. Human hands had done that. She reeled, tried to retreat, but Lacey's hand was in the small of her back, pushing her up the stairs.

"Get to the wall. I'm right behind you."

Dee stumbled forward, clutching her skirt. Her tiny evening bag swung down her wrist and banged against her thigh. She jumped back. Lacey shoved her up against the varnished logs and moved past her. Watching her slink toward the chair, her silk dress shimmering in the harsh white light, Dee swallowed a tendril of hysteria. She turned her head and stared out at the dark drive, the impenetrable shadows beneath the trees. Who was out there? Or were they inside her house, waiting for her to walk into a trap? She stretched out a hand to grab Lacey, stop her from walking into it, but found no silk dress there. Lacey was gone.

CHAPTER THIRTEEN

Lacey stepped around the corner into darkness. The motion-activated light sat dead on its bracket, barely visible against the eaves. The dogs leaped at their gate, howling to raise the dead.

Behind her, Dee screamed.

Lacey raced back to see Dee huddled by the wall where she'd left her. "What's wrong?" she yelled over the dogs' racket. "Did you see someone?"

"I turned around and you were gone. I panicked."

"You made that quite clear." Lacey put her hands over her ears. "If I go with you, will you get the dogs out? They'll keep you safe while I check out the house." *And they'll shut up so I can hear anyone else moving before I walk right into them.*

The dogs settled as soon as Dee spoke to them. A smart prowler would be half a mile away by now. Unless they were gaslighting Dee with this trick; they might be lurking to see the effect. Lacey pulled Dee with her to the dog pen and then hustled her to the mudroom door. The dogs picked up the mood and hung in close. A cold nose poked at the back of her knee.

Using the flashlight on her phone, Lacey examined the lock before putting her key in. No scratches or sign of forced entry. The front door hadn't been noticeably disturbed, either. Should she check the French doors before opening this one, or was it more vital to get the lights on? With Dee clinging to her and the setters panting loudly in the darkness, she opened the door far enough to get her hand in and flipped every switch she could reach. The deck, the terrace, the yard all flared into view. Nobody on the grass or on the paving stones. Nobody on the drive …

But wait! There was movement out there, barely visible in the glow of the LEDs along the road. She pushed Dee behind her, not into the house, but against the wall. One of the dogs barked. The other whined. The movement on the drive became Terry and Rob running flat out.

"Who screamed?" Terry shouted, passing Lacey's car at a dead run.

"Me, sorry," Dee called back and stepped away from the wall. She stood tall and spoke clearly. No cowering in front of the neighbours. "I tripped over this chair and thought we'd had a bear, or something."

Lacey have her a sideways glance. *Or something? Why doesn't she tell the truth?*

Terry lifted the chair easily and swung it onto one shoulder. "Jarrad must have forgotten to put it back."

"Jarrad was here?" Lacey yelled. "When?"

Rob got to Dee as she swayed. "You're done in, honey," he said. "How about I take you inside and fix you a drink?"

"Not yet," Lacey snapped. "When was Jarrad here, and why?"

"Yes, why?" Dee had recovered her voice, if not her poise. She shrugged off Rob's hand.

Terry set the chair back by its fellows. "He and Mick were out on the trail this aft and Mick's heart conked out a bit. Jarrad got him as far as here, and then Mick rested while Jarrad brought up the car. Dee, I know you hate his guts, but surely he did the right thing for Mick?"

"Of course I don't begrudge Mick a rest. Why didn't you tell me he'd been here?"

"It slipped my mind. Are you sure you're okay now? Don't want us to search the house for intruders?"

"We're fine," said Dee. "But thanks for rushing to our rescue. I hope Jan didn't hear me or she'll be worried."

"If she had, she'd have already phoned when your new lights came on. What's up with them, anyway?"

"Something's been disturbing the dogs," said Dee before Lacey could answer. "She hasn't seen anything around here, has she?" To Lacey she added, "Jan can see right down into my yard from her sunroom. She watches the place when I'm out."

Could Jan be the one creeping around at night? "Do the dogs like her?"

"Love her to pieces," Terry answered. "She keeps an eye on them and they on her. She thought Mick was a bear this afternoon. She almost had me fire off a banger to save them. It would have scared the life out of him."

"Maybe literally," said Rob.

Lacey turned away. "I left my sneakers on the back patio this morning. Might as well get them while the lights are on." The French doors, as expected, were still securely locked. The temporary lights in the back came up as she passed the sensors. The whole incident was a non-event started by a sick neighbour leaving a chair out of place. On her way back, she could see dust lines where the chair legs had been dragged right across an extension cord, pulling it from the wall. Jarrad, intent on helping his sick old friend, probably hadn't noticed. She plugged it back in for the sake of thoroughness. The sensor picked up an arm wave from Rob and promptly illuminated Dee's silver dress, shimmering like moonlight on water. The men, in their black tuxes, were pillars of formality beside her. Between them and the varnished logs, the scene could have been a movie still or an ad for luxury homes.

Tonight of all nights would have been a perfect opportunity for someone bent on mischief. Yet it looked as if nobody had come. She reached Dee in time to hear Terry say that Jan had been too sick tonight to leave the house. Ah, that was one suspect who couldn't be ruled out. Come to think of it, the other suspects — except Neil and the Beal brothers — had all been down at the museum. So, existence of prowler still not proven … nor disproven. Nobody could be ruled out yet. Even Terry and Rob might have sinister motives of which she was unaware. She added her goodbyes and watched them walk away along the dimly lit drive.

"I'll sit out here," Lacey said, "until you get the dogs back in their pen."

Dropping into the chair Terry had replaced, she tipped her head back. Once the front motion-sensor lights clicked off, the stars blazed with a vigour too often dimmed in the Lower Mainland by sea haze and car exhaust. Not even a mosquito buzzed in the clearing. Dee's murmurs and the dogs' shifting feet were all she heard. The quiet seeped into her bones. She breathed deep of the heavy scent from the hanging flower baskets. She could get used to this peaceful country living, especially if the alternative was a return to Tom's crowded child-centric house in Calgary.

Off to the west, thunder. A cold chill wafted down her neck. What was that Terry had said about the snow-pack coming down if it rained?

"Dee," she said, sitting up and searching for clouds past the corner of the house. "Almost done there? Feels like it might rain." She blinked. A red dot had briefly lit up near the window of Dee's home office. Like a marker from a laser sight, but not tracking across the wall or window. Just on and off. Still …

"Dee?"

There it was again: high up on the far front corner of the window.

She walked over for a closer look. Tucked right up into the corner, secured with brown tape to mimic the dark stain on the window frame, was a small silvery slab about the width of her hand. The edge of a control button was visible past the tape.

"Hello?" she said experimentally. The red light gleamed, reflecting from the glass for a fraction of a second. The reflection was what she'd seen. "Son of a bitch! Dee, come over here, please."

The light flickered with every slow click of Dee's shoes on the deck planks. Lacey put out a hand to stop her, and with the other, pointed up. "Can I assume you did not bug your own office window?"

CHAPTER FOURTEEN

It was a couple of hours before the storm blew itself out. Rain still drummed on the roof, but lightning no longer crackled between the hills. The storm inside the house had subsided, too. Dee crept up the stairs on wobbly legs, watching Lacey's green gown glide ahead. Two hours of spinning through all possible combinations of shock, grief, even relief, had left her as limp and creased as that silk. After the initial horror of confirming that someone had been sneaking around her house at night, corrupting her dogs, she finally had proof she was not losing her mind. The prowler was real.

And now she knew what was behind it, although not who or why. The prowler wasn't some shadowy figure driven by hate or lust, someone in her small circle wearing a friendly mask. The prowler wasn't even out to do her harm, except as a by-product of doing some good for their own interests. The main reason for bugging the office of a real estate lawyer was strictly and simply business. Lacey believed anyone who would invade your privacy to that extent was surely a physical danger as well. In the policing world, that was as likely as anything to be true. But in business it was information, not physical coercion, that held the real power.

What Lacey didn't understand was exactly how much was at stake if it got out that Dee's office had been compromised. The East Village deal, for starters. Lawsuits, Law Society hearings, her professional reputation. With all that on the line, she could not phone the RCMP tonight. She had, instead, uncased her good work camera, the one she used to document jobsites, and taken photos of the undoubtedly illicit bug from every angle. She had downloaded the stills and sent copies to her work email, as well as Lacey's for backup. She had put copies on a thumb drive to take to her safety deposit box on Monday morning. She had recorded herself and Lacey each recounting how they had discovered the bug taped outside her window. She had sent those files to several places, too. If the shit hit the fan over this, there was very little cover to be had, but she could at least do this much. Doing it gave her a sense of control.

After a long shower, Lacey headed downstairs and put her half cup of forgotten tea into the microwave. Then she opened one set of drapes on the great wall of windows and leaned her forehead on the cool glass, watching the last of the night's rain trickle down the driveway.

The nearest trees were visible in the growing light. If only she could see the way forward as clearly.

The little digital recorder that had been duct-taped to Dee's office window sat in a Ziploc bag on the coffee table. A second bag held all the scraps of rust-brown tape that could be cut away without disturbing any possible fingerprints. The recorder was a basic piece of equipment, smaller than a smartphone, with simple controls: record, playback, fast-forward and rewind, and a button to switch between voice-activated or steady recording. She had seen these before. Wayne used one for talking to himself on jobsites. The screen that displayed file names, date/time, and such was still covered by tape.

It might have stayed up there undetected for weeks if they hadn't come home after dark, if she hadn't sat in that exact spot and looked at the house from that specific angle and spoken loud enough to activate it. Maybe it had been there for weeks already. She sighed. Dee couldn't take much more right now, but they had to come up with an action plan, or neither of them would sleep.

When Dee came down, her hair in a towel and the rest of her in flannel pajamas decorated with penguins, Lacey said, "Doing nothing is not an option. Somebody is actively spying on you. It's not a professional bugging or we'd never know it was there. For all we know there might be a webcam out there, too. I'll take a look when there's more light. Meanwhile, this is evidence. The prowler's fingerprints might be on it, for heaven's sake. The police could find that out for you by lunchtime. It's their job."

Dee raised red-rimmed eyes to her. "You know it's not that simple. If any of my clients turn out to have lost money because confidential information was leaked out on that recorder, I'll be the one in trouble. In this market, millions are at stake every day. I could lose my house to lawsuits, face a Law Society hearing." She sat, tucking one foot under her, but the schoolgirl pose couldn't mask her determination. "Nobody can know about this until I've listened to the recording and figured out how to cover myself legally. If I even can. But you won't let me play the damned thing because of fingerprints that might not even be there, will you?"

If Lacey hadn't left the Force, she could have asked a friendly crime scene tech to do the job. Someone would have been happy to take ten minutes out of their routine day, even on a weekend. But she was cut off from those tools as a civilian. Or was she?

"Okay, here's a compromise. I'll ask Wayne if there's a way to copy the recording — any recording, not mentioning you — onto a laptop. Hopefully we can do it without messing up any fingerprints. You can listen to every note it recorded, figure out what you have to do to protect yourself from legal action. Meanwhile, I'll take the recorder to Tom. He was going to check with Cochrane detachment about the original prowler complaint. He could get the prints checked by saying there's a possible person of interest." It would be true.

"But the police would want to listen to it."

"Not if he says the evidence could become inadmissible without proper authorization. No officer likes to risk a case falling apart on technicalities. They'll wait for the prints, and then wait longer while the prosecutor's office chews over the file, deciding whether to apply for an audio warrant or not."

Dee put the heels of her hands over her eyes. "You would do that for me? Tom would? And not tell anyone I've been compromised?"

Lacey knelt by the chair and put one arm over Dee's shoulders. "Of course we will. Nobody has to know unless it goes to court. So, deal?"

"Deal." Dee sat up straighter and blew her nose. "When we wake up, you phone Wayne. Once I know what's recorded on there, I can review my files for the past several weeks and assess the risks. If only I hadn't worked from home so often. I may have commented on dozens of files in that time. But it will be clear very soon if this is something Neil could dream up. God knows how many times he might have traded on information he picked up from me or my secretaries while we were married. How soon can you get Tom on it?"

"This afternoon. I want to collect my mail, anyway, in case my pension transfer paperwork has appeared. I'm supposed to go to his shift breakfast early Sunday, but no way I'm leaving you alone after this. You'd better come with me this afternoon, too."

"I have to be here. There'll be post-gala details to take care of and the party at Jake's. And I have to get the Lexus from the museum, plus some groceries." Lacey argued, but Dee was adamant. "It'll be daylight. I'll be surrounded by neighbours. I'll bring the dogs indoors when you leave. They might not bark, but they sure as hell won't sit by if someone tries to hurt me."

"I hope you're right." Lacey paced to the window and back, thinking. "The RCMP will need Neil's fingerprints for comparison — unless they're on file for some reason?"

"Not that I know of." Dee bit her lip. "Oh, wait … that stupid pen."

"Huh?"

"He got them made last year as giveaways. *Your Dream Home at My Fingertips*." Dee scrabbled through the end table drawer and came up with a fat ballpoint pen. She tossed it to Lacey. "Push the little knob by the pocket clip." Lacey pushed. A small, blurry beam of light shot out the back end. She lowered the pen until the blur came into focus on the table. It was a fingerprint. "Neil's right thumb," said Dee. "It took him a whole evening of inking and pressing and scanning to get the image, and all for a one-sentence sales gimmick. Typical Neil, over-focussing on the tiny details and ignoring the overall impact. He'd have used his thumb to hold that recorder, wouldn't he?"

"Uh-huh. This might not be a clear enough print, but I'll pass it along. If he did this, we'll make him suffer."

Dee dragged herself up to bed. Lacey went through her door-and-window check and took another hard look at the office window from the inside. A decorative valence had hidden the recorder from anyone in the room, and the curtains had mostly stayed closed. But if she were the one spying, she'd want an eye on the scene, say, a webcam on the garage eaves. This amateur might not have thought of that. If they had, chances were they'd use something just as low-tech as the recorder. Probably not a live wireless webcam with dark-sight, which would have told them instantly their scheme had been blown. That garage eave would be her first search area in the morning. Or rather, after some sleep. It was already morning.

CHAPTER FIFTEEN

In the early afternoon, Jan woke from a fitful sleep to the faint sound of the theme song from *The Road Runner Show* down the hall. Saturday cartoons: Terry's secret vice. Was Rob still here, too? She lay listening, picturing the Road Runner and the Coyote in their endless game of tag. The familiar pain behind her eyes magnified as her pupils resisted the bedroom's shadowy light. Terry was right. Those pills, even at a half dose, messed her up. She'd skip Jake's party tonight. The food smells alone would probably make her puke.

After a cup of anti-nausea tea and some dry toast, she settled on the sunroom lounger with her dark glasses on and her binoculars in hand. Down at the museum, a dozen vehicles remained from last night, the red Corvette most visible. Jarrad had probably walked to Mick's place. She could see the Hardy house plainly from here. Mick was stretched out on a lounger on his terrace, eyes covered by a panama hat. Whatever his heart trouble had been, he hadn't been kept in the hospital for it.

Rob came to sit on the floor beside her. Sunlight danced on his frosted tips, but his expression was gloomy. "Ready to hear the highlights of last night?"

"Looks like there were lows. Terry didn't mention any, except Mick's heart trouble."

"Yeah, poor guy." Rob fidgeted. "I think I've lost the permanent contract because of him."

"Why? You did what was needed, right? Got him some help ASAP?"

"Yeah. But —"

Terry appeared with the coffee pot and refilled his and Rob's mugs. "But what? He won't blame you. Assuming he survived."

Jan pointed down the hill. "He's on his deck right now. So it couldn't have been that serious. What has Mick's heart got to do with the permanent contract?"

"Not Mick. His wife." Rob turned his mug in his hands. "When I went looking for her last night, I tried the stage and then went down the backstage stairs to the dressing rooms. The lights were low. It didn't look like anyone was down there."

"And?"

"I was halfway into the women's dressing room when I realized it was occupied."

"Camille?"

"Uh-huh. And she wasn't alone. I mean, she *really* wasn't alone."

Jan pulled her glasses down her nose. "She was making out in the basement while her husband was having a heart attack upstairs?"

"Uh-huh." Now that the worst was out, Rob relaxed a

bit. "Her and her co-star. They were groping each other all week at rehearsals, so it wasn't really a surprise. But it didn't dawn on me that anyone would … well, I'm no prude, but really, there's no graceful way to greet a woman whose bare ass is bent over the makeup table."

Jan blinked. "*Ew.* Thanks for that mental image."

"You asked. Anyway, you can see why our sitting at a board meeting together will be awkward. She's a rich board member; I'm a lowly temporary employee. Guess which of us won't be around after my contract is up next month."

"I see your point." If Rob left, if his contract wasn't renewed, not only would he be unemployed, but her last link with her old life would be gone.

Terry stretched out on the carpet in the sunshine. "Dee wants you there. If Jake sides with her, Camille can suck it up. Er …"

"Terry! Between the two of you, I'll never look at that woman again without thinking about her sexual athletics." Jan picked up her mug. It wasn't as much of an effort as the first time, but it still hurt to move. "You're right, though. She can't tell him the truth about why she doesn't want you. Jake's a tad sensitive about cheating wives."

"Problem," said Rob. "I've only met the man about three times. His donation was done long before I hired on. I doubt he'd recognize me on the street, much less overrule the board for me."

Three horses trotted down the road. Jan popped up her shades again and shielded her eyes to identify the riders. Young men, well muscled. Some of Jake's hockey guests taking advantage of the amenities. She would meet them tonight if she went to the Finals party. If she went, she could talk to Jake about Rob. But she had to convince Terry she was fit to go out, and without sneaking a quarter pill first. She sat up, channelling the surge of dread at the prospect of losing Rob.

"Come to the party tonight. Meet Jake on his own ground."

"Not invited," Rob pointed out. "I can't just show up on his doorstep."

Terry shrugged. "One more won't matter to Jake. He loves a houseful. If you can stand to socialize with the ladies of the board for the second night in a row, that is. Including Camille."

"Are you sure you can simply drag me along to an oil baron's hockey party? I'd totally die to be there with all that hot stuff on the hoof."

"Aren't hockey players a bit out of your usual line?" Terry asked.

"A gay art historian can't appreciate a manly sport? I was a serious Canucks fan in university, wasn't I, Jan? Besides, one of those hunks last night was giving off ambiguous signals. Him I'd like a second look at."

"Hussy," said Jan. "Just don't pull a Camille in a dark corner. I'm pretty sure that's one thing Jake would not tolerate."

"No fear. This job is much more important than any piece of tail could be. Even one as ripped as that guy last night. But what's the dress code? I can't go in Terry's leftovers. No offence, old man, but your clothes were not designed with seduction in mind."

"Glad to hear it," said Terry. "Think business casual — golf shirts and khakis."

"If Dee takes you as her date," said Jan, "it will be an extra boost in Jake's eyes. He thinks she can do no wrong."

"First I'm to crash the party and now I'm to tell the woman who signs my pay slip that she's helping me do it?"

"She'll be fine with it," said Jan. "Somebody get me a phone and I'll fix it." It crossed her mind as she punched buttons that Dee might be having a leisurely visit with her dear old friend and not appreciate a museum-related interruption. Today's brain wasn't up to holding that worry for long, though. By the time Dee picked up, Jan had almost forgotten why she was calling. "Oh, right. Dee, can you take Rob to Jake's party with you? It's a cunning plot to circumvent Camille if she tries to block him getting the permanent curator job." She listened for a moment and hung up. "Told you she'd be delighted. Meet her at her place around four. Faceoff is at five and there's schmoozing to be done first. Not to mention eating. The food will be fab."

Rob looked at his watch. "I'd better get my skates on. Too bad I left my car down the hill."

Terry went for his jog, Rob went for his car, and Jan rested in the sunroom. More cars left the museum parking lot as their owners rose from the fumes of last night's event. If only she could be as certain of rising above the pill hangover. For Rob, she would make the effort, maybe sneak the quarter pill a bit before. Jake liked her as much as he liked Dee. If he saw how much they both wanted Rob to stay, Camille wouldn't stand a chance.

CHAPTER SIXTEEN

As soon as she got into Tom's car, Lacey took a good-natured swipe at his hay-thatch head. "Jackass. You made my fingerprints your excuse to duck out of an afternoon with Marie's parents."

Tom flashed teeth too perfect to be natural in a mouth that had met half a dozen immovable objects during their patrol years. "Thanks for backing me up, McCrae. If I'd realized we'd see them every single weekend, I might have stalled on moving back here."

"You've only been here a couple of months. The novelty will probably wear off. If not, there's always work."

"I can hope." Tom wheeled expertly into traffic and Lacey settled back in the passenger seat. Only with other cops could she really relax as a passenger. Civilians were either too tentative or clearly outdriving their reaction time. "To keep this off book for now, Sergeant Drummond will meet us on his supper break. He says he knows you."

"Not Bulldog Drummond? What's his real name again? Steve? We went through Depot together." Another old pal still on the Force, ideally placed to support her in uncovering Dee's stalker. "I'll let Dee know I won't be back for a couple of hours. After last night, she's got to be freaked about being alone out there. Even though there was no other spy equipment that I could find."

She dialed, and after three buzzes Dee answered. Before she could say a word, Dee jumped in with, "Lacey, you're on speaker. I'm driving. Should I pull over?"

"Is someone with you?"

"Rob from the museum. He's coming to Jake's party with me. Say hi to Lacey, Rob." He did so.

Lacey said hi back, mentally revising what she'd been about to say. "I'm on my way to Cochrane with Tom. An old pal of mine wants to meet for an early supper. I can ask him about this morning's thing, plus he knows those brothers we were curious about, what kind of work they do and all that." Hopefully Rob would think she was talking about contractors for renovations or something. He would be too polite to ask, anyway. "I expect to be back well before dark. What time does your party end?"

"You can take your time," said Dee unexpectedly. A hint of steel entered her voice. "I think I know who played that prank on me, and it will not be happening again."

"You know? Uh, should I not go ahead with the, uh, other thing?"

"Oh, please continue," said Dee, so sweetly that you had to know her deeply to realize she was bleeding pure rage through the phone. "You know what they say: there is no tragedy here, only ammunition."

The only thing Lacey could think of was that Neil had left his voice on the tape. If it was him, he was busted but good, and without need for fingerprinting. But why wouldn't she say his name? Would Rob recognize it and tell the wrong person, giving that rat the chance to cover his sleazy paw prints? "Um, do you want to call me back when you have a minute?"

"No need. We're here. But man, will I have things to tell you when you get home. This is going to be one hell of a party."

"Don't do anything crazy." Like confronting someone warped enough to bug your house. Especially if that someone was Neil. But surely he wouldn't be at Jake's. Dee had constantly told her he didn't come around the neighbourhood anymore, that he only sleazed around the office. Of course, if he was the one bugging the house, then Dee was simply wrong. Or in denial. "Promise me you will be … okay."

"I'll be fine. Say goodbye to Rob."

Lacey hung up and stared at Tom. "Well, what the bloody hell? She knows who planted this bug, can't say because she's not alone, but she's not scared anymore. She's flat-out furious."

"Do I have to go back to my in-laws now?"

"No. She wants us to keep to the program. Said something about ammunition. Could Neil lose his real estate licence if he's got a criminal conviction?" And how far would he go to prevent that happening?

Tom grinned. "I like her style already."

"What am I not getting?"

"You always were too girly for your own good," said Tom.

"I can kick your ass six ways to Sunday."

"She means having his fingerprints on that recorder, in police hands, is her big gun, and she's not afraid to use it. He messed with the wrong woman."

Lacey puzzled over the situation while Tom wove confidently through the westbound traffic on Highway 1. The Rockies were clear greys and browns, their tips white against the sunlit sky. White. That remaining snow might come down all at once if it rained again tonight. Nothing she could do about the weather, but the thought of crossing that river while it was in full spate gave her cold chills. Nothing she could do, either, about whatever Dee did in the next few hours, except get back quickly after her errand.

"How far is Cochrane?"

"Another fifteen minutes. About the same distance north on 22 as Bragg Creek is south."

"We're almost at Bragg Creek? I could have brought my own car and gone straight home from there."

"Yeah, but then I'd have to go straight back to my in-laws' place." Tom passed a line of semis and dodged back into his lane, barely ahead of the front grille of an RV. "This way, I have to drive you back to our place first, and the boys might be bored enough to come home by the time I get over there. No Xbox at Grandma's house."

"Does your wife know what a skunk she married?"

"Not for lack of you telling her."

Cochrane was a mellow town with a roofline that rarely protruded above the second storey. Old character homes had been revitalized into commercial properties, and the Old West main street thronged with shopping families. Tom pointed.

"RCMP post is up a couple of blocks, but we're meeting Drummond at an old-timey saloon. He says the burgers are good and we're buying."

Lacey expected to pay. She hadn't expected the qualms she felt walking into the plank-floored, rustic-themed restaurant to meet another member of the Force that she'd left behind. She and Bulldog had toughed out all those months of training together, but only he was still taking it in stride. Maybe if she hadn't married Dan, if she'd been free to take transfers to anywhere in Canada.... Policing couldn't possibly be as grim out in these quiet prairie towns as it was in the Lower Mainland. It might have its moments, but not every second of every shift. Was every member she met from here on going to give her the same cold stare as Wayne, waiting for her to reveal whatever flaw made her not tough enough? She set that thought aside and concentrated on how to convince Bulldog to lift and file those prints ASAP without starting a file on them.

At a table near the saloon window sat a huge man in uniform, his neck muscles bulging above his collar. More bull than dog, more mountain than both. She remembered suddenly that she didn't need to argue for anything except a slight delay in paperwork. Whatever her ex-training buddy might think about her leaving the Force, he had grown up under a wife-beating dad and had a permanent down on domestic abusers. All she had to do was tell him.

Once her summary was out there, he said, "It's almost always the ex. And that ex, who I interviewed myself, if I remember right — and I do because I glanced over the file this afternoon — was the slimy kind whose left hand never meets his right because one or the other of them is always in somebody else's pocket. I'd enjoy pinning something on him." Bulldog slurped down his coffee to make way for the refill the waitress offered as she brought their plates. Once the woman was out of earshot, he said, "There's a chain of custody problem or something with this item you want printed?"

"Admissibility of evidence issue." Lacey described in brief how she'd found the recorder duct-taped to Dee's office window and transferred the recordings to a laptop. "Whatever's been recorded is speech protected by lawyer-client privilege. We'd need a judicial order to overturn that, and I don't see it being granted if we have a simpler way to identify the individual responsible."

"I want a signed statement of where you found it and what steps you took to protect any prints. Photos in situ?"

Lacey nodded.

Bull grunted his approval. "Won't kill off the doubts if it comes to trial, but you'll be a credible witness. Ex-officer and all." The pause that followed was the closest he'd come to asking why she'd left.

"Now I know where you are, I'll come back for coffee one day and tell you the whole damn story."

"Make it a beer," said Bulldog. "Anything else?"

"The Beal brothers, Eddie and Eben. It might still be them, over this museum business."

The meal passed with Bulldog recounting the Beal brothers' colourful history of mostly harmless encounters with law enforcement, both the RCMP and the RM's bylaw officers. Lacey was briefly distracted by the possibility of working as a patrol sheriff for the RM, but stopped short of asking for particulars. Time enough for job hunting after Dee's prowler was on ice.

"No gun offences," Bulldog concluded. "Eben's a family man, careful for his kids' sakes, and Eddie picketed to keep the gun registry, if you can believe it. Got egged for that by his neighbour. Eben went over with a couple of flats of eggs and pelted the guy's truck good, with him sitting in it. They shook on it after. Washed the truck together."

A rural gun owner picketing to keep the registry? Astounding. She stored up the egging and other funny bits of Beal history to pass on to Dee, but she couldn't find anything in that history to suggest either brother was more than a homegrown crank whose agenda was right out in the open. Bulldog saved the only surprise for last.

"They'll soon be witnesses for the prosecution, for a change." He scraped his last fry through the ketchup dregs.

"Yeah?"

"A dangerous driving and assorted from last winter. Goes to court next month. The hotshot hockey player that nearly creamed your friend? He just missed the Beals' truck a bit farther along the same road. They live nearby and ID'd the car."

That put a new twist on things. Maybe the Beals had been bought off by Jarrad or Mick. Even a time change of fifteen minutes in their testimony or any expression of doubt from them could get charges dropped or bargained down. But it would look obvious that they'd altered their testimony unless Dee's could be discredited as unreliable. As a motive is was thin as onion skin. Hard to see what they could hope to gain.

"Was the driver drunk?"

Bulldog shrugged. "He hid his car and lay low. Then a month later, in he trots with a lawyer to confess. We tested him for substances and got zip. No surprise by that time."

"If he was going to confess anyway, why delay?"

"Needed time to find his nerve, maybe." Tom waved for the bill. "Or he could have been taking a banned performance enhancer. The league might've tested him when they learned about the charges. The wrong positive could cost him big."

"Trial will show," Bulldog said and pushed back his chair. "Gimme the evidence, McCrae. I'll trust you for the statement." He eyeballed the Ziploc bag with the date/time/location all marked on it in approved fashion. "Good to see you remember some of your training."

Back in the car, Tom announced he was taking the scenic route back. "Give you time to digest."

Lacey rolled her eyes. His boys wouldn't be ready to go home for another two hours. That was the real reason. How soon until Dee would be going home? After six now and night was still miles away over Saskatchewan, but soon enough the shadows of the spruce trees would be creeping toward Dee's French doors. She pulled out her phone, hesitated, then stuck it back in her belt. Dee would barely be sitting down for supper at the grand hockey party. Let her eat in peace. The next check-in could be made from Tom's, before Lacey started back to Bragg Creek. Damn Tom and his in-laws-shirking ways. She could be halfway home by now. And what would she find when she got there? Dee with a triumphant solution or a whole new set of problems?

CHAPTER SEVENTEEN

Jan got ready early, then lay down on the couch until she heard Terry start the shower. She dragged herself to the kitchen, picked half an Adderall out of the pill bottle, whacked it in half again with her pill chopper, and sucked one of the tiny quarters into her mouth. The other quarter, no bigger than a crumb, went into her supplements travel box. If she started to crash at the party, she could take the second crumb and hope the buzz wouldn't be obvious to Terry. She put her purse and sweater by the door and went to the sunroom to watch for Rob's arrival at Dee's. If they all arrived at the same time, the positive impact on Jake would be stronger.

Terry was ready by the time Dee drove up the hill. As he helped Jan to her feet, he congratulated her on resting before the big event. She smiled, leaning on his arm, hoping he would attribute the tremble in her hand to the usual fatigue. They drove through Jake's main gate and parked in the turnaround behind Dee's SUV. Her legs were shaking again already. She'd pushed herself way too hard this week. If a wheelchair had magically appeared to spare her the walk around to the terrace, she'd have been tempted to use it. But none did. Instead she took Rob's arm when he came over and walked with him and Dee to where Jake was greeting people at the top of the shallow terrace steps. The house was Spanish style, with red-clay roof tiles, one large storey on this frontage, and three levels down the hillside on the other side to the pool deck. She'd lost count of the number of parties they'd attended out here. At least he had an elevator indoors, installed a decade ago for some visiting relation's convenience.

Jake shook hands vigorously and congratulated Rob on the success of the opening. "Jannie, good to see you. When you didn't make the gala, I thought you'd be out for this one, too. But you look okay."

If "okay" meant brain-fogged, blinded by the sunlight even through dark glasses, deafened by the gravel crunching underfoot, and with all her muscles twitching randomly due to the pill, then yeah, she was okay. She smiled, all the answer he was looking for, and followed him around the house to the main terrace. The view gave her an excuse to pause and catch her breath. She wasn't the only one looking. The mountain panorama spread from behind the west wing to the distant peaks of Waterton Park and the U.S. border. Jake, who saw it every day, ordered a couple of people out of loungers in a sheltered nook and installed Jan in one of them before hurrying off to greet more guests.

Jan sat, wriggling backward across cushions so soft they sucked her in. Terry brought her a sparkling water.

A few dozen people milled about with glasses in hand. There were buffet tables along one wall, a full-service bar between the sets of French doors, and a half-dozen immense television screens along the walls and railings. No excuse for missing a great play today.

While she waited for Terry to bring her some food, Mick Hardy came over. He was no longer the robust man she remembered from the Mardi Gras party last winter. His hair was lank, his face grey, and his sports jacket hung off shoulders that were more bones than flesh. His left arm was tucked protectively against his chest, cherishing a glass half full of ice and amber fluid. His other hand held a plate. He stared helplessly at the lounger beside Jan's.

"Here," she said, working her way up to a sitting position. "Hand me your stuff and then sit down. These loungers are fatally soft."

Mick smiled, lines creasing his drooping cheeks. "But great once you're in, huh?"

"Uh-huh." She watched him ease cautiously into position and returned his food. "How's the pacemaker holding up? I heard you had to leave the gala last night."

Mick swallowed half his drink and coughed, carefully. "Looked worse than it was. I didn't want a fuss, so I was waiting until most people were gone. Then the curator blew the whistle on me, so to speak."

"I was glad to see you were home this morning. Was the hospital able to tell you what went wrong?"

"The wires didn't heal into place properly in my heart. Or they pulled out when I stretched the wrong way. I'm supposed to take it easy and see if they connect better. If not, I'll need a repair job." He grinned, a ghost-ly imitation of the old Mick Hardy charm. "I don't know whether to hope the game's tame for my heart or root for Jake's team regardless."

Terry came back with plates of food and sat at the foot of Jan's lounger. "I introduced Rob to a bunch of the play-ers," he told her. "I had no idea he was such a fan. He knew all their stats, which ones have the Stanley Cup ring, and so on. Stuff even I don't know, and I see them all the time."

"He probably did his homework when he went home to change clothes."

"Rob, that's the curator, right? I want to thank him for helping me out last night. Nice young fella, even if he is as queer as a plastic toonie." Jan exchanged glan-ces with Terry. So much for keeping Rob in the closet tonight. Mick caught their look. "Oh, don't worry about me. I learned the 'don't ask, don't tell' rule a long time back. In hockey, there's more of it than some folks want to think."

Dee arrived with a plate of food and a tall glass. "Can I share your footrest, Mick?"

"Your friend didn't come?" Jan asked her when she was settled.

"She had to go into Calgary." Dee nibbled at a dry rib. The tension in her thin shoulders ran all the way to her hands, and she gripped that rib like it was some-body's throat.

"How did things go last night?" Jan persisted. "You look exhausted."

"What you'd expect," said Dee. "You missed some memorable performances, but they'll be on the video."

Mick sat forward, his plate tilting. "There's a video?"

"DVD, eventually," said Dee. "Those roving camera people will make a compilation DVD of the evening as a souvenir for the board members and big donors, and cut some footage for YouTube advertising."

"I'll enjoy that," said Mick, wheezing as he leaned back. "I wasn't at my best last night, might have dozed off a time or two. When will it be ready?"

"Next week, I hope. My last job as interim president will be writing tasteful notes to send out with the DVDs."

"You're leaving the board?" Jan jerked upright. "You can't go yet."

"The chair, anyway." Dee pushed back her hair with one wrist. "I've done my bit. I want to get on with my own life, socialize with less-myopic people for a change. Present company excepted, of course." What a mercy Jan had swallowed her pride and the quarter pill to make sure Rob got a good introduction to Jake. If Dee wouldn't be there next year to ride herd on the trophy wives, all the more reason to have a skilled curator who knew the politics going in.

Jake, standing by the bar, tinkled his glass for silence. His big voice spread happily over the deck. "Friends. Welcome all of you to the first game of the Stanley Cup Finals. In a minute, the sound on all these TV sets will come up for the pre-game. But don't fret — plenty of time to fill your glasses and your plates. I want to say how pleased I am to see you all here, celebrating with me that I've got a piece of a team in the finals for the third time. My money was made in Alberta, so it was only fitting that I put some back into the Calgary Flames" — huzzahs from one contingent of hockey players — "and then the Edmonton Oilers" — louder cheers from the other side of the terrace. "This is the first time I've owned a piece of Chicago, and they made the finals, too. Teams are gonna be bidding for me next year."

Someone yelled, "But none of them win!"

After the laughter, Jake added, "I never would have bought into this team without the advice of a good friend and neighbour who knows hockey as a player, coach, and manager, a man whose contributions to hockey in Canada and through the World Hockey Federation have not gone unnoticed. A man who, we learned just this week, has been nominated for the Order of Canada: Mick Hardy. Wave to the folks, Mick." Mick waved. The hockey players yelled and whistled. Camille came over, all smiles, to accept her share of the glory. Dee, faced with Camille's deliberately turned derriere right at her eye level, moved over to sit beside Terry.

"What are you two smirking about?" she asked as Jan covered a smile with her napkin.

"Nothing," said Terry.

"Tell you later," said Jan.

Jake yelled and everyone quieted down. "So, if the Order of Canada selection committee phones, you all say nice things about him, okay? Lie if you have to."

As the next wave of laughter died down, the giant screens and speakers came to life. People refilled plates and glasses or, in the case of non-fans, snuck into the house to wait out the first period by playing billiards. With the usual amount of pomp amid the screams of the crowd, the teams skated out and stood for the American anthem. The puck dropped.

Half an hour later, the first-period horn startled Jan out of a TV-induced trance. She'd had her eyes closed the whole time, except when the noise level rose to signal a breakaway or brawl. Now she'd have to interact with people again. Why had she thought this was a good idea again? Oh yeah, Rob and the job. Was there anything else she could do tonight to help it along? A word with Jake, maybe? But he wasn't in sight. All over the wide terrace, people jumped to their feet, streaming toward the bar or the bathrooms. The meats and salads had disappeared, and now a tempting array of desserts graced the buffet. Terry went off to make a sampler for her. Rob followed to replace everyone's drinks.

A hockey player approached, holding a cellphone to his ear. "He's right here; I'll ask. Mick, seen Jarrad today? He missed the plane."

Mick shook his head.

Jan leaned forward. "His car was still at the museum two hours ago."

Hockey grinned. "Must have got a better offer." He wandered away, telling his caller that Jarrad was off getting his stick polished. Jan, admiring the easy muscles in his departing thighs, wondered if Camille knew her sex toy was shacked up with someone else for the weekend.

Terry approached with small plates containing a selection of bite-sized desserts. He handed her one and said, "You okay, Mick?"

Mick was absentmindedly massaging the left side of his chest. "Huh? Yeah, I'm all right. Say, those chocolate things look good. Give me a hand up, would you, Terry?"

"I'll fetch some for you," said Terry. "You stay here." He went back to the scrum around the dessert table. Jan saw him lean close to Camille and speak into her ear.

She came over, storm clouds on her perfect face, and sank gracefully onto the lounger at her husband's side. With her back to the terrace, she probably looked like the caring wife, but face-on and low-voiced, she dropped any pretence of concern. "Christ, Mick, quit milking this. I'm not leaving early again over your imaginary pains. Go home!" She walked away, smiling at acquaintances.

As the second period began, Terry came back with another plate, but Mick only picked at the mix of desserts on it. Rob went to get a plate for himself. Five minutes later he was still at the buffet, chatting to a handsome hockey player in every break of the onscreen action.

The second period was half over when, during a long delay while video of a suspect goal was being reviewed, Dee's voice sounded angrily from inside the house. Jan looked up to see a window cracked open over Mick's head, and caught the phrases "bloody unethical" and "first thing Monday." The exchange rumbled on a bit longer, and then a few phrases burst out.

"Don't you dare bug me again. Or speak to me, either!"

The puck dropped, the game started up, and Dee strode out of the house, her face set in a rigid half smile. She stopped near the loungers as if she couldn't decide whether to stomp off or go back indoors to let loose another blast. She finally looked around, saw Jan, and came over.

"I'm going home."

"Take me, too, please." It was Mick, almost inaudible under the renewed roar from the TVs. His face had sagged, as if all the life left in him was oozing down his cheeks.

Dee crouched beside his chair. "Is it your heart? Do you need an ambulance?"

Mick moved his head slightly. "No. Just tired. Need to get home to my own bed." He struggled to sit up.

"Are you sure?" Jan started wriggling out of her squishy cushions. "I'll help you."

"I've got him," said Rob, coming over to slip an arm behind Mick's shoulders. "Take it easy there."

Mick found a smile. "Thanks, young fella. Mind giving me a hand to Dee's car? Through the house, please. I don't want to cause another scene like last night."

"No problem." Rob smiled back. "I'll ride down the hill with you and make sure you get inside okay." He hoisted the older man upright and eased him through the French doors. Nobody turned from the game.

Dee bent down to Jan. "Guess I'd better tell Camille. She'll be spitting."

"Don't bother. She already said she wasn't leaving early for his imaginary pains. Direct quote. You won't leave him alone, will you? Until you're sure he's all right?"

"I won't."

CHAPTER EIGHTEEN

After a winding drive back to Calgary on Highway 1A, Tom pulled into his driveway and pulled out his phone. "I'll just check if they want me over there." Lacey pulled out her phone, too. It was after seven; surely Dee would be finished eating. If not, she could let it go to voice mail. Dee answered on the third ring.

"Hi. How's the party going?"

"I'm not there anymore."

"I thought it would be going on for hours. You're not home alone, are you?"

"No. I'm down at Mick Hardy's place. He needed a ride home. After this I'm going home, too. No more party for me tonight."

"I'll get there as fast as I can."

"Don't worry about it. I am totally not worried about being alone now. Besides, Rob is coming back with me for a drink. Or several. We can sample everything in the liquor cabinet and think up snarky slanders about everyone we both know. Sound like fun, Rob?"

In the background, Rob yelled, "Absolutely!"

"Does this mean you confronted whoever planted the bug? Was it Neil?"

"I can't talk about that now, Lacey. But don't you worry about me tonight. In fact, don't you have a picnic or something starting early tomorrow? If you want to stay overnight in Calgary, I'll be fine."

Lacey protested, but Dee insisted. Honestly, it sounded like Dee didn't want her back. Would tomorrow bring *Thanks for coming but now move out*? She hung up and stared at Tom. "Far from being paranoid about being alone, she practically insisted I stay here tonight."

"She got a hot date?"

"The guy she's with is gay, so I don't think so."

"Maybe he's bi. You're welcome to the couch, if you come back with me to the in-laws' first."

Lacey drove up the hill after noon on Sunday and was relieved to see Dee's SUV right where it should be. She went around to the kitchen door, mentally preparing for the outburst from the dog run. No barking. The dogs weren't sprawled over their usual half acre of terrace, nor in their pen. In the kitchen, Dee's purse hung from a stool back. A note on the counter said, *Took the boys for a long run. Pick out something from the freezer to thaw for supper. Did I mention I hate arrogant assholes? Sister, have I got a story for you!*

Lacey ignored the freezer for the time being. Instead, she made a tall glass of iced tea and wandered out to the terrace. When was the last time she had simply sat out on a shady terrace, smelling the flowers? Not that she could smell the ones in the pergola with the breeze at this angle, but the spruces and those low, scrambling bushes in front of them sent spicy green scents toward her. Sunlight smiled on every trunk, shrub, and blade of grass, from just beyond her toes to halfway up the little path. Everything was so fresh and sweet, warm and dry. The Lower Mainland had been shrouded in fog and rain when she'd left nearly a month ago. Not even the daily winds off the ocean could completely blow away the airborne residue of industry, manure-sprayed fields, and high-density traffic. Those had formed the background in her nostrils during her years in Surrey. This foothills air was like having her soul gently washed.

She woke with a start sometime later. Had a door snapped shut? The sun was still high, but her patch of shade had moved, and the top of her head was cooking. The dog pen remained empty. She picked up her iced tea, saw dead flies floating in it, and dumped it over the railing.

"Hello? Anyone here? Dee?" A man's voice. Mick Hardy stepped slowly around the corner of the house, breathing hard.

"Oh, hi, Mr. Hardy. I don't think Dee's here. I'm a friend of hers, Lacey McCrae."

The lined face smiled at her, a bit shakily. "Didn't I meet you on Friday? You're the young lady who got me an ambulance, for which I forgot to thank you. I didn't realize you were with Dee."

"We're old friends. I'm glad to see you're on your feet again. It wasn't serious, then?"

"Not so much," said Mick, leaning against the wall to catch his breath. "My pacemaker got its wires crossed, kinda. I'm taking it easier now, driving everywhere. Say, looks like I just missed Jake Wyman. Was that old hound down here trying to find out why the lovely Dee left with me last night?"

"I must not have heard him knock." Had the whole neighbourhood stopped by to watch her sleep in the shade? "Have a seat. Can I get you some iced tea?"

"No, thanks. I only stopped to ask if Dee saw my billfold in her car. I can't put my hand on it this morning. I can phone her later."

"I'll see if her keys are here, and we can take a look now." She took the glass into the house and saw the clock over the stove. Five thirty already? She'd been asleep for two hours.

Dee's purse lay on the counter by her note, but the spare keys were on their hook by the back door. Lacey took them outside and walked with Mick, very slowly, around to the drive. They checked the creases of each soft leather seat, but no billfold turned up.

"Another long shot misses the net. I don't know if everyone with heart trouble loses their memory, but mine's downright awful lately."

Lacey watched his car crawl down to his own driveway before she went back indoors. Two hours. Dee was taking a really long walk. Maybe she had detoured over the bridge to that little wine bar. There were always dogs tied to that railing while their owners enjoyed the shady patio. The delay would give her a chance to be a good houseguest and cook supper for a change. She hung Dee's purse on the stool back and stared at it for a moment. Hadn't it been hanging there before? Had she moved it to the counter without remembering? She couldn't be sure. She poked through the fridge and freezer, found some bacon ends and a handful of veggies, and whipped up the one dish she could manage without screwing up: a crustless quiche. It would take a while baking, and there were enough salad greens around to supply a rabbit farm.

Now she could check her email in hopes there'd be one from her realtor saying he had an offer on their house. And not another one from Dan, complaining about the awkward position he was in whenever people asked him where Lacey was, telling her that keeping her location secret was irrational, and trying some new and creative way to guilt her into believing she had over-reacted to what he called a little argument that got out of hand. After his first flurry of emails, she could have pretty much written them herself and saved him the trouble. But they always left her feeling queasy, uneasy about whether she had been too quick to pull the plug. If she had stayed with the Force, or with him.... But speculation served no purpose. She had made the best decision possible at the time, and now she was here to help out Dee. When that ended, when the museum job ended, then she would re-evaluate.

In Dee's office, she groped under the middle desk drawer for the key to the filing cabinet, retrieved Dee's laptop, and waited for the erratic Wi-Fi to stabilize.

Then she dredged up Dee's complicated password, an amalgam of the dogs' names, and was finally able to open a browser to view her inbox. Nothing from the realtor, which was bad, nor from Dan, which was a deep relief on a day she already felt slightly off-kilter. She stared at the screen, trying to think of some friend or relative she hadn't already emailed in the first lonely weeks in Calgary. Then she searched real estate listings for affordable Calgary condos until the oven timer went off. She shut down the browser, debated putting the laptop away, and then decided she could have another session after supper, this time looking for apartments to rent. She must be prepared if Dee gave her a strong suggestion about moving on.

Six thirty and still no sign of Dee. This was their first weekend as housemates. Dee might have a regular Sunday routine that Lacey knew nothing about. She tried Dee's cellphone and heard its gentle chime upstairs. So much for that idea.

At seven she ate half the rubbery quiche. Afterward she sat out back with her tea, listening for the dogs to come panting up the trail after a long day's romp. Clouds piled up behind the hill. Would there be another downpour, like on Friday night?

At eight o'clock, driven indoors by mosquitoes, she paced from room to room, wondering if she had overlooked some sign of trouble. Nothing was obviously disturbed, but drawers didn't seem as neatly closed as usual. Why would anyone search the napkin drawer in the dining room? It wasn't an obvious hiding place for anything of value. She checked it, anyway, in case someone had planted another bug. Just napkins. The house's emptiness was sending tentacles of fear into her paranoid brain.

She had been home for nearly six hours and there was still no word from Dee. The sunset was getting lost behind the clouds, taking with it the dregs of hope that nothing was wrong. She called Dee's phone again and tracked it by the chimes to the upstairs hallway table. Fortunately it wasn't locked, and she was able to retrieve Rob's cell number. She hit dial.

"Not Dee," she said when he answered. "It's Lacey McCrae. You were with Dee last time I talked to her, last night. I've been home for hours now and she's not here, although her phone is. Did she say anything to you about her plans for the day?"

"Far as I know she was taking the dogs for a run. Something about reclaiming her old route. Is that any help?"

"Maybe." It would be a place to start looking. And did Rob know anything he didn't realize he knew? The cop technique: get him talking and see what falls out. "So you had a good time last night? When did you finally leave?"

Rob laughed. "About ten this morning. We made a lovely night of it."

"Just the two of you?"

"Yup. Believe me, the things we said about board members, we wouldn't want anyone else to hear. Dee is some lady. Even when mega snarky, she could match a Hepburn for class. Is her bike back? I got it down for her."

"I'll go check. Thanks." The bike was not in the garage, nor in the yard. Lacey looked up the hill, where the lights had just come on at Terry Brenner's. Would they know if Dee had a regular Sunday port of call? Maybe not. Jan might be higher than a hawk or passed out cold after a weekend's worth of uppers. The phone number would be in Dee's phone, but walking up there felt more productive. She turned over Dee's note and scribbled on the back, *Gone up to Jan's, back ASAP.* Just in case.

The sound of the rushing river assailed her when she stepped outside. The path Dee would take along the river might have washed away under her feet, dropping her into the roaring waters. *Please, not that.* Lacey could face anything except her best friend's body being tumbled along in the muddy, churning water.

Terry answered the door. "Lacey? What's up?"

"Dee's missing. At least, I wondered if you'd seen her today."

"Dee's missing? Come in. Tell us what happened."

Lacey followed him into the living room, where his wife was flat on the sofa, covered with an afghan. Jan struggled to sit up. It looked like a major effort. He said, "Dee's gone AWOL. Did you see her today, hon?"

"She went up the trail about, oh, one thirty. On her bike. The first time in a while. Usually I hear the dogs when she gets home. I just assumed I'd missed her today because I was resting."

Resting. Right. Speed crash.

"But she normally would go for an hour or so and then come home?" Lacey asked.

"She used to. Not this year, but with the bike she could get a lot farther. Did you try her cell?"

"At the house."

"Oh, no, Terry. What could have happened?"

"Chill, honey. She might have bumped into Jake and been dragged home. The hockey squad is off at a camp for underprivileged children today, and you know how he hates to be alone up there." He turned away, pulling out his phone.

Jan slumped back. "Yeah, that's probably it. Jake won't eat alone if he can help it. And I'm convinced he has designs on Dee. He drags her name into all our conversations, trying to casually find out what she's up to."

Terry came back, shaking his head. "He hasn't seen her. If we don't track her down in an hour, he wants to mount a search. You said she was on her bike; did it get a tune-up this spring, do you know?"

"I don't think so. It was hanging in the garage until last night."

"Could be tire trouble," said Terry.

"Sure," said Jan. "Or she lost the chain. She wouldn't be able to walk all the way back. You have to go look for her. It's supposed to rain."

It wasn't clear whom Jan had intended the order for, but Terry nodded first. "Lacey, do you know the road north of here, by the boarding stables?"

"Where the trail crosses? Uh-huh."

"Good. You drive around that way. I'll take my bike along the trail and meet you. She's bound to be back there somewhere, hungry and furious at herself. She'll yell when she sees my bike light. Or the dogs will knock me down. I'll give you my cell number. Phone if you see her before I do. And take a flashlight, in case you have to go in from the road to help haul her out to the car."

"Phone me, too, please," said Jan. "I may not be much use, but I can start tea and spread blankets. She'll be chilled to the bone if she's been sitting on wet grass all this time."

"Thanks. Both of you." Lacey hurried down the hill in the deepening gloom, extraordinarily relieved that she wasn't alone with this situation. She had always been self-assured on patrol. Why now did she feel like a panicky civilian?

Wilderness, that's why. No handy paramedics or nosy bystanders, no security cameras recording every back alley. Dee was her only friend in Bragg Creek, and she was missing. Was this how all those frightened people who reported missing persons felt? They would usually be a little bit calmed and reassured as soon as she, the officer, said she would look into it. Imagine, having to leave the Force to gain insight into the value of a calm presence to a frightened civilian.

She drove down the hill and turned left onto the river road, watching the shoulder even though Dee would surely have been helped if she'd been stranded along this busy stretch. Unless the Beal brothers had found her. Nothing in their history suggested an attack was likely, but then, nobody had a criminal history until they got caught committing a crime. No obvious sign of a riverbank washout along here, but the churn and rumble of the water ate at her nerves. In the depths of her mind the riverbank moment with Dan played on a loop. She ignored it as best she could, concentrating instead on scanning the ditches and bushes for red dogs, pale clothing, and the chrome gleam of bicycle parts. Nothing.

Around the bend, the white fence of the boarding stables glared in her headlights. Left onto the dirt road, around the toe of the hill. The road rose and fell more than she remembered, forcing her to slow down, keep her eyes on the ditches and not on the dark wooded hillside. Slowly, slowly, with the windows down, she strained to see past the tall grasses or to hear a setter's howl. She stopped and got out, hoping to hear better with the engine off.

"Dee? Beau? Are you out there? Boney? Dee?"

Nothing.

She got back into the car, drove down into the little dip and up the next ridge, and repeated the performance. Nothing but the sound of the wind in the trees.

"Boney? Beau?" she called again.

A familiar howl curled faintly along the rain-scented breeze. She jumped back into the car and drove until the dog appeared in her headlight beams. He stood belly-deep in the weeds, facing the car. Blue collar meant Boney. Where was the other dog? The bike? Where was Dee? She pulled the car half across the road so its headlights lit up the tall grasses. "Quiet, Boney. Dee? Are you there? Dee?"

No answer, and the dog, as usual, didn't obey her. She went back for her flashlight and played it across the overgrown roadside. Even with the light, she almost missed Beau, crouched in the tall grass beyond the ditch. He was growling softly toward the trees. Almost unseen in his shadow lay a pale streak that looked unnatural in the environment.

Lacey turned the flashlight full on it. Starting with a jogging sock on one end — no shoe — the white light played along a calf unnaturally twisted, and above that, a lax thigh that ended in the hem of Dee's faded Mem U running shorts.

CHAPTER NINETEEN

"Dee? Dee, can you hear me?" Lacey scrambled down the ditch and stopped abruptly as Boney sprang in front of her, teeth bared. "Oh, you idiot, get out of the way."

She took another step. Boney growled. Beau turned from the woods to add his threat. After a couple more attempts, Lacey retreated to the road and groped in her bag for her cellphone. Terry couldn't be far away now. Maybe the dogs would listen to him.

"Terry? I found her. She's in the ditch along the back road. Unconscious, I think. You'll see my car headlights. Hurry. The dogs won't let me near her."

"Call 911. I'll be there in three minutes."

The minutes she stood there went on forever, her flashlight shining on Dee and Beau while Boney blocked her path. The last soft light of twilight vanished behind the clouds. The wind rippled along the treetops, sounding too much like rushing water. Rain scent hung in the heavy air. It wasn't here yet, but soon Dee would get wet. A devoted dog was no substitute for a raincoat. What an idiotic thing to be thinking of. Shock was taking hold of her brain. God, just like a civilian.

A bike light bobbed into the road not far away. Terry dropped the bike beside her car. "Boney. Here, boy! Beau. C'mere, old fella." Boney growled. Beau stayed where he was, looking from them to the trees. Terry pulled out his cellphone. "They'll move for Jake if anyone. Jake? Hi, it's Terry. Dee's hurt and we need you to call off the dogs … Up past the boarding stable. Ambulance is on its way. Try not to run them over getting here." He shoved the phone in his pocket. "I'll ride to the intersection to direct the paramedics. Unless you want to go?"

Lacey shook her head. She was not leaving this spot until she had Dee safe. As Terry pedalled down the hill toward the main road, she shivered. What if she was too late? Dee had been out here for hours, unconscious or worse. Had Neil ambushed her as she came off the trail? Had the Beals? They were witnesses to the earlier accident. They must live nearby. But why would they hurt Dee? There was no answer to that question, nothing she could do for Dee until Jake and the paramedics arrived.

Nothing except think like a cop.

There would be traces of the perpetrator: tire tracks on the shoulder, maybe footprints. Standing here staring at Dee would not find and protect those traces. She forced herself to pull the light away. That small act felt like an overwhelming betrayal, like she was leaving her best friend to the wild animals, even though, technically, the headlights' glare was more than sufficient to scare them off.

Edging around the car, staying in the hard ruts where no tracks would show, she shone the flashlight along the softer shoulder. Not far from her front fender were deep gouges in the dirt. A car, moving fast, had swung out of the ruts almost into the ditch and been violently pulled back.

Hit and run.

Failure boiled up in Lacey's throat. It tasted of vinegar and ashes. If Neil had done this, she would kill him.

No. The law was the law. She would see him convicted instead. She stabbed a couple of long sticks into the ground beyond each end of the raw earth, marking the evidence. Dee had been flung forward, landing on who knew what rocks or stumps. Her odds of survival weren't high. And where was her bike?

Lacey played the light over every piece of ditch, looking for a gleam of chrome, but didn't dare leave the gravel lest her foot crush a vital clue. Did she just hear Dee moan, or was that only the wind? Knowledge of the odds duked it out with hope and denial until the first sirens wailed in the distance. Still a long way off, they bounced between the hillsides all the way, making the distance difficult to estimate. Eventually, the cherry lights came bobbing up the road, the welcome revolutions splashing along the treeline. A fire truck stopped first, its siren dying mid-wail, and immediately washed the scene with brilliant white from two rooftop spotlights. Two men jumped out and ran toward her. She pointed toward Dee.

They stopped at the dog, tried to flank him. He lunged whenever either man got close. EMTs bounded from their vehicle, saw her pointing, started over, and got the dog treatment. The patrol constable, following them, pulled his radio out. If they had to wait for dog handlers this far from Calgary, it could take another hour to get to Dee. She might not have that long.

Someone hopped out of an SUV behind the cruiser. Boney stopped barking. Beau raised his head. In under a minute, they were both sitting beside Lacey's car while Jake Wyman talked softly to them, his arms around their necks.

The EMTs bent over Dee. In the surreal white glare they performed the rituals Lacey had seen countless times on patrol, but never from this distance. They could be on a stage and she in the audience. The air crackled with messages, but no words were clear past the pounding of her pulse. Was Dee alive? The impatience to rush over and see warred with a fear of disrupting the delicate dance of lifesaving procedures. An EMT strapped a mask over Dee's face, and a wild surge of hope wiped out the ashes in Lacey's mouth before she remembered she was not a civilian and knew better. Paramedics rarely called someone "out" at the scene unless they had injuries clearly inconsistent with life, such as decapitation. In all other cases it was the doctor's job to make that decision at the hospital. How could the system make bystanders wait? It was inhumane. How had she never realized that before?

When they moved Dee, it would be clear. If they thought she'd survive, they would stabilize her and be as careful as possible getting her out of that ditch, maybe call in a chopper for air evac. If they thought she was going, diesel fuel was their best friend. They'd get her in the rig and work her on the way in. How long had they been down there? She tore her eyes from the stage play and looked at her watch, which told her nothing. She had no idea what time she had found Dee, much less how long it had been since the first responders arrived.

A fine mist touched her bare arm, sending goosebumps along her skin. In the ditch, someone looked at the sky. Rain would complicate all their jobs, and getting soaked would be really bad for Dee. If she was alive to feel it.

The constable came over to take a preliminary statement. When pressed, he admitted Dee was alive. Lacey could have cried on his shirt. Instead, she blinked hard and answered his questions.

"Yes, I found her. She's Dee — Deandra Sharon Phillips." She gave Dee's address and then identified herself. "McCrae, Lacey. I'm a guest staying at Dee's. You'd better see what's back here." She led the way around her car, pointed out the two sticks and the gouged earth between them. When the cop went back to his car for another light, she stayed on the dark side of her car and squeezed her eyes very tight, not moving until the tears retreated. She had never broken down at a crime scene, not even that bad night in Surrey when Tom had bled all over her shirt during a drug bust gone wrong. The night that had cemented their friendship beyond shift buddies and brought her all these years later to Calgary and Bragg Creek and this wilderness road that Dee might not leave alive.

As she rounded the car again, Terry headed for her, followed by a burly young man who promptly draped her in a soft leather jacket several sizes too big. "Best sit down," the youngster said and opened her car door for her. Lacey slumped against the seat, snuggling the jacket around her. So this was what it was like to be a civilian. A bystander wrapped in a warm jacket. Terry put his hands on her cold ones.

"I guess you'll want to go to the hospital. I'll drive you in. Jake will settle the dogs for the night. Don't worry about a thing here." He went off to scrounge for news and soon reported back. "They're pretty sure she's got broken bones — legs and ribs. Her head is the big concern. A stump caught the back of her head, just below the helmet, and may have cracked her skull. Her blood pressure's steady, so they're not talking internal bleeding. Which is a miracle, considering."

Extra patrol cars arrived to close off the intersection below, waiting for a crime scene team from Calgary. Lacey hadn't yet mentioned Neil, but the police would want to know Dee was being stalked and that she was recently divorced. The two things were paired in thousands of police reports annually. How long before Dee was alert enough to give a statement on her own account? Tonight? Ever?

Against the brightly lit backdrop of forest, the EMTs moved Dee onto a stretcher. Lacey stood up to get a better look. Firemen clustered around and lifted. As they shuffled carefully through the briars and grasses, one person bagging and the other holding a fluid drip, the tight ball in her chest began to expand. Careful meant alive, and likely to stay that way. The dogs sat beside Jake, but watched the EMTs every step of the way as they carried their mistress up to the road. When Boney started to stand up, a word from Jake stopped him.

Lacey said, "They sure listen to you."

Jake nodded. "I walked 'em when Dee-Dee sprained her ankle. Took 'em out with the horses, too, so they had to learn to obey whistle signals. Can't control the reins with leashes in your hands. That pair could have pulled me right outta the saddle at the first deer crossing the trail."

"Terry said you could take them home tonight?"

"I'll put 'em in their kennel and do the usual, and come down in the morning if you're not home yet. We'll stay until Dee-Dee's taken away, though. They won't want to leave her out here."

"Thanks, Mr. Wyman. I'm sure Dee would be very relieved."

"I owe her. Anything she needs, you let me know."

As the ambulance lights spun up, the mist thickened into serious rain, battering the car roof, the ditch, and the trees, kicking up small dusty puffs where it splattered on the road. Lacey scrambled back into her car to wait for the emergency vehicles to move. Feeling as if her nose was pressed against the invisible barrier between cop and civilian, she watched as the first responders beyond it succoured the friend she had abandoned last night.

CHAPTER TWENTY

Terry returned in the drenched dawn, his borrowed SUV's headlights sweeping up the hill into Dee's driveway. Jan, wrapped in a comforter in the sunroom, watched through the last of the thunderstorm as Lacey McCrae went up the steps. When the living room windows glowed, Terry pulled away. She met him at the front door, submitting to a hug so intense it hurt. "You're so cold," she said when he let go. "Do you want a hot drink? How's Dee?"

"Out of surgery. Stable." Terry yawned. "Hot choc would be great … with booze. Man, what a night." He followed her into the kitchen and slumped on a stool while she put the kettle on. "Did you sleep?"

"Not a chance. All my stress hormones went into overdrive, and that thunderstorm was intense." Not to mention the quarter pill she'd taken when Terry and Lacey first left on their hunt, so as to be functional if Dee needed her. "I've been lying awake wondering if Dee would survive and wishing I weren't such a wimp. I was useless last night, and I won't be able to visit her in hospital."

"You're not a wimp. Charging around the trails would not have helped Dee. And it's not your fault that you can't tolerate the hospital smells or those endless corridors."

Jan stirred cocoa and sugar and cream into a paste. "I didn't mean to beg for reassurance. I just feel really useless. She's my only friend, besides Rob. How bad is it?"

"One leg fractured below the knee. Lacey said that likely means a car, not an SUV, an older model since the bumper had a narrow impact point. Rounded bumpers diffuse the damage more and an SUV hits higher up the leg."

Jan brought the kettle and filled their cups. "Is that it?"

"I wish." Terry waved the Kahlúa bottle. "You want?"

"It's poison to me, but yeah, give me one spoonful. What else is wrong?"

"Broken ribs. Might get pneumonia. They'll treat for that. The real concern is her head, a depressed skull fracture behind her ear. Two inches different and the helmet would have taken the blow. They fixed it already, but there'll be swelling. Might mean more surgery. They're keeping her sedated for at least twenty-four hours. I brought Lacey home so she could get some sleep. She can take Dee's car into town when she wakes up."

"What's the matter with hers?"

"Hers is surrounded by crime scene tape. She said they won't move it in the dark in case it runs over evidence."

"Good point. It must have been in broad daylight, the hit. Some yahoo hunting out of season, or driving drunk?"

"If they were heard hunting near the Beals' land, they'll already be sorry. Those guys are big on gun safety, especially on a weekend, when their kids are in the yard." Terry yawned and shook out his shoulders. "Here's a weird thing: Lacey knows Eddie Beal. He called out to her by name as we were creeping out through the police barricade. She just glared at him and kept moving."

"She glares at lots of people." Jan stirred her cooling cocoa and took a cautious sip. "So what happens next?"

"Police try to find the driver, I guess. For now, I need to sleep for a week."

"No work today?"

"Jake wants me handy for whatever Dee or Lacey might need. Makes sense since I'm the only one Lacey knows. He's edgy about dealing with her himself. Maybe he thinks she's a gold digger."

"He's made enough bad choices with women that it's almost a sign of good character if he doesn't like one."

"He likes you."

"Brat."

Terry fell asleep almost immediately, but Jan, spooning against his back, lay awake as birds took up their morning chat fest beyond her blackout curtains. Who in their mellow, rural area could crash into a cyclist and keep going? It was tempting to blame someone from outside, a transient or joyriding kids from Calgary. Respectable, responsible women like Dee were unlikely to be deliberately targeted. Camille, now, there'd be drivers bidding for the privilege. Not that a person would wish that on Camille. Well, maybe Mick would, although he was too nice to ever say so.

The phone rang soon after noon, catching them at breakfast. Jan picked it up. "Rob. What's up? Yes, she did. Yesterday, but she wasn't found until late. Broken leg, broken ribs, and they operated on a depressed skull fracture last night. We're waiting on more news now, but it will be a long haul any which way. What? Sure, come on up. Bring extra coffee and milk." She hung up. "The river's rising again. Rob wants to sleep here so he can be sure to get to work tomorrow. You'd better tell Lacey. She might want to stay in Calgary overnight rather than risk getting stuck on this bank."

"How'd you know she was paranoid about the river? I only realized after the gala. She kind of freaked out about the bridge maybe closing."

"I didn't know." *So, the judgmental ex-Mountie has a weakness after all.* Trying not to be glad of that, Jan went on, "I was thinking of her being able to get to the hospital."

"Off to your lounger while I shave," said Terry. "Sing out if you see Lacey moving. I don't want to phone while she's still asleep."

When Dee's dogs sent up howls from their kennel, Jan looked down the hill to see Lacey on Dee's porch. She called out to let Terry know and heard him on the phone. But Lacey had no news to share and was soon away in Dee's Lexus. Back to the hospital, surely.

Jake passed with the setters an hour later. Jan knew Terry had already updated him on Dee so it wasn't a surprise that he merely waved and rode on. His guests, if they knew about the possible bridge closure, weren't making a mass exodus. Jake could get supplies in by helicopter. His west lawn was big enough for a whole flock of whirlybirds.

Rob arrived before supper, bearing food and news. "The Mounties still have the stable road blocked. They're going door-to-door seeking witnesses, too. Poor Dee. What's the latest?" Jan filled him in while he chopped, stirred, and seared dinner. All fresh foods, no preservatives or colourings to trigger her food sensitivities. Dear Rob. He said, "I hate to seem selfish by worrying about my job, but do you think they'll extend me without Dee to push for it?"

"That lot? Until they've got another party planned, you'll be lucky if anyone shows up to countersign the checks. Just keep on keeping on as long as you can. How's the place look after the big bash, anyway?"

"It looks fine, but I think that high river is pushing back on the sewer system. There's an intermittently foul odour wafting up the elevator shaft. I might have to get the plumbers in." He dragged out another pot and slapped in a slab of butter. "At least the vault temperature controls are settling. Today's facilities readout shows them almost back to normal range. One less thing for that vault guy to complain about when he finally gets back here to fix the racks."

As supper ended, a Mountie's arrival shook them all out of their exhausted silence. Terry brought him to the kitchen. "He wants to know if any of us saw any red vehicles in the vicinity yesterday."

Jan thought. "Eddie Beal's old truck is reddish, though that's mostly rust. There's a couple of dark-red SUVs around in town. As for cars, the only one I can think of is Jarrad's Corvette."

"He's not here," said Terry. "He went south on the Stanley Cup golf junket. His car is probably still sitting at the museum."

"No, he missed the plane. Someone phoned the party looking for him. And his car wasn't in the parking lot when I got up yesterday."

Terry shook his head. "I saw it on my run yesterday. It's impossible to mistake a classic Stingray."

The Mountie was taking notes. "A red Corvette Stingray? And the owner's name? What time did you notice it gone, ma'am?"

"Sunday morning."

Terry shook his head. "The car was still in the parking lot at four."

Jan shrugged. "Maybe he went back, took a walk along the river, or looked for his picture in the hockey paintings."

"Jarrad looking at art. That'll be the day."

"Guys," said Rob. "The nice man is waiting. If this particular car is important, its movements will be on the museum's security footage. Anyone else with a red car?"

Jan bit her lip. "Dee's ex has one. But he lives in Calgary now."

"He used to drive a red Grand Am," said Terry, giving her a sideways glance that wasn't altogether friendly. After showing the Mountie out, he came back and glared at his wife. "Why'd you bring up Neil? Have you seen him out here lately?"

"Not for months. But he has a red car."

"Did. He may be a greedy prick, but he wouldn't hurt Dee."

"He's an asshole. Even if he didn't do it, he can sweat for a bit."

"You sent the cops after him for proxy revenge? Dee won't thank you."

Rob's head was flipping between them like a tennis spectator's. "You two suffering from adrenalin poisoning? Uncle Rob recommends you both go pick a nice escapist movie, and I'll make tea."

When he brought a tray to the living room ten minutes later, he went right back to his chief interest: gossip. "Divine Dee has a nasty ex? What on earth did he do?"

"Didn't like it that Dee made more money than him," said Terry. "So the slimeball took up with her secretary and let everybody in the company know it. When she found out and tossed him, he sued for spousal support. No-fault divorce rules mean he's living high off the woman he cheated on. The no-class bastard."

"No shame," Rob agreed. "Dee's too good for that. She was showing me around her house the other night. Her office has maps of battlefields, model ships with all sails flying, even a bust of Admiral Nelson. Or was it his stuff?"

"It's hers," said Jan. "She's the only woman I know who has every line of *Master and Commander* memorized. The dogs' names are a clue, too. Boney, for Napoleon — blue collar, like his uniform. Beau, as in Beau Douro — did you know that was one of the Duke of Wellington's nicknames? I didn't — has the red collar. And Duke, also as in Wellington, the poor old beastie."

"I must have missed Duke. There were only two dogs the other night."

"Duke died last winter," said Jan. "Jarrad's fault. He nearly creamed them all and didn't even stop, the punk. Hid his old car to avoid charges. Then Mick bought him the Corvette. Talk about rewarding bad behaviour.

Scary, Dee getting hit again so close to the site of the first accident. I hope she'll be okay."

Scary didn't begin to cover it, but Jan knew if she let herself go, she would cry and rage until she was too exhausted to move again. She was barely able to get her feet under her as it was.

CHAPTER TWENTY-ONE

The bridge over the Elbow River was still open on Tuesday after lunch, when Lacey returned from Calgary. She white-knuckled over it, trying not to look at the churning brown water so close to the bridge deck, then drove up to the house and sat, too tired to get out of the car. The night nurses had turned a blind eye to her snoozing at Dee's bedside, but this morning's guy said Dee would not be waking today. Lacey was free, he added, to go home for a shower.

What would she find in the house this time? Monday morning she'd found all the drawers in Dee's bedroom open, their contents tumbled about. Lacey hadn't looked in the room since Friday, so she couldn't say if Dee normally left it like that. The napkin drawer on Sunday still nagged at her, as did Dee's purse. Had it been moved, or had she imagined it on the stool because that was where it usually hung? Dee wasn't awake to ask and probably wouldn't remember how she'd left things, anyway. This was all too reminiscent of the weeks Lacey had spent after

Dan moved out, walking from room to room to look for evidence he'd been snooping around while she was at work. She couldn't afford to install security to watch this house while she hung out at the hospital watching Dee. Maybe Wayne would lend her alarms temporarily.

She got out of the car and almost fell right back in as Boney headbutted her in the stomach. "Oof! What are you doing out?" She reached for his collar without much hope, sure he'd run off. Instead, he abruptly sat down beside her, tongue lolling and head cocked. Jake Wyman and another man rode up the drive on glossy brownish-red horses, with Beau strolling sedately alongside. Jake threw his reins to his younger companion and dismounted, tucking a silver whistle into his sleeve as he landed.

"G'day, Miss. I hear Dee-Dee isn't awake yet?"

"No. They'll start easing off her sedation tonight, so maybe tomorrow."

"How come they tell you so much, and give me nothing but 'stable condition'?"

"I said I was her sister." She hadn't hesitated to lie, not with Dee's next of kin being her sick mother in St. John's and her only local semi-kin being that skunk, Neil.

"Smart. You'll keep Terry in the loop, right?"

Taking her agreement for granted, Jake snapped his fingers and went off around the porch, the dogs following.

After some silent fidgeting with the loose end of his reins, the young man said, "I'm real sorry about this. None of us thought Jarrad would go this far. He said he was coming home to do a dance on somebody, but we never guessed it was Ms. Phillips. I mean, it was only a windshield."

"What windshield?" When he chewed his lip instead of answering, Lacey fixed him with her best cold cop's eyeball. "Tell me the about the windshield. From the beginning."

"Yes, ma'am. Jarrad killed Ms. Phillips's dog last winter — an accident, honest, but still, he should have owned up right away and said sorry. Next time he came home, she was at the golf course parking lot when he drove in. I don't know what was said, but she put a five iron through the windshield of the Stingray. That car was like his brand-new baby. She paid for the repair, though. So it shoulda been over, right?"

Calm, collected Dee had put a golf club through Jarrad's windshield? Talk about handing his defence lawyers ammunition. "You think he ran over Dee to get back at her?"

"You didn't hear? Oh, shit. Sorry, ma'am. The cops came up looking for his car last night. I just assumed ..." The hockey player looked beyond her and closed his mouth.

"You assumed too much."

How Jake had come so quietly across the planks in cowboy boots was anybody's guess. "Ma'am, I'm sorry if this young fella upset you. It was police routine, checking up on red cars, and someone told them about Jarrad's. I'll make sure he talks to the police as soon as he surfaces. But he won't have anything useful to say." He touched his hat brim and remounted his horse. "I'll be down in the morning for the dogs. Good day to you, ma'am."

Lacey stared at the horses' rumps as they receded. The investigators should hear about the windshield. Her money was still on Neil, but the odds had changed. She found the card for the officer in charge on Dee's hit and run, left a message about Jarrad, and asked if they had checked the whereabouts of Dee's ex-husband. Then she called Tom.

"Got anything for me from Cochrane yet?"

"Nice to hear your voice, too," said Tom. "Got some prints — left and right thumbs, index and middle — but they're not on record. That penlight print is blurry. Drummond needs clean prints to compare."

"Don't real estate agents have to be printed for security purposes or something?"

"Not that I know of. Get those prints and we'll help you nail this guy."

"I'll figure out a way and get back to you." She'd be taking Neil's fingerprints post-mortem if she had to speak to him right now. No, she wouldn't. Asshole or not, dangerous or not, he was innocent until proven guilty. She would have to see him face to face and hope he touched something that would take a print. She opened Dee's cellphone to get his number, which went to voice mail.

"Neil, it's Lacey McCrae. Long time. I don't know if you've heard, but Dee's in hospital. Give me a call for the details."

Her phone rang three minutes later. Neil was all charm and apology. He hadn't realized she was visiting. How badly hurt was Dee? Which hospital? Sure, the nurses would let him in. He was sort of still family. And could he interest Lacey in a spacious condo in Marda Loop? Priced in the low fours, a steal for that part of town. No? Okay, tonight at the hospital, then. Bye.

Fucking creep. Trying to sell real estate in a crisis.

Lacey stopped walking. If he was after Dee, he had a half-hour's head start to the hospital. She had to get there before he talked his way past the nurses.

RM sheriffs' cars and Highways Department trucks sat by each end of the bridge, keeping traffic to one lane. She had too long to watch workers take soundings while the muddy brown water swirled past, carrying branches and, occasionally, whole trees. The Fraser River had been the same murky colour on that dank February day, but this one was running twice as fast. Would they close the bridge today? Should she go back to the house for more clothes? No time. A sheriff waved her forward. After the traffic circle, another delay as a crane lowered cement dividers into a ditch to divert runoff that was already pouring down the hillside. Should she send Tom to the hospital? She should have gone up to Highway 1 instead. Or not phoned Neil yet. *Stupid.* The traffic moved again. Speeding might buy her three minutes, but if a sheriff pulled her over, she'd lose five times that.

Twenty minutes later, she hurried into the hospital, up the familiar stairs, turned left at the nursing station, and skidded to a halt outside Dee's observation room. Someone was in there now, wide shoulders bending over the bed. From the back, in the dim lighting, all she could see was pale clothing that might be a nursing uniform. The man straightened as she entered, his linen jacket sliding easily over his six-foot body. His beefy good looks and tousled blond hair were all too familiar. Neil had beaten her to Dee.

Swallowing her fear and fury, Lacey looked at the bed. Dee seemed just as she had been that morning, head swathed in a white gauze cap, oxygen tube beneath her nose, heart monitor clipped to her finger. The scrapes on her face shone with invisible Band-Aid solution. The monitors all gave their regular, irritating beeps. The IV tube dripped undisturbed. She was okay, or at least as okay as she could be.

"I thought you weren't coming until tonight."

"I had a cancellation. Poor little Dee. Driving too fast, was she?"

"The police haven't talked to you?"

"No reason why they would, but anyway, we were in Radium for the weekend."

Radium was four hours away. He could have come back. "We?"

"My girlfriend, Dani. Her father owns a resort down there. We spend most weekends with him."

Dani? The name would fit right in with Camille Hardy's posse. Maybe she deserved Neil. Now, to get his fingerprints.

"Tell me about this resort."

His enthusiastic description was typical Neil, all about appearances. He'd always had a good line of patter for a guy not quite as deep as a dollar bill. Hopefully he would touch something besides the bed rail. She couldn't very well walk out with that. "So," she said when his self-centred babble slowed. "What are you driving these days?"

"A Hummer. It belongs to Dani's dad's company."

"Isn't that hard on gas? Don't you have a smaller car for getting around town?"

"I'm making serious deals these days. Can't drive up to a five-mil Mount Royal property in an old Grand Am."

Lacey cranked up her calm friendliness. "Oh, you still have that? Red, wasn't it?"

"Sitting in my garage. Well, Dani's garage. The house-keeper uses it." He chatted — bragged, really — for a while more, looking harmless and touching nothing. Eventually he said, "So, what happened to Dee? She's sure sleeping sound."

About bloody time he noticed.

"She was hit by a car. Broken leg, broken ribs, skull fracture. She's being kept sedated, but they'll let her wake up gradually." Nearly too late, she realized that Dee's waking up, being able to give a statement, could precipitate another attack. "Maybe by the weekend."

"Oh." Neil sat in the only chair, his hands dangling between his knees. "Tough luck. You looking after the dogs?"

"No. Jake Wyman is."

"Oh, sure. Hero Jake. Always riding to the rescue."

"He seems nice enough to me."

"Yeah, well, he didn't badmouth you to your boss, did he? Just because I sold his ex-wife a couple of properties to invest part of her settlement. Dee's managing them for her, but you don't see him dissing her. Oh no. He's all over her, inviting her to his parties, introducing her to everybody. I'd make a fortune with those contacts."

What a charmer. It had probably never crossed his mind that Jake would side with anyone else whose sleazy spouse had cheated on them. Was this all that lay behind the bugging — trying to mine her telephone conversations for business leads?

"Look," Neil was saying, "Here's my card. Call me if there's anything I can do. And I'll give you my home number." He whipped out a card and scribbled on the back with one of his fingerprint pens. "Just do me a favour. If Dani answers, say you're calling about a property. She's not cool with me seeing my ex."

"Even when she's in a coma?"

"I doubt she'd believe that."

So Dani had his number already. Still, his fingerprints were on the card, and that was what mattered. She accepted it by a corner he hadn't touched. Paper didn't always yield the way it should. What else could she get? "Got a spare pen? I could do crossword puzzles while I'm hanging around here."

"Good idea." He put a couple more pens beside it and flashed his charmer smile. "Give one to the doctor for me. See you later, Lacey."

See you in handcuffs, asshole.

She waited until he was in the elevator before she folded a paper towel loosely around the pens and the card. Then she followed him to the lobby, saw the Hummer pass the parking gate, and pulled out her cellphone.

"Tom? I've got Neil's prints. Can you come by the hospital and pick them up? I can't leave Dee now that he knows where she is."

Tom came after supper, bringing his wife, an ex-Emergency nurse who took in the equipment with a practiced eye. Marie offered to sit with Dee while Tom took Lacey downstairs for a meal. When they were sitting in the cafeteria with Tom's coffee and Lacey's soup, he said, "Okay, gimme what you've got." Lacey unfolded the paper towel. "Pens again? I told you that fingerprint isn't good enough. It's not going to be clearer on a different pen."

"He took these pens out of his pocket and put them on Dee's bedside table. No gloves. His perfectly fresh finger-prints — the real ones — are on all three pens and the business card."

"Oh. So what else you got on this guy?"

She summarized the conversation with Neil, ending with, "He still has an older red Grand Am, kept in his girlfriend's garage."

"You really want it to be him, huh? So does Drummond. Why didn't you call him direct?"

"I can't afford to. Next time he might be off duty, and his bar tab would break me." She slurped up her soup while Tom left a message. With Dee under Marie's more-than-competent eye, she could go back through the line again for a sandwich to take upstairs for later.

"I'll call you when he calls me," he said, pocketing the phone. "Are you really staying here all night again?"

"I left Dee alone on the weekend when she needed me. I can't risk him coming back to finish the job."

CHAPTER TWENTY-TWO

Rain again on Tuesday. The endless drizzle drove Jan in from the sunroom by midafternoon. Sunday night's adrenalin was long gone, leaving her weak and miserable. A quarter pill would fix it. But that would leave her worse off tomorrow, when Dee might be awake and needing her. Better save the pills for emergencies. Terry phoned to say he was staying late at work. She warned him the police had barricades ready at the bridge, then went back to huddling under her comforters. If this was what stimulants did to her after only a short trial, she could not afford them anymore.

Rob appeared on the deck shortly after five with a grocery sack. She uncurled herself from the heap of comforters and opened the glass door for him. He propped his dripping umbrella on the mat and draped his jacket over a chair.

"I'll mop up in a sec," he said. "Just let me find a stiff drink first. Get you anything?" Jan waved her water glass as he disappeared into the kitchen. He was more a wine guy than a hard drinker, so today must have been more trying than usual. When he came back, she asked.

"Oh yeah, lousy." Rob flopped onto the loveseat. "Mrs. Ass-in-the-Air has lost her key card, but she wouldn't speak directly with me, just left a message yesterday with the secretary about getting a replacement. When I phoned her back to ask about when she last saw it and so on — because we have to block it in the computer if it doesn't turn up — she got all snippy with me for daring to question a board member. So it's anyone's guess if the place has been insecure all weekend. And she won't wait to see if her card turns up, just demanded a new one and told me to leave it with the secretary for her. Doesn't even want to look at me. Bloody sexual politics. You'd think I could avoid them by being gay."

"Maybe she'll be embarrassed enough to resign."

"Fat chance. She'll get me bounced and forget the whole nasty incident. Especially with Dee out of the equation. How is she today?"

"The same, Terry said. Just you and me for supper."

"Not hungry yet. You?"

"Not yet. So what happened besides Camille?"

He groaned. "Everything. Did I mention that stink?"

"The river pushing up the sewer line?"

"The plumber says it's not the high water. He thinks a workman might have left his lunch-bag in a ventilation shaft. Says it's happened on other jobsites. Or it could be our protester up to mischief. The vault racks are still not fixed, so I had to delay more paintings in Calgary. Maybe the vault guy will be back Thursday, says that sweet-voiced wench who I'd strangle if she wasn't in their

Vancouver office. And then, just to really cap my day, the Highways fellow wants to park a backhoe on the terrace. Guess what that will do to the Rundle-stone paving."

"Why do they want a backhoe?"

"There's a massive snag in the river. Whole trees piling up. If it gives way and crashes into the bridge, it could mean a long-term closure. Ergo, backhoe."

"Okay, you deserve that drink. Have another if you need it."

Rob turned the glass in his hand. "Nah. Hard liquor's not really my thing."

After a bit he went into the kitchen and threw stuff into a pot for soup. While it was simmering and sending out savoury aromas of tomato and nutmeg, they watched the Calgary news for the latest on the flooding. Rain and the melting snowpack had swelled every river from Highway 1 to the U.S. border. Normally tiny creeks were ripping out culverts, cutting range roads, turning saturated slopes into mudslides. With the flood news out of the way, the announcer went on, "RCMP are asking for the public's help in locating a red 1969 Corvette Stingray like the one in this picture." A photo splashed up beside his head.

"That's Jarrad's car," said Jan.

"Damn if I didn't forget. Yeah, it's his, and you put them onto it."

"Me?"

"You told the Mountie last night, when you and Terry were sniping at each other."

"So?"

"They did whatever it is they do with paint scrapings and figured out they were looking for that type.

Two Mounties spent all afternoon looking at our outdoor security recordings to figure out when the 'Vette got there and when it left. Isn't there a song? 'Gimme the Red Corvette' or something like that? Anyway, the cops are singing it today. The car left late Saturday night and showed up in a different parking spot the next day. After Dee was hit. Its nose was stuck in a spirea bush that hid any damage to the bumper."

"Oh my god. So they're looking for Jarrad, too?"

"Presumably. The car disappeared again in the middle of that thunderstorm on Sunday night. You know how lightning flashes fuck up a camera's sensor for a few seconds? Well, somebody got into the car and then there was one of those whiteouts. After the reset it was gone."

"But when it came in on Sunday, it was daylight. Couldn't they tell it was Jarrad?"

Rob shrugged. "He had a ball cap on both times. The cops pulled some still photos to show around for a proper identification."

"God. The Mounties actually think he ran into Dee and left her there to die? The same way he did last winter?"

"Seems so. Who is this guy, anyway? I must have seen him if he was at the gala."

"You saw him all right," said Jan. "His bare ass behind Camille's, over the makeup table."

"I wouldn't want to stand in her satin flats today," said Rob. "Imagine knowing you screwed a would-be murderer."

Attempted murder. Jan had not framed the attack on Dee that way. Easier to believe it was an accident, a mischance of fate that had brought the bike and the car together. If Jarrad had done it deliberately, she would do her utmost to make him pay. The surge of rage was almost a pill's worth. She leaned back on the cushions and breathed deep, willing the fury into her brain where it might unlock the resources she needed. Surely she, who watched and listened to everyone in the neighbourhood, could figure out where he might be hiding. But her stupid, sluggish, useless brain refused to co-operate. The rain trailed down her cheeks, too tired to keep up with gravity.

CHAPTER TWENTY-THREE

"You can go home now."

"Huh?" Lacey sat up. It was morning. Tom's wife, Marie, was bending over her. In the bed, Dee seemed unchanged. "What are you doing here?"

"I'll stay with Dee today, and you'll go home to sleep. A neighbour will pick up my kids from school, but I need to collect them by five. And listen to your voice mail."

"My voice mail?" Lacey repeated, yawning. Every muscle griped about her disturbed night in the chair. How could she have stiffened up so badly when she had hardly slept for nurses entering to check on Dee?

"Tom left you a message. Dee will be fine with me. See you by four thirty."

Outside, Lacey turned on her cellphone and checked her messages: one from Terry asking for an update and one from Tom an hour ago. "Those prints don't match the ex-husband. Meet me at that museum place at one. I'm bringing the recorder."

She navigated the tail end of the morning rush on autopilot. If Neil had not bugged the office, then who? Who hated Dee enough to attempt vehicular homicide? The sun strengthened as she drove, adding an extra layer of strain to her tired eyes. She hadn't taken sunglasses yesterday because of the rain, and there were none in Dee's glove compartment. When could she get her own car from the stable road?

Despite the let-up in the rain, the river had crept closer to the bridge deck. She kept her eyes relentlessly on the centre line as she crossed. It was bad enough driving exhausted without being sucked away by the hypnotic patterns on the river's surface. She turned up Dee's driveway and braced herself for the dogs' threats before realizing they weren't in their pen. Hopefully that meant they were out with the neighbour and not running loose on the muddy hillside. She was too tired to even think of looking for them.

By the time she was out of the shower, the dogs were back. She watched out the bathroom window while Jake put them in their pen, checked their water, and patted them over the fence for a couple of minutes. Then he came toward the house. He had to have seen the Lexus out front. There was nothing for it but to go down, even though every bone of her body longed to crawl into bed. She scrambled into her clothes as the kitchen door opened below.

"Miss McCrae?" he called. "Can we talk?" She found him leaning against the counter, quite at home. "Sorry to barge in," he said. "But when I saw Dee-Dee's car … what can you tell me about her today?"

"They'll let her slowly wake up over the next twenty-four hours so they can test her reflexes and cognition. The doctor doesn't expect trouble since the brain didn't swell much at all. She'll be in a wheelchair for a few months. I don't know when she can come home. This house isn't exactly wheelchair friendly."

"I can send some fellas over to install ramps. Maybe one of those platform chair lifts up the stairs. Think I should ask her, or do it for a surprise?"

"That would be quite a surprise."

"Fitted out my ma's house twenty years ago. It's bound to be easier nowadays." He straightened up. "Ma'am, I owe you an apology for yesterday. I shut down that young fella when he was only telling the truth. It looks mightily like Jarrad Fiske was the driver of the car that hit Dee-Dee. You know about that incident last winter?"

"Only that Jarrad was driving the car that hit her dog."

"Mick, I regret to say, helped the kid by hiding the car and getting Jarrad on a plane back to his team. Now I hear from the grapevine that the young fella was already off his game by then, breaking training and mouthing off at his coaches. Then he started drinking too much and fighting with his teammates, yelling about getting his own back on somebody, for something. It sure sounds like he brooded on Dee-Dee over that windshield, and maybe he blamed her for reporting him over her dog. When he saw her out bike riding, he didn't stop to think. I'm real sorry."

So Jarrad had been making threats. Had he spied on Dee, waiting for an opportunity? But if the record-er had been installed around the time Dee had started to suspect a prowler, that would have been when Jarrad was away. He'd have needed a confederate, someone to bug Dee's window and find out where she was vulnerable. Maybe Mick? He lived practically next door to Dee and might even have visited over the winter. It was easier to see Camille as an active accomplice than poor old Mick. Even if she had no suspicion of how far Jarrad might go for revenge, Camille would revel in the chance to get some dirt on Dee.

"Then there's no doubt Jarrad deliberately ran over Dee?"

"Not much. The Mounties came around with photos of him abandoning his car at the museum. The youngsters identified his jacket, even though he wore a ball cap and kept his head down. There'll be a whatchamacallit — all-points bulletin?"

"Canada-wide warrant. Would Mick aid Jarrad in evading charges this serious?"

"I'd like to think not, but he probably would. Except he's not able. Heart's bad and the pacemaker isn't helping much. Camille found him collapsed in the den Sunday night and took him to hospital. They didn't keep him in, but he's got a private nurse at their place in the city. Camille won't have him out here when the bridge might close any hour. I said I'd fly him out if he needed medical attention, but she wouldn't have it."

"Wouldn't Camille help Jarrad just as much as Mick would?"

"Nah. She hates the little punk." Camille hated Jarrad? Not by anyone else's report. If she had helped the new prime suspect escape to the States to evade arrest, it would please Lacey mightily to see her charged as an accessory. Jake added, "I expect you'll be staying here awhile, once Dee-Dee's out of the hospital. You don't worry about looking after her. Medical insurance will pay for private nursing and I'll cover what it doesn't. We stand by our neighbours out here."

She thanked him and showed him out, locking the door this time. Two hours left to nap before lunch and then Tom. Was he coming to stand by while Wayne fired her ass for not working this week? Wayne had sounded quite understanding on the phone, but you couldn't always tell with ex-cops. Job loss. Wouldn't that put the icing on her mud pie?

She didn't fall asleep easily. When she woke to the noon news on the radio, the police were asking for the public's help in locating Jarrad Fiske. Last seen on Sunday afternoon in Bragg Creek, he was thought to be driving a 1969 Corvette Stingray, bright red with a white convertible roof. Anyone with information on the whereabouts of either Jarrad or the car was asked to call ...

CHAPTER TWENTY-FOUR

Jan ate her toasted bagel in the sunroom, keeping half an ear on the TV news in the living room. The first sunny day in nearly a week and the first she could stand up without pain. A good day. Except she still had no idea how to track down Jarrad, other than keeping an eye on the Hardy house in case he was there. Not that she thought he was. He'd have hopped the first available flight back to the States, or even driven through the border to catch up with his teammates by Sunday night, and been perfecting his putt at some resort. Well, there was a Finals game tonight. If she spotted Jarrad in those stands, cheering on his friends like nothing was wrong, the police would know where to apply for extradition.

Or had he left the car at Mick's townhouse? Could she ask Terry to drive by there on his way home from work? If he got to come home at all tonight. The snow-pack was still melting, raising the river terrifyingly close to the level of 2013's massive flood. The slow rise was almost worse than that sudden mass of water. Harder on the nerves of every person for a hundred miles. Maybe she should send Rob on a grocery run in case. Dear Rob. He'd do it, too, despite all the work at the museum and worry over his job. If he lost that he'd have to move on, and her life would be that much lonelier. She appreciated Rob. She could show that by taking him last night's left-over soup for lunch. The road was dry, the day was lovely, and it was only a five-minute drive downhill. No need for the magic pill. She could phone him from the parking lot and not even leave the van. Meanwhile, she could ponder Phase Two of the Get Jake on Rob's Side campaign.

At the museum, she parked facing the wild, whirling river, looking for familiar faces among the anxious watchers along the bridge and far bank. A diesel engine rumbled and a belch of black smoke rose from the riverside terrace. The backhoe's arm stretched out from the stone parapet, bit deep into the turgid waters, and brought back a soggy mass of pine branches. It dragged them up on the muddy bank below the terrace, dropping them with a ferocious squelching, and dipped again into the brown swirl. A small poplar came up next, with a few young leaves clinging to its waterlogged branches. Beyond the tree, something pale broke the surface before being sucked back under.

Rob climbed into the passenger seat and sniffed. "Mmm, soup."

Jan said, "What was that?"

"What?"

"Where the backhoe is working. Something whitish, like cloth, is caught in that pile of trees." They both watched the backhoe's next reach. This time the white was plainer: a large flap of paleness that slid off a branch and back underwater.

"Garbage?" Rob suggested. "A tarp from some building site upriver?"

"Maybe. Do you want to reheat that soup in the museum kitchen?"

"Not a chance. It's unsanitary in there. The area near the elevator has more flies than a trout-fishing derby. I keep spraying, but they just keep coming. There might be a screen missing on the ventilation system somewhere."

While Rob unscrewed the soup Thermos, Jan watched the backhoe arm make another dive. This time the diesel engine's deep bass rumble deepened. The machine was really working, possibly dragging the root of the whole snag. There was the white thing again, folded around the backhoe's jaw. With a bigger, fouler belch, the machine kicked up another notch. Whatever was down there was not coming up easy. Water whirled in new patterns over something red, larger and smoother than any tree. The backhoe shuddered and the red thing slipped away. The operator had lost his big fish, whatever it was.

"I'm going out to look," she said. She perched on a bench by the building, hardly noticing as Rob and his soup arrived at her side. There it came again, with greater caution on the part of the backhoe's operator. Red, metallic, with water coursing down its fenders, it slid toward the muddy shore and stopped with its once-bright chrome bumper resting on the tangle of dredged-up trees.

"Holy shit!" Rob bounced to his feet, soup spilling over his hand. "That's the car, the Corvette."

"I'll call the police." Jan fumbled for her phone with shaking hands. "You get down there and tell them to stop. Jarrad's body might be inside."

CHAPTER TWENTY-FIVE

Lacey flopped microwaved scrambled eggs and cheese onto a bagel and ate it in the living room, staring downhill at the horrible river. If a person was body-checked down that crumbling bank, nothing would save her. How long before the torrent covered the bridge and cut off her access to Dee? She should head back to the hospital immediately, but Tom's message had her on edge. Wayne might be letting her go entirely. She would be hard-pressed to put a deposit on a cheap apartment at this rate, much less convince any bank to give her a mortgage. Maybe she should go down a bit early, sound out Wayne before Tom arrived. So it didn't look like she needed the backup. The last bite of bagel landed in her mouth as an RCMP patrol car sped across the bridge far below. Was Tom driving a marked car today? She hurried out, brushing crumbs from her hands.

When she arrived, the museum's atrium was empty except for a handful of people staring out the riverside windows. A blue band flickered across their faces at intervals. The police action was outside. Probably nothing to do with Tom, then, or Wayne, or her job. She tracked Wayne down in the kitchen, glowering at his sandwich and batting at a half-dozen flies that threatened to land on it whenever it wasn't moving. He nodded at her.

"What's up, McCrae?"

"Not much. I came to see if you had an ETA on the vault guy and how soon you will absolutely need me to return to work." She mentally crossed her fingers against him running her off on the spot.

Wayne waved his sandwich again. "Friday morning. Can you collect him at the airport at eleven thirty? I'll text you the flight info. We'll finish the vault right after lunch if you can stay that long, and leave the rest until next week. Bring bug repellent."

Okay, she still had a job. That was good news. Now to hang around until Tom showed. "What's with the patrol car out back?"

"Huh?" Wayne looked through the kitchen hatch toward the office windows, where the backhoe's long arm was intermittently lit by the cruiser's light bar. "Can't be much. I didn't hear a siren."

"I'll go see what's up," she said, leaving Wayne to his sandwich. The elevator door opened as she reached for the button. "Whoa, Rob! Where's the fire?"

Rob barely slowed. "Hi, Lacey. Excuse me."

She followed him back to the kitchen. "What's with the police?"

"We found, well, they found — the backhoe guy, I mean — he found the hit-and-run car in the river. The red Corvette. I just came in to get Jan a cup of tea."

"Are they sure it's the right car? Never mind. I'll ask the constable." She ran up the nearest stairs, past the knot of gazing ghouls and out the terrace door. The tail end of the red Corvette lay on the bank, the backhoe's metal mouth resting on the rags of its white roof. The patrolman stood by his car, talking on a cellphone. Slime coated his boots, and his pant legs clung wetly. Had he found a body in that Corvette? Lacey made a mental bet on no. With the leather roof floating, even a seat-belted driver could have been tugged free by the evil, brown water — a nice mess for a crime scene team. She turned away from the memories of other bodies, of her terrifying struggle to free her tank strap in that sunken boat on the dive-training exercise. Underwater bodies were not her business, not anymore. She was just a civilian with a question.

"Hi," she said when the officer closed his phone. "I'm the housemate of the hit-and-run victim. Is that the vehicle of interest down there?"

The constable sized her up. "Crime scene unit has yet to verify."

"No driver inside?"

"Not now." He said it with resigned gloom. The RCMP would bring in a crane and a flatbed to haul away the saturated vehicle. The first cop on scene would have to stay until he could follow it to an evidence-processing facility. She had all afternoon to find out what he knew about Dee's investigation.

"Looks like you'll be stuck here awhile. Want a coffee or something?"

"That'd be great. Cream, two sugars."

As Lacey reached the kitchen, Tom arrived, his face ten degrees grimmer than usual. She sent the constable's coffee out with Rob.

Tom refused coffee. "Someplace private. Both of you."

Lacey led Tom and Wayne to the art library beyond the classrooms. It was fly free, but maybe not for long, the way the miasma of decay and diesel from the backhoe's work was seeping through the windows. Wayne shut the door and stood by it.

"This an official visit, Tom?"

"I hope it doesn't have to be." Tom pulled out a Ziploc bag. "Recognize this?" Whether Wayne did or not, Lacey did. She started to speak but, seeing a minimal headshake from Tom, stopped.

"Digital recorder. I use one for on-site notes," said Wayne. "This the one McCrae asked about on the weekend?"

"Looks the same," said Lacey. "But is it?"

Tom dumped the little device out of the bag. A faint shimmer of dust puffed around it as it landed. Fingerprint powder.

"We should have the latest comparison soon," he said, "but it might not be necessary. Wayne's going to explain this to us." He flipped open the battery compartment. Under the lid was a narrow printed label bearing a serial number and a familiar name: *AWL Security Services Ltd.* Wayne's company.

Wayne looked at the gadget like it was an interesting species of insect. Then he said, quite mildly, "I hope you didn't drive out here expecting me to confess to illegal intercepts, Tom. I need to check that serial number, but I believe it went with an installation I did a few months back."

"Near here?" Lacey asked.

Wayne scratched one ear. "Get my laptop from the van, McCrae. The serial number will be matched with the jobsite."

She ran, her brain buzzing. If the device came from Mick Hardy's house, that clearly pointed to Jarrad. If not him, then who? Did Neil's rich girlfriend use Wayne, too? Neil's fingerprints weren't on the recorder. Could he have paid a local to plant and monitor the bug, to spare him valuable deal-making hours in Calgary? She came back with the laptop bag and watched impatiently while Wayne logged in. He typed the serial number into the search function.

"Jake Wyman."

CHAPTER TWENTY-SIX

"But Jake doesn't like Neil," Lacey told Dee's sleeping face a couple of hours later. "He said so, you said so, and even Neil said so. Why would he have lent Neil a recorder? Or Jarrad? Although Jarrad could have lifted it during some hockey thing up there. But he'd still need someone to go check on it, download the recordings, while he was away with his team."

Dee, naturally, did not hazard a guess. Lacey studied the half-healed scratches and scrapes. The bruised bits were slowly easing from vivid reddish purple to yellowish grey. The duty nurse said they had decreased her level of sedation, but the improvement, if that's what it was, wasn't obvious to the naked eye. Marie's word was the one Lacey trusted. Marie had read the charts with her old Emergency nurse's eye and sworn to the reliability of Glasgow Coma Scale scores. The important thing was to keep the brain slightly stimulated, despite the drugs. That's why you talked to people in comas. Their brains could register voices, and their vital signs often responded to the calming presence of a loved one. It was all reassuring nurse-speak, a side of Marie that Lacey had almost lost sight of. So Lacey held Dee's hand and talked, although Marie would probably not have approved of the topic. Reminding a comatose woman about the car that ran her down would be bad form, but talking about the recorder seemed safe enough.

"Wayne said Jake saw him using one last winter and asked how it worked. He mastered the buttons and liked it, so Wayne gave him a spare out of the van. Good customer relations on a job that size. Anyway, would Jake have given Neil the recorder, or a chance to steal it? You'll suggest I ask Jake himself. But you're not thinking this through, Dee. He's now as much of a bugging suspect as Neil." *Or Jarrad*, she thought. "Except I have no idea why Jake would do that to you, and I can't exactly go ask him that. Even Tom and Wayne aren't ready to do that, not until they get the fingerprint results from the recorder. It's sheer luck that the plaque you presented him on Friday night had been so well polished beforehand. Jake's prints are almost the only ones on there. I'm still betting on Neil, though. I wish the cops had given the nurses that rat's photo. I'm glad you gave him the boot, even though it cost you. I'm pretty sure Jake sees right through his smarm."

Jake Wyman, the nice old ranch-hand type who had dropped two million dollars into the museum to please a wife with one leg already in someone else's bed. Women were obviously his Achilles heel, but otherwise, he hadn't gotten that rich by doing dumb things. And yet, he would fit the "arrogant" part of Dee's last note.

He had walked into the house uninvited while Lacey was upstairs. He'd been at the house on Sunday afternoon while Lacey was napping out back. That was the same day the drawers and Dee's purse were moved, the day Dee was hit by Jarrad's car. He could have tried to recover the bug. He wouldn't have known Lacey had taken it to the RCMP. If Dee had shot that fact at him on Saturday night, he would have had no reason to search the house, and no reason to ... well, that was the next logical assumption. No reason to hurt Dee.

If Jake was the prowler and the attacker both, silence was his best policy as long as Dee wasn't awake to tell anybody. The nub of the matter, though, was why. Why would someone that rich and powerful bother with a simple bug on a neighbour's window? It made no sense.

Back to Jarrad. He might have done the hit and run, but he was away playing hockey when the bugging seemed to have begun. Could Camille have taken the recorder from Jake's and planted it herself, maybe hoping to further diminish Dee as a witness against Jarrad? Mick might have noticed the recorder in his wife's possession. Lacey could hardly ask him if his wife had helped her lover terrorize and then try to murder the neighbour. His pacemaker would blow a fuse.

It was all a blurry mess of people she hardly knew and had no official right to question. Unofficially, she could ask Terry Brenner. He'd known these people for years. There was no suspicion attached to him in anyone's mind. Which, in the world of detective fiction, probably made him the villain.

Oops! She wasn't talking to Dee. Those last few years with Dan, who'd only ever answered her in order to twist her words, had left her unused to talking beyond the necessary exchange of information. Okay, talking out loud some more.

"I think I have a plan. I'll slip out after supper and phone Terry Brenner. He'll know if Neil was at any Wyman parties this spring. Meanwhile, I was thinking about our trek through the Algonquin Trail. Do you remember those two German guys and the bobcat …?"

CHAPTER TWENTY-SEVEN

"Searching those unstable riverbanks is really not your business." Jan glared at Terry as he bolted down his supper while standing at the kitchen island.

"I have to help out," he said between mouthfuls of pasta. "This is what we train for."

"You train to rescue living people. If Jarrad went into the river Sunday night, he's not alive now."

"If his battered corpse is washed up on the bank downstream, would you rather I find him tonight or leave him for some young family to find next weekend, after he's been partially dismembered by wildlife?"

"Besides," said Jan, ignoring his speech, "I'll bet he never was in that car. He probably pushed it over the bank to confuse the trail and then Mick or Camille drove him to the airport."

"You might be right. But the Mounties asked us to check along the banks, so that's what we'll do. Quit fussing. You know I'll be roped to two other guys near the water."

"Some of those SAR volunteers are rank idiots who only show up for the beer. If they fall in, you'll go with them. And it'll be dark soon."

"It's nearly the summer equinox. It won't be dark for hours. Just chill, honey."

"Yeah, chill," said Rob. "Think of it as just another training night, only if he finds what they're looking for, he gets bragging rights for a decade. Think of the money he'll save on other people buying his post-meeting drinks."

"You saying I'm a boozer, guy?"

"Nah. Mickey Mouse could put you under the table. Ready to go?" Rob helped Terry load his gear and then drove him down the hill. Shaking her head, Jan rinsed her teacup. Guys. The phone rang as she was moving to the sunroom to watch the searchers gathering in the museum parking lot. She scooped up the handset and kept walking.

"Hi, can I speak to Terry Brenner, please? This is Lacey McCrae."

The woman who had called her a drug addict, the one who hadn't bothered to say hello this afternoon on the museum terrace. The cow. *She's had a stressful week, too*, Jan reminded herself firmly. *And you want to know how Dee's doing, so be polite.*

"Hello, Lacey. Terry's out. How's Dee? Is she awake yet?"

"Uh, hi." In the pause that followed, Jan had a moment to start panicking over Dee before Lacey went on, "Dee is doing as well as can be expected. That's the official line they always give out, but a nurse friend of mine confirmed it this afternoon. They'll ease her off of the medication overnight and start checking her speech and stuff in the morning. Only …"

"Only what? If there's bad news, I'd like to know about it. Dee's my friend, too."

Lacey's reluctance — or uncertainty? — came through clearly in her voice. "Only … well, I don't know if you're friends with Dee's ex, Neil?"

"Not hardly. I'm sorry if you like him, but I don't think he was ever good enough for her."

"Something we agree on," said Lacey, suddenly sounding more cheerful. "Then you won't mind not telling Neil she's about to wake up.'"

"I'd be surprised if he knew she was hurt."

"He knows. He came to her hospital room last night. And —" Again the hesitation. "Look, Dee didn't want anyone to know this, but someone was stalking her. It might have been the hockey player they're looking for, but it might equally have been Neil. I'm not accusing him of anything at this point, but a whole lot of women get stalked, and sometimes hurt or killed, by their ex-husbands."

"Jesus." Jan sat down on her lounger. It was a wonder the phone didn't slide from her hand. She clutched it tighter and automatically pulled an afghan over her lap. "Are you sure?"

"We couldn't quite pin it on Neil. But I don't want Neil, if it was him, to have another shot at her before she can tell the police what happened."

"God, I had no idea." Everybody protected poor, feeble Jan from stress or worry. It wasn't as if she could be any practical use in a crisis, anyway. She realized she was clenching her jaw so tightly it ached. She breathed deep before saying, "I'll make sure he doesn't hear it from any of us. What else can I do to help?"

"Would you be willing to answer some questions about the past few months? I'm trying to get a feel for whether Neil could have pulled some specific stunts, and I don't know anyone else well enough to ask."

"Is that what you were going to ask Terry about?"

"Yes. I understand you don't socialize as much as he does because of your … health issues."

It was obvious Lacey was really, really trying to be courteous. If Jan hadn't heard her say it, she might not realize what Lacey really meant by "health issues." If this woman had been even the tiniest bit nicer that first day, Jan could have explained. But not in the face of that snap dismissal, those few words that reduced her life-crushing issues to a self-inflicted mess that inconvenienced everyone around her. Rob would advise her to pretend she didn't know, to keep the focus on what was best for Dee. In other words, keep her thoughts to herself and co-operate. Much as it galled her to admit it, Lacey was in a better position to protect Dee from a stalker. Anger at her own helplessness made Jan's chest hurt. She took another deep breath.

"Ask me anything you want."

When Rob returned home, Jan was curled up on the lounger under her afghan, absentmindedly holding the phone, staring out the window with her head in a whirl.

"What's up, doc?" he asked.

"I think my brain cracked under interrogation. You wouldn't believe what that Lacey woman was asking me."

"Ooh. Do tell."

"Only if you get me some tea first. It might be June but it feels like October inside me."

Rob returned with two mugs and settled on the carpet. "Give."

"Would you believe Dee's ex was stalking her?"

"No!"

"That's what Lacey told me. She wanted to know about every time Neil has been in this area since Christmas. Any parties? Not even one of Jake's extravaganzas? She must have meant the All-Star week, but he wasn't there. Dee left with that defenceman from the Hurricanes, and she would have been more discreet, not to mention more irritated, if Neil had been there." She paused for a sip of tea. "Then lesser events. House sales? Social calls? Is Neil on good terms with any neighbours? Does he have any other business that might take him up to Jake's place?"

"And?"

"Across the board, no, I told her. He's not on visiting terms with us, Jake, the Hardy household, or anyone else I could think of. He was a glad-hander and elbow-bender with the rest when he lived here, but once he moved out, nobody noticed his absence. Or if they did, they were glad. He had a habit of saying quite snarky things to Dee. It made people uncomfortable." Jan shifted to look down at the log house below, basking peaceably in the sunset's glow. If Neil had been that unpleasant in public, how nasty had he been at home? "Jarrad, on the other hand, has been everywhere. I didn't think of it during Lacey's interrogation, but maybe he was stalking Dee to get revenge for his windshield."

"Huh." Rob stared down the hill. "Hard to think of the delightful Dee being at anybody's mercy. Which one does Lacey think ran her down? Neil doesn't square with the use of Jarrad's car."

"Maybe Neil stole the car."

"Wouldn't Jarrad be howling for blood if his precious Corvette went missing?" Rob answered his own question. "Nope. He left it at the museum after the gala, when he presumably went off with some woman for a dirty weekend. He'd missed his first flight but eventually he flew away to catch up to his teammates without a thought for the car. Likely assumed sick old Mick would collect it for him. If he's not the one who ran over Dee, that is."

"The game." Jan struggled upright. "I want to watch tonight, try to spot him in the audience."

"You'd know him from a brief glimpse? I wouldn't. Half the time he was in the theatre he was sucking face with Camille, and apart from that I've only seen his naked ass and the top of his hat."

"That's a weird combo. Why the hat?"

"Our security tape. The Mounties picked out still photos: the car arriving and leaving and returning, the driver getting in and out wearing a jacket and a hat that hid his face. It was Jarrad's jacket, I heard. He was identified from it."

"Jarrad was on there? So much for your theory that some puck bunny drove him to the airport. Unless …" Jan lay back and closed her eyes. The excitement of all this detecting was making her heart race. "What if Jarrad left his jacket in the car on Friday night? It was warm out, and he'd probably had a bit to drink."

"So?"

"Anyone could come along Saturday night and steal the car to use on Dee. Then, when they brought it back, they used his jacket to fool the security cameras and send the police after Jarrad."

"Anyone meaning Dee's ex, I assume? Is he the same size as Jarrad?"

"Now that you mention it, I think Neil's taller. Although when Jarrad's on skates, he's nearly as big."

"You should tell Lacey about this. She could check Neil's alibi through her Mountie pals."

"Not tonight. Talking to her is so exhausting, Rob. You have no idea. No matter how polite she's being, she gets under my skin, makes me furious at my own weaknesses. I'm not phoning her until we have something more to offer than the suggestion that Neil might have been wearing Jarrad's jacket. If you think of some concrete way to test that theory, I'll phone her when we have something."

"What if I brought you copies of those security stills? Or you could come down and look at the tapes yourself."

"Not tonight. I'm not sure I want to go down there tomorrow, either. Bad things happen whenever I set foot on that property."

"Okay. I'll try to make copies tomorrow. The vault guy isn't coming until Friday, and we're extending storage contracts for another week. Bad time to be a curator. I don't suppose Jake said anything about the job, or me?"

"I haven't seen him today," said Jan, but her mind clung to the problem of Jarrad and the photographs. Even with her trained, artistic eye, she wasn't sure she would be able to tell if it was him or Neil in his jacket and hat. She hadn't seen either of them for months, except for a brief glimpse of Jarrad at that rehearsal, and never together. How could she enhance her chance of making an accurate identification? "The last Olympics' hockey game recordings," she said suddenly. "The CBC camera crew talked to Mick several times, and I'm sure Jarrad was with him sometimes. I know Mick's about six inches shorter than Neil, so I can estimate from him beside Jarrad. Now, can I remember whether those were the men's games or the women's?

"Anyway, it's more important to know where Jarrad is now. The Stanley Cup game is about to start. Cameras will pan around during the pauses. He might get his face on the Jumbotron, seeing as he's a player." Jan flipped back the afghan and sat up, waiting for the blood to drain from her head before she stood. The pills could keep those wobbles at bay. Would they help her concentration through hours of videotape? Probably not. She'd survived without for the past few days. No sense starting again if she didn't absolutely have to.

"I'll brew fresh tea for you," said Rob. "And if you don't mind, I'll just get back to my social media whirlwind instead of watching with you."

"Not so much of a hockey fan when there's no hot guy to impress?"

"Maybe half." Rob headed for the kitchen. She heard the sink run and then he called back, "Look at the bright side: if Terry comes back with news of Jarrad's bloated corpse on the riverbank, you won't have to spend hours looking at old hockey footage."

"Some bright side that is." Jan finished her move to the living room couch and brought up TSN for the game. The crowd noise and camera shifts tortured her overtired brain, but she forced herself to keep watching for the audience pans. No Jarrad that she could spot, although she recognized the hockey player Rob had been chatting up last weekend. Rob hadn't mentioned him since and she decided not to ask if it had fizzled out. He was lonely enough these days with only Jan and Terry for companionship.

When the game was over, the long dusk was over, too. Terry came in before she had time to work up another good fret about his safety. He shook his head in answer to her question. No Jarrad.

CHAPTER TWENTY-EIGHT

Morning found Lacey brushing her teeth in Dee's hospital bathroom, peering at her bloodshot eyes in the mirror. Sleeping in a chair again. How would she cope at work tomorrow? Come to that, how could she go to work if Marie couldn't come to sit with Dee? She spat into the sink and decided not to face that bridge yet. If Dee woke up coherent, if she could tell the police about the car or driver, maybe Neil would be arrested by nightfall. Then Lacey could have a good night's sleep and a good day's work, her first of either for nearly a week.

The nurse came in to check Dee's vitals, working through the now-familiar routine that included the Glasgow Coma Scale as Marie had explained it. Only this time, when the nurse spoke to Dee, there was a soft mumble in response.

Lacey lurched from the bathroom. "Did she say something?"

The nurse, focused on her task, said Dee's name again. Dee groaned. Her head moved on the pillow. Her eyelids crunched up. When the nurse spoke her name for the third time, she opened them.

"And I thought my eyes looked bad," were the first words out of Lacey's mouth.

Dee's head turned toward her. "La-ee?"

"I'm here." Lacey reached for her friend's hand, careful not to disturb the attached tubes and wires. Tears stung her overtired eyes.

"Lee," said Dee, and zoned right out again.

"Uh, is this a bad thing?" Lacey asked the nurse.

"Quite normal. When she wakes up again, please buzz right away. Don't give her anything to drink until her swallow reflex has been checked out. Make a note of anything she says. It will likely be a few more words each time." The nurse jotted something on the chart and departed, leaving Lacey prey to new fears. What if Dee didn't wake again? What if she didn't have a swallow reflex? What if she didn't remember the attack? What if her brain was more damaged than the Coma Scale predicted? More bridges to be faced. The Bragg Creek bridge with its rushing, rising water was a paper tiger compared to all that could still go wrong for Dee. Lacey wouldn't be expected to appear at work tomorrow if the bridge was closed. So that would be okay.

She nearly laughed out loud. One easy step from fearing the bridge would be flooded to hoping that it happened by tomorrow.

Later, when it was plain that Dee was just sleeping deeply, she let go of her hand. In the bathroom finishing her minimal toilette, Lacey stared at her face. She was smiling for the first time since last Sunday afternoon. She went downstairs, called Terry Brenner, and passed on the glad tidings. Terry confirmed that Neil wasn't friendly with the neighbourhood and certainly not with Jake. He asked immediately what Jake had to do with anything.

"He gives a lot of parties that Neil might have used as an excuse to spy on Dee," Lacey said. She asked about the river search for Jarrad.

"Unfruitful," was the reply.

Afterward, she ate a full tray of breakfast hauled up from the cafeteria and wondered about the hit-and-run investigation. Had her official notebook still been in her pocket, she would have jotted down some questions. Had Tom postponed telling Bulldog about Jake's owning the recorder? Would Bulldog check Neil's alibi for last Sunday? Did the RCMP have leads on Jarrad that they weren't making public? Was Jarrad oblivious to the whole mess, off on some extended boozy orgy with one of Camille's posse? Maybe the best question to ask was which trophy wife had suddenly gone "on vacation" after the gala. Jarrad might be romping at a villa in Invermere. Or he might be right here in Calgary with old Mick, watching the local TV news to track the police search.

Speaking of Mick, surely that was his head showing in the window. He rolled through the doorway in a wheelchair pushed by a brawny male in dark-blue scrubs.

"Miss McCrae. Good morning."

"Hello, Mr. Hardy. What brings you here? Not more heart trouble, I hope."

"Just running a tickertape through the electronic ticker," Mick said, wheezing slightly. "Make sure the gizmo's connected to the whoozit and all that. This is my pal

Ron. Hired by my wife to keep me out of trouble. You go get a coffee, Ron. I'll visit with this young lady for a bit." Ron left without a word. Now Lacey had two invalids on her hands. If Dee woke up enough to incriminate Jarrad, Mick's next round of heart trouble would happen right here. He didn't look quite as bad as last weekend, but his face retained that grey underlay, like wall primer imperfectly painted over with beige. At least he was able to smile this time. She smiled back.

"How are you doing, Mr. Hardy?"

"Call me Mick, please. Doing as well as expected. What they always say. That's what they said about Dee when I phoned, and I look a sight more alive than she does." Mick frowned at the bed. "Has she woken up yet?"

"Sort of. She said my name this morning, but it might have simply been the word last programmed to reach her lips." Better not to mention she would most likely be more lucid each time she woke. He might have contact with Jarrad. "If she wakes again, they'll start investigating how much brain damage she's suffered."

Mick's face grew more wrinkles while she watched. He blinked a few times. "I'm real sorry people think Jarred would do this. Sure as I'm sitting here with a battery pack in my armpit, that boy would never deliberately hurt a woman. If he was going to, wouldn't he have done it when she smashed up his windshield? Huh? But he didn't. He stayed clear, just yelled at her to stop, that he was sorry about her dog. My boy does not hurt women."

"I know you have faith in him," she said gently. "But it looks bad that he took off. He can't be cleared until the police have heard what he has to say. If you know how to reach him, you really should urge him to show up and answer their questions."

Mick's face drooped toward his collar. "God help me, I haven't seen or heard from him since last weekend. I had no idea the police were looking for his car until I saw it on the news last night. Pulled from the river. I can't stand to think my boy might be in that river himself."

Lacey didn't like to think of it, either, or of Mick fretting his weak heart over that spoiled, sulky young man. She patted his hand. "Likely he's gone off with friends and hasn't seen the news for a few days. Didn't they have big plans for a lot of golf and boozing?"

Mick's chin firmed up a bit. "You're right. Just because I phoned everyone I know doesn't mean I know everyone I should have phoned. I left messages all over. Sooner or later he'll sober up and call me. He always does."

"How's your wife holding up with all this stress? She must be worried half to death with you ill and Jarrad missing."

"Oh, she's fine. She's not that fond of Jarrad. Just as well she's out at the river house, or she'd be telling me twenty times an hour how inconsiderate he's being."

So Camille was staying home, supposedly alone. Terry and Jan could check that, and they might know if Mick and Camille owned any other properties at which to conceal their wayward protege.

"You're a good friend to our Dee, Miss McCrae. I guess you've been stuck in this hospital room for a couple of days now. If you want to stretch your legs a minute while I wait for Ron, I'll sit here with my finger on the button in case she opens her eyes."

It was tempting, but Mick looked so frail. Even if she alerted him about Neil, he couldn't stand up against a man half his age and a head taller. He wouldn't believe, either, that Jarrad might be a threat to Dee, not until damage was done before his eyes. A kind offer, but she couldn't take it. She said no, with thanks.

"Well, then, can I fetch you anything from Dee's house? Ron's gonna drive me out there to round up a few things before the bridge closes."

"I think I got everything on my last trip." If she went anywhere from here, it would be to Tom's place for a nap. If Marie came today, that was exactly what she would do. All her limbs were shaky with bone-deep fatigue. She would soon be too whacked to comprehend whatever broke next in the investigation. She forced her wavering thoughts together and got down to the business of sifting through Mick's memory of all the parties last winter.

The only new thing she learned was that Jarrad had not gone to the All-Star party in January, although he was at Mick's that week. Mick was starting to look at her oddly every time she mentioned Jake Wyman. It was a relief when the burly nurse returned and wheeled Mick to the door. The old fellow twisted in his chair. "Missy, Jake Wyman may be a generally good neighbour and a happy host, but don't you mistake that simple rancher act he uses. If his interests are affected, he'll stop at nothing to come out on top. That's why he's rich and we're not. I think Dee mighta forgot that. She was cussing him out something awful at the party."

"Wait, Mick. When was this?"

"Finals party last Saturday. Guess they didn't know the window was open. I was sitting right by it, kinda accidentally eavesdropped before I realized what I was listening in on. She was real upset after, and left the party right away. She drove me home."

"Thanks. I didn't know that. Was she angry with anyone else, do you know?"

"Not that I could tell, but I didn't ask her about it, either. Not my business. And young Rob from the museum was with us."

"Well, thank you for passing that on," said Lacey, smiling at him as he left.

As soon as he was out of sight, she let the smile drop. Dee could not have known the recorder came from Jake's unless something on the recording had tied him to it. His post-accident helpfulness could all be cover. Why had Lacey not asked Mick exactly what he'd overheard? Shock, probably. She had been so sure Neil or Jarrad was the villain that she had not investigated Dee's last evening. Another black mark against her investigative skills.

Her head was still splitting from the possibilities when Marie arrived an hour later. "Go away," said Marie. "I left bedding on the rec room couch for you. I'll phone you if anything happens here."

"Thanks. You're a good friend." Lacey submitted to a brief hug. "What if I don't wake up in time for you to pick up the kids?"

"I'll phone Tom to get them. Just go. And promise you'll sleep."

"No fear." Lacey yawned. "Nothing could keep me awake today."

Nothing, that is, except Neil grabbing her arm as she stepped out of the lobby elevator. He swung her sideways. When she stumbled over a newspaper stand, he yanked her upright. He shoved her against the wall, his flushed face crowding hers. His breath was damp on her skin.

Lacey's training, and her temper, kicked in. She twisted herself beneath his arm and came up behind his back. Her free hand forced his elbow up his spine until his grip on her forearm loosened. She applied that hand to his shoulder and put the pinch on. Hard.

"Goddamnit! Let go, bitch."

She pushed his face against the wall. "What the fuck do you think you're doing, Neil?"

"Ball-breaking bitch. You sent your Mountie pals to Dani's father's place. If he throws me out over this, I'll be coming after you."

"What could you possibly do to me? Send some thugs to beat me in a dark alley?"

"I'll tell everyone you screwed your partner, you adulterous slut. Get you in shit with your Mountie bosses."

Neil knew about her and Tom? Dee must have let that slip sometime before their marriage turned sour. Trust Neil to remember any little factoid that might someday come in useful. If he told Marie … no time to burn that bridge now. Better to convince him his ace wasn't a weapon at all.

"Who do you think will care, asshole? He wasn't married then, I'm not married anymore. I'm not on the Force either, so they won't sanction me for conduct unbecoming. I'm going to release you and step off, but if you try to touch me again, if I even see your overfed face up in Dee's ward, I'm charging you with assault. Explain a court date to Dani and her rich daddy."

"Go fuck yourself," said Neil, but he didn't move when she lifted her hand from his neck. She lowered the arm behind his back, stepped well clear, and only then noticed the hospital security guards on either side of her.

Neil saw them, too. "She pinned me up against the wall, goddamn it! Arrest her."

"I saw you grab her," said one guard. "Security cameras saw it, too. Please leave the building quietly or we'll have to call the police." Lacey waited with him while the other guard followed Neil to the door. He said, "You related to him?"

"Not me. His ex-wife is upstairs on a trauma ward with injuries from a so-far unidentified assailant." No lie there, but she hoped the guard would make an assumption.

He spoke into his radio. "Get a photo if you can, Chuck. This guy's going up on the wall."

Perfect. Each guard shift from now on would see Neil's photo on their bulletin board and watch out for him around the place. It wasn't much security, but it was more than Dee was getting from the police. Running into Neil down here was a stroke of luck despite the bruises she was sure to see on her arm tomorrow. She thanked the guard and went to get herself a cafeteria tea. If Neil was waiting for her to come outside so he could tackle her again, she wanted him to have a long, conspicuous wait.

CHAPTER TWENTY-NINE

Jan found Terry's note when she wandered out to the kitchen midmorning. *Dee woke up*, it read. *Looking good, but they'll know more later.* A small bit of tension slid out of her shoulders. She started the kettle and sat on a stool, sorting her morning supplements onto a saucer, a smaller list than last year — ten things instead of seventeen. Last year she wouldn't have made tea, either. Last year, Terry had left her tea in a carafe by her lounger each morning, along with the tray of breakfast and the array of pills. That was where she had stayed until lunchtime, or sometimes straight through until supper, neither awake nor asleep, doing nothing and yet not getting rested, either. Back then, she had wondered if she would ever leave the house by herself again. Now she could go out to the deck at will, could sometimes drive herself around their quiet rural neighbourhood. Things to be grateful for today: Dee waking up and Jan being healthy enough to drive down to the museum later to pick up the security stills Rob was making for her. What a glorious day!

It was equally glorious outdoors. Sunlight danced on fresh green leaves. Planters filled with flowers splashed their vivid hues against Camille's varnished log gateposts and the museum colonnade they mirrored. The view was an Impressionist painting waiting for the brushstrokes to capture it. How fitting that Dee should wake up on such a day. On impulse, Jan uncovered her camera and took photos of Dee's house glowing in the sunshine. The spruces surrounding it waved friendly limbs. No hand tremors today.

Jake rode by with Beau and Boney loping along behind. The dogs bounded up the outside stairs and drooled over her skirt. She fussed over them to make up for Dee's absence, soothing Boney's ears the way he liked and scratching under Beau's collar. Then she told them to sit while she snapped several close-ups. Dee would like to see those, too, to know everything was all right at home.

After a bit, Jake whistled the dogs back, using the ultrasonic, horse-friendly whistle that he'd trained them with last winter. Jan whipped the camera around again and got a few shots of the trio as they trotted down the road, and again when they reached Dee's porch. She would email a slideshow to Dee. Lacey could take Dee's laptop to the hospital so she could watch it. Mental note to suggest it when Lacey next phoned. Dee's whole life was in that laptop. She would feel better with it under her eye.

After a few more photos of the summery day, Jan tore herself from the bright, sweet outdoors to go through old Olympics' hockey footage. Finding a shot of Jarrad to compare with the security stills had seemed simple before she remembered that, in her mental fog during the last Winter Olympics, she had been overwhelmed by Terry's new PVR system and returned to the old, familiar VHS setup in the bedroom. Now she would pay. Fast-forwarding through every game would take ages. Men's and women's games both. Sheesh. At least Terry had incorporated the other old VCR into the living room's new entertainment complex, though with considerable grumbling. Otherwise she would have had to spend the whole lovely day hiding in her bedroom.

She was halfway through the Canadian women's final when a shadow fell across the deck doors. She hit pause and waved Jake in.

"Mornin', Jannie. No need to ask how you're feeling today. Always a good sign when you've been out on the deck."

"I was photographing Dee's house so she could see it in the hospital when she feels homesick. You came along with the dogs at just the right time."

"You're a good friend to Dee-Dee. I want your opinion."

"On what?"

"Getting her house ready for when she comes home. If we start now, it could be mostly done in a month. My architects are on notice."

"Architects? You can't make major renovations to her house."

"Not major. An elevator up from the mudroom. Ramps up to the porch, front and back. Might expand some doorways, too. Do you think I should show her the plans or do it for a surprise?"

She was used to his sudden enthusiasms, but an elevator? "That's one hell of a surprise. You know, I've been sick a lot these past few years, and I really need my familiar space around me. I expect Dee will feel the same at first." His face lost its light and she added, "If you arranged for a portable ramp up to her front door, and maybe one of those temporary stairlifts, those she could appreciate right away."

"And get the plans drawn up for the rest? I won't show them to her until she's feeling stronger."

"Plans couldn't hurt. But it might be weeks before she's able to concentrate on detailed drawings."

"They might take weeks. If I can have your key to her house, I'll get the fellows measuring Monday morning."

"That's really sweet of you. But I don't have my key. I gave it back to Dee when Lacey moved in. She was going to get another cut, but then the accident happened."

Jake clucked his tongue. "Next time Miss McCrae phones, ask for that key back, Jannie. I promise I won't knock down any walls until Dee-Dee's on board with it."

"Okay." As he turned to leave she said, "Leave the door open, would you? I want to at least smell the great outdoors while I'm stuck in this gloomy room."

The tapes were as boring and time-consuming as she had expected. Although she got a good refresher in Mick's trademark vitality from two years ago — his enthusiasm and the intricate knowledge of hockey that made him a natural for the Order of Canada. However, in not one of those interviews was Jarrad visible. Camille appeared often, hanging on Mick's arm, wearing a loose leather jacket in a buttery shade that almost matched her hair. One of her Italian purchases, no doubt. Camille had come back from the Olympics with a dozen designer outfits suitable for an Italian winter or a Canadian Rockies spring. If the Olympics had a shopping event, she'd be a gold medal contender. Jan left the last tape running through the post-game while she scrounged up some lunch.

Returning with her plate, she stared. There on the screen was Mick again, seated rinkside at some miscellaneous practice session of the men's team, looking fit and athletic in a navy-blue fleece. In the row behind him were Jarrad and Camille, both wearing butter-caramel leather jackets. They sat so close the matching buckles on their shoulder tabs overlapped.

Her first reaction was scorn. How like Camille to flaunt her boy toy on international television, literally right behind her husband's oblivious back. At second look, a thought popped fully-formed into her brain: was this the jacket Jarrad was wearing on the security video? He earned enough to own a dozen leather jackets, but if it was this jacket, then it might not be him or Neil on that tape at all. It might be Camille.

CHAPTER THIRTY

Hidden from the day in Marie's basement rec room, Lacey fell deeply asleep in the middle of Tom's old cuckoo clock squawking through its noon sequence. The adrenalin rush of manhandling Neil had quickly evaporated. Not even the *FOAD cunt* scrawled in dry-erase marker on Dee's windshield had the power to do more than briefly annoy. Neil would get his, and soon.

The thought kept Lacey company in dreams filled with images of her old life: endless patrols in the rural-urban sprawl of Surrey, multi-unit raids on gang houses, tramping the wooded areas for home-less camps, driving smelly old Gracie down to the street mission for hot coffee, the occasional post-shift drinks at the RCMP's unofficial clubhouse. Arresting Neil with extreme prejudice at the end of every dream cycle, only to have him turn his battered face up from the squad car and say, "Gotcha this time, McCrae. I didn't do it."

"I said, he didn't do it," Tom repeated.

Lacey jolted awake. Upstairs, a multifooted monster trampled the kitchen. The boys must be home from school. If Tom was here with them, then Marie was stuck at the hospital. "Oh god, sorry. I overslept."

"You needed it." Tom sat in the rocking chair by her head. "Did you hear me?"

"You said he didn't do it. I thought you meant Neil. I was dreaming about arresting him."

"I did. His alibi for Sunday checks out. His girlfriend's father told the Invermere RCMP that Neil was on the golf course with him last Sunday. He was continuously in sight of multiple witnesses between nine a.m. and eight p.m. He's not your guy."

"Jesus bloody fu—" Swearing wouldn't help. She wanted it to be him but it wasn't. "If Neil's out for both the surveillance and the vehicular assault, who's left?"

"Just the hockey player. If you make the bug investigation official, we can ask for a legal opinion on releasing the recordings to the investigation."

"If Dee's not able to give permission in the next twenty-four hours, I'll consider that option. Have they checked into Camille Hardy's recent activities? I'm told she's been bonking Jarrad for years, and she used her husband's bad heart as an excuse to move him to Calgary first thing Monday. Jarrad could be hiding at the Bragg Creek house, or she and Mick might own other homes elsewhere."

"I'll pass that along. The CSU needs Jarrad's prints to match to the car, and the Hardy residence is a likely place to find them. I'll get them checked against the recorder prints, too. You grab a shower and head to the hospital. I need my wife back before the boys wreck the place." A shriek came down the stairs. "Or each other."

She was halfway back to the hospital through the thickening pre-rush traffic when she remembered Mick Hardy's warning. Dee had argued with Jake the night before she was run down. Well, Dee might soon be able to tell her all about it. When she got to the room, though, she found Dee soundly asleep and Marie talking to Terry Brenner in the corridor. Lacey slumped into the hard plastic chair beside him.

"Your friend was telling me the good news," he said.

"She doesn't know yet," said Marie. "I haven't left the room to phone anyone. Because of Dee's ex-husband, we don't leave her alone."

"I heard there were issues with Neil."

"Maybe not, after all," Lacey said. "His alibi checks out for Sunday."

"Well, good," said Marie. "Then you can get a decent night's sleep for a change. Want me to leave the bedding on the couch for you?"

"I don't know. Maybe. What's your good news?"

"Dee woke up several times. Her eyes track. Her fingers and toes respond to stimuli. She can swallow. And she can talk coherently, with only minor aphasia."

"Oh my god." Lacey shut her eyes. She didn't realize the tears were leaking out anyway until Marie pushed a Kleenex at her and Terry put one warm hand on her shoulder. Then, instead of their comfort locking her up the way it normally would, she sobbed, the tissue pressed to her mouth to muffle the sound. It didn't last long, but it surprised her. She hardly ever cried, and never in front of people. Where had her self-control gone?

After a good nose-blowing, she asked, "Did she talk to the police? Did she remember anything about the accident?"

"No and no. The doctor asked her if she knew why she was here. She didn't. So there's nothing to tell the police until she comes further up from the drugs. Maybe by tomorrow. You go eat. Not hospital food, either. I'll stay here until you come back."

Terry held out his hand. "I'll take you myself. There's fast food three minutes away, or steaks five minutes farther."

"Steaks," said Marie. "I'll enjoy sticking Tom with supper duty for a change. You can call him when you get outside."

"Terry, won't Jan be expecting you?"

"Rob's there. He'll make sure she eats. Oh, and I have messages for you from her. She said to pick up Dee's laptop from the house. She made a photo montage of the dogs today and emailed it to Dee, to keep her company while she recovers."

The laptop. Lacey's brain came together again. The laptop held the copy of that recording. She and Dee could listen to it tomorrow. "I'll go in the morning. Anything else?"

"I'm too hungry to remember right now. Let's go."

With every intention of grilling Terry about Dee's Saturday evening, Lacey found she was a zombie. She forgot to phone Tom until she was seated in the steakhouse with tea on the way. Then she stared at the menu, unable to make sense of it. She'd coped with higher adrenalin daily on the job for eight years, and now a four-day hospital vigil had left her half dead. All she could do was nod vaguely when Terry suggested which side dishes and steak she might like, while the waiter's question about cooking preference left her blank. She settled on "medium" as the safest option and gripped her teacup as if the summer day was forty below.

After a while, when the hot tea had seeped from her stomach to her brain, she said, "Sorry. I'm usually competent enough to order my own meal, but right now I feel completely whacked."

"I'm used to it. Jan's like this half the time."

"Like what?" Forgetting how she liked her meat cooked? Exhausted to the point of every joint aching? Unable to string two consecutive thoughts together? None of that sounded like drug withdrawal symptoms. "What's wrong with her?"

"Myalgic encephalomyelitis — sometimes called chronic fatigue syndrome. I thought you knew."

"Yuppie flu? Dee told me she was sick but we never got into specifics. So much else was going on right up to the gala." And then finding the bug had occupied all of their attention, but of course she couldn't say that to Terry.

"Nothing to do with yuppies. Or with flu. There are defects in her immune system, though. Sometimes it overreacts and other times it ignores stuff. Her cells don't produce enough energy — something interferes with normal mitochondrial function. Her brain wiring fritzes in and out like bad satellite reception. No known cause or cure. There's probably a genetic predisposition involved, and then some toxic insult like a virus or chemical exposure tips the person's metabolism past the point of recovery. In Jan's case, it was likely all the volatile organic compounds she used in art school."

"She went to art school?" Repeating things was idiotic, but Lacey's exhausted brain needed time to process the new information.

"A visual arts degree and an art history one. She'd love to be working at the museum, but she was really sick when they needed someone. She's better now, but still too sick to cope with any kind of job."

Lacey took another big swallow of tea. "I'm sorry to hear that. Dee said she had health issues, but I had no idea it was such a big deal."

"It was a complete reversal of her previous life. One whiff of solvents or paint and she can't stand up by herself, much less concentrate."

"Was that what happened the day I found her at the museum?"

"Pretty much. She was trying a new medication and it backfired." Terry unrolled his utensils. "Stimulants do help some sufferers some of the time, so she figured she should try them. They gave her a temporary surge, but also wild mood swings, and she crashed big-time afterward."

"Why didn't she explain? I'd have helped her."

"Why didn't you order your own steak five minutes ago?"

A solid point. "God, and I said she was a prescription drug addict. Do you think she heard me? How can I make it up to her?"

"Try treating her like she's as intelligent and competent as I am. More, actually. I was barely a B-level geology student and she graduated with honours in art history."

"You're very supportive of her."

He shrugged. "She's more interesting on an average day than half the women I know on their best days."

Lacey's steak arrived. She pounced on the meat like a tiger on a tethered goat, her stomach growling. After half the plate was empty, her brain shifted to a higher gear. "What were Dee and Jake arguing about at the Finals party?"

Terry swallowed his mouthful. "Was that him she was yelling at? We caught a few words, but no details."

So much for that line of inquiry … for now.

An hour later Lacey walked into the hospital feeling 90 percent more human than when she'd wobbled out. She found a security guard sitting in the corridor near Dee's room.

"When did he show up?" she asked Marie. "The best I could do was get a photo of Neil taken, and that's a waste if he wasn't involved."

Marie gave her a smug grin. "I speak hospital."

"Huh?"

"Witness to a crime, just now conscious, might be at risk before she can make a statement. If anything happened to her here, it would be bad PR for the hospital. Plus reporters are trying to find out what floor she's on, whether she's awake yet, if she's made a statement to police. Haven't you seen any local news?"

"Not for days. What does the hospital tell them?"

"The usual. Patient's condition is stable. No visitors permitted except family. They could sneak in to see for themselves. The hospital doesn't need a media scrum on a ward, ergo security guard nearby until further notice."

"I love you, Marie." The trite phrase came from the heart.

"I know. You sleeping over tonight?"

"I think I'll go out to Dee's. I've got to fetch her laptop, and I really should try to get friendly with those blasted dogs."

"With that attitude, I can see why they don't like you. Let me know if you want me to come over tomorrow. Not that there's any real need, but I like being back in a hospital atmosphere. It smells like home."

CHAPTER THIRTY-ONE

An hour later, rewarded for her days and nights of vigilance with a weak smile from a briefly waking Dee, Lacey left the city, reminding herself every few kilometres that her friend would be fine. The hospital had woken up to the fact that it had an interest in keeping her safe, not merely alive. Hurray for a full night at home.

Home. When had she started thinking of Dee's house as home? Well, it would be for a while yet. Even after the museum project wrapped up, Dee couldn't be abandoned in that huge house, dependent on the neighbours. That reminded her of Jan Brenner. Of course the woman must have heard Dee talking to Wayne. Smooth move, McCrae. She tried out words of apology the rest of the way to Bragg Creek. No barricades yet, thank goodness.

The westerly sun sparkled off the river, almost disguising the treacherous muddy current that roiled below the bridge. From here, the back side of the new museum stood tall, its atrium windows reflecting the cool blue of the sky. Dredged-up heaps of muddy debris marred the line of the blue stone terrace. The Corvette was long gone to an RCMP crime lab, where unlucky techs no doubt crawled over the squishy seats looking for fingerprints and other evidence. Drying and restoration were not in their job description. Not that the owner would be putting in an insurance claim for water damage. He was either in hiding or in the river. Much simpler for all concerned if he opened Mick Hardy's front door to the CSU when they went there in search of his fingerprints. She turned up Dee's road, half hoping to see cruisers surrounding Mick Hardy's house. There were none. A movement from above caught her eye: Terry, waving from his deck. She drove on and met him in his driveway.

"I hoped you'd come out tonight," he said. "Jan found something you should see. You'll know if it's worth reporting." He led her to the deck, where Jan and Rob lounged beside the remains of grilled salmon and salad. "Tea? Beer? Something harder?"

"Beer, please." No need to drive home from here.

"Bottle or glass?"

"Bottle's fine."

Rob gathered up dishes before following Terry into the house.

"Sit down, Lacey," said Jan. "You must be exhausted. How was Dee?"

Lacey seized the moment "Listen, Jan, about the other day. I'm really sorry if I … I mean, I didn't understand how sick you were. If I'd realized … I should have helped, not jumped to conclusions. I apologize."

"Yes, well, it's over." Jan didn't look totally displeased, but not completely won over, either. "What about Dee?"

"She woke up for a minute again before I left, said a whole sentence. And the hospital finally put a security guard near her room. That's a big relief. I wasn't sure I could take another night on that fold-out chair."

"I thought Terry said Neil was in the clear."

"Yeah, but Jarrad isn't. He could walk in unchallenged if he carried a bouquet. He doesn't seem that well known up here."

"Not like the Flames and ex-Flames are," Jan agreed. "If Iginla or Kipper walked into that hospital even now, half the staff would swoon and the other half would rush for autographs. So you don't think Jarrad went over the riverbank with his car?" She talked like a rational person when she was relaxed and in her own space. She might have useful ideas about the situation, if she would forgive Lacey enough to share them.

"I don't know Jarrad. What do you think?"

"I think he pushed the car in to cover his tracks. Probably threw Dee's bike in there, too. If it even was him on the security camera."

"I thought it might have been Neil, but he's been ruled out."

"What you said about Neil stalking Dee was what got me started. If he'd found Jarrad's jacket in the Corvette, he could have used it as a disguise. I couldn't remember if Neil and Jarrad were the same height. My Winter Olympics tapes had some footage of Jarrad. I'd hoped to compare his height to Mick's and by that to Neil's. Also to compare his shape to the person on the security stills."

"And?"

"I didn't find one of Mick and Jarrad standing together. Plus Terry said Neil was cleared, so I shelved that angle. But I've got another suspect."

"Yeah?"

"I'll show you." Jan uncurled from her lounger and led the way to the living room. She pointed at the security stills on the coffee table. Then she picked up the television remote and cued up a videotape. Lacey glanced through the photos, the same time-stamped grey images she had seen at the museum: an individual in a loose-fitting, light-coloured bomber-style jacket, wearing a dark ball cap that hid his face. From the daylight picture of him beside the Corvette, she estimated his height at five-ten to six feet.

Terry brought Lacey's beer. "Want anything, hon?

"Not right now. Where's Rob?"

"Getting ready for his date."

"Is it the one he met at the Finals party?"

"Didn't ask."

"Me neither. I figured he'd tell us voluntarily." Jan forwarded the tape a bit.

Lacey looked up. "About that party? Dee's argument with Jake?"

"Dee told some guy off for making a pass at her, or that's what it sounded like from the little I heard. Who said it was Jake? He's far too much of a gentleman."

"Mick Hardy told me."

"He'd know. He was sitting right under the study window, close enough to hear every word. Here's what I wanted you to see." The TV screen showed an arena, with hockey players skating desultory circles on the ice. Mick

Hardy chatted with some men in the players' bench while, in the row above, his wife and sulky Jarrad sat shoulder to shoulder. They wore matching jackets. "Look at the shoulder buckles on the one in the photo."

Lacey was already doing a point-by-point comparison. It could be either jacket in the security stills. During their dreadful performance at the gala, Camille had been almost Jarrad's height in her satin flats.

"You'd better show this to the investigating officer. Can you lift stills from the videotape, or maybe copy the tape for him and mark the time on it?"

Terry was already moving. "Whole tape, not just this piece?"

"Whole tape. They'll need the context if it's to stand up in evidence. Although, once you show them yours, they can pull the original footage from the network that filmed it." Lacey took a swig of her beer. Camille might be far more than Jarrad's accessory after the fact. She might have been the primary mover behind the attack on Dee. But why? "Camille had nothing to gain by running Dee down."

Jan settled on the couch and pulled an afghan over her legs. "Especially since using Jarrad's car implicated her lover in a crime. Unless …"

"Uh-huh?"

"Unless she did it out of spite. The woman scorned. She'd have heard at the party about Jarrad missing the plane Saturday morning. The hockey players at Jake's were speculating which woman he'd gone off with. Dee didn't go to the post-gala supper; neither did Jarrad. If Camille thought … surely she wouldn't?"

"Who wouldn't what?" Rob was back, looking shiny clean and sleek.

Terry spoke up. "They're assassinating Camille again."

"I'm so in for that! What wouldn't she do?"

"Run over Dee with Jarrad's car because she thought Dee snatched her boy toy."

Rob shook his head. "She'd go after a man of Dee's, if there was one. If not, she'd bide her time."

"It's all speculation at this point," said Lacey. "What I want to know, Rob, is if Dee said anything to you on Saturday night about her argument with Jake Wyman. You left with her, right?"

"Right." Rob settled on an ottoman. "She was clearly going to need help getting poor old Mick back into his closet."

Jan frowned. "His coffin, you mean? He may look like the undead right now, but he's not there yet."

Lacey charged ahead with her next question. "Did Dee say anything while you were together? About the argument, I mean."

"The divine Dee has far too much class to kiss and tell. Or slap and tell. She was utterly gracious when I took her home from Mick's. When can she have visitors, please? I'm dying to see her reactions to the souvenir DVD."

"From the gala?" said Jan. "Are they ready?"

"Monday, babe. You'll have your copy first, I swear." With that, he drifted to his feet and left.

Terry looked at Jan. "Bet?"

"Nope," she said. Lacey looked from one to the other. Jan promptly explained. "We're wondering if Rob's date is the one whose phone number he got at the Finals party. I thought it was quite self-sacrificing of him to help Dee with Mick instead of staying there with the hottie, but he said leaving first is a superlative seduction technique. He's really looking forward to tonight, so it obviously worked." She glanced at her husband and back at Lacey. "Want another beer? You can tell us stories of Dee's university days. She has the reputation of never putting a foot wrong, and we're dying to know if she has a disgraceful episode or two in her past."

"Now that she's out of danger, of course," Terry added. "Yesterday it would have been in terribly bad taste, but today we can start collecting things to tease her with later."

Lacey guessed she was forgiven for her earlier slur against Jan. "Yeah, I'd love another. Do you know if Jake fed the dogs already?"

Jan nodded. "He threw the ball for them a few times down the drive, too, just as we ate supper. He does not scoop, though, so watch out for doggie land mines. Oh, and he asked if he can have a key to Dee's house. He wants his architect to draw up plans to make the house easier for Dee when she comes home."

"Easier?"

"Uh-huh. He mentioned an elevator, among other improvements. I'm to ask you whether it would be better to let Dee approve the plans or surprise her with a *fait accompli*."

"He doesn't think small." No way in hell was she handing over a house key until Jake was cleared beyond doubt. If he'd bugged the place once, he might get surveillance wired right into the walls next time. But she wasn't going to advertise her half-formed suspicions in front of Terry. "I'll try to get keys cut this weekend. It's been a hell of a week."

The casual conversation filled a void in Lacey's post-Force life. She didn't talk about leaving the RCMP or her husband, and the Brenners didn't ask. Instead they talked about non-stressful common events, like their university days. Jan, it turned out, was at SFU the year Lacey finished her English degree there part-time. They might have passed each other in the halls. It was a small connection, but a welcome one, and Lacey got up to leave an hour later with a comforting sense of tiny tendrils anchoring her in the post-RCMP world.

It was quite dark outside. The long evening had trailed away on a stiff breeze that chilled her bare arms. She swung them for warmth, wondering how people got used to all this rural quiet. Nighttime in Surrey meant lower traffic noise, louder-sounding sirens, occasional gunfire, and greasy food in shabby cafés that poured liberal coffee to make up for their culinary shortcomings. The sky there was a low ceiling of smoggy dark above the endless streetlights, not a vast velvet void sprinkled with glimmers of distant light. Not this peaceful, alien world of widely spaced houses, whispering leaves, rustling grass and … raging dogs?

Boney and Beau were barking loud enough to rouse the dead. She took the shadowy drive at a cautious run, scanning the clearing around the house for possible threats, pulling out her cellphone and wishing it was her duty Glock. Was that a faint light moving in Dee's office? Two steps farther on, it wasn't there. A reflection of a star, or a distant vehicle's headlights. Nonetheless, she crept across the stones, flattened against the house, and slid along to the office window.

Bam! The front door slammed against the outside wall. She ran to the front porch. Nothing. No running figure on the drive or rustling leaves that would mark movement through the bushes. The dogs' barking rose to a new frenzy. She sped around the house in time to see a two-legged shadow vanish under the trees beyond the dog pen.

She couldn't be sure whether it had run up the trail or down, could barely be sure she had seen someone. Pursuit was out of the question. Searching alone in unfamiliar terrain at night was like begging to be ambushed. She returned to the house. After a quick reconnaissance through the open kitchen door, she went inside and turned on all the ground-floor lights. Then she locked the front door, shutting out the night wind that had seemed her biggest problem ten minutes ago.

While waiting for the RCMP from Cochrane, she stood in the doorway of Dee's office, staring at dumped-out drawers, scattered papers, and, with a sinking feeling in her stomach, the empty spot on the desk where, last Sunday at suppertime, she had left Dee's laptop instead of locking it back in the filing cabinet.

CHAPTER THIRTY-TWO

Having slept through Rob's departure for work, Jan phoned the museum after her late breakfast. When he picked up, she said, "I just wondered if Lacey said anything today about her break-in last night."

"She's not here. She's picking up the vault programmer at the airport. This adjustment could have been done over the internet a week ago. But no, the old prez was afraid we'd be hacked if we let the guy install remote software. As if any thief would need to move our vault drawers by remote control. They'd have to hack the elevator security and those double-backstopped electronic door locks before getting to the storage drawers. And then they'd be looking right at the unsecured remote control. If it's good enough for Arab oil billionaires to protect their mega collections, it should be good enough for our little collection of cowboy art. It's not like somebody's going to donate us a lost Cezanne."

"Sorry I asked. I take it today's not going well, either?"

"The smell is getting to me, that's all. We have a school group in the Natural History Gallery and the little beggars are making jokes about what exactly the stuffed coyotes are stuffed with."

"Still no clue where it's coming from?"

"I'm thinking it's the elevator shaft. That's where the flies congregate, anyway. I sprayed the elevator three times this morning, but we're sure to end up with some getting into the vaults. We might have to fumigate. More expenses and we've hardly taken a cent in entry fees yet." He hissed in frustration and then said, "How are you doing? I thought you'd sleep until noon after all the excitement last night."

"I wish. I laid awake for hours, worrying about Lacey down there by herself. Then I had nightmares of Jarrad's car, dripping wet and covered in river mud, roaring after me with Camille at the wheel doing a Cruella De Vil impression."

"Wearing a white mink coat and ropes of jewels?"

"No, in that leather jacket we stared at for half of yesterday. Instead of black and white, her hair was red and white to match the car."

"Do you think it's a sign from your subconscious?"

"Yes. It's telling me to stop fussing about things I can't control. My nerves are so shot. When you came home last night, I practically landed on the ceiling with my claws extended like Sylvester the cat."

"I'm sorry. Do you want me to move back into town?"

"That's not what I meant. You might volunteer to sleep at Dee's place, though. I'd feel better if Lacey weren't there alone."

Rob snickered. "Now you're worried about her? Two days ago you'd have made her the main course at a barbeque."

"Not worried, exactly. But she came straight out and apologized to me for that thing last week. She's pretty human, when you get to know her."

"I already know her."

"You were awfully late. Good date?"

"Not hardly. He talked about Jarrad the whole time. I was quite cast down."

"This was the guy from Jake's party?"

"Yup."

"A close friend of Jarrad's?"

"More than a friend, darlin'. You never told me Camille's main squeeze was the hockey equivalent of a switch hitter."

"What? Are you sure this guy is telling the truth?"

"Yup. He was pretty cut up about Jarrad going missing. If Jarrad is pulled from the river, he'll have at least one mourner."

"Mick must have known." Jan stared downhill at the Hardy house. "Maybe that's why Camille and Jarrad got away with it for so long."

"You know these hockey folks better than I. Would it matter if Jarrad was outed? I mean, would he lose his job, be subjected to dressing room beatings, or forced to take segregated showers?"

"Gosh, I don't know. I don't think so, although I don't recall any male hockey players who are openly gay. Are you thinking Dee might have found out, and he tried to silence her to save his reputation? Not that she would have outed him, anyway."

"Yeah, but would he know that? I mean, Dee is a class act and I adore her, but she did do that nasty thing to his pretty car. He might think she'd happily destroy his career."

Rob was right. Jarrad, immature as he was, could have run over Dee on a misguided mission to save his reputation. But could he bring himself to drown his beloved Corvette? Possibly Camille had covered up for him by ditching the car after he was safely away. Wearing the same jacket might be accidental. Would the security photos show any difference in body composition between the night and day shots? She wished Rob well with the vault repairs and went to apply her artist's eye to the photos.

CHAPTER THIRTY-THREE

"I searched along the trail first thing this morning," Lacey finished, "and there was your laptop, wide open in a puddle. Filthy water dribbled out of every crack when I picked it up."

"So it's useless?"

"Maybe not. Wayne recommended a data recovery specialist and I dropped it off there once it was fingerprinted. You might get some data back."

Dee nodded sleepily. "Mostly legal templates. Easy to replicate from the company database."

"What about the sound file from the bug?"

"What bug?"

"The recording device we found on your office window. Don't fall asleep now, Dee. Can you tell me what was on it, or give me permission to lift another copy direct from the recorder?"

Dee looked at her blearily. "Oh, I forgot. Not Neil."

"I know that. His fingerprints didn't match. But whoever did that to you, don't you want them to pay for all the stress they caused you?"

No answer. Just like that, Dee had blinked out again. She might wake up in ten minutes or in hours. Lacey was due at the airport to collect and feed the vault guy, then have him on the jobsite by one o'clock. Dee had hidden the thumb drive copy somewhere Lacey couldn't find, or it, too, had been stolen. Tom could copy the recording today as insurance, in case the laptop file wasn't recoverable. Making a mental note to ask him about that, she went out to the corridor where an RCMP constable waited to take Dee's statement. "Sorry, she zonked out again."

The cop sat down. Lacey nodded to the security guard on her way out. Dee was really well protected now, if Jarrad or Camille showed up. Or Jake. Although she puzzled over things all the way to the airport, she couldn't make Mick's warning fit with anything except the recorder being from Jake's place. Camille had ample opportunity to take it, although her motive was a mystery. Maybe Mick's warning about Jake was an attempt to deflect suspicion from the wife he seemed to love.

Nobody could love the "master" programmer of the vault software, Lacey soon decided. A paunchy computer geek with an exaggerated sense of his own importance, he kept shoving his hand up to his pasty forehead while shoving his complaints down her throat. First the wait for his luggage, which she didn't instantly pick out when it appeared on the carousel. Then the absence of a limo — he always got a limo. The restaurant. She had simply turned in at the first chain she saw that separated its tables from its chairs. Yeah, the food was slightly plastic, but not as bad as it would be at the gas station by the junction of Highways 1 and 22. No doubt she could have driven him all the way to Bragg Creek, except that lunch in one of those places would take an hour longer. Wayne would blame her for their lateness. Her, not the vaultmaster. Well, the vaultmaster could eat as upscale as he wanted tonight, after the vault was fixed, and no doubt he would charge the meal to the Bragg Creek facility along with his flight and his deluxe room at the elegant bed-and-breakfast across the river. And his limo to the airport in the morning.

She ushered him and his tiny tool kit — a laptop bag, really — into the museum at two minutes to one. The atrium smelled strongly of fly spray and faintly of decay. A dozen flies crawled along the gap in the elevator doors with their wings waving excitedly. The vaultmaster gazed at them with his fat lower lip sucked disapprovingly inward. Or maybe it was the odour disagreeing with his plastic salad and petrified croutons. The elevator door opened and a swarm of new flies appeared. Rob dashed over with a spray can upraised.

"Not now," Lacey said. Rob sprayed anyway and reached in to press the door-closing button.

"I'm trying to keep the flies out of the vault. Can't have them breeding down there and eventually laying eggs on a loaner painting."

The vaultmaster sniffed. "I should say not. Have you joined the present century in any other ways? Such as permitting me to install a cyber-link so that future problems can be adjusted from my clean, fly-free office in Vancouver instead of repeatedly being dragged to this rustic village?"

"Put in the software. I'll let you know when I have approval to activate it. Okay?"

"Thank you. Now where is this Wayne person, who couldn't follow a few simple directions correctly by telephone?"

A faint growl answered him. Wayne stood beside the elevator. "Let's go."

Rob looked at his watch. "Another couple of minutes to let that blast settle and a jiffy to sweep out the remains. Anyone like a cup of tea?"

Wayne curled his lip. The vaultmaster sniffed. Lacey rolled her eyes. It was going to be quite the afternoon.

When the elevator doors opened on the vault level, the stench hit Lacey's nose a nanosecond before the humming hit her ears. The metal door to the vault was home to hundreds of flies, all buzzing madly. Rob gave them a hefty blast from his spray can. While Lacey held her breath, waiting for the spray to settle, her eyes met Wayne's. She had seen enough locked doors crawling with flies to know something substantially bigger than a rodent was rotting in that climate-controlled vault.

Wayne glared at the door. "Got gloves, McCrae?"

"Yes, sir."

"Then get on it." He waved his key card over the master lock and entered the code with the tip of a tiny screwdriver instead of his fingers. When the door whooshed softly open, leaving a one-inch crack, he put the handle of his hammer in at the top corner and eased the door open wider, scraping aside a swath of fallen flies. The smell seeped out, stronger and more intensely familiar. Lacey snapped on her latex gloves, stamped her feet to shake off any loose dirt or fibers, and stepped forward.

Rob, one hand over his mouth and nose, muttered, "Please tell me some workman forgot his liverwurst sandwiches in there."

The vaultmaster, finally cluing in, paled. "Is there a … something in there?"

Wayne nodded. "What's left of something, it seems. Thank god for air conditioning, eh, McCrae?"

The vaultmaster backed away as the foul odour flooded the small lobby. He turned his face to the corner and puked up his lunch. Lacey shrugged. He wouldn't have to digest any more of the plastic salad now. She took a couple of deep sniffs to desensitize her nose and walked through the door.

In the sterile wash of overhead lighting, it took her only a moment to spot the misalignment of a rack at the end of the row. It was the same one she'd been trapped behind. She shivered, then refocused on the job at hand. "Flashlight?"

Wayne handed one in and she edged along the wall, watching the floor for any trace evidence before she could step on it. By rights she should be wearing a Tyvek bunny suit and slippers, as well as the gloves, but that wasn't her job any longer. Before calling in the pros, she only needed to know what — or whom — she was calling them for. She made her way to the last rack and ran the light along its edges, looking for obvious stains or fingerprints. Then she gingerly turned the light and her eye to the narrow gap.

At first she saw only steel mesh and the limited flashlight ray. She bounced the light off the white-painted ceiling for better diffusion. The first half-length of the mesh floated in the dark, bare except for the posters she'd seen before. The light spread farther back and then she knew, if she had doubted before, what had stopped the drawer from closing flush with its neighbours. In the same spot where she had narrowly escaped being crushed ten days ago, someone else had not been so lucky.

Jarrad Fiske's bloated face hung in the shadowy space between two end plates.

CHAPTER THIRTY-FOUR

Half an hour later, Lacey sat in the museum's administration offices while RCMP officers took over the vault. Once again, she was on the civilian side of a police incident, banished to a distance while real cops handled a situation. Cops who hadn't quit the Force.

Those six months of training at Depot were all about weeding out the quitters. You weren't supposed to quit after that. You were supposed to serve faithfully until your honourable retirement. Her leaving the Force reinforced the stereotype of women not being tough enough to stick with the job. The duty cops would take their tone from Wayne, who had retired honourably and could be trusted. Lacey was an outsider. Here was a straight-up investigation for which she had possibly crucial background on the deceased, and she had forfeited the privilege of saying, "Sergeant, I've discovered …"

The glass wall facing the lobby muted the police voices out there. It also reflected her face and the room behind her, where Rob and the vaultmaster waited. Wayne had impressed on them both that discussing the scene or transmitting news of it before giving their statements to the police was practically a hanging offence. The vault-master sucked in his pouty lip and commandeered the secretary's desk, where he sat tapping away on his laptop as though uploading his remote-control software was the only task of import in the place. Or he was tweeting what he'd been asked to keep quiet. Rob was in his office, phoning the art storage place to put an indefinite hold on shipments that were supposed to arrive Monday. The delay in using the vault seemed to bother him more than the reason for it. He had only said, "Will the smell go away when the body does?" and then asked Wayne about crime scene cleanup companies.

For Lacey, Jarrad's corpse was a giant question mark. How long had he been in there? How had he gotten in there? Had he set the touchy rack in motion himself, or had someone else done it? Accident or murder? He might have been alive for hours or days, trapped in agony where nobody could hear his cries for help. What a thought!

Wayne walked in. "This has fucked my schedule backward over a barrel. You good, McCrae?"

"No worries." *Well, except for whether I'll have any job hours coming after this disaster or if I'll be scavenging out of Dee's freezer for the next month while looking for other work.*

"Good. I've gotta start the next job on Monday. If I leave you a detailed diagram, can you run camera cable through the ceiling tiles below the theatre? You'll have to work around whoever is using the classrooms down there."

Paid hours. Whew. "Sure. Just leave me whatever tools I'll need. Do you care if I don't wait until Monday to start? I've got a few days to make up."

"Long as you don't charge me double for Sunday."

Lacey leaned closer. "Did they get you to check the elevator log? Can you say how long he's been down there?"

"Need-to-know only, McCrae, and you don't need to. Get used to it." He pulled up a wiring diagram on his laptop. They spent the next half hour going over it, then bringing in cable spools and tools from the van. A pair of reporters followed them across the parking lot.

"Is it true there's a body in there? Is it connected to the car from the river? Is it the missing hockey player?"

Lacey kept on walking. She had never made enough seniority to talk to the media while she was on the Force, and she wasn't going to start now. Let Wayne handle it. Which he did by shrugging and walking past the outstretched microphones. No more than the vultures deserved. And just how had they got onto this so quickly?

Constables were waiting for them at the office, annoyed that Lacey had not sat meekly in a chair until wanted. She shrugged off their frowns. Until a month ago, she had outranked both of them. She followed one constable into the little meeting room and sat across the table from him without being told. Nor did she wait for him to ask a question.

"You do know Jarrad Fiske was wanted for questioning in a vehicular assault last Sunday?"

"We know all about that, ma'am. Please confine your statement to the discovery of the body."

So much for giving them useful background on the deceased. But then, she had never made the special investigations team out in Surrey because, as her sergeant repeatedly told her, she had too much imagination and was prone to going off on tangents. Most of the men she tested with went on hunches, too, only their tangents led to a by-the-book solution, whereas Lacey's equally correct solutions leaned toward interpersonal elements. Despite her recent lapse into linear thinking about the dangers of ex-husbands, she was not about to ignore the interpersonal elements of Jarrad's very odd death.

Whatever had taken him into that vault, into that space behind the massive steel rack, it was not an accident. It was the result of who he was, who he was involved with, and whatever was going on in his life. Not potentially criminal activities, but emotional ones. No stranger could have forced a robust young hockey player into that unlikely death trap. It was someone he knew. Someone with a key card had either given him their card or gone down there with him. Therefore it was someone connected to the museum. Every board member had a key card, and so did the staff, but only a few had vault access. That was the suspect pool in a nutshell.

The constable didn't ask for her inside knowledge, not of the relationships or of the vault access. He only wanted to know whether she had touched anything and how she had recognized the deceased. She gave him a step-by-step account of finding the body. She also gave him her fingerprints, hair, and a sample fibre from each item of her clothing, to eliminate any traces she might have left in the vault today.

Dismissed, she picked up the tools Wayne had left for her, climbed upstairs to the theatre level, plugged in the little gizmo that read elevator logs, and downloaded everything from Friday afternoon forward. She might not be able to link card numbers and card holders at a glance the way Wayne did, but Rob had a complete list in his office that she could check. Whether Jarrad had run over Dee himself or merely let his car be used, whoever had gotten him into the vault had some explaining to do.

When she got back to the office, Wayne was heading out. He handed her a sheaf of diagrams, warm from the printer. "Any questions, call my cell."

"Yes, sir. Have a good weekend." The other constable left Rob's office. Lacey looked at the meeting room, where the vaultmaster was giving his statement — and doubtless a litany of complaint — to another constable. He could talk as long as he wanted, so long as his voice covered her chat with Rob. She folded Wayne's diagrams and leaned into Rob's office. "I have to check the elevator logs against the key cards. Can you give me a copy of the cardholders list?"

"Sure." In a moment the office printer whirred beside the secretary's desk. Rob came out as she was scanning the list of names and stood fidgeting beside her until she lifted her head.

"What's on your mind, guy?"

The curator rubbed his neck with one hand. The gesture was old and tired, but the worried face looked younger than his estimated thirty years. "Uh, are you about done for the day? Now that Wayne's gone and all."

"I could be."

"Because, well, I'm supposed to be meeting a friend of Jarrad's for a drink after work, and I don't want to be the one to …"

"To tell him his friend is dead. But you don't want him to see it on television, either."

Rob nodded. "I realize it's an imposition, but you've got experience giving people bad news. If you'd come with me, at least long enough to explain the situation …"

Lacey looked down at her plain, dark cargo pants and tan T-shirt. Not grubby — she hadn't worked enough to get dirty — but not fresh, either, and faintly tainted by the pong in the vault. She wanted a shower and a drink and some thinking time. Yet a chance to meet a friend of Jarrad's, to question him while he was in shock and off guard, was not to be ignored.

"Where are you going?"

"He's meeting me outside the wine bar."

Lacey made up her mind. "It's not the kind of news that should be broken in a public place. Why don't you hop over to that liquor store beside the wine bar and pick up whatever you think he'll drink? When he shows up, say you have to bring the stuff up to Dee's. We can tell him there."

"That'd be great." Rob's worry lines eased. "I'll go right away."

"I'll go home and get out some glasses."

A couple of minutes past five, one of Jake's BMW convertibles whizzed up Dee's drive, carrying Rob and another man. Lacey went out to meet them and stopped in surprise. The hockey player behind the wheel was the same man who had told her about Dee and the windshield.

He got out of the car. "Ma'am. How's your friend?"

"Recovering, thank heavens. Call me Lacey."

Rob came to stand beside her. "Meet Chris." His eyes appealed to her to take it from there.

"I see you brought my supplies, Rob," she said. "You know the way to the kitchen, right?" Rob took the hint and carried the bags around to the mudroom door. Lacey leaned on her Civic and looked at Chris. "I got the impression the other day that you knew Jarrad pretty well."

"As well as anyone, I guess. I still don't think he would run over your friend. Not sober, anyway."

Sympathy softened Lacey's voice. "We might never know now."

Chris frowned. "Why not?"

"I'm sorry to tell you this, but it's bound to be on the news soon. Jarrad has been found. He's dead."

The hockey player recoiled. "That's not true."

"I'm afraid it is. I found him."

Chris slumped against the Bimmer. "Was he … in the river?"

"No. He didn't drown. Why don't you come inside and I'll tell you what I know." A small voice belatedly niggled about contaminating an interested person before the police got to him, but the constable hadn't cautioned her not to talk about her find. He had probably figured it was too late, that those reporters in the parking lot had winkled out all she knew before he'd gotten his hands on her. As if. She steered Chris to the living room, where Rob handed him a drink. Chris accepted it and drank half, apparently without noticing. Then he looked at his glass and sat down heavily on the couch.

"You knew about this, Rob?"

"I was with Lacey when she, uh, found him."

"Did you see him?"

"No. But I understand it was very fast. He didn't suffer." Rob waggled his eyebrows at Lacey for a confirmation she couldn't quite give.

"His face looked about the same," she said, not quite truthfully. "Are you ready to hear what happened?"

"I guess." Chris finished his drink. Rob took the empty glass away and refilled it while Lacey gave a sparse description of Jarrad's death. "I know how easily it can happen," she finished. "A rack nearly caught me a few days earlier."

"The place should have been locked if it was that dangerous."

"It was. He shouldn't have been able to get into that room at all."

Chris turned his new drink in his hands. The glass made a *tink-tink* each time it contacted his heavy ring.

"Stanley Cup ring," said Rob. "From four years ago, right, Chris?"

"Huh? Yeah. Long before Jarrad. God, I can't believe this. If he'd wrapped the 'Vette around a tree, I could see it. But this … it doesn't make any sense."

"No, it doesn't." Lacey seized her chance. "When was the last time you saw him? Was he up at Jake's for that party last weekend?" She already knew the answer, but what would he say?

"He never showed. The guys were all betting which of the women he'd gone off with. He always flirted for show, but he never followed through. Hadn't been with a woman in years."

Lacey didn't miss the flicker in Rob's eyes. He said nothing, so she went on. "The last time you saw Jarrad was when? At the gala?"

"Yup. Doing that dumb act on stage. He'd have done anything for old Mick, but he shoulda said no to this. The guys were all primed to give him a hard time afterward. He never showed then, either." *Tink-tink* went the ring.

If Jarrad had left the building with a straying trophy wife, she wouldn't answer a public plea for information. Lacey might be able to find her, though, via the museum's external cameras record from Friday night. "So you hadn't seen him since he left the stage? Not a phone call, either?"

"He wouldn't call me, anyway." The words were flat, the voice heavy. "He was losing his grip all last winter. I tried to reason with him, even talked to the coaching staff, but he was furious. He fought everyone who tried to help. Word spread. St. Louis had a hard time getting rid of him in the last trades. Then Pittsburgh didn't play him once."

"He really hit the skids, huh? Any idea what started it?"

"I can't tell you any more than I did the other day. He was coming home after the season, ready to pull a dance on somebody, clear the air for good, he said. He wouldn't talk about it last winter, and he wouldn't talk to me last week when we were all hanging by the pool at Jake's."

"Was he staying up there, too?"

"Nope. With Mick, always. He was afraid the old man would give him a bad rep with the other owners."

"I didn't realize Jake had that much influence in hockey."

"He could break us with a word in the right ear, but he can get a young player some chances, too. That's why nobody refuses his invitations." The glass rolled in his hands again. *Tink-tink.* "Don't get me wrong, Mr. Wyman is a good fellow. I have a lot of respect for him."

The resemblance to Mafia-speak might be unintentional, but it seemed apt. Jake was the godfather of the local hockey community, the last known owner of the bug in Dee's window. He could have seen Jarrad's conspicuous car left behind and used it against Dee. What if Jarrad had found out? Maybe it wasn't the first time Jake had expected a young hockey player to cover for him. But Jarrad's career was dying anyway; maybe he'd decided not to play along. Did Jake have a key card with vault access? An alibi for Jarrad's last elevator ride, whenever it was? Her old sergeant would have called this a tangent born of imagination, but she would investigate Jake Wyman to the best of her ability nonetheless.

Chris turned his Stanley Cup ring in his strong fingers. "Jarrad wanted one of these so bad. Maybe I'll give this one to Mick, let him be buried with it. He'd have got one himself, eventually."

"Mick?" Rob set down his glass. "This will kill him. Should we go down there?"

Lacey shook her head. "Mick is staying in Calgary until his heart is stronger. He has a private nurse. He'll be looked after. What about Jarrad's parents, Chris? Did they know he was missing?"

"I don't know. Maybe Mick got in touch. He must have met them in the early years."

"You didn't? Not even when you and Jarrad played for the same team?"

"I never met them. You've gotta understand, in hockey our real family can fall away fast. Kids from small towns get scouted in the minors. If you're picked up by a junior team at sixteen, you end up billeted with strangers a thousand miles from home. Finish high school between road games, see your family twice all winter, spend half the summer at a training camp. You're closer to your teammates than your brothers. Obey your coach before your mother. The guys you billet with, play with, are your family. Not your old family in some two-lane mining town. Sounds harsh, but you don't succeed in hockey without sacrificing something."

"And Jarrad sacrificed his family?"

"Traded it for a better model, more like. Jarrad billeted with Mick for some regional tournament in Ontario, and his road was paved with gold from then on. Mick coached him, bought his equipment, got him into the nearest minor team, and billeted him through high school. He taught Jarrad all the tricks a little guy needs to draw penalties and avoid hits, things that take years of poundings to figure out on your own. Mick managed him until he got farmed for the NHL, and then he found him a decent agent. Mick and Jarrad were totally tight, even after Mick got married. Better than family."

"How'd Mick's wife get along with Jarrad?" Lacey felt, rather than saw, Rob's twitch, but he didn't interrupt.

"They put on a good show for Mick, but Camille hates Jarrad. She resents every penny spent on him. Not that it was much lately, with Jarrad's salary rising — just a trip, or maybe some clothes. Mick says ... used to say, if he didn't buy Jarrad a coat now and then, the kid would freeze to death. And there was the Corvette, but that was special. It was Jarrad's dream car. I think Mick hoped it would give him something to hold on for. It seemed to help, anyway. That and the trade. I never thought I was a bad influence, but Jarrad straightened up some after he moved. So I must have been." He blinked hard and emptied his glass. "I must have been."

Rob reached a hand toward Chris's shoulder, hesitated, and went for the glass instead. "You want another?"

"I'd better go see who's still up the hill," said Chris. "Any idea when the funeral will be?"

Lacey shook her head. "In cases like this, it might take a couple of weeks before the police release the body."

"Thanks." Chris stood up. "And thanks for not telling me this in public, Rob. I guess you'll understand I'm not up for that dinner now."

"I know." Rob rose from his chair with less than his usual grace. "I'll walk you out." Lacey waited until Chris drove away and then went out to the drive. Rob stood, hands in pockets, looking forlorn. "He's done with me," he said. "He'll never look at me again without hearing you say Jarrad is dead."

"He said he only knew Jarrad 'as well as anybody.'"

"He lied. That bit about the bond hockey players form with the guys they're billeted with? Well, he and Jarrad were closer than most. They were lovers until last winter. He never understood why Jarrad called it off. I figured that was Camille. Jarrad wouldn't be the first guy to swing over the centre line when an experienced woman took an interest."

"So that's why you twitched when he said Jarrad hadn't been with a woman for years."

"For sure. I also know why the little shit never came upstairs after the gala. He was in the dressing room fucking Camille, pardon my language. They were at it when I went to find her after Mick's heart trouble."

"So that's why she had a supersized snit that night? *Coitus interruptus*?"

"Yup. She'll never forget I saw her *in flagrante*. I expect to be fired any day. Probably at the emergency board meeting I'll have to call ASAP to address the PR fallout from Jarrad's highly inconvenient death. Dee would have looked calm and gracious on television saying, 'We extend our deepest sympathy to the young man's friends and family.' Camille in the role won't have the same class."

He glowered at the sunny evening a bit longer. "Any plans for supper, Lacey? Jan and Terry aren't expecting me, and my date just went off to organize a wake."

CHAPTER THIRTY-FIVE

After a quick supper with Rob in Bragg Creek, Lacey went to the hospital. Dee was awake, more alert than she had been earlier. Carefully, watching for signs of emotional distress, Lacey told her about Jarrad.

Dee couldn't quite follow that he might be connected to her accident. She had heard a car engine, called the dogs to stand, then nothing. She thought someone had called her name while she was lying on the ground, but couldn't be sure it wasn't a dream. Assured that Boney and Beau were being looked after and the house was okay after the break-in, she soon faded.

"Dee, stay focused. We've got to talk about that recording device. Who bugged your window?" Dee closed her eyes and said nothing. "Well, was there anything confidential on the recordings or can I listen to them?"

"I thought the lapel ... lap ... computer was still drying out."

Having been warned by Marie about aphasia, Lacey didn't comment on Dee's difficulty finding the right word. "The laptop will be ready Monday. But think about this, Dee. It's too much coincidence that we find the bug on Friday night and thirty-six hours later you're run down by Jarrad's car. Then your laptop is stolen and he's found dead. Somebody else knew about that record-er on your window and might have killed Jarrad because he knew, too. Don't you want to know what the connec-tion is before they come after you again?"

Dee muttered that she was too tired to talk about it. Then she dozed off, or appeared to, leaving Lacey little option but to go home and catch up on her sleep. Except that, alone in the huge house, she kept hearing the creak of spruce boughs and the sigh of the wind around the eaves and wondering if the burglar had found what they came for or if someone was out in the dark right now, ready to sneak back in the instant she put out the final light. Three weeks of waiting for Dan to creep in while she was sleeping had very nearly broken her; how had Dee stood it, living alone for three long months with the prowler out there?

If any stalker or potential burglar came to the house overnight, the dogs, as usual, didn't bark at him. Saturday morning, Lacey woke feeling surprisingly rest-ed and mostly clear headed. Today she would get Dee's permission to listen to the recording. But first, author-ized by a voice mail from Sergeant Drummond, she'd retrieve her car from the crime scene. She threw her town sandals and wallet into a backpack, laced up her joggers, and headed out past the dogs' pen. Boney and Beau didn't bark at her for a change, but watched her so mournfully that she felt compelled to lean on their fence for a moment's chat. Boney placed a red ball before her, on his side of the wire, and sat tidily beside it. Beau ambled over to join him.

"Don't you guys try the puppy eyes on me. You've had miles and miles of good running this week with Jake, and I'm not springing you from this pen until I'm sure you'll listen when I call you back. Got that?" They sat, heads cocked as if they understood every word. She gave the wet noses a daring pat and her own head a mental smack for projecting her buoyant mood onto dumb animals. "Tell you what. When I get back, I'll throw the ball for you inside this pen, and if that goes okay, we'll see about opening the gate. Deal?" They kept up the hopeful pose until she was at the trail. Then Beau flopped to his stomach with a hefty sigh and Boney nosed the ball away. Experts at guilt, those dogs.

The short route, the one she'd slunk back on the other day, went over the hill and straight down the other side. She ignored it, turning downhill on the main trail. This route should have been explored days ago for places the prowler might be parking a vehicle. Too late for that now, but Terry had assured her it was the most direct route to her car. The path meandered through shrubby stretches between access paths to the houses below Dee's. Both were occupied by young families who seemed to spend most days and evenings at home, and therefore were not good parking spots for someone trying to avoid notice. She jogged gently onward in a cathedral of birdsong and dappled sunlight, shaking off a bit of the week's tension with each step, following the red-gravel trail around a rocky outcrop and through a shady copse until it popped out onto a long, narrow lane through the trees.

Across the way, the trail continued. To her left a brighter space showed the road she was aiming for. The other way, deep and mysterious in tree shadows, led to the gigantic Hardy house, now sprawling in a pool of sunlight. Her gut lurched. This lane was likely Jarrad's route on Sunday, and on that awful January night. Out there on the open gravel road was where he had careered past Dee and the dogs. Had anybody ever asked him what had set him off that night? Maybe he was drunk or using drugs, as Tom suggested. Maybe a lovers' tiff with Camille. Maybe racing to be with his friend up at Jake's place. He would never have his day in court to explain, apologize, redeem himself. At twenty-three, he was out of chances. Here in this green, shaded lane, she could almost feel sorry for him. With a small sigh she set off toward the road and the brighter sky above it.

She was not quite out of the woods when she heard the rustling of something large. A bear? A deer? She was poised to speed on past when Eddie Beal stepped out from behind a large spruce trunk, his clothing filthier than before, his beard more matted. In his left hand he swung a large claw-foot hammer.

CHAPTER THIRTY-SIX

Eddie raised the hammer.

Lacey's cop brain, fuelled by instant adrenalin, read his emotional state (disturbed), physical status (bigger than her), and familiarity with his weapon (held it like it grew from his wrist). All this came to her before her other foot touched the ground. Her body shifted into field stance, arms down and slightly out from her sides, fingers partly curled, weight poised to shift her in any direction in a hurry.

"Hi, Eddie," she said, with all the old calm of her patrol days.

Eddie's beard quivered. What light there was glinted on his red-lined eyes. He turned his head away like a bear about to charge. She held her ground.

He snorted wetly. "I thought you were old Mick Hardy," he said. "Wanted to say I'm sorry about his boy."

"About Jarrad?" As long as he was talking, he wasn't tackling. Her specialty on patrol had been de-escalating. Please let it work now, alone in the woods with a hammer-wielding nutter.

"Yup." Eddie sniffed hard and swallowed. "Heard he was dead. I want to tell old Mick that even though me and Eben were set to testify against the boy, we had no ill will and we're sorry he's gone." He tucked the hammer into the crook of his arm and tugged at a grimy hankie sticking out of his pants pocket.

As he blew his grotty nose, Lacey eased down from high alert. "Why'd you need the hammer for that?"

He stepped back a pace and pointed to the tree he'd been hiding behind. Lacey moved up, keeping half an eye on him, not sure yet what to expect. A dead animal? But no. He had nailed up a picture. Under a double layer of plastic sleeves was a blow-up of a shaggy golden dog, with part of a human leg and the Memorial University logo cropped off beside his head.

"Is that Duke? Dee's dog? The one that was killed on this road?"

"Yup. A good old dog." Eddie sniffed and honked his nose again. "Didn't deserve to end like that. I was wait-ing for the trial so he would have justice, but that can't happen now. A higher power saw to it in his own way." Did Eddie really believe God had killed Jarrad for injur-ing the dog? Beyond that ...

"How did you get a close-up picture of Dee and her dog?"

"The camera lady," said Eddie sorrowfully, gazing on the dog's happy face. "She had some on her table when I took the eggs one day. That's what give me the idea. I asked her to cut the people out and she did. Fixed him up real nice, didn't she?"

"What camera lady?"

At her sharp tone, Eddie pulled his eyes from the picture. "The sick one up the hill. She takes pictures from her deck. We sell her free-range eggs every week, organic meat and vegetables in season. Bring you some if you like. Early greens are coming on nice."

"Thanks. I'll think about that." It figured that Jan Brenner knew Eddie Beal. This wasn't the Lower Mainland, where people actively avoided getting to know their neighbours. She likely knew his brother, too, and his nieces, nephews, parents, and in-laws. She could have told Lacey all about the Beals if Lacey had only thought to ask. That's what came of looking for police sources first. A mistake she wouldn't make now, having found Eddie already softened up and ripe for questioning.

"You were nearby the night the dog was hit, right?"

He nodded.

"Can you tell me about it?"

"The car skidded around that curve by our lane just as I started to pull out. Young fellow been driving that brown beast for going on five years, of course we knew it, and him."

"You didn't go look to see what he was running from?"

He shrugged. "Thought he was just speeding. They do that. Damned hotshots. Anyway, we weren't coming this way. We headed for the highway to make Eben's plane. Didn't know a thing was wrong until I came home and the cops had the road closed."

"Where was Eben going?"

"He works up at the oil sands since the chicken plant fell through, only gets home four times a year. Had extra weeks after Christmas, but he ain't been back since."

This encounter put a different complexion on the threat posed by the Beals. Eddie, it appeared, was a dog-loving farmer. Eben was hundreds of kilometres away when Dee was being run over. Eddie blew his nose again and stowed the hankie. "You going for your car? I can give you a lift that far."

After nearly a week of Dee's Lexus, Lacey's five-year-old Honda bounced like a pop can on the highway, blown about by semis and vibrating through the construction zones. No mid-range car had the solid ride of a luxury SUV, but then, a ten-year Mountie didn't make nearly the salary of a corporate real estate lawyer. She arrived at the hospital to find Dee's door shut. An RCMP constable stood before it. Through the glass she could see another officer placing a small recorder on Dee's bed table. Statement time.

No more than ten minutes later, the officers went away. Lacey went in. "More questions about the hit and run? Or did they learn about your window being bugged? At this rate, they'll know what's on that tape before I will."

Dee closed her eyes. "If you can't wait for the laptop to be fixed, get the recorder back from Tom. There isn't a criminal case and I won't talk about the person who put the recorder there because that would lead to my legal affairs, and they are still confidential." No words lost or missing in that whole speech. That must be a good sign.

"Is it Jake Wyman?" Silence. "I know the recorder came from him."

Dee turned her head away. "I can't do this."

"I'm sorry if I'm pushing you. But it's important to be sure the person who hurt you doesn't get a free pass." Tears trickled down Dee's cheek, pooling in her ear. Lacey reached for a tissue. "Oh god, I'm really sorry. What can I do?"

Dee wiped her face with her non-IV hand. "I have a bigger worry now. Last night I didn't really take it in that Jarrad's death had anything to do with me."

"What changed your mind?"

"The police said he hasn't been seen alive since I was last seen going down the backstage stairs at the end of the gala."

But that was the Friday night. He had to have been seen somewhere after that. "Maybe you misunderstood?"

"I don't think so. They asked about the end of the gala, how long I was off stage alone, where I went, did I see anyone else downstairs. My heart went crazy. If I'd still been hooked up to the monitor, the room would have swarmed with nurses."

"But Jarrad was caught on tape on Sunday night, moving his car. That was two days later, and several hours after you were hit. What did you tell them?"

"I said I went downstairs before my speech to check my makeup. I didn't see anybody then, but when I left the dressing room, Jake was there to take me upstairs."

"Then Jake is your alibi." Or Dee was his.

"That's what I thought. But they didn't care about him. They know Jarrad killed my dog. They know I smashed his windshield." Dee groped for Lacey's hand. "They think I killed him."

"That makes no sense." It really didn't. Jarrad was on the security recording long after Dee was unconscious in the ditch. "Are you sure they said that?"

"Not those exact words. But they made it plain. You always told me, 'If I ever have to question you, get a lawyer first thing.' So I said I had nothing more to say to them without a lawyer present. You have to find me a criminal lawyer."

"I'll phone your office and ask." Lacey's fingers were going numb, but pulling them away would upset Dee even more.

"No! Keep my work out of it as long as possible. Call my divorce lawyer and ask her to recommend someone. The number's on my desk at home." Dee wept harder, all her faded bruises puffed up and streaked with tears.

"I'll get right on it. You just calm down. They won't arrest you while you're in this bed." If they really thought she was guilty, they'd collar her on the hospital's front steps in full view of the media. It's what any PR-concerned police force would do in a high-profile case.

When the physiotherapist came in, Lacey left. She couldn't quite break her old conditioning enough to call and cuss out the homicide investigators for harassing an injured woman. It was the job. Not so long ago, she'd done the same, not exactly accused a hospital patient of murder as soon as their heart monitor was removed, but leaned on bed-bound suspects. With no justifiable target for her ire, she called Tom instead, hoping to learn whether the investigators had anything regarding Dee or were only fishing. Marie said Tom had taken the boys out to the lake. She thought the recorder was in his locker downtown; it wasn't loose around the house, anyway. Did Lacey want to come over for lunch and look for herself?

Lacey should have enjoyed a peaceful visit with Marie, but the first words out of the ex-nurse's mouth were, "Why does Dan think you're in Newfoundland visiting your folks?" When Lacey only stared, she added tartly, "You and your family are as tight as polar bears are with penguins. You'd never go to them when you're exhausted and looking for shelter."

"Did Dan call here? What did you tell him?"

"Relax. He hasn't called. I got that in an email from another Force wife out in Langley." Marie headed for the kitchen, assuming Lacey would follow. "There are things you haven't told me about that breakup, Lacey, or why wouldn't you tell Dan where you are?"

"It's, well, I just needed time to clear my head. I didn't tell him I was going east, just that he could have the house back until it sells." She could feel Marie's eyes on her. Would she have to explain about Dan coming after her in their own house, or the probably irrational dread she'd had of him since the riverbank? Marie knew Dan. She wouldn't believe him capable of putting his wife in danger — even accidentally. She'd say Lacey had read too much into it, that she'd overreacted. Hell knew how many times Dan had accused her of overreacting, until she'd made herself numb from trying not to react at all. If Marie did believe, that would be almost worse. She'd surely tell Tom. He would never again look at Lacey without doubting her, without wondering if she needed protection like any other weak woman. That would show through in every job recommendation he gave going forward. If he gave any. He'd had her back for years, and vice versa, but when it came to the male world of the Force versus a female — now a civilian — she had moved herself to the wrong side of the loyalty bar.

Whatever she might have thought or seen in Lacey's face, Marie didn't push. She turned away to pull coffee mugs from a cupboard and said, "It's not up to me to report on your whereabouts. If I'm asked directly when I last saw you, I'll say you stopped here on your way east and leave it at that."

"Thank you."

It was a reprieve only. Sooner or later, Tom or maybe Wayne would mention her presence to some other old buddy in the Lower Mainland. Word would spread. Eventually Dan would track her down to Dee's. He might show up there. And what would happen to Dee if Lacey fled to avoid him? She would have to face him.

The things unsaid loomed over their lunch, stilting the conversation and turning every bite of her well-stuffed chicken wrap to so much packing material in her mouth. Eventually Marie sent her downstairs to look for the recorder. A cursory glance over Tom's cluttered desk revealed nothing, and she didn't feel right opening the drawers. She thanked Marie for the lunch and drove off, facing a long, hot weekend afternoon with nothing useful to do, until she remembered the museum. In the rush to question Jarrad's ex-boyfriend yesterday, she had left the key card list locked in her tool box. She could work on that angle right away. On to Bragg Creek.

Lacey pulled into the museum parking lot and found several luxury vehicles that could have been here for the gala last weekend. Were there honest-to-god art fanciers among the gold-plated guests? She parked at a distance from the shiny new rides, flashed her key card at the employee door's card reader, and descended into the classroom wing. Ahead of her, women's high voices chattered.

"Ooh, Tami," one squealed. "That's so harsh." Tami? Ugh. If she was here, the rest of the posse was, too. Working unobtrusively near them, Lacey might learn who'd gone off from the gala with Jarrad. Camille Hardy might be with the chattering horde, too — a good chance to eye her up and see if Jan's theory's had legs. Could Camille have been disguised as Jarrad on the security video?

She took the stairs to the office level with renewed enthusiasm, and caught sight of Camille coming down the other staircase. The woman hurried across to her posse, who were clustered by the kitchen.

"Sorry I'm late, darlings. My key card wouldn't work, and I had to come in the front door like a bloody tourist. When are the Mounties going to give us our elevator back? Crime scene tape on the keypads is really going too far. Is Rob ready for us yet?"

Oh, right, Rob's emergency board meeting. A corpse on the premises had at least gotten him a good turnout.

Camille saw Lacey. "You. Aren't you a security person? Find out what's wrong with my card. That Rob probably forgot to activate it."

Lacey took the card by a corner, wondering if there was any substance handy with which to lift Camille's prints. Not that she expected they would match the set on the recorder, but getting something, anything, on this arrogant female was rising on her priority list. It occurred to her that Camille was demonstrating a complete lack of concern about Jarrad's death. If she had wept behind closed blinds, she was disguising it very well.

Rob appeared in the meeting room doorway. "Ladies, if you please. Refreshments are ready. Please take a minute to look through my report before we start." He stepped out to allow them in and came over in response to Lacey's wave. "What's up?"

"Camille Hardy says her key card doesn't work. Can I use your computer to check its status?"

"Sure. It's logged in and you know which icon, right? If that's the new card I coded for her on Monday, I tested it myself." He looked past her, around the lobby, and his shoulders drooped. "I was hoping Jake Wyman would show up today to speak for my job, but he's left me out to dry. Wish me luck in there."

"You got it." Lacey hurried to his office. She had to scroll down the index twice before she was sure about the card. Then she went back to the boardroom.

Camille spotted her instantly. "Did you fix it?"

"This is your old card, Mrs. Hardy. The one you reported lost. It was cancelled as a security precaution. Your new card should work just fine. If you don't find it today, please tell Rob immediately so he can cancel that one, too."

"My old card? It can't be. The police thought Jarrad took it." The last was directed to the posse, not to Lacey, and she quietly stepped out of Camille's line of sight. Jarrad, or someone with him, must have used that card to access the vault. Then who put it back? And who had the new one now?

Camille wasn't worried about that, though. She said in thrilling tones, "Girls, I may be a suspect."

The others leaned forward, their perfect noses quivering like chihuahuas. One of them — Twyla, or was that Chareen? — asked breathlessly, "The police questioned you?"

"They said I might have been the last person to see him alive. They asked if I lent him my card. The silly thing obviously doesn't work, anyway, so I couldn't have got him down to that vault, could I? I didn't get the new one until Monday." Except it would have been working all weekend, until Rob cancelled it on Monday. Analysis clearly wasn't Camille's strength. She likely hadn't noticed it was missing sooner, what with the gala and the Finals party. Then on Sunday she came home from somewhere to find Mick collapsed in the den. Had she been out partying then, too? And did she have an alibi for Sunday afternoon, when Dee was run down?

A collective "ohh" encouraged Camille to continue. "I'm sure I wasn't the last person, really. I never saw him Friday except during our act, and I have a witness who can tell the police I was otherwise occupied right up to when I left with Mick."

But she had been with Jarrad when Rob went down, hadn't she? That made her more of a suspect, not less.

The one Lacey thought was Tami giggled. "But weren't you with *him*? What would Mick say?"

"Mick wouldn't care if I did it on the stage." Camille smiled. "Rob, have the police asked you about the gala yet?"

Rob paled. "Yes."

"Did you tell them where you found me? And with whom?"

"Yes." A lesser man would have flinched, but Rob kept his smile while he waited for the axe to fall.

"There. Isn't he a dear? I'm as good as cleared."

As she turned away, Rob lifted a bemused eyebrow at Lacey. He made a tiny shooing motion and she left, still holding Camille's old key card. So the police had used a similar technique on Camille as they had on Dee, claiming she was the last person to see the hockey player alive. If they had found prints besides Camille's on her card, they'd have kept it in evidence. Unless they'd kept her new one. Meanwhile, their looking at cards confirmed that Jarrad had not been found with one. Since he'd been unreachable once he was behind the rack, the card must already have been in the killer's hands. It was past time Lacey went through those elevator logs. It wasn't a job she could charge to Wayne, but she would more than repay the time if it cleared Dee.

She spent the next hour working backward through the elevator printout, starting from when the body was found. Nobody had gone down on Thursday, but that wasn't unexpected. No vault access Wednesday, nor Tuesday. Nor even Monday. Jarrad had last appeared to a security camera outside the building on Sunday night, presumably just before he pushed the car into the river. Had he used Camille's new card to wait inside the building until that violent thunderstorm passed? No, that new card was only issued on Monday. She turned back a page to Sunday, wondering why Jarrad had gone to the vault at all. Had someone suggested the hiding place to him, knowing it was off limits until the vault-master's arrival? Camille could have taken him down there and left him, and he might have messed with the racks before accidentally getting trapped — unlikely, but possible. Why wouldn't she have gone back to look for him, and raised the alarm? Chris claimed she hated Jarrad, yet Jan and Dee were convinced she'd been having sex with him for years. Which was it? Both?

There was no vault access on Sunday, either. Lacey started on Saturday, working from midnight back to morning. Still nothing. Then she found herself looking at the long list of elevator uses on Friday evening, during the gala. Most had no key card number. They represented gala patrons moving from the atrium to the theatre lobby and back again. Were the police being truthful when they told Dee Jarrad was last seen alive that night?

A line with a key card number caught her eye: 10:27 p.m. When the performance was ending, the elevator went to the vault from the studio level, stayed less than five minutes, then went all the way up to the theatre mezzanine. The key card number was Camille's — her old card, now lying on the desk.

Lacey sat back in her chair, grappling with the implications of the elevator logs. Nobody had taken the elevator down to the vault between gala night and the vault-master's arrival. If Jarrad had gone to the vault at the end of his performance and never returned, he couldn't have run over Dee on Sunday.

Furthermore, if he was dead or dying by ten thirty on gala night, then who was in the dressing room with Camille an hour later? Rob might have lied for Camille, claiming Jarrad was alive when he and Camille came upstairs. He could then blackmail her to secure his job. It might even be Rob on the security tape, wearing Jarrad's clothing. In fact, Rob might have lured Jarrad, the bisexual hockey player, into the vault using Camille's lost — or stolen — card. He could have urged Jarrad behind the rack for a tryst, below the camera's all-recording eye … and Jarrad could have been crushed accidentally? Could Rob have come to work every day and complained of the smell and the flies if he knew what caused them?

Her purely imaginary theory could fit the facts. Where it did not fit, she quickly realized, was with Dee. If Rob had left Jarrad in the vault, behind the rack, he couldn't have gotten the Corvette's keys. Were Jarrad's keys missing? Besides, Rob had no reason to go after Dee two days later. He'd had all the opportunity necessary when he spent the night drinking with Dee. If he'd learned then that Dee had seen him and Jarrad slinking downstairs, he could have dumped the hockey player's body into the river long before the vaultmaster arrived.

Lacey gave up and stood up. The circumstantial evidence against Rob was a figment of her too-eager imagination.

The yipping of the chihuahuas penetrated the glass walls. She watched as they tittered away up the stairs. Rob and Camille stood for a moment in the meeting room doorway. They were very close to the same height. Jarrad, if Lacey's mental image of the stilted gala performance was accurate, was about as tall as Camille in her gold-toned evening flats. Ergo, he was about as tall as Rob. Disguise her hips or his shoulders, hide their hair under a ball cap, and it could be either one of them in those security stills.

Camille followed her posse upstairs. Rob came to the office and dropped into a chair. "Thank god that's over."

"I take it you still have your job."

"Yes. The little darlings gave me a free hand to cope with the press as I see fit. They don't want to be seen on television commenting on corpses. I don't think they realize this could be bad for our attendance, and thus our earnings. The idea that the directors are financially responsible for any budget shortfall at year-end hasn't quite penetrated their sweet little *têtes*. I'll do my best for them all the same. If this facility can't make a go, it's my reputation on the line as well as their money." He looked exactly the same as he had earlier, concerned but not in the least overwrought. Maybe she was the one who was overwrought.

"Last night, you said something about a souvenir DVD of the gala. I'd like to buy one as soon as they're ready."

"I picked them up in Calgary this morning, hoping to sweeten up the board harpies. I'll get you the one for Dee. She might find it amusing, all that terrible acting. Although Camille's main squeeze wasn't half bad. Quite a stage pro he turned out to be." Jarrad had been anything but a pro on stage. Rob's sarcasm, if that's what it was, seemed out of character for him as well as in bad taste. She was about to call him on it when he added, "Oh, I forgot! We're watching it up at Jan's tonight. She wants to invite you to dinner and the movie. I suppose she left a message at Dee's."

"Much good that would do me," said Lacey, activating the half of her brain that wasn't busy comparing Rob's casual mention of "Camille's main squeeze" to the sex-gone-wrong scenario lingering in her brain. "I don't know Dee's voice mail code. I haven't checked her mailbox either. I don't know where her postbox would be, or its number."

Rob explained which super-box of the three across the way served their road. "The key will be on her ring. A fiddly thing of cheap metal, stamped with a number. So, can I tell Jan you'll come?"

Checking out a suspect's alibi in his presence wasn't ideal police procedure, but then Lacey wasn't with the police any longer. Rob, if he turned out not to be a suspect, could be invaluable at filling in other people's whereabouts.

"I'll call Jan to make sure," she said. "Don't want to wear out my welcome."

CHAPTER THIRTY-SEVEN

Two hours later, Lacey leaned back in her chair and licked salad dressing from her finger. "Great supper. Thanks." And it was: thick steak, salad, crisp whole-wheat rolls, none the worse for being her second steak dinner in three days.

"It's great company that makes it." Jan waved a hand inclusively at everyone, including the mutts. "I'm glad you didn't mind us coming down to get the dogs. They miss the regular social round they had with Dee." Boney and Beau did look happy. They lolled on the deck, tongues dragging and tails gently thumping whenever someone said their names or patted them in passing.

"They sure do behave better with you than with me. I'd never let them leave the kennel on my own."

"Years of acquaintance," Jan said. "Dogs can't fake warm fuzzies, like humans do. Camille Hardy and her set are the fakest people I know. All smiles when they're together, but if you ever talk to one alone, you can soon see the others' shredded flesh hanging from her fingernails. I swear they'd poach each other's husbands without a second thought."

"Camille would trade hers in a millisecond." Rob set down his steak bone for Boney and started stacking dishes. "You should have heard her this afternoon, sneering over Mick for being cut up about his protege's death. What a bitch."

Jan sighed. "She's not upset, I suppose?"

Lacey threw her bone to Beau, who eyed it and her with suspicion for a moment before the aroma seduced him. "She seemed completely taken up with whether she was a suspect. What was she gushing at you for, Rob? Did you ever figure it out?"

"Not a clue."

Jan handed her plate to Rob. "Do tell."

"I was expecting her to be after my blood, but she nearly drowned me in syrup. She seemed to think something I said had cleared her of suspicion in Jarrad's death."

"Did you tell the cops you saw them having sex in the dressing room?" Jan asked.

"Not in so many words, but yeah. For her to think that that somehow clears her ... Does it make sense to you, Lacey?"

Lacey shook her head. It didn't make sense on more than one level. Rob had obviously told his story to Jan and Terry before spreading it to Lacey or the police. Either he believed it himself, or he was deceiving his long-time friends. Except that what he said he saw was impossible. Jarrad was already down in the vault by that time last Friday night. Where had her other suspects been during those critical five minutes?

She stretched. "Too bad we can't watch the DVD out here. It seems a shame to take the dogs home just so we can sit ten feet closer to the TV. But I'm eager to see how Dee looked on film."

Terry held out his hand for her plate. "They'll be fine on the deck if we only close the screens. And they'll come back if Jan calls them. They like her much better than me. Probably because she makes a fuss when she photographs them. The big sucks lap up the attention like rock stars." Jan was making a fuss now, smooshing their ears and murmuring a mix of baby talk and growls that they seemed to understand and appreciate. When she got up, they followed her to the door, stood hopefully for a minute, then settled down outside with heavy sighs. Everyone else had to step over them. At least this time they didn't growl at Lacey when she passed. She sighed as heavily as they had before she followed the other humans indoors.

Terry set up the DVD and Rob brought more beers and snacks: two kinds of chips and dip, peanuts, and Smarties. "Watch out for these chips in the blue bowl," he told her. "They're salt free, trans-fat free, organic imposters. Jan's fave."

Jan was already on the couch, half-draped in an afghan. The men did all the table clearing and guest-attendance chores as if nothing was out of the ordinary. Maybe it wasn't, for them. How could a woman be as sick as Terry said, and yet look so normal?

The TV screen woke up. The show was on. But Lacey's hope of isolating the exact time when Jarrad had disappeared was doomed. The gala disc was not the cheesy production she had half expected. In this digital age, when any festivity might be captured by amateurs armed with cellphones, the professionals had to provide something glossier than mere reality. The gala disc held only the most flattering footage of the board ladies, soft-focused the gnarled tycoons and aging media people, and panned panoramically to emphasize the spaciousness of the building. It was also not chronological. Instead, the scene bounced between the actual event and earlier footage of the building at various stages of construction, with sound bites from board members interspersed between group moments at the gala. Rob appeared briefly to discuss the significance of the biggest painting in the gallery, the Joe Cadot. He made sure to mention the oil baron who had loaned it by name. Good schmooze. Interspersed in the mix were praises sung for the facility by the provincial minister of culture and a rep from the RM of Rockyview, whose comments were tinged with faint *damn*s that the new cultural showpiece was not in Springbank.

Rob remarked, "He's grumpy that they'll have to bus Springbank kids down here once in a while, instead of Bragg Creek always sending their kids out."

When not trained on the stage, the cameras roved the audience to mark noteworthy faces. It was impossible to figure out the order or time of performances, much less where every suspect was when. As it wound toward the end, Lacey knew pretty much what she had known before: that Jarrad and Camille were on stage about fifteen minutes before he went into the vault. He was the same height as Camille, give or take a centimetre, but did that matter anymore?

Rob said, with obvious satisfaction, "See, I told you Camille's chew toy could act. Better than the other guy, by far. He could have a second career in theatre." This time it was clear Rob wasn't being sarcastic. He truly believed that.

Terry snorted. "I've seen better acting by a broken broomstick."

"Must be love if you think he was even mediocre," said Jan.

"You guys are watching too much reality TV. He was the star of the evening. That bit from Thomas Mann was totally inspired."

Terry laughed. "Jarrad didn't do the Mann monologue, doofus. That was the pro actor from Calgary."

"That was Camille's main squeeze, honey. I should know. They were groping each other in dark corners all week long. Hell, Jan, you're the one who told me his name."

"I said we all thought Camille was way too hands-on with Jarrad."

"Well, she was all hands with this guy. You also said, just last week if I recall, that Jarrad was back and acting in the gala with her. Nobody introduced me to him. I just assumed."

Amid exclamations from the Brenners, Lacey leaned forward. "You lived here all last winter and never met him, even though he was making waves over killing Dee's dog and her smashing his windshield?"

"Divine Dee beat up his car," Rob mused. "I still have trouble with that picture. Anyway, I wasn't moving in those exalted circles. I never got invited to a fabulous Wyman party until Jan and Terry dragged me along last weekend. Then I ended up leaving early to help tote that old guy back to his closet." Rob set down his beer with a thump. "Oh my god, I told the Mountie Jarrad was the guy bonking Camille in the dressing room. Lacey, are they going to use thumbscrews on me if I tell them I was mistaken?"

"I think you'll find they already knew. What exactly did they ask you? And what exactly did you tell them?"

"They asked when was the last time I saw Jarrad on the night of the gala, which I thought was odd because he was seen on the security video at least three times after that. I said I'd seen him with Camille in the dressing room when her husband was about to be hauled away in an ambulance. They asked if I was sure it was Jarrad, and I said, 'I didn't see his face, just his back, but it was the same guy she was rehearsing with all week.' Oh, you mean they already knew it was the other guy? But how?"

"Because Jarrad was already in the vault by then."

"What?" came from three mouths simultaneously.

Lacey held up her hand. "Whoa! Yes, Jarrad was in the vault before we put Mick in the ambulance. I checked the elevator logs myself. Jarrad went down there at ten twenty-seven p.m., according to the computer printout. My best guess is it was during the Mann monologue, but I can't be sure. What I need to know from you, Rob, and you, Terry, is where everybody else was for, say, ten minutes either side of that time."

"Everybody? Can you narrow it down?" Terry, the voice of calm.

"For the sake of argument, let's say Camille, Jarrad, the pro actor, and the chihuahuas — sorry, I mean Camille's pals from the board. Oh, and any audience members who came backstage before the final curtain."

She didn't want to say Jake's name, lest loyalties be conflicted and information withheld. If they brought him up unasked, that would be a different story.

Rob bounced upright. "Are we helping you solve the crime? Sweet! Cue up the DVD, Terry. Take us to Jarrad's final bow and I'll walk you through the backstage action."

Terry ran back the DVD while giving a succinct account from his own vantage point. "Dee left us during the Tristan and Isolde bit to get ready for the presentation. Jake left his box a minute or so later, but I'm pretty sure the rest of the hockey contingent stayed put. They were talking during the monologue and I glared at them a couple of times. Jake came back barely before the presentation, when Camille escorted him down, but I don't know where she was between leaving the stage and appearing in Jake's box. From my chair I could see the other board ladies clustered in the wings, but whether they were all there all the time I can't say. Rob?"

"I think they were. But you're confusing me. I know, I'll draw you a plan of the stage." He bustled around gathering paper and felt pens. "Now, here's the stage, audience out this way, and the wings. These squiggly lines are the standing curtains. This ladder-y thing is the stairs down to the dressing rooms."

Jan was picking out Smarties from the bowl. "We'll make the yellow ones the Chihuahuas. That's such a great name for them, Lacey. I'm going to laugh every time I see them. Twyla, Tami, Chareen, and Tiffany. Camille can be orange, to stand out from them. Jarrad red, the actor blue. Who else?"

Rob put on a pout clearly lifted from the vaultmaster. "I want to be blue."

"Fine. He can be brown," said Jan. "Who else?"

"Wait a sec. Let me get organized." Rob spread the designated candies around. "Camille and Jarrad behind the curtain, actor dude in front, the board babes here, me there. Jake can be green, up there in his box. We're missing Dee."

Jan selected another Smartie. "Dee can be pink. She'd hate it, but pink is a good people colour. Where was she during the monologue?"

"Backstage," said Rob. "Rather, she came up the stairs during Camille's onstage emoting but didn't stay. That scene ran a bit long because of young Jarrad's long pauses while he tried to remember his lines. I can't believe I didn't realize he wasn't the same guy."

"When she didn't stay," Lacey asked, "where did she go?"

Rob moved the pink Smartie. "Back down these stairs to the dressing rooms."

"Okay, the skit is over and the monologue on. Camille and Jarrad are offstage. Where do they go?" But at the end of moving about a lot of candy on Rob's little chart, they weren't much further ahead.

Lacey summed up. "So four people visited the dressing rooms during the monologue — Dee, Jake, Jarrad, and the MC."

Jan interrupted. "Wait. Jake was down there?"

"Yes. Dee ran into him when she was touching up her face, and had to hustle him upstairs to his box before the plaque presentation. Camille would have passed through not long after, catching up to Jake so she could be on his arm going down to the stage."

"Arm decoration is her life's ambition," Jan muttered.

Lacey ignored the sneer. "That timing seems too tight for any of them. Does anybody know of a connection between Jarrad and the MC? Maybe he's a hockey announcer or sports journalist?"

Her witness pool looked blankly at one another.

Rob shrugged. "As far as I recall, we wanted a media personality and Dee's boss suggested his friend. None of us met him before that week."

Jan ate the orange Smartie with a snap of her teeth. "Nothing useful here, unless you think Dee did it, which I don't. Jarrad could have reached the elevator via the classroom corridor or through the clay room's locker corridor. Or he could have met up with someone anywhere on that level and gone with them."

Rob nodded. "The school kids and teachers were gone. Everyone else who wasn't needed on stage would be in one of three places: watching the finale, warming up the bar, or out for a smoke."

"One person must have been unaccounted for." Lacey ate a handful of Smarties from the bowl while she worked out the possibilities. Jake had gone downstairs around the critical time. If Camille's evening bag was in the dressing room then, he could have taken her key card. Dee might have seen him with it, or with Jarrad. She might have been run over to silence her before people started asking questions about those critical few minutes downstairs. Car keys? If Jarrad's had been in his pocket, Jake had had all of Saturday to drop by the

Hardy house and look for a spare set. He could also have slipped the card back into Camille's purse, either then or at his Finals party. If he knew Dee was awake and able to answer questions …

She jumped up. "I've got to call the hospital."

Terry pointed her to the hall. "Number two on the speed dial. We check daily, for all the good it does."

Although Lacey got through to Dee's ward rapidly, the nurse on duty would not forward the call to the room. "It's after ten," she said severely. "Mrs. Phillips is down for the night. Call again in the morning."

"Is the security guard still in the corridor?"

"Yes."

"Good. She needs protection." Tonight maybe more than ever. "Please make sure the guard doesn't fall asleep."

The nurse sniffed.

Back in the living room, Rob and Jan had come up with a plan to cement people's whereabouts. "We know the guy who made the DVD," Jan explained. "If he kept the raw footage of the gala, it will have time-stamps. I'll ask for a password to his secure editing website, where I can look at the uncut versions. By this time tomorrow we ought to be able to confirm who was on stage at what exact minute, and maybe spot anyone else out of their seat at the critical moment. Like, for example, Jarrad's ex-boyfriend. Sorry, Rob, but you know a spurned lover is bound to be suspected."

Lacey walked home an hour later with Rob to "protect her" while Terry drove Jan and the dogs. Rob offered to come in and check for burglars under the beds. From any other man it would be the prelude to a pass. She invited him in for tea, just for a few minutes more of company.

"Should I invite Jan and Terry in, too?" she asked.

"Nah. They could use an hour without me. Pretty soon I'll be out of excuses to stay up there keeping Jan company. I hope you'll visit her once in a while, like Dee used to. She's stuck at home so much, and she gets a bit depressed sometimes." He went out to send the Brenners home.

Lacey put the kettle on. When he came back, she asked, "Is Jan really so ill that she can't reliably walk to Dee's and back again? She's seemed so, well, stable the last few times I've seen her."

"In her own low-chem house, staying warm and resting a lot, she does pretty good. Sunny days are better than cloudy ones and summers are easier than winters. When it's colder, her body can't create enough energy to both stay warm and run her immune system. Not to mention her brain. For weeks on end, she can barely hold a coherent conversation. Basically, from November through March, Terry rolls her up in a blanket on the couch and brings her soup at intervals. She goes nowhere and sees nobody. Some life, huh?"

"How long has she been like this?"

"Getting on for five years now, with a worse spell in the middle. And before you ask, no, there's nothing the doctors can do. They don't know what caused it and they can't cure it. They can't really fix the symptoms, either, just medicate people enough that they no longer feel the grief at all the things they've lost. I've gotta tell you, I thought Terry might leave her when he realized the full scope. It wasn't the money she was no longer earning, or even that their great travel plans evaporated. It was giving up hope of having kids. Nobody knows if her illness is genetic, or how her body would cope with being pregnant. If she ended up needing full-time care, Terry would be on his own, with a newborn and a drastically sick wife to look after. So they can't risk it. They just hope there'll be a cure, or at least a reliable treatment, before she's too old. He watches Saturday morning cartoons faithfully on his own, and I think it's his way of keeping the torch alive for the kids that might someday come. A little ritual of hope, if you like."

"Rob, you're a very perceptive man."

He blushed. "What I am is an old gossip. I shouldn't talk about my dearest friends' innermost concerns. I'm just worried. This year has been hard on Jan, with the museum opening and all. It should have been her job, you know. Mine, I mean."

"Terry told me. He said it's killing her trying to pretend it doesn't matter, or words to that effect."

"He did? I wasn't sure he really got that. It was one thing for her to lie there looking out her window all day when all the arts jobs were far away in Calgary. Now there's a whole gallery and museum and weekly arts events right under her windows. It's like looking through the glass at a world you're no longer allowed to enter and yet can't avoid seeing."

"I know what that feels like," said Lacey. "From the moment of Dee's accident, I've been outside the glass myself, watching the RCMP work the hit and run and the vault. A month ago I was handling those kinds of incidents. I dealt with road rage results between lunch and coffee. If I chased down a subject, I had an army at my back. Now I'm on the outside, working alone, can't even get a fingerprint checked on my own. My only friend here is thirty miles away in a hospital bed while her damned dogs won't give me the time of day. I can't find out who hurt her, or keep my former co-workers from harassing her in her hospital bed. I'm useless when she needs me most." Sobs welled in her throat. She forced them down. She couldn't cry in front of someone for the second time in two days. That was just weak. "I'll manage. It's just a lot of adjustment."

Rob looked at her with sympathy. "Sure it is. You and Jan have that in common; you're both good at adjusting. You want a pot of tea, or bags in mugs?"

CHAPTER THIRTY-EIGHT

On Sunday morning, Lacey cleared away their teacups, reflecting on her unusual moment of weakness with Rob. He was easy to talk to, utterly non-judgmental. Except about Camille Hardy, but then, denigrating Camille was a communal pastime. Anyway, he was right that she and Jan both had glass-wall syndrome in common. Lacey stared at the cops the way Jan hungrily watched the museum. She must find out who had placed that bug, though. Dee's safety was her responsibility, and this house was, too — not just for this crisis, but until Dee could manage alone. So she might as well start looking after things around here, starting with clearing Dee's postbox, which was probably overflowing by now. Where was the key?

Dee's purse still sat on the counter by the sink. Lacey opened it, feeling as guilty as if she were invading a private domain. There'd been no need before; the spare car keys lived on a hook by the back door. Like many private spaces, Dee's purse was a mess. She pawed through it and finally shook the shambles out onto the counter. No keys. She scanned tables and shelves near all the doors, ransacked the pockets of any coats or sweaters Dee might have worn lately, and still no keys. A shiver ran over her scalp. Somebody could have lifted the keys. It would explain the lack of forced entry when the laptop was stolen, and maybe the clothing littering Dee's bedroom. Someone could have entered the house while she was sleeping.

Nonsense. Dee had probably had the keys with her last weekend when she was hit. They'd be at the hospital, or the police had them. No need to panic.

The phone rang, sending her hot-wired nerves through the roof. A month off the job and she was freaking out like a civilian. She picked up the handset, recognized Tom's home number.

"Morning, McCrae. You sound buzzed. Skip your run this morning?"

"Haven't got out the door yet. How was the lake?"

Tom summarized his day with the boys before asking, "What's up with this recorder? More prints to check against?"

"Nope. Dee says there won't be a criminal case. I can listen to the recorded notes any time and then the matter is closed."

"*Sheesh.* After all that. She could have left you a note last week and saved us the trouble. She say who put it there? Someone should throw some payback at that guy."

"She won't confirm, but I think it's Jake Wyman, who got the recorder from Wayne. I haven't the slightest idea why he would do this, but a neighbour warned me he's ruthless beneath that good-ole-boy folksiness. And hockey rumour has it that he could kill a player's career if he got pissed off. I wish I knew if either of the investigations — into Dee or into Jarrad — looked at Wyman."

"If I hear anything, I'll let you know."

"Will you also let me know if Dee's a suspect in Jarrad's death? The cops leaned on her until she lawyered up on them."

"I'll check. You keep your hair on."

"I haven't done anything."

"Yeah, but I know you."

"What do you know about the vault death?"

"Crushed chest. He didn't live long. Is that the same spot you went in last week?"

"Nearly."

"Could have been you."

"Uh-huh."

Tom paused. "Then you won't want to know what could have happened to you."

"I have a fair idea already. Go ahead."

"Okay, you asked. He knew it was coming, tried to push back. Ripped ligaments, arms cracked, and the back end of that rack mashed his wrist bones into his chest wall. Dead in seconds."

"God." Lacey shuddered. Not a thing anyone could have done, either, once the rack started rolling. "Still could be an accident," she said, "unless someone out in the main vault knew how to cut the power rather than mess around with the control pad and was as fast as Wayne doing it."

"You think accident, not homicide?" Tom asked.

"Dunno. Every trail leads somewhere that doesn't make sense. You hear anything else, I want it, okay?"

"Sure. Can I drop this recorder with Dee? We're off to a ball game soon, but Marie is feeling responsible for her only patient, so we have to stop in there."

"Thanks, Tom. I don't know how I'll ever return all these favours."

"You've had my back before, and you will again. Be safe, McCrae."

Lacey changed her Tweety Bird pants for jogging shorts, stretched out her legs, and set off uphill along the trail. It all came back to Jake: the recorder, the visit to the theatre basement at the time Jarrad died, the argument with Dee on Saturday, maybe the hit and run on Sunday. Mick had said he'd seen Jake leaving Dee's drive as he came up. Jake might have taken the house keys while Lacey was snoozing out back. He had opportunities for all the crimes, as far as she knew. He wasn't even half a head taller than Camille, about right for the hatted man on those security stills. But although he seemed vigorous for his age, was he strong enough to push that car into the river? How could she go about investigating a man as powerful as Jake Wyman?

When she reached the back road, she paused a moment by Duke's memorial. Beside Eddie's photo, someone had tacked up a baggie with a bone-shaped dog biscuit. A nice thought, but it wouldn't survive the first passing squirrel. She jogged on, keeping an eye out for cars and for Dee's missing bike, although it, too, had likely been tossed into the river.

When she reached the highway, the brown, swirling water was several feet farther down the bank. Some
gravel bars were almost breaking the surface midstream.
The bike might be cast up far along the rocky riverbed,
mangled beyond recognition, and never be linked to
a hit and run way out here. But the lower water level
eased her mind. Although she left the riverside trail to
less traumatized people, she was able to jog along the
road shoulder all the way to the museum without al-
lowing the mental loop of Dan's body slam to take hold.
Then it was a fast uphill to Dee's, a quick shower made
tense by those missing keys, and a bagel to eat in the car.
Hospital visiting hours would begin in half an hour and
she really, really wanted to hear that recording.

CHAPTER THIRTY-NINE

Dee jogged in place on a patch of ice-free gravel, her breath misting the blue evening air. Duke lumbered along, far behind as usual, while Beau and Boney romped ahead, leaping over the snowbanks on either side of the trail with effortless glee. She wasn't running fast enough to keep warm in her thin jogging clothes because she kept pausing to let Duke catch up. Maybe it hadn't been a great idea to take all three dogs out tonight.

Still, it felt good to be out among the trees for the first time in a week, surrounded by sleeping winter woodland instead of office walls and laptop screens. Now that the East Village development was nailed down, she could truly take a weekend off. Maybe by Monday the staff would have forgotten about Neil's latest incursion into the office. Trust him to pick the day of her biggest victory to be smarming through the secretaries while her back was turned. She'd walked in from a billion-dollar lunch, on the pinnacle of professional success, to be greeted by sideways glances, dropped conversations, and that damned single rose on her own assistant's desk. All unmistakable signs of Neil, all reminders — in the midst of triumph — of her biggest error in judgment. She picked up the pace, running herself clear of the miasma that was Neil's legacy.

When they could see the open ground by the road, the younger dogs happily yipped and slithered down the trail. Dee jogged on the spot, waiting for Duke, watching Boney and Beau romp along the road allowance below, their gangly legs easily leaping the drifts and the smallest spruces, their rusty setter's tails flying. The last late rays of sunlight blipped behind the peaks and were gone, leaving the vale in blue winter shadow.

She turned at a yelp from behind. Duke, his shaggy golden head hanging, was slumped with one front paw sticking out at an awkward angle. "Oh, poor old boy. Did you slip?" She crouched beside him and ran cold fingers over his foreleg. Beyond a ball of ice in the pad, there seemed nothing wrong. She helped him to his feet and held his collar as they navigated the rest of the slope together.

On the road below, a black Escalade kicked up gravel in passing. Some NHL hotshot extending his All-Star break, no doubt. After hockey season the peaceful foothills around Bragg Creek would be overrun with them, all driving too fast between the golf course and the beds of their latest conquests. Best to enjoy the peace while she had it.

As she left the woodland trail for the gravel shoulder of the road, a chill breeze gnawed through her lightweight clothes. The first stars appeared in the dark-blue eastern sky. Yesterday's chinook had melted the road clear, but up against the trees, the snow lay deep, dirty, and uneven, its purity long since lost to jagged chunks cast up by passing plows. Leftover Christmas lights flickered to life in glades where houses interrupted the forest. Somewhere a car door slammed, the sound alien in the still wilderness.

Under the spruces, the shadows were deep enough to hide anything. No bears in January, but elk or the bigger wildcats were common out here year round, and neither appreciated her dogs. With all three dogs trotting to heel, she hoped she looked big enough to avoid a confrontation. She sped up, anxious to get down to the highway with its lights and traffic. So much for enjoying the peace.

A motor raced. She glanced back. The beams burst onto her face as the vehicle slewed out from a side road. The back end swung wide. Gravel sprayed. The driver overcorrected into a skid the other way. Her way.

She scrambled up the snowbank, yelling for the dogs. Her foot came down on an ice chunk and she fell hard, rolling down the far side into the ditch. Boney and Beau landed beside her in a shower of snow. The car slung more gravel, its reflected headlights vanishing along the ranked trees. Then it was gone, chased by her yell of "Asshole!"

Beau whimpered, licking her face. She tugged his ear reassuringly and pushed up to her knees. "All right, I'm getting up."

The moment of pain. The wind rose, drawing an icy tang down from the high country. The chinook was passing. The temperature could plunge as fast as it had risen. She shivered. Boney pressed against her, blocking some of the breeze. From the road, Beau whined, his shoulders dark above the snowbank. But of Duke there was no sign.

"Duke? Where are you, boy?" The crawl across the snow, following Boney's agitated cries. Duke lay on his side across a tire rut. His fur was coated with dust and gravel, but there was no visible blood. He raised his head a tiny bit and tried to lick her hand.

She was cold, so cold, huddled in the velvet-grey dusk with the soft fur of dogs pressed against her arms. The wind whined down the road from the high peaks. The darkness deepened and the silence spread around them. She wavered between an invading fear of freezing to death and a creeping, uncaring drowsiness.

Someone called her name. A familiar voice. The snow was gone. Not cold. Had she gone beyond feeling at last? Her legs wouldn't move, nor her left arm, either. Dogs lying on her. But the dogs didn't sleep in the house. She tried her right hand and felt her fingers flex. Her wrist moved. A hand touched hers.

"Dee-Dee? Can you hear me?"

A strange echo. No more forest sounds. The smell was wrong, too. Chemical. She was lying on her back, on something soft. Lying tight over her body were the dogs or … blankets?

"Dee? Dee-Dee?"

The voice. The hospital. The bug. That voice.

Outraged, she opened her eyes. A familiar face loomed over her, too close. A pillow was clutched in his raised hand. She screamed.

CHAPTER FORTY

Highway 8 was down to one lane where the concrete water-diversion barriers in the right-hand ditch were being removed. Thanks to the heavy weekend traffic, Lacey sat unmoving in the hot car for twenty minutes. Visiting hours were well underway before she reached the hospital. On the top floor, she was surprised to see the security guard missing from his chair. She hurried toward Dee's room. A nurse was coming out. Beyond her, Dee lay in the bed, eyes closed.

"Where's the guard? What's going on?"

"Shh," said the nurse. "She woke up screaming. Trauma patients often have nightmares. I just got her settled down."

Dee's right hand waved. "I'm awake," she croaked.

"All right. Go in. But don't upset her."

Lacey pulled a chair up to the bedside and took Dee's hand. "Bad day?"

"Did you find me a lawyer? The police may be back any time."

"I'm not as concerned about that as I was. Camille Hardy has been asked the same questions. She was rather thrilled about it, actually."

"She's not smart enough to be scared," said Dee weakly. "Or maybe it was my imagination. Now I've made myself look suspicious by refusing to answer."

"You did what I told you to," Lacey assured her. "Without a cast-iron alibi for those five minutes, you're better off shutting up. Anyway, we're trying to find anyone else who was down there when you were. There might be someone visible on the gala video footage who can clear you. Or who saw Jarrad after he went downstairs."

"I only saw Jake." A tear rolled from the corner of Dee's eye and trailed down to her ear. "He's here somewhere. You can ask him yourself."

"Here? When? Why?"

"He woke me up."

"You woke up screaming. Are you afraid of him? Where is he now?"

"He's gone somewhere with the guard. He'll be back."

"Are you sure that's a good idea?"

"It's over now," Dee said. Afraid of disturbing her by pressing that question, Lacey asked about the house keys instead. Dee turned her head on the pillow. "They should be in my purse. I take a bracelet for jogging with just the kitchen door key."

That key was in the bedside drawer two feet away. The main key ring, however, was not in the purse. It was gone. It would not do to tell Dee that today, though.

"I probably just missed them. I was in a hurry. Is there another postbox key, just in case?"

"Main drawer in my office decan—" An odd look crossed Dee's face. "Dog … the table thing in my office. Now, are you ready to hear this recording? I can't comment on anything that might lead to a client being identified, so you'll have to draw your own conclusions."

"Sounds like you want me to know who set this up, but your legalistic scruples won't let you tell me. Okay, I'll listen."

Hearing Jake's voice was anticlimactic. "Testing. Testing." The date and time followed: ten after six on gala night. The dogs began barking at a slight distance, then abruptly quieted.

"How'd he make them shut up?" Lacey asked.

"Ultrasonic whistle," Dee whispered. "I should have realized. He trained them with it for running with the horse. Horses can't hear it, or don't care."

Hands fumbled with the recorder. The dogs started up again. Boot heels thumped. A car motor started, then faded. Mere minutes later, Jake had walked into the museum gala to greet Dee with that folksy cowboy charm. Lacey unclenched her jaw with an effort. The two-faced skunk. Did he have the faintest idea how much terror Dee had been through because of him?

More footsteps, a clutter of them, came too soon for the voice-activated recorder to shut itself off. Chair legs scraped, barely audible above the setters' outraged howls. That would be Jarrad moving the chair, when he inadvertently unplugged the motion-sensor cord. This action made sense to Lacey at last: he'd shifted Mick out of sight of the dogs, in hopes they'd stop barking. And, after another half minute or so, they did.

"That better?" Jarrad asked.

"Yeah." Mick Hardy's voice, breathless and strained, recorded with perfect clarity. He'd have been almost directly under the recorder at that moment. "Just need to sit."

"You're sure?" After a pause, "Was that Mr. Wyman leaving?"

"Probably. He's got Dee Phillips in his sights."

"Better him than me. You doing okay?"

"Just need a rest after that uphill."

"I'll go get my car and drive you down."

"No, wait, Jarrad … about this idea of yours. Why do you have to do it right now?"

"I just want it finished, behind me."

Lacey could picture the sulky young hockey player, his stubborn mouth and inner tension. This was mere hours before he died. What had he wanted to finish?

Jarrad said, "You know I love you, Mick. You and Camille are my family. I'd never want to pull a dance on you. But I need to figure out —"

"Is that young Fiske's voice?"

Lacey pushed the stop button. Jake stood in the doorway, staring at the slim little recorder. She reached for the call button pinned to Dee's bed.

"No need for that, little lady. I'm not here to hurt anybody. I was trying to put a pillow under her head when she screamed and they all came running." One gnarled hand waved in the direction of the nursing station, reminding Lacey of his effortless power over those reporters. Did he have that power here, too? Was he a real threat to Dee? He didn't look it, standing with his hat in his hand, the very picture of an old-time cowboy respectfully addressing the schoolmarm, a refugee from *Gunsmoke*. "I'm only here to see if Dee-Dee's ready to accept my apology."

"Don't call me Dee-Dee."

"Yes'm."

"I haven't decided if I can afford to forgive you. Tell Lacey about it; then we'll talk."

"Can I sit down first? These old bones …"

Dee flapped her hand. He sat. Lacey kept her finger at the call button. If he tried anything, she'd both push it and yell for the security guard. Then she'd clock him a good one.

"Tell me what?"

"I put that recorder on her office window."

"I gathered as much."

"Started a few months back." Jake's shoulders and jaw firmed up, like Lacey had seen in witnesses about to reluctantly tell an unpleasant truth. "It wasn't set loud enough at first, only went on when the dogs barked. I can listen to a dog bark any day, but I needed to hear her voice when she was on the phone. So I kept sneaking over to check it and adjust the volume. I went at night most times because that little Jannie, she's up there in her sunroom watching over the neighbourhood all day. I never thought about Dee hearing me and being scared. That's the honest truth, Miss McCrae."

"You admit you placed that device to record confidential telephone calls between Dee and her clients? Have you ever heard of unlawful intercepts, Mr. Wyman?"

Jake turned his battered hat carefully in his hands. "I know it was wrong. But I don't need her real estate tips.

That's not why I did it. She knows that." Lacey looked at Dee, who nodded, her head-gauze rustling over the pillow.

"Go on."

"It isn't enough that I told you, honey? Do I have to tell her, too?"

"Everything." Dee looked half dead lying bandaged in that bed, her face yellow from aging bruises, but hers was the voice of a woman who could take a five iron to a windshield. "Or kiss your ass goodbye."

"Honey …"

"Tell her or tell the Law Society."

He half-smiled at Lacey. "Never piss off a lawyer. They're about as forgiving as a rattlesnake in a corner." He set the hat down on the bed and opened his hands. "I meant no harm to anyone. I bugged Dee's office window hoping to hear her talking to my ex-wife. That woman would never forgive me if I put detectives on her trail, so I was being sneaky. When I found her, I could say I overheard Dee on the phone to her. That wouldn't have been a lie."

"You went to all this trouble, broke who knows how many laws, and drove Dee to the brink of a nervous breakdown to track down a woman who left you?" Domestic violence: the most fatal time for a woman is in the year after she leaves her abuser. Jake didn't look like a batterer, but then, so many of them didn't. He was used to having unchallenged power, and psychological abuse didn't leave visible signs. A lot of money had vanished in his divorce; that had to be a factor, too. Would he get it back if his ex-wife died? All questions that would bear further investigation if he didn't have satisfactory answers. Lacey stood up. "What were you going to do when you found her?"

"No harm, I said, and that's what I meant. I never laid a mean hand on that woman. She was a nice little thing, easy to have around. I was comfortable with her." He set his hands on his knees. "I'm getting old, Miss McCrae. I don't like change as much as I used to. If she'd told me she wasn't happy, we could have arranged something. But she up and went one day, and left all the talking to the lawyers. I just wanted to hear her voice. I guess I let myself get carried away. There's no fool like an old fool."

The man who had everything was too ashamed to hire private detectives to find his errant wife? Dee clearly believed his story, but then Dee didn't know about the missing keys or those missing few minutes downstairs at the gala. And yet … all those years of being lied to on the job had left Lacey with a pretty good bullshit detector, and this story, improbable as it was, didn't set off the alarms. He believed what he was saying, and he was, to say the very least, deeply ashamed he had to admit his motive at all.

Dee was whiter than the sheets, tears trailing from beneath her closed eyelids, but her voice was calm. "Thank you, Jake. You go now and leave me to talk to Lacey."

"Yes'm. Can I come back tomorrow? I've got some ideas about your house."

"I'll let you know in the morning."

"Wait," said Lacey. "Mr. Wyman, when you went downstairs during the gala, just before Dee's speech, did you see anyone else down there? Or hear anyone?"

"Not that I recall. I went to the men's room and then looked for Dee."

"Neither of you saw Rob downstairs during that time?"

Dee's bandages slid as her head waved from side to side. "He was backstage when I went up. Both times."

Jake said, "Never saw him down there. You don't suspect young Rob, do you? He's a nice fella."

"Just crossing him off."

Jake left. Lacey watched him until he got into the elevator, then she came back and sat on Dee's bed, careful not to jostle her casted leg.

"That story sounds fantastic, and I don't mean great. Not the bugging part, but the reason for it."

"Not if you knew him. He's an utter sap over women. He convinced himself that if he played the right cards, Miss Hockey Chippy — who was well known for entertaining the visiting players behind his back — would come home and cuddle up to him like she used to. He can't accept that she stayed exactly three days past the five-year mark that turned her miniscule pre-nup into a generous life annuity. He was a job and she held on long enough for the retirement package. Barely. But he'd hate for any other man to know that. Especially in Calgary, where his name makes ruthless tycoons tremble. So, no private investigators. He just wouldn't."

"Why are you managing her property if you dislike her so much?"

"No lawyer can afford to take only the clients they like. I needed the extra income to get my second —" she made several tries at *mortgage* before settling for *loan* "— to buy Neil out. In hindsight, selling up would have been simpler, but I didn't want to move the dogs back to the city. God, what a mess."

"You're tired. You sleep. I'll come back later." After she had made a start on the camera wiring, so she had something to report to Wayne tomorrow. She'd have to find out more about Jake, too, and about his dealings with Jarrad. Whatever Dee believed about his motives for the bugging, he was still the most viable suspect in Jarrad's death. "Meanwhile, don't talk to the police if they come. They can't haul you down to the station from your hospital bed."

Dee put out her hand. "Thanks for everything. If you hadn't been here when all this fell on me, I don't know what I'd have done."

CHAPTER FORTY-ONE

When Jan could no longer tolerate staring at raw video on her laptop screen, she rolled off the couch, stretched, and headed out to the deck to look at birds instead. The only alibi times she could confirm were Dee and Jake's departures from their respective boxes, and those were essentially non-alibis, putting each of them downstairs very close to when Jarrad had been taken to the vault. Jarrad's ex-boyfriend, whose photo she had found online as soon as Rob had coughed up his last name, had stayed in Jake's box throughout and left with the crowd at the end. Who knew what the cluttered footage from the third roving camera would bring to light? Examining it would require more mental and visual focus than she could summon right now.

The magic of the June day wasn't clearing her head, either. She was restless, even outdoors, jumping at sudden noises, twitchy fingers jerking her zoom lens past any nest or blossom she tried to focus on. She knew why: too much living like a normal person. Too many

visitors, too much conversation, too much rowdy playing with the lonely dogs, plus the mental exertion of
working out alibis. Every one of those activities was
interesting and welcome on its own, but cumulatively
they destabilized her delicate balance between making
energy and using it up. She would need to be firm with
herself after today, stay home and stay quiet until at
least next Wednesday.

She was zooming in on that grosbeak's nest near Dee's
house when an odd gleam struck her lens. A vehicle was
parked halfway up the driveway, invisible in the trees
except where a trace of sunlight touched it. If that was a
legitimate visitor, why didn't they drive up to the house?

She focused in her camera and moved it slowly over
the porch and windows. Everything looked normal,
but intermittent barks floated in on the fluky southeast
breeze. The dogs were stirred up. Had the laptop thief
returned, or was it merely walkers on the woodland trail?
Boney and Beau didn't take kindly to other dogs trotting
past while they were stuck in their pen. They preferred to
spend their weekend days on the deck, where they could
amble out to the trail to greet their pals or warn pushy
new dogs off their territory. She moved the viewfinder
on down the hill, looking for dogs or people, but the trail
disappeared behind the next house without a sign of
movement except for tree branches shifting in the wind.

Farther downhill, Camille's Bimmer sat in her driveway with its top folded away. Serve the woman right to
have her car fill up with water if those wisps of cloud
creeping past the mountain peaks boiled up into a violent
summer storm. Or would it? Camille might be weeping

in private, but more likely the heartless slut had moved on from Jarrad's death without a second thought and was touching up her nails while her husband did the grieving. How much was Camille acting a role, and how much was she really not upset? She had not, after all, been groping Jarrad in the week before his death. She'd thrown him over for the actor. Did it all come down to a lovers' tiff?

The phone rang. Jan abandoned the tripod, hurried indoors, and with the phone in her hand, realized that answering it was another sign she was way too far from her resting mode. Normally she would save her steps and let the answering machine get it, only pick up if the message sounded urgent. But she was here now. She pushed the talk button.

"Hi there, Jannie. You see any sign of my surveyors down at Dee-Dee's? They were supposed to quote me for the outside ramps yesterday." Ah, that explained the vehicle. Only Jake could command surveyors to work on a beautiful June Sunday. Naturally they wouldn't park by the house, where they'd need to be measuring.

"I think they're down there now."

"Good. I didn't get a chance to ask Dee-Dee about the plans, but she was almost back to her old self this morning. Feisty. I'll spring the ramps on her before we talk elevators. Don't you spoil my surprise if she phones you."

"You're a good friend to her."

"I owe her. If you see those surveyors leaving before I get there, try to flag them down. I'm feeding poor Mick lunch up at my place. He's some cut up about the boy. Needs taking out of himself, and that wife of his won't be any help."

"You're a good friend to him, too, in spite of Camille."

"Hell, Jannie, we all make mistakes over women. Can't hold that against my friends, or I wouldn't have any. Bye, honey."

While she had the phone in her hand, Jan called Lacey to report her morning's footage review. She got voice mail and summarized her few findings while wandering aimlessly about the living room. Out of nowhere, lethargy sloshed over her, oozing her toward the soft couch and her comfy afghan. She resisted, heading out to cover the camera in case of later thunderstorms, and stared vaguely downhill at Dee's drive, where Mick's Buick was just backing out. Mick's car … why would that be important? Something she had been thinking about Camille before the phone rang … but her brain wouldn't make the connection. She watched the sedan go uphill with one person in it. Camille was not, it appeared, invited to lunch.

A door banged open, sending her nerves into overdrive. Only Terry coming into the kitchen for a drink. She listened to his movements, hoping he wouldn't come to check on her. He'd think her jitters were pill jitters. It was past time to stop pacing around and lie down. She surrendered to the couch and the afghan, closed her eyes and tried to calm her breathing. The phone rang again. She forced herself to be still and lay waiting until the phone kicked over to the answering machine.

"I was just wondering," said the caller, over the sounds of highway noise.

"Lacey, I'm here."

"You sound out of breath. Are you okay?"

"Sure, fine," Jan lied. "Are you calling while driving? You'll get a ticket. Or be in an accident."

"I've been taking radio calls while driving for years. It's ingrained now. And a ticket is worth it if you can help me sort something out."

"I'll try. What were you wondering?"

"Only whether you could tell from the raw footage where Camille was. I know Rob thought she was still on stage when Dee came up those backstage stairs. Could she have slipped away without anyone noticing?"

"I can't tell from the video I've seen so far. The chihuahuas were dressed too much alike to for me to be sure she was with them in the wings."

"Did Rob have any reason to pay her whereabouts particular attention?"

"Probably not. She wasn't a threat to his job until later. You know, I've just remembered how he gushed about the Mann monologue. He was probably enraptured by it and not noticing much backstage at all."

"Could be. Not that I'm saying Camille's guilty, just that she's almost the only one left who might have a motive for wanting Jarrad dead."

Through Jan's tired brain wafted that half-forgotten impression of Lacey thinking much more than she was saying. "Almost?"

A deep sigh. A long pause. Then, "Just how smart is Jake Wyman about women?"

"The world's prize chump. The more he likes a woman, me and Dee apparently excepted, the more likely she is to be a traitorous, lying tramp."

"Really? So he might do something incredibly stupid because of a woman?"

"Don't see why he'd change now. The last two wives were utter disasters, yet he never once said an ill word about either of them. I never met his first one. But if you're thinking he helped Camille in some nefarious scheme to do away with Jarrad, you're dead wrong." His loyalties were firmly with Mick. They'd been pals for decades. Mick got him to buy his first team share. All those jerseys, all the colours and logos and ... She realized her mind was drifting and pulled it back. "Camille was his last wife's best buddy. He might reasonably suspect she helped plan the woman's midnight flit. You're either loyal to him and entitled to the same in return, or you're not."

"You'd know better than me. I'd never heard of any of these people two weeks ago. But you can't rule out Camille's being downstairs when Jarrad went into the vault?"

"Not so far. Only one camera left to review, the shoulder-mounted roaming one that was gathering colour and movement at the event. I don't know if it ever went backstage, much less downstairs. Is it important to know right now?" *Please say no.* It was hard enough to keep concentrating on this conversation.

"Not immediately," said Lacey.

Jan let out a sigh of relief. "I need a break, but I'll get back to it later this afternoon, I promise."

"Thanks. I didn't think of asking Dee about Camille, just if she'd seen Jarrad downstairs. Hopefully Camille doesn't take it into her head to visit Dee in the hospital. Until I know what Jarrad meant by 'pulling a dance,' I won't feel easy about that woman."

"Dee would smell a rat if Camille appeared at her bedside bearing flowers. Unless Jake was there to be impressed."

"He's been already today and tired her out. I left her falling sleep."

If Lacey was angling for an invitation to hang out for the afternoon, Jan couldn't give it to her. "I'll let you know when I've anything more on Camille or anyone." She hung up, found an eye mask in the end table drawer, and let herself fade. Sometime later, she realized people were talking in the kitchen. She called out, "Hello?"

Terry came. "Sorry, did we wake you?"

"Not to worry. I got carried away looking at the gala footage and my brain went numb, if that makes any sense."

"Only because I know you. Want some lunch?"

Jan yawned. "Yeah, maybe. Call me when it's ready." Then she drifted off again to the faint clatter of kitchen utensils. When Terry came back with a tray and the aroma of cinnamon French toast, she struggled into a half-sitting position. "Gosh, I really went out of it for a bit there."

"Must have needed it." Terry set the tray on the coffee table next to her laptop. The screen woke up, showing the frame she had paused on. "Find anything interesting?"

"Nope. I was trying to pin down Camille."

"Don't trust my memory?" Rob set down plates and cutlery.

"Just checking. If she offs people, don't you want to know before you get back on her bad side? I mean, you could end up a witness in a nasty divorce case, unless the stress of living with her kills poor Mick." She picked up her dish of digestive supplements and the glass of water Terry had supplied.

"That brings up a good point." Terry loaded up his plate and drizzled maple syrup over everything. "Why would she kill Jarrad? I don't buy the whole woman-scorned thing for a second. Especially since we now know it wasn't him she was screwing last week."

Rob placed a sliver of butter precisely in the centre of his toast. "Maybe that's how she disposes of her leftovers. Poor Jarrad. And poor Mick. Or should I say poor Chris? He's the one suffering alone in silence. I doubt there's another soul alive who cared about Jarrad like he did."

Jan reached for a plate. "Do you think you'll see him again?"

"Not likely. Apart from the sheer bad taste of pursuing a guy over his ex's grave, I've realized that being an intermittent hockey fan isn't enough grounding for involvement with a player. They have their own dialect. Words and phrases that I think mean one thing say something entirely different to them."

"Such as?"

"Well, this line about doing a dance or pulling a dance on somebody. I thought it just meant to fake them out, get around them on the ice. I could see that meaning translating to situations off-ice, couldn't you?"

"Sure. But it doesn't?"

"No. Chris used it a couple of different times in the context of targeting someone or doing them ill. Vague, I know. It was more in the way he said it."

Something was trying to claw through the fog in Jan's brain. Had Lacey talked about a dance? "How, exactly, did he say it?"

"Just, 'I was afraid Jarrad was coming up here to do a dance on somebody.' Stuff like that."

"Faking out Mick over Camille, maybe?" That thought wasn't even denting the cotton balls in her cranium.

"Nope," said Terry. "Camille had moved on by then. Maybe it was Camille he was after, was going to punish her for dumping him after he dumped Chris for her?" The men went on discussing while Jan concentrated on getting food to her mouth. Finishing a single slice took forever. By the time she pushed her plate away, Terry and Rob had demolished the French toast and the case against Camille and were kicking around a plan for launching pumpkins off the deck come Halloween. "But could we hit Dee's porch from here?" Terry asked, and then, "And what would she do to us if we did?"

"You don't want to know." The mention of Dee reminded Jan of Mick's car leaving there earlier. Why was he at Dee's when nobody was home? And what exactly had been on Lacey's mind earlier when she fretted about Camille going to the hospital? She couldn't seriously think Camille would kill Jarrad, run over Dee, ditch the car, steal Dee's laptop, and then go after her in the hospital? It was far too much effort for a woman who didn't walk anywhere she could drive to. Jan swallowed the last of her cold tea to wash down the last bite and wished her head would clear. "Somebody tell me if Camille's Bimmer is still in her driveway."

Rob went out on deck. "Nope. Looks like she's at the museum. Guess I should go down and find out what the hell she's mucking with now. That woman tangos to her own drummer. "

Tango music pulsed in Jan's brain. For sure Lacey had said "dance" earlier, on the phone. Not tango, but dancing? Oh, curse this flaky memory. Jan lay back and put both feet up on the back of the couch, hoping the rush of blood to her head would access that half-formed thought. According to Chris, via Rob, Jarrad was pulling a dance on somebody. What did hockey and dancing have in common? Something was crawling persistently through her mind, but it couldn't break through to the surface where she could see it. She couldn't finish the videos in this state of exhaustion, either. She spoke out loud before her sluggish brain could stop the signal to her tongue. "I need a magic pill."

Terry looked up. "No! You're half dead already, and you haven't recovered from the last time."

"Please, Terry. I only need half. Or a quarter." He glared at her. Should she insist? Was this dance thing really important enough to start a squabble with the husband who did everything he could to make her life bearable? She subsided on the couch, eyes closed, trying to relax and let the urgent information rise naturally up her train of thought. But it didn't. Her mind wandered, drifted, from one image, one half-formed thought, to another. Vaguely, she was aware of Terry and Rob resuming their conversation about pumpkins flying off the deck. Like the dancing pumpkins in a Halloween cartoon. What cartoon? Dancing ... dancing with

Terry at somebody's wedding. A tango with Rob at the fine arts faculty's annual masquerade. An Ice Capades tango on skates. Hockey. Hockey players don't dance. The Calgary Hitmen with ice dancers? Something was important about that. What? It skimmed tantalizingly close, and then away again, like a forward circling the net. She opened her eyes.

"A quarter pill. I've got what might be a vital clue flopping around in my head, and I have to jack up my brain to get it out."

Terry said, "You can't do that. You know the rebound exhaustion will be ten times as bad."

"I have to. I need my brain firing on all cylinders. If Camille is a murderer, she might be at the museum right now tampering with evidence."

"Lacey would notice," said Rob. "She's working there today."

"I still want it. Something is wrong. I can feel it. Please."

"Rob, don't move," said Terry. "Jan, if you try to take that pill, I will flush the whole bottle down the can. I'm serious."

"So am I." Jan struggled to sit up, desperate to communicate her creeping terror, to make him see how vital her brain's locked-up information might be. Something in all those hockey tapes had flipped a switch, but which one? Dee's life, Lacey's life, might be at stake. Those were way more important than anything anybody thought of her, including Terry. Why hadn't she taken him up on that wheelchair? She could have powered down the hill herself to see what was going on.

She slapped her hand on the coffee table. "All right, here's the deal: I get one measly quarter of a pill today and tomorrow you can flush the whole lot. Then you can take me shopping for a wheelchair. I'll try it your way for a while."

CHAPTER FORTY-TWO

The cable crimpers were not in the tool box. Lacey gathered up the various implements strewn along the stair and returned them in batches to the box. Each handful landed with a collection of clacks, clanks, and clunks. Amplified against the metal elevator door and the clay room's wide window, they assaulted the silence of the empty building. Today was the last day she could spread cable to hell and back without inconveniencing anyone. If she could just find the crimpers to put the screw ends on.… Where had she used them last?

She'd been carrying them Friday, on the way to the vault. Those, and the replacement for the little plastic stool the killer rack had torn apart. The vaultmaster had been pouting — but then, when wasn't he? — while Rob sprayed the cluster of flies around the elevator. If she'd left the crimpers in the vault lobby, behind the police tape, she was screwed. She'd have to ask Wayne for a spare pair or go buy replacements. First the stool, then the crimpers. That vault was damned bad luck for her. And the cameras still weren't wired. Something she would have to face again after the police tape was removed, and who knew how long that would take?

Wayne's voice popped into her head. "This has fucked my schedule backward over a barrel." He'd been holding the crimpers at that moment. She had handed them to him before stepping into the vault that reeked with the ineffable odour of decaying flesh. Where had he said that? No, not down in the vault. Somewhere with light and air and the sound — she shivered reflexively — of the roaring river as it churned by outside the windows. The administration suite! If he'd put them down before leading the crime scene team to the vault, they might still be in the office area. That would save her Sunday afternoon's work and save her some face when Wayne wanted a progress report in the morning. She set the toolbox by the yellow-taped elevator to be out of the way and dashed down the half flight to the administration level.

The crimpers were in plain sight on an end table between two chairs. It was a measure of the day's disturbance that Wayne hadn't counted his tools at the end of the day's work and retrieved them himself. She swiped her card over the pad and stepped through the glass door to be met by the river's rumble. Her eyes told her the water level outside was lower by far than it had been a couple of days ago, but in this deserted space, with the torrent roaring not far enough below the office windows, the sound was as ominous as ever. Ragged piles of mud and debris made a jagged mess. The Corvette's front tires left ruts gouged into the bank. Had that been only Wednesday? Had it been only a week today that Dee had been struck down?

A lifetime's worth of a week. She suddenly felt exhausted, too tired to move her tool box, much less the ladder she would need for running cable above the ceiling tiles in the classroom wing. As the glass door closed her out, away from the river noise, she headed not up the stairs, but across to the kitchen. Refill the tea, regain some perspective. The flood was falling. Dee was recovering. The job here was almost finished.

So few hurdles left: finish the cabling, get a lawyer for the next time the police questioned Dee, find Dee's attacker. If that hit-and-run driver was the same person who killed Jarrad — and it seemed improbable that two violent criminals had made tiny Bragg Creek their target in the past week — then Dee wouldn't need the lawyer. And Lacey would have atoned, in some measure, for leaving Dee alone last weekend. She would also be doing a public service, one worthy of the ideals she'd used to serve before they were burnt out of her by those last months on the Force.

The time had come to clear away the mental debris and the eliminated suspects and see what was left. After filling the kettle, she hiked her butt up onto the countertop in the bland grey kitchen and checked her mental investigative notebook. Suspects in Dee's attack only:

1. Jarrad, formerly #1, was ruled out due to being dead at the time.
2. Jake could have wanted Dee dead or injured to avoid accountability for bugging her office and could have gotten Jarrad's car keys to do so. His friends were inclined to be understanding over

his attempt to contact his ex-wife, but his alibi for Sunday afternoon had not yet been looked into.

3. Camille had access to Jarrad's car but, unless she thought Dee could implicate her in Jarrad's death, had no known motive for attacking Dee. Jarrad's death was a separate category, for now.

4. Eddie Beal, despite Lacey's initial suspicion, had no history of violence, no known motive beyond disapproving of the museum, and no known access to Jarrad's car. His hothead brother was far away at the oil sands during the whole affair. They were most likely not involved.

5. Rob had had plenty of other opportunities to harm Dee and no discernable motive for doing so. In fact, his job was only tolerable because of Dee, which gave him a compelling motive for wanting her fully functional.

6. Neil … honestly, there was no evidence to support his involvement. Lacey's ongoing suspicion of him had been part statistical, part policing experience, and almost certainly part of her ongoing worry that Dan had actually tried to kill her that day on the riverbank. But Dan was a separate category, to be dealt with when the current crises had passed.

Not all of Dan's impact could be set aside so easily, if she was being honest. How quickly had that unacknowledged emotion of hers overturned all her investigative training! If she had faced up to her fear from the first, she might have been quicker to eliminate Neil as the prowler, instead of clinging to him as the chief suspect. Might she have identified Jake as the prowler sooner, and then pinpointed the real source of danger in time to save Dee from being run down? She mentally apologized to her RCMP trainers. They had been correct that linear procedure must be observed and all suspects thoroughly checked out, even — or especially — when a gut instinct pointed to a particular suspect.

The kettle clicked, so loud in the stillness that she half-slid from the countertop. She dropped the teabag into her to-go mug and set her phone timer for five minutes to brew. Then, since she was up anyway, she paced the length of the kitchen and back along the other side of its central island. In the building's hush, her boots on the tiles were preternaturally noisy. Somewhere, an air conditioning duct whispered, and a breath faintly tinged with decay drifted down from the ceiling. A lone fly followed it. The building was taking its time clearing out the odour of death. Once the cleaners could get into the vault and wash everything down, there'd be nothing left for the flies to follow.

And so to Jarrad's murder. If she couldn't hand the police a viable suspect for that by tomorrow morning, Dee would need a lawyer, which she could ill afford, and she would face highly stressful questioning, for which she had no resilience to spare. How she must be regretting that golf club through the windshield! It was the one tangible incident showing her fury and grief. She'd never have done it if she hadn't been chronically sleep deprived from Jake's prowling. Since they couldn't tell the police, much less a jury, about the bug or the prowling, she would come off as ragingly unstable and therefore capable of killing Jarrad. She had full vault access and knew better than any other suspect — because Lacey had gone home and told her all about it — that the rack was potentially fatal.

So, suspects in Jarrad's death, excluding Dee:

1. Jake had been downstairs during the crucial time and could have lifted Camille's key card, but he had no known motive for killing Jarrad.
2. Rob was hardly in the picture, save for that wild stretch of imagination that put two gay men who had never met each other into a compromising situation in a place and time where both had a lot to lose by being caught, and having it go fatally wrong. Some of Lacey's ex-colleagues would have run with that scenario just because homosexuality was involved. She wasn't one of them. There was no evidence against Rob at all.
3. Camille had time, between leaving the stage and escorting Jake, to go to the vault and back; furthermore, it was her key card that accessed the vault and only her word that it had ever been missing. As to motive, was she afraid of what Jarrad would do or say once he realized she had thrown him over for the actor after he had betrayed Mick and thrown over Chris for her?

The timer went. Lacey fished out the teabag and tightened the lid. Picking up the crimpers, she headed back to the classroom wing, trying to think of any other suspects in Jarrad's death. Only the Camille theory ful-filled Occam's razor; it was the simplest explanation that fit all the known facts.

As Lacey dragged the ladder into position and ran the guide pipe up over the ceiling-tile support, she tried to look at Camille's motives and behaviours from all angles. Could it have been self-defence? Maybe Jarrad had accosted her once they were downstairs with no-body around. Maybe she had taken him to the vault so they could thrash out the issue without being overheard. Maybe it had been an accident, after all … except that she'd left him there to die while she carried on with her affair and her weekend partying.

Down, then, to two suspects for Jarrad's murder: Jake and Camille. Which of them was most likely to have attacked Dee? Dee had probably seen one of them down-stairs in the theatre with Jarrad. She might not remem-ber now, but on Saturday she could have said something in front of either of them which would only have been important to whoever knew Jarrad had not left the vault the night before. To that person, it was vital that Dee never have the chance to tell anyone else. Into the men-tal notebook went the notation to pick through Terry's, Jan's, and Rob's memories of the Saturday evening at Jake's for any overheard conversations between Camille and Dee and what exactly Dee had yelled at Jake. There might have been phone calls, too, but those could have been follow-ups on the gala, and anyway, she couldn't re-create the conversations.

She moved the ladder along the loading bay corridor, climbed up, lifted the ceiling tile, and groped for the end of her guide pipe. As she shoved it farther along between the roof and the tiles, the next piece of the puzzle came to her: the break-in at Dee's and the attempted destruction of the laptop. Who would know that the laptop held recordings from the bug beyond Lacey, Dee, Tom, Bulldog, and Wayne? Dee might have let that slip to Jake in her tirade, but the dogs wouldn't have barked at him. How would Camille have found out? Jake wouldn't have told her for fear she'd tell his ex-wife what he'd been trying to do.

Down the ladder, move the ladder, up the ladder. The laptop had been found on the downhill trail that crossed Camille's back lane three houses farther on. The recording had to contain some clue, or why would Camille — assuming it was her — try so desperately to retrieve the thing and to silence Dee, the only person who had listened to it?

Mick! He had overheard Dee yelling at Jake during the hockey party. Everybody talked to their spouses, even police officers who should know better. Even lawyers as canny as Dee, who definitely should have known better than to discuss Lacey's lone indiscretion with that slimeball, Neil. Yes, Mick would have told his wife that his and Jarrad's conversation might have been recorded. Camille, having killed Jarrad twenty-four hours earlier, would have been horrified to learn that her secret — whatever it was — was not yet safe. A chance recording of a sunny afternoon's conversation might well reveal her motive. Nothing Lacey had heard in the hospital was a motive. Before moving the ladder to its final position, she pulled the little recorder from her pocket and settled down with her tea to listen to the whole thing.

The recording began as she remembered: Jake talking to the dogs, his car leaving, the scrape of that patio chair when the other men arrived. Jarrad sounded so concerned for his mentor. A kinder, gentler Jarrad than Lacey had seen at the pre-gala reception.

"You know I love you, Mick," said the dead man's voice. "You and Camille are my family. I don't want to pull a dance on you. But I need to figure out who I am. Get it all out in the open, deal with all my feelings. Then I'll know."

"Sounds like a *Dr. Phil* episode." Mick took a few wheezy breaths before asking, "You been talking to somebody about this?"

A long pause followed. The wind blew mournfully through the spruce trees. A hawk shrieked.

"Anonymous online group. No names, no details."

Lacey tried to picture Jarrad's face. In an interrogation, during a long pause, there would be body language to show his state of mind, whether he had taken that time to decide whether to lie or to tell the truth. Which was it? Had he spoken to someone else? And about what specifically?

"Jesus. Anybody could have traced your email address." Was she hearing a trace of panic or was it her imagination?

"I had to risk it. I needed something, or I'd have killed myself."

"My poor boy. I had no idea it hit you so hard." Mick breathed a few more times and coughed. "Maybe you do need to talk to somebody. A doctor. I'll pay for one. But you should keep this private until you're back on firm ice. A media shitstorm won't help anybody."

"Keeping it quiet got me cut from my team. Going public could get me another chance. It worked for Fleury."

Even hockey-blind Lacey knew what Theo Fleury was latterly famous for: a book about having been sexually abused as a young player. Things were falling into place.

"You're not a thousand-game NHL star," said Mick. "The press'll tear you apart. Only way to save your career is to buckle down and work hard. In a year this will all be behind us. You'll see."

"It's not about the contract."

"Then what?" Mick sounded less fatherly, more … angry? Scared? "You're going to destroy all our lives, humiliate Camille in front of the whole world, and for what?"

Camille. Lacey lifted the recorder closer to her ear.

"For love." Jarrad sniffed. "I was so young when we started. How can I be sure I love Chris now when I'm not even sure if I'm gay?"

Mick sighed like a leaky air mattress. His voice dropped, all the heat gone. "I'd never want to deprive you of love, boy. You do what you have to." More breathing. "Only, can you wait until after the weekend? Camille worked really hard for tonight, and I don't want this to spoil it for her."

Camille again. She had the key card, the knowledge of the killer rack, the timing, and now here at last was the real motive: protecting herself from charges over the sexual abuse of a minor. Just how young had Jarrad been when she first seduced him?

"Sure, Mick." Jarrad's voice betrayed relief, and maybe a little fear. Coming out with this would have been difficult even with Mick's support. Victims of sexual abuse were still too often judged as having asked for it, and many people found it incredible that sex between a teenage boy and a walking sex-bomb like Camille qualified as abuse. "Two more days won't matter. But … thanks for your support, for putting me first this time. You sit still. I'll go get my car." His feet pattered away as the sound of a vehicle engine rose on the recording. The vehicle receded. The next sound after that was Mick's harsh sob. Lacey let the recorder play on in case there was more conversation, but it was only Mick gasping and the wind whispering in the spruce boughs. The revelation that would humiliate his wife had only been deferred. Camille was a scant decade older than Jarrad, but she'd been almost a stepmother to him while he was billeted in her house. A media shitshow whether it went to court or merely to the newspapers.

Jarrad had thanked Mick for "this time," implying there had been other times when Camille's desires had taken priority. Perhaps Mick had condoned the abuse, maybe thought he was doing Jarrad a favour by giving him experience with an older woman. And yet, at the last, he had agreed to support Jarrad in going public.

Had he warned his wife when they reached the museum that evening, unwittingly precipitating Jarrad's murder?

Thinking back, Lacey was sure Camille had been her usual sleek self during the pre-show schmoozing. She must have visited her husband in his lonely box before the show. Her shrill voice on stage: was that stage fright, or the strain of pretending to adore the man who was about to ruin her?

All through Lacey's musings, the recording was clicking off to silence, clicking on again for sounds: the Corvette's throbbing engine, the dogs barking at times during the evening. Then her own voice. "Because you're shorter than me." And it spooled out from there, doubtless carrying on right up to the moment she'd turned the recorder off inside the baggie, in the living room, after she'd realized it was still recording during her argument with Dee. She wouldn't erase any of that; it was all evidence now, though it would probably never be worth introducing in court.

By the time they discovered the bug, Jarrad was three hours dead already.

So much had happened since that moment, and all stemming from an accidentally taped conversation on a porch between two people who would never normally have sat there. The homicide investigators would need to hear this. It pointed right at Camille for murder, attempted murder, and burglary. Wouldn't Jake Wyman be floored when he had to explain to the RCMP how he'd happened to make this recording? But there was no protecting him now.

Fishing out the lead officer's card, Lacey left him a voice message that she had new evidence in the Fiske murder. She dropped the phone into her light tool caddy with the crimpers and put the little recorder back in her pocket.

She was up on the ladder by the loading bay doors, hooking up a camera to the new cable, when faint clunks rattled along the corridor. This building was too new to have ghosts. Was loose ductwork vibrating as the air conditioning started up? She put the last twist on the cable connection and angled the camera to approximately where it should be facing. Then she climbed down the ladder and stood under the nearest air vent. Nope, no airflow. The clatter came again, sounding like tools. Another tradesman finishing up? For her own peace of mind, she would identify who and where.

The clatter increased as she headed along the studio corridor. Her tool box, which should have been sitting by the elevator, was gone. Now the sound was more metallic, echoing like someone was tossing pop cans into an empty dumpster. The only metal container that big was the coffin-sized sink in the clay room. In the muted light from the stairwell, the window reflected her own wide-eyed gaze. She shielded her eyes and pressed her face against the glass.

Mick Hardy stared back at her from the far side of the immense sink. Her tool box was tipped on its side, with pliers and screwdrivers strewn over the galvanized steel. Screws and washers tinkled, rolling toward the huge drain hole. She made a mental note to tell Rob about the incursion of metal objects into the special clay-trapping drain and walked into the room.

"Hi, Mr. Hardy. What are you doing with my tool box?"

The man's bony shoulders drooped under his golf shirt. His collarbones stuck out like the hips of a dead horse. If ever he had been a brawny hockey player, it was all gone now. "Miss Lacey. You caught me red-handed. I was going to borrow a screwdriver."

"If you need something fixed, I'd be happy to help. But please don't mess with my tools. They belong to my boss." *Screwdriver? Like hell.* Nobody searched for a screwdriver — which was kept in the top tray, in plain sight — by dumping the whole box out onto the nearest flat surface. If Camille had come seeking the recorder, it wouldn't have been a surprise, but sending sick old Mick? He must have her new key card. Did she know each use was recorded? "What really brought you here on a Sunday afternoon when the building is closed?"

Mick leaned both hands on the metal sink, his breath wracking his chest. "Helping out a friend."

"You want a chair, Mick? I can bring you one, and then you can tell me all about it."

"I'll sit here." Mick edged half his scrawny butt down on the sink's wide lip.

Lacey perched on the opposite lip, more than an arm's reach away. "I'm listening."

"Right. Well, I had lunch up at Wyman's place today. Jake is a very old friend. To put it bluntly, he said you had something of his, something that was likely to cause him some bother, but he was honour-bound not to try to take it back because Dee would be angry. We all know he's sweet on Dee. First nice lady he's courted since I don't know when. D'you know how she thinks of him?"

"I'm not here to matchmake. Let's go back to Jake saying I had something of his. You came down here to see if you could find it for him?"

"That's about the size of it."

"Did he tell you what it was?"

"It's one of those little dictation machines. Goes on when you talk to it."

"Did he tell you why I have it?"

"He put it on Dee's window, hoping to catch his ex-wife phoning her."

"He told you that? I thought he was determined never to tell anyone else."

"We both made mistakes with women. Can't hold that against each other."

Mistakes with women. That had the ring of truth. He was making another mistake right now, by trying to cast the blame onto Jake.

"I don't think he did tell you, Mick. I think you've known since you heard him and Dee arguing at that hockey party last week. And I'll bet you're not looking for the recorder to give it back to him."

"I'm not?" Mick stood.

Lacey stood, too. "You're trying to protect your wife, aren't you? Jarrad was going to expose her for sexual abuse of a minor. Surely you know it's gone way beyond that now. She must have killed him."

A shiver ran over Mick's bony shoulders. He clutched at the sink. "Then it's all for nothing. My poor boy."

"When did you guess?"

"I came down after the performance to congratulate them, but I missed them backstage. They were just getting on the elevator when I came around the corner. I waited for it to come back and took it up to my chair. I never saw my boy again. Then the detectives came and asked where she was right after the gala. That's when I knew. My poor boy." Tears got lost in the creases down his cheeks. He groped his way to a corner and leaned there, pretending to study a miscellany of wood chunks left behind by some contractor.

Lacey's phone buzzed. She glanced at it, saw Jan's number, and let it go to voice mail. Nothing short of a police return call was as important as keeping Mick on track. He had to tell the whole truth about the night Jarrad died, for his sake as well as Jarrad's. His poor boy, indeed. Poor Mick. He had probably come downstairs hoping to prevent a premature, too-public confrontation between his wife and his protege. Missing them had been one more failure in his relationships with both Jarrad and Camille. This time his failure had proven fatal.

Those constables would surely have asked the pro actor if he was with Camille after the performance ended, but did they realize he'd still been on stage after she left it? He could have lied for her, same as Mick. What was it about that woman that made men willing to perjure themselves for her?

After a long minute, Mick blew his nose with an old-fashioned hanky and hobbled toward her, using a sturdy piece of dowelling as a walking stick. "I guess I've gotta tell the truth, huh? Do we just phone the RCMP, or is it better to go down there? I don't think the post in Cochrane is staffed on Sundays."

"It would be the Major Crimes investigator, anyway. I've got the number. Can you get to the office okay? We can wait in comfort until they get here." She went around the sink to lend him an arm.

"Can't you phone from here? If I take any more stairs today, I'll have to be carried out again. No elevator, you know. It's still locked up." His left hand, clutching the stick, was tucked against his chest as if holding his rib-cage together. He shivered, his face as grey as the walls.

Would his heart conk out even with the pacemaker? "Can you pass me my jacket? It fell off the tap."

Although he looked harmless, he might yet be an even bigger fool for love. And he was holding a big stick. Lacey kept her eye on him as she dragged up the dusty black windbreaker.

"Say, Mick, when the elevator came back, was anybody in it? If someone else saw Camille and Jarrad together at that particular time, they could testify." She didn't add "instead of you." Why rub in the humiliation and grief he must be feeling?

"It's a good thought, and I thank you for it, but the elevator was empty."

Lacey thought back to her intense study of the log covering those crucial minutes after Jarrad left the stage. The elevator had gone from this floor down to the vault and stayed, presumably unable to move while the vault door was open. Its next move had been straight from there up to the top floor. All on Camille's key card. It had not stopped at this level again until after the presentation to Jake. Mick misremembering, or a lie?

"How long did you have to wait for the elevator?"

"Not long."

"Less than a minute?"

"About that. Why?"

A second lie. The elevator had sat on the vault level for nearly five minutes, by the log. If he was lying about the elevator, was he also lying about seeing Camille with Jarrad? Was he trying to get her arrested?

Mick looked so frail standing there. Yet he had been physically fit all his life until very recently. He had pleaded with Jarrad to delay any action until after the weekend. He could have learned about the oversensitive racks via Camille. He could have lifted his wife's key card at any time. He could have lured Jarrad to the vault, tricked him into the narrow slot somehow, and been back in his chair upstairs, genuinely exhausted and grief stricken, by the final applause.

The rest of the week rushed back at her: Mick on Dee's deck last Sunday afternoon, asking if that was Jake he'd seen driving away. There was no independent confirmation that Jake had been to the house at all. Mick probably had spare keys to Jarrad's car. He could have come straight to Dee's after the hit and run, searched for the recorder while Lacey snoozed on the deck. No wonder he looked so ill that day; he'd been a busy fellow.

Then visiting Dee at the hospital while she was sedated. What luck that they had not been left alone together! Telling Lacey how ruthless Jake could be. That same evening, Dee's laptop was stolen, mere hours after Lacey had told this man she would be staying in the city overnight. Poor, feeble Mick with his wonky pacemaker. Everybody overlooked him. And now she was alone with him in a deserted building.

Well, she had taken down larger and fitter men than him without incident. Just let her get within reach.

"Do you want your windbreaker?" she asked, and held it out. Keeping one eye on his hand that was clutching the dowel, she took a step forward.

The dowel's bottom end tangled between her legs. Mick's shoulder slammed her in the ribs, sending her backward. The sink lip caught her thighs. She landed with a crash, her back bending painfully over the tool box. The far lip of the sink smacked her temple, stabbing streaks of red through her vision.

The red mercifully faded.

So did everything else.

CHAPTER FORTY-THREE

Jan took a glass of water from Terry and rinsed down the crumb of pill. She lay back on the couch, waiting for her face to flush and her heart to pound. If Camille was the villain of the piece, she wouldn't be going after Dee as long as she was at the museum. Lacey would not turn her back on that woman. She would two-step all over the building to keep a potential murderer in sight. Two-step. Dance. Back to that problem: what did dance and hockey have in common? The drug crept toward her brain, agitating nerve endings. Her legs and arms tingled, like ants crawling up the insides of her veins. *Please let this be worth it.*

Not dance. *Dants.* Now the cylinders were clicking. Dants had played for the St. Louis Blues a few years back, overlapping with Jarrad by one season. What about him? Had he played for the Calgary Flames or Hitmen? No. He'd *hired* a hit man.

"Rob, could Chris have said 'pulled a Dants?' D-A-N-T-S, not D-A-N-C-E."

"I dunno. What's a D-A-N-T-S?"

"Not what. Who." She had him sorted now. "Mike Danton, a.k.a. 'Dants,' was a promising young hockey player with a troubled personal life who hired a hit man to try to kill his agent. I'm surprised you didn't hear about it."

"God, how do you remember this trivia when your own name is irretrievable some days?"

"My entire social life for the past five years has been Jake and his hockey players." Jan bounced upright on her cushions. "Dants and his agent, though. Danton pleaded guilty to the attempted hit, avoided a trial, and wrote to the press from prison, professing his agent innocent of any wrongdoing." She shivered. "But the FBI was absolutely sure that Mike Danton had wanted his agent killed."

Terry set down his mug. "You think Jarrad was hiring someone to go after Mick?"

"I can't see that. I mean, Mick's not like Danton's agent, all controlling and arrogant. And Jarrad was kind to him on that last day, when we saw them down at Dee's. He wasn't furious then. But if he had ever been angry enough to mutter about hiring a hitman, there must have been something to be upset about." The creeping was all over her body now. She stood up, shaking out the ants. More pieces fell into place. "After the Finals party, what did you say about taking Mick back to his closet? Did you get the impression he was gay?"

"Not entirely." Rob stacked the last sticky plate onto the tray. "But the deepest, darkest, most rat-infested dungeon of the closet … probably never so much as kissed a man. Peeked a few times in locker rooms and thinks his fantasies are his own private vice. No wonder Camille has to get hers in the basement of the theatre! Her husband is secretly rooting for the other team. If she were anyone else, I might feel sorry for her. As it is, my sympathies are all with Mick. And with Jarrad."

Jan shook her head. "Don't waste your sympathy on Mick. Mike Danton, who hired the hit man? His agent was way more than a business partner. He was closer than family. Danton's father wanted to sue him for alienation of familial affection. His name was on the deed to Mike's condo. And this is the clincher: rumour was he'd lured Danton into a homosexual relationship when the young man was barely in the minors."

"So, underage and in a power dynamic as well." Rob shook his head. "Tell me the agent was charged?"

"Not then. Danton wouldn't testify. But the point is, there's only one person who fills such a big part of Jarrad's life. If Mick's not 100 percent heterosexual, and if he thought he could keep Jarrad from ever telling …" She reached for the laptop and zipped backward through the footage to a camera angle of Jake's box full of hockey players. Jake was absent. "Look at the right side of the screen. What do you see?"

"Mick's box," said Terry. "He was behind the curtain, avoiding the stares of his acquaintances after his wife's little drama on the stage."

"My god, he wasn't!" said Rob, staring. "There are only four chairs and we can see them all. He wasn't in that box when Jarrad died."

Terry shook his head. "Why would Mick, of all people, kill Jarrad?"

Rob answered before Jan. "Why did Mick buy him a hugely expensive vintage car when he was going off the rails last winter? Buying his silence. Chris said Jarrad billeted with Mick for a minor-league tournament and lived with him afterward. Even after Mick got married, which means, in other words, that it started before he got married. Camille didn't seduce the kid. It was Mick."

Jan nodded. "Mick, who's been nominated for the Order of Canada. The crowning moment of his career, when his heart is failing and his chance to make his mark is almost gone. One whiff of a sex scandal involving an underage hockey player and he'll not only lose the Order of Canada, he'll go to jail."

"Jesus," said Terry, "and he might be in the museum right now."

"Yup. He took Camille's car. Lacey won't be leery of an old guy with a bad heart. We've got to warn her." She dialed not only Lacey's cellphone, but every telephone number that rang anywhere in the facility. They all went to voice mail. "We're going down there. Terry, get the truck. Rob, call the Mounties."

Terry left. Rob swiped his phone. "And say what, exactly?"

"Tell them you're the curator at the Bragg Creek Museum and you've got a report of an intruder. Your on-site security person isn't answering the phone and may be in danger. You're on your way there now and could they please send a car ASAP."

"You're that sure about Mick?"

"Yes. Too many pieces fit and he wasn't in his box." She zoomed across the room. "I need a sweater."

CHAPTER FORTY-FOUR

Lacey woke to a cold splash on her cheek, her face stinging where it hit. She gasped as blood-tainted water rushed into her mouth. She was lying on her side while water pooled around her head, rising slowly toward her nose. She tried to sit up, but pain slammed her from her ribs and her head. A hand pressed her cheek back into the water. The flow from the tap splashed into her ear. That hurt.

Assessment: she was injured and someone else was controlling her movements. Bad situation. Had she called for backup before getting into it?

As the water rose, she concentrated first on keeping her lips closed and breathing through her nose. Where was she and who was standing over her, patting the pockets of her half-soaked jeans? She cautiously opened the eye that wasn't in the water and saw a disorienting pattern of jagged light. Concussed again. Was a second concussion more dangerous? She would have to ask Marie.

When the flashes settled, she saw a flat, metallic surface above the wavering water. She was in the clay room sink. She was lying almost as she had fallen, and the pale light coming in the big window had not changed. Chances were good she had only been completely out for a few seconds. With that much sorted, she remembered who she had been talking to: Mick Hardy.

Remembering was good news. Probably not a skull fracture. But she also remembered she was not RCMP now. No backup.

Her waistband jerked as Mick tried to wiggle the little digital recorder out of her pocket. Too bad for him he'd turned on the water first. Everything was sticking. But the jiggling sent stabbing pains through her head and her ribs. It was almost worth wishing the recorder would slide out easily.

Someone called her name. The watery echo put her, for a brief, disorienting moment, back at Depot, during a torturous swimming-pool session. That hard-nosed training officer didn't call her Lacey. She was McCrae. Or Pansy-Ass. Or Pond Scum. These were auditory hallucinations. The water turned off. Good. A hand came over her mouth. Bad. Someone called her name again. Not Mick, and not the drill instructor. Backup was coming after all!

She tried to yell. The hand on her face tightened painfully, cutting off the sound. She tried to kick, to bang the metal sink loud enough to echo. Another hand pressed on her ribcage, sending shockwaves through her torso. Broken ribs. Like that time she and Tom broke up that brawl outside a biker bar. She could recover from that again. The water was trickling down the drain beneath her ear. Soon she'd be able to breathe through her mouth, if the hand went away.

Just then, it did. Good. Open mouth quick and breathe.

A smelly, greasy cloth was crammed between her lips. She gagged, gave a muffled shout, and was promptly punished for it by another jab on the ribs. While she was fighting the pain, trying to spit out the cloth, she was dragged headfirst out of the coffin-like sink. Pain crashed through her skull, ricocheted down her ribs, leaving her dizzy.

When the waves subsided, she was chest-down on a rough stool, her legs still in the sink and Mick squarely in her light-streaked line of sight. He was taping her dangling arms to one leg of the stool. Not stool. Sculpting cart. After a moment he stepped back, yanking her and the wheeled cart with him. Her legs fell to the floor. She scrabbled to get her feet under her, but he dragged the cart too fast for her wet boots to grip. Then he spun her around, cart and all, and shoved her backward into a dark space.

"I'll be back to finish this tonight," he whispered as he wrestled the recorder out of her pocket. The door clicked shut, taking the dim light with it.

By force of will, Lacey lifted her head, ignoring the stabbing pain in her head and torso. She was in a sculpture locker, a dark, enclosed space that might trigger a claustrophobic panic any second. She, a trained ex-law officer in peak condition, had been tricked, wounded, tied up, and locked up, all without having lifted a finger to save herself. No wonder she had left the Force. She really couldn't do the job. Quitter. She was a failure at the RCMP, a failure as a bodyguard for Dee, a failure at even protecting herself. Quitter.

Once the first rage at her helplessness had passed, Lacey found the dark and stillness a relief. Her eyes stopped sending conflicting signals to her brain. Her body, no longer being pushed, pulled, poked, or half-drowned, eased up on the pain flares. If Mick Hardy thought she was sufficiently damaged and cowed to lie here in the dark, waiting for him to come back and murder her, he was in for a surprise. Ignoring the jabs in her side with every movement, she got her feet against the back wall and edged her torso forward on the cart until she could touch the bottom shelf. Please, just one tool with a point.

No tools, at least not within her fingers' reach. That was a blow, but it showed her the tape was stuck only to her arms, not to the cart. More contortions brought her tied hands in reach of a dangling corner of the cloth lodged in her mouth. After that, it was a race between the tingling numbness spreading up her fingers and the gag's increasing looseness.

With a final, choking spit, she cleared her mouth. Somebody had called her name. Were they close enough to hear her yell?

CHAPTER FORTY-FIVE

Jan sat in the sun-baked truck, staring at the staff door. For the third time, it swung open in the breeze. Any minute now, the shoe would fall out of the hinge and the door would slam shut. No police cars were in sight, no welcome sirens came to her on the wind. The cellphone in her hand showed that ten minutes had passed since Terry and Rob had gone into the building. What was taking so long? They just had to find Lacey and come out to wait for the police. She'd give them another two minutes before panicking.

Where were the Mounties? It took barely this long to get here from Cochrane at the speed limit. A "possible intruder" might not have merited their priority attention. Should she phone them again and say Jarrad's murderer was in there? She scanned all the other doors she could see and came back to the staff door for approximately the hundredth time.

The extra two minutes were up. Now what? Where in the building were they? Still chasing around the hallways looking for Lacey? Locked in a life-and-death struggle with Mick? Could she get as far as the atrium on pill power, in case she was needed?

Incredibly, families happily biked past while her husband and her best friend might be fighting for their lives inside the beautiful new museum. Asking the bikers for help might put their children in danger. Patience. Terry or Rob would phone her when they'd found Lacey or Mick. She had to be here to direct the police. Anything but sitting would only exhaust her, to no useful purpose. She looked over the bridge toward the village, hoping for the sight of police lights. When she looked back at the museum, the staff door was moving again.

This time it wasn't the wind.

Fingers gripped the door at about shoulder height, showing a forearm in a pale long-sleeved shirt. Rob and Terry were both wearing T-shirts. The door opened wider. In a shaft of sunlight, Mick stood, blinking. She pushed open the passenger door, ready to stop him, her phone already calling Rob's. As soon as the truck door moved, Mick ducked back into the building. The door swung hard, then bounced off the sneaker.

"He's at the staff door," she yelled as soon as Rob answered. "He went back inside." Then she dropped the phone and turned the ignition key. No way was Mick getting the chance to use his getaway car.

CHAPTER FORTY-SIX

Time to take stock. Feet free, mouth free, hands tied to a rolling cart. Ignore the trickle of water — at least Lacey hoped it was water — down her forehead. Could she roll to the door and get her hands to the lock? She pushed off from the back wall too hard and smashed into the door. Shock waves shot through her head and ribs. The cart rebounded in the narrow space, bashing her bruised hip. When her head cleared, she tried again, creeping instead of lunging. But the cart sloped upward like a flat-topped pyramid. The bottom shelf reached the door and stopped. Her groping fingers nearer the top touched only dark, empty air.

She backed up the two feet or so to the rear wall, braced herself for the inevitable damage, and shoved off as hard as her legs could push. Crash. With a lightning storm behind her eyelids, she rebounded, banging against a side wall. The cart skewed sideways, but the door didn't shift.

"Shut up in there, or I'll have to come in and knock you out."

Mick was back. Or he hadn't left. She had only been in this closet for a matter of minutes, with the dripping clothes and hair to prove it. If he needed her silent, somebody else must be in the building.

As the pain of her last attempt receded, she backed up to the wall again, braced her feet, took as deep a breath as her ribs would allow, and yelled for all she was worth. The closet rang with her voice for a couple of seconds, but it was enough. The lock clicked. He was coming in.

As soon as dim light showed in the crack, she pushed forward as hard as she could. The cart hit the door and slammed it back. Lacey followed it, swinging around into the little hallway. As Mick staggered back, she got her feet under her, tucked her head to one side, and rammed her shoulder into his midsection. He fell against the opposite bank of lockers. His shirt caught on a latch, holding him for a microsecond. She rammed the cart's wide lower shelf into his shins and backed off, twisting the cart around so she could stand almost upright. She gripped the wooden top and, ignoring the dizziness, rammed him again. The bottom shelf caught his ankles, and the top, tilting dangerously, slammed into his stomach. This time, when she staggered back to regain her balance, the duct tape parted. Hands freed!

Mick scuttled sideways, lit by the faint light from the open door to the packing room. While she stood swaying, he grabbed the doorframe, hauled himself through, and started across the big room, clinging to the wide tables to stay on his feet. Lacey lurched after him, the cart keeping her upright. Its base bumped against table legs and chairs, setting the lights dancing in her eyes. She kept moving on sheer adrenalin, stalking him, hunting him down, the way he'd hunted Dee.

CHAPTER FORTY-SEVEN

Ignoring the stabbing pain of every breath, fighting nausea with each bob of her head, Lacey clung to the cart and staggered across the shadowy room. Mick was almost to the far door, wheezing like an old steam engine. If he got out to the hall, he could go either way. She wouldn't have the speed or stamina to search the whole building. She could have gone for her phone instead, but rage had propelled her those first dozen steps, and now she was committed.

Slanted sunlight came in high on the west wall, gleaming on a smear of blood at the edge of a table. A handprint stamped in Mick's DNA. If he managed to get clear of the building but she didn't, that was evidence enough to link him to her death. Heartened by that thought, she pushed faster and caught the door before it swung shut. She shoved the cart through and eased her head around to the right, closing one eye to limit the distortion in her vision.

The backstage stairs. How had he dragged himself up to the third step already?

She shuffled over as fast as she was able, lifting one arm from the cart long enough to swipe her forearm over the sludge oozing down her right eye. When the bottom shelf hit the bottom step, she clung with her left hand and reached with her right. Puke rose in her throat from the pain, but just a hand span farther.... Snatching the back of his loose shirt, she held on.

His foot slipped from the fourth stair and he fell to his knees, wrenching the cloth from her fingers. His hand scrabbled for the railing, and he managed to be more or less upright when his feet hit the cement floor. His free hand swung for Lacey's gut. She got her arm across to deflect but that meant letting go of the cart, and he pushed it farther away as he stumbled past her. She swayed, lurched forward to grab her wheeled life support, and then, clinging to it, vomited.

A thin trickle of tea drained from her throat. Oddly, although it tasted foul, it cleared her head. She raised her face cautiously, wiping the renewed sludge from her right eye. If the tea was still liquid, part of her brain said calmly, then this endless struggle wasn't more than a quarter of an hour old. Now, where had Mick gotten himself to?

Not far away at all. Leaning heavily on the wall, leaving streaks from one hand, he hadn't made it to the corner yet. Ahead, up just six stairs, was the employee entrance, its door bouncing in the breeze, light and air swirling the dust motes up from the treads. At least, she hoped they were dust motes. If not, she was hallucinating something rather pretty. But she couldn't let him climb those six stairs out of the building. Straightening up, shoving the cart in front of her for support, she shuffled along the hall.

She heard her name again. At first, between shallow panting breaths, she thought it an auditory hallucination. But Mick was staggering on at twice his previous speed. Grabbing the stair rail, he began to pull himself up. She doubled up her panting and her footsteps and hit the bottom step with a rib-screaming thud. She and the cart tipped forward, crashing against Mick's legs. His ear smacked the railing as he fell. They tumbled together, cart and legs and arms all sliding in a heap to the floor.

Mick lay still, face down, groaning. Well beyond the last of her strength, Lacey rolled over onto his back, pinning him by the sheer dead weight of her broken body. She heard her name again.

CHAPTER FORTY-EIGHT

The cop car was just peeling off the bridge when Terry burst through the staff door, his arm streaked with something red and glistening. Jan climbed out of the truck to meet him.

"Lacey?"

"Rob's with her. Get paramedics." He grabbed the truck's little first-aid kit and ran back inside.

Jan sat down quite suddenly.

CHAPTER FORTY-NINE

The paramedics insisted on giving Lacey a stretcher ride up the few stairs to the parking lot. Their procession came out in the warm June afternoon to the sort of scene she'd usually seen from the active angle: a pandemonium of police and paramedic lights and enough superfluous passersby to give the show a circus flavour. Too bad the blood wasn't a show-biz effect. She was tucked and strapped in enough that her bloody T-shirt didn't show, but some of those raised cellphones were surely recording her bloodied face and matted hair for YouTube, or for possible sale to the evening news. As she was rolled to a stop by the rear of the ambulance, she saw she wasn't the day's only casualty. Jan Brenner lay on a second stretcher, covered with a blanket.

"Jan! What happened to you?" That much breathing hurt, but not as much as it had a few minutes ago. Lying still was heavenly.

Jan opened her eyes, squinting in the sunlight. "Might have swooned a bit when I heard you were alive.

I was afraid he'd kill you before we found you. He killed Jarrad, you know. What happened?"

"I fell for a stupid hockey trick." Lacey reached out slowly with her bloody hand to squeeze Jan's shoulder. "Thank you for sending them in. Whoever yelled my name saved my life. Another minute in that sink and I'd have been a goner."

"Least we could do for a pal," Jan murmured. "What sink?"

"The coffin-sized one in the clay room. He tried to drown me." Lacey couldn't turn her head far enough to see the muddy grey-brown water, so much lower than it had been, but she could hear it. "I guess he intended to drop me … in the … river. Like … the car." A sob ripped up through her ribs.

Jan's hand crept out of the blanket and pressed cold fingers to hers. "It's okay. It didn't happen. No river. It's okay."

The paramedic got between them, flashing his little light into Lacey's eyes, asking her name, giving her the whole head injury rundown she had pretty much memorized in Dee's hospital room. The routine was something to focus on, take her away from the tearing pain in her chest.

"If you pinch me for my reflexes," she said, as firmly as she could without taking a deep breath, "I'll kick you really hard."

"Yes, ma'am." The paramedic wrote a number on his little chart. "You're awake, responsive, and not garbling your words. Those are all good signs. Any more visual disorientation?"

Just a blur from more welling tears. Lacey blinked them away. What was with her, crying over a few cracked ribs and a concussion? She'd felt worse any day of her six months' RCMP training and at least twice a year ever since. Soft, that's what she was getting. All this civilian living. Not that it had been noticeably more mellow so far. Lying out here in the sunshine — this was peaceful. She could take a nap right here, except that the paramedic was still talking.

"What?"

"I said, we're going to take you into Calgary, get you stitched and wrapped. They'll probably keep you overnight for observation."

"Oh great. They'll come around and flash lights in my eyeballs every half hour."

"I see you know the drill. Let's get you loaded up."

"Wait. Jan?"

"Uh-huh?"

"Did they get Mick?"

"They have him." Jan smiled. "Don't worry about anything. I'll send Rob to the hospital with clean clothes."

CHAPTER FIFTY

Lacey woke, still in hospital. Her first thought was to get to Dee. They hadn't let her go visiting yesterday, just sewn her up, washed her, and tucked her into a clean hospital gown and then into bed. She didn't remember the flashlight-and-questions routine waking her more than twice. Was that a good sign?

She tested all her limbs. Everything that should move moved, though under protest. Apart from a great wad of gauze on her head and a hundred miles of strapping around her ribcage, she seemed okay. The rest was just bruises and minor punctures from the rough cart. Her hands were stained with disinfectant.

Breakfast came and went, doctors and nurses, too. The morning crawled by. Rob showed up, bearing not only clothes, but also her toiletry kit. He helped her sit up, got her to the bathroom, undid her gown ties while holding the garment discreetly together over her bare butt, and sat himself down on a chair right outside the door.

"Don't lock it," he warned. "I want to be able to leap to your rescue if I hear a crash. And don't scream when you look in the mirror."

Of course she had to look then, propping herself on the sink ledge with both hands, wincing from the splinter holes in her palms. She was missing some hair around the gauze on her temple. A ring of swollen purple spread from it to include her eye, half her cheek and as much of her ear as she could see through the netting that kept the whole disaster together. If she had spent yesterday brawling with bikers, she wouldn't have looked any worse. She could see why Rob had yelled for help when he'd found her, her head slick with blood, her T-shirt torn, and every inch of visible skin bloody, bruised, or filthy. Although the nurses had cleaned her up already, her skin felt sticky. Or maybe it was the memory of the blood and pain. She dropped the gown and began gingerly to wash everything she could reach without putting any twist on her damaged torso.

By the time she was dressed, Marie and Tom were waiting by her bed. Tom said, "Wayne told me to say you shouldn't worry about finishing the museum job right away."

"Or ever?"

"No, he means come back to work when you're ready."

"Really? I expected every day to be told to go."

Tom fidgeted. "That's just his way. Doesn't mean anything."

"Yes, it does, Tom. Tell me."

"Okay, have it your way. He figured you for a quitter because you left the Force when you could have stayed on. After I gave him the rundown last night, he said,

'Anybody who's half drowned, concussed, has broken ribs, is tied to a cart, and still takes down the suspect is no slacker.' So you're good with Wayne."

"Next time, I'll try to get beat up on my way to the interview." Lacey tried to keep the smile off her face, mainly because it hurt. She had a job waiting. The hospital had accepted her B.C. health card without a blink. She had a home at Dee's for now, if she could struggle up that long staircase. Too bad Jake hadn't gone ahead with his elevator. "Can we go see Dee?"

"Have to wait for your official release."

The nurse bustled in, interrupting Rob's bare-bones account of the events immediately following Mick's arrest. She whipped through her discharge routine and loaded Lacey into a wheelchair.

"I'll drive," said Tom.

When they arrived in Dee's room, Jan and Terry were already there, the former slumped in a wheelchair. "Are you worse?" asked Lacey at the same time as Jan said, "You're looking better." They both laughed.

"Thanks," said Lacey. "You're about the only person who'd think so. Why the chair?"

"I've resisted for years. But I really wanted to be here this morning, to see Dee and drive home with you. There's no way I'd make it through all these miles of corridor, so they snagged me a chair from the lobby."

"You don't fool me," said Dee from her pillow. "You knew Lacey would get one and you had to compete."

Jan grinned. "I feel surprisingly okay not walking, though how I'll get up to Elbow Falls to throw a coin in, I don't know." At Lacey's puzzled look, she added, "It's a thank-you to the river kind of thing. Since it didn't destroy the town this time. I'll show you."

Dee nodded. "Throw one for me, too. And now that Lacey's here, can someone please tell me how it all went down yesterday?"

Rob dived in. "So, the part Lacey doesn't know: it was Jan who sounded the alarm over Mick being in the museum with her. We all thought he was too sick at the gala to have left his box, plus it was well known that he adored Jarrad. So naturally we didn't think of him as dangerous. But Jarrad's pet phrase, the one Chris quoted all the time, about pulling a dance on someone, or doing a dance —"

"He used it with Mick, too," said Lacey without thinking. Tom coughed. Dee waved a warning. She stumbled, backtracking. "I accidentally recorded a conversation Mick and Jarrad had last week. Back then I suspected Neil, and what they said meant nothing to me. Later it seemed like Jarrad was a threat to Camille, not to Mick. I never suspected Mick of anything until it was too late."

Terry looked at her curiously. "Will the recording be evidence against him?"

"Gone now," said Lacey, and saw Dee relax. "Mick took it yesterday. It's probably in the river."

Tom stepped in. "It wouldn't likely be admissible evidence, anyway." And that neatly closed the subject of Jake's illicit intercept. "Go on, Rob."

"Right. Well, after her morning of reviewing video footage, Jan was flat on her back with her brain gone begging, muttering variations on the theme of *dance*. I swear her head is a repository for more disconnected information than Wikipedia is. Eventually she sat up and said, 'Dance? Dants. Mike Danton.' She showed us the video that showed Mick conspicuously missing from his box, ordered us all down to the museum, and the rest is, if not history, then certainly becoming a local legend as we sit here."

Lacey reached for Jan's hand. "Great work!"

Jan turned red. "What else are friends for?"

"Great work," Tom echoed, and shook Jan's other hand. "You saved one of my best friends. What I don't understand, McCrae, is how he got the better of you. The guy's a runt. And sick."

"A pacemaker." Marie shook her head. "If you'd asked me, Lacey, I could have told you the number one problem with pacemakers is that the recipient feels so much better with blood finally pumping again that they overdo it. His symptoms were from doing far too much hard physical work, hauling bodies and pushing cars and whatever else. Not because he was in danger of heart failure."

"He wasn't stupid, that's for sure," said Lacey. "I expected him to hit me with his little stick and was watching the top end very carefully. Then the bottom end flipped up between my ankles and I went down."

"But you already knew he was the Iago of the piece?" Rob gazed at her wonderingly.

"He gave himself away talking about the elevator."

Jan lifted her eyes from Dee's face. "I still don't quite believe that Mick killed Jarrad. I'd have sworn he loved that kid more than anything."

"Not wisely, but too well," said Rob, and looked at Tom. "Am I right?"

Tom nodded. "The investigating officer got on the phone with Jarrad's team psychologists yesterday. They had already referred him to a specialist in sexual abuse. It's also clear now that Mick only took up with Camille after questions were raised about Jarrad living with him."

"Oh," said Jan. "And then Mick found out he was getting the Order of Canada."

"He was?" Lacey winced at the pain of suddenly turning her head.

"Uh-huh. Jake announced it at his Finals party. But it's not the kind of news that comes on weekends. Mick would have heard earlier in the week. And the Order nomination would be dead in the water if even a rumour of child molestation surfaced."

Terry shook his head. "A lifetime of work for hockey down the drain over one mistake."

The room went silent, or maybe it was the roaring in Lacey's ears that seemed to go on forever. A man excusing another man's violence. She'd heard it so often from Dan, from others on her shift and his, from the higher-ups. She wanted to yell at Terry, set the record straight. How Mick had violated Jarrad's trust as well as his body, how he'd tricked Camille into marriage to cover his ass. That wasn't one mistake. That was a lifetime of choices. But if she yelled, if she told off Terry, she'd be alienating the people in this room who were his friends. People Dee needed very much right now. Was silence always the price she would pay for being accepted?

Rob coughed. "It's not one mistake, old man. He took gross advantage of his position of power over a vulnerable kid. Who knows how long it went on for, or if he'd done the same to other youngsters? He was destroying Jarrad long before he murdered him."

Terry was already turning red when Jan added, "And he married Camille under false pretenses, as surely as if he'd used a fake name. I wonder when she found out about him and Jarrad. She may be the town bitch now, but she wasn't like that when they first moved here. Something hardened her. And maybe I was wrong about her reasons for sticking close to Jarrad. Maybe she was trying to protect him once she realized."

Relief surprised Lacey into a deep, painful sigh. She didn't have to choose this time. Instead, she watched the others' faces. They were nodding; those aspects of Mick's deeds hadn't escaped anyone but Terry, and he eventually nodded, too. If only Jarrad had gone public sooner, he'd have found support here. From what was on that recording, Mick had kept buying him off with cars, clothes, and promises of help he never intended to fulfill. Was it desperation that had sent Jarrad speeding out of Mick's back lane that January night, killing Duke and injuring Dee?

One other thing she hadn't figured out. "How did Mick get Jarrad behind that rack?"

"He sent the kid back there to sign his poster," said Tom. "A fine-point marker had rolled under an adjacent rack. It had Jarrad's fingerprints on it."

Simplest thing in the world. Lacey could see it all: Mick intercepting Jarrad as he came off stage, congratulating him on his performance, telling him his poster needed autographing if he had a minute. Whether the rack killed him outright or not, Mick had calculated that nobody would go down to that level all weekend. If he'd intended to move the body into the river, he was foiled by Lacey's locking the vault when she recoded the elevator after the gala. If she had checked the vault itself, would she have found Jarrad still alive? She swallowed. No. Tom had said he'd died quickly, his chest wall crushed. To be certain, though, she would ask him again when she got him alone. No sense sharing that nightmare with people who had known him.

Rob shuddered. "No wonder old Mick was *in extremis* when I found him in the theatre box. He'd just killed the kid he had loved and nurtured for ten years. He'd probably convinced himself it was mutual, or even that Jarrad seduced him first."

"If he'd just kept his head," Tom said, "and done nothing after leaving the vault, he might have got away with it. Suspicion would have centred on his wife, even if she never came to trial."

"Almost makes me feel sorry for Camille," said Dee. "Anybody know how she's holding up?"

"Fine, I'd say." Terry's lip curled. "Jake invited her to stay with him until the media stops camping on her doorstep. Wanna bet she'll be the fourth?"

Jan groaned. "Please, no. Even he couldn't be that blind."

Shaking off her vision of Jarrad's puffy face behind the rack, Lacey forced a smile. "Five bucks says she's still there at Christmas. You said yourself, the worse a woman is, the better Jake likes her."

"Yeah, well," said Jan, "Camille may be a bitch and a tramp, but she's not a liar. She told Mick right in front of me that she didn't believe his much-flaunted chest pains were serious, and she was right. If he hadn't been spending his spare time murdering people, pushing cars into the river, and rushing up to burgle Dee's house every second day, his pacemaker would have been fine."

"I'm starting to think he didn't have a heart," Lacey said. "If you'd heard him trying to pass the buck, first to his old friend and then to his wife … I'll never believe in sports ethics again." She groaned. "Ouch, my ribs. I need rest. Hope I can bend far enough to reach into your freezer, Dee."

"No worries on that score," said Terry. "You're going home with Rob as babysitter, and Jake's cook will send down meals daily, fit for a woman who can't chew, but needs red meat to rebuild. We'll have you ready to go rafting before the summer's out." He stood up "Rob, bring the van to the front doors, would you?"

Rob nodded. "We laid the last seat flat for Jan. Lacey, will you want flat or merely a steep recline?"

"Recline," said Tom. "She's done in ribs before and couldn't lie flat for the first week. We'll wheel you out, McCrae."

The cluster of visitors moved out to the hallway, leaving Lacey alone with Dee for a moment. She squeezed her friend's hand. "Guess I won't get back to see you for a couple of days. Sorry about that. And I'm really sorry I got so focused on Neil that I didn't spot the real threat before Mick got to you."

Dee smiled sleepily. "Don't worry about that. You've had a lot on your plate. And at least now we'll have plenty of quiet evenings together to thrash out our miserable divorces. Two out of three's not bad."

"Two out of three?"

"When you moved to Calgary, you were divorcing, jobless, and homeless. Now you have a secure job and a home, for as long as you'll stay. Nothing I can do about the divorced part, but I'm really glad you weren't off having a fling with some hockey stud while I was getting run over in a ditch."

"I don't have the stomach for the hockey crowd. All that money, and the power the team owners and agents and coaches have over those young men. It's just asking for trouble."

"Not all of them are like Mick, thankfully. Sport does a lot more good than harm." Dee yawned. "I feel so calm now. It's like a flood washed all the hidden dirt to the surface, yours and mine, Jake's, Mick's. Now we can shovel it out and move on with a clean floor. Or some of us can. Say thanks when you throw that coin into the falls."

"I'm just glad the water's gone down." It would take Lacey a lot more than shovelling or wishing to clean up the mess from her marriage. She realized Dee was drifting off again and reached out one hand to smooth the blanket. "Let's have a nice, gentle float for a while, okay?"

ACKNOWLEDGMENTS

It takes a village to make a book. In this case, it started with the village of Bragg Creek, Alberta. To the denizens of that lovely region, I apologize for the liberties I've taken with the geography, specifically adding that extra land at the western end of the Balsam Avenue bridge to build my dream arts facility on, and that massive hilltop estate looming above it. There's no road up that rocky cliff and never will be, but I've imagined it for so long that its absence is always a shock when I cross the bridge. Apart from those amendments, I've tried to be true to the fabric and feel of your lovely wilderness community. I'm thankful so many familiar homes and businesses did recover from the 2013 flood, and I sure understand why every June there's that communal breath-holding until the whole snowpack has come down peaceably.

Although it's set on the edge of trackless wilderness, this book is at heart about relationships and, contrary to the image of the solitary author in their garret, the same is true of my writing life. The people who helped get my book from concept to publication are legion.

Some have become long-term friends, from Fiona, my first crime-writing buddy, to Ilonka, my most constant one. Early encouragement and guidance flowed from Melodie Campbell, longtime point-person for Crime Writers of Canada (now retired). Cheryl Freedman and Caro Soles ran Bloody Words, the Canadian crime writers convention where I met so many generous authors. Phyllis Smallman, Peggy Blair, and D.J. McIntosh blazed a trail for me through the Debut Dagger contest, the Unhanged Arthur award, and the process of publication. Louise Penny cheered me on at the Debut Dagger and helped start the Unhanged Arthur contest that eventually brought my work before Dundurn's editors, designers, and publicists, who are bringing it to you. My delightful agent, Olga Filina of The Rights Factory, came into my life through the good offices of mystery author Alex Brett. Generous authors who critiqued parts of this manuscript along its journey include Gail Bowen, Barbara Fradkin, Phyllis Smallman, and the late Lou Allin. Thank you all.

I'm grateful for the encouragement and wisdom of my Sisters In Crime, especially the Guppies, the Toronto chapter, and the new Canada West chapter. To my pals at Calgary Crime Writers, thanks for having my back. To my new pals at the Comox Valley Writers Society, thanks for welcoming me. Specific to police and paramedic procedures, I deeply appreciate the insights offered by a number of serving and past members of the RCMP and the Calgary Police Service (who prefer to remain nameless). Special thanks to fellow author and retired paramedic instructor Dwayne Clayden, B.H.Sc.,

M.E.M., for the accident-scene walkthroughs and many patient explanations. I'm grateful to Rosemary, in whose serene green winter home most of my writing happens.

More than anyone, I'm thankful for Kevin, who has driven and walked me around Bragg Creek dozens of times in the name of research, and who keeps my home fires burning while I wander in fictive dreams.

MYSTERY AND CRIME FICTION FROM DUNDURN PRESS

Birder Murder Mysteries
by Steve Burrows
(BIRDING, BRITISH COASTAL TOWN MYSTERIES)
A Siege of Bitterns
A Pitying of Doves
A Cast of Falcons
A Shimmer of Hummingbirds
A Tiding of Magpies

Amanda Doucette Mysteries
by Barbara Fradkin
(PTSD, CROSS-CANADA TOUR)
Fire in the Stars
The Trickster's Lullaby
Coming soon: *Prisoners of Hope*

B.C. Blues Crime Novels
by R.M. Greenaway
(BRITISH COLUMBIA, POLICE PROCEDURAL)
Cold Girl
Undertow
Creep

Stonechild & Rouleau Mysteries
by Brenda Chapman
(FIRST NATIONS, KINGSTON, POLICE PROCEDURAL)
Cold Mourning
Butterfly Kills
Tumbled Graves
Shallow End
Bleeding Darkness

Jack Palace Series
by A.G. Pasquella
(NOIR, TORONTO, MOB)
Coming soon: *Yard Dog*

Jenny Willson Mysteries
by Dave Butler
(NATIONAL PARKS, ANIMAL PROTECTTION)
Full Curl
Coming soon: *No Place for Wolverines*

Falls Mysteries
by Jayne Barnard
(RURAL ALBERTA, FEMALE SLEUTH)
When the Flood Falls

Foreign Affairs Mysteries
by Nick Wilkshire
(GLOBAL CRIME FICTION, HUMOUR)
Escape to Havana
The Moscow Code
Coming soon: *Remember Tokyo*

Dan Sharp Mysteries
by Jeffrey Round
(LGBTQ, TORONTO)
Lake on the Mountain
Pumpkin Eater
The Jade Butterfly
After the Horses
The God Game

Max O'Brien Mysteries
by Mario Bolduc
(TRANSLATION, POLITICAL THRILLER, CON MAN)
The Kashmir Trap
The Roma Plot

Cullen and Cobb Mysteries
by David A. Poulsen
(CALGARY, PRIVATE INVESTIGATORS, ORGANIZED CRIME)
Serpents Rising
Dead Air
Last Song Sung

Strange Things Done
by Elle Wild
(YUKON, DARK THRILLER)

Salvage
by Stephen Maher
(NOVA SCOTIA, FAST-PACED THRILLER)

Crang Mysteries
by Jack Batten
(HUMOUR, TORONTO)
Crang Plays the Ace
Straight No Chaser
Riviera Blues
Blood Count
Take Five
Keeper of the Flame
Booking In

Jack Taggart Mysteries
by Don Easton
(UNDERCOVER OPERATIONS)
Loose Ends
Above Ground
Angel in the Full Moon
Samurai Code
Dead Ends
Birds of a Feather
Corporate Asset
The Benefactor
Art and Murder
A Delicate Matter
Subverting Justice
An Element of Risk

Meg Harris Mysteries
by R.J. Harlick
(CANADIAN WILDERNESS FICTION,
FIRST NATIONS)
Death's Golden Whisper
Red Ice for a Shroud
The River Runs Orange
Arctic Blue Death
A Green Place for Dying
Silver Totem of Shame
A Cold White Fear
Purple Palette for Murder

Thaddeus Lewis Mysteries
by Janet Kellough
(PRE-CONFEDERATION CANADA)
On the Head of a Pin
Sowing Poison

47 Sorrows
The Burying Ground
Wishful Seeing

Cordi O'Callaghan Mysteries
by Suzanne F. Kingsmill
(ZOOLOGY, MENTAL ILLNESS)
Forever Dead
Innocent Murderer
Dying for Murder
Crazy Dead

Endgame
by Jeffrey Round
(MODERN RE-TELLING OF AGATHA
CHRISTIE, PUNK ROCK)

Inspector Green Mysteries
by Barbara Fradkin
(OTTAWA, POLICE PROCEDURAL)
Do or Die
Once Upon a Time
Mist Walker
Fifth Son
Honour Among Men
Dream Chasers
This Thing of Darkness
Beautiful Lie the Dead
The Whisper of Legends
None So Blind

Border City Blues
by Michael Januska
(PROHIBITION ERA WINDSOR)
Maiden Lane
Riverside Drive
Coming soon: *Prospect Avenue*

Cornwall and Redfern Mysteries
by Gloria Ferris
(DARKLY COMIC, RURAL ONTARIO)
Corpse Flower
Shroud of Roses